PRAISE FOR THIS SEA WITHIN

"A stirring reminder that love lies at the heart of every revolution. The prose is marked by lyrical imagery and visceral depictions of exotic landscapes, along with an unflinching dive into taboo ideas, making this an impressively timely and radical read." ***SPR Review***

"Lena is an incredibly relatable main character. Besides meticulous character work, the worldbuilding is a reward in itself. *This Sea Within* is an intimate coming of age novel perfect for readers who appreciate artful, poetic fiction with the highest stakes." **Nicky Flowers, Indies Today** ★★★★★

"*This Sea Within* kept me turning pages late into the night. This is a character-driven novel told from Lena's POV, a coming-of-age story and a love story about freedom, rebellion, and living up to one's principles. I highly recommend it." **D. W. Peach, award-winning fantasy writer**

"*This Sea Within* is a sweeping and emotionally charged novel that immerses readers in a world of revolution, forbidden love, and personal awakening, capturing the fierce courage it takes to fight for identity, justice, and the life you were meant to claim." **NewInBooks**

"*This Sea Within* is an epic, page-turning tale filled with passion and beauty, political intrigue and revolution, about a young woman's journey to connect to her past and find her future." **Mark Paxson, author of *The Jump* and *The Dime*.**

"*The Sea Within* simultaneously juggles romance, revolutionary politics, displacement, political conscience, and cultural belonging. Deborah Brasket crafts a story that is both intimate and politically charged, leaving readers with questions that linger long after the final page." **Aimee Bittourna, *Rockin' Riverview Book Club***

"A passionate affair, a heroic rebel, thrilling dangers, a magical locale, masterful writing—what else could a reader want? This is a book you will feel and long remember." **Harvey Ardman, author of *The Final Voyage*.**

"This *Sea Within* features complex and revolutionary characters, exciting prose, and streams of consciousness that lay bare the psyche of the key characters. Fans of *The Red Sparrow* trilogy and *The Kite Runner* will enjoy how this book explores the way personal passion becomes inseparable from the cataclysm of history." ***Readers' Favorite*** ★★★★★

"*This Sea Within* slowly pulls you into its world and makes you feel emotionally connected to the characters and their journeys. What stood out was how beautifully the story balanced emotion, romance, history, and self-discovery. The writing has a cinematic quality to it, and the atmosphere stays with you even after you finish reading." ***The Reading Lane***

"A political thriller about a young woman discovering who she truly wants to be as she tries to reconcile her pacifist leanings to the freedom fighter mentality needed to overthrow the government. This is a must-read!" **Teri M. Brown, author of *Peg, Unhinged***

"Lena's riveting love story with Raoul kept my attention to the very end and wishing for more. I can't wait for the sequel." **Carole Wagener, author of *The Hardest Year: A Love Story in Letters During the Vietnam War***

THIS SEA WITHIN

A Novel

Deborah J. Brasket

Sea Stone Press

Sea Stone Press, Paso Robles, California, USA

www.DeborahJBrasket.com

Cover design by Barış Şehri

Hardback ISBN 979-8-9920103-5-0

Paperback ISBN 979-8-9920103-6-7

Ebook ISBN 979-8-9920103-7-4

Library of Congress Control Number: 2026913711

Printed in the United States of America

This sea that lies within, without, all things,
All bodies, minds, soaring hearts and grasping hands,
This ceaseless stirring, this Siren's call,
These turbulent thoughts
And tireless rhythms that know no end.
This urgent quest.

—From "This Sea Within All Things"

CONTENTS

The hour of the garden must wait
When the hour to arms calls,
The hour of blood ever flows in its wake
When tyranny rises and freedom falls.

PART ONE

Hour of the Garden

May – August 1971

There is, one knows not what sweet mystery about the sea,
whose gently awful stirrings seem
to speak of some hidden soul beneath.
—Herman Melville

We must return to the Garden of Eden,
To the innocence we once understood:
Where destroyers become dolphins
And bullets butterflies
And Serpents sing sermons of good.
—From "Back to the Garden"

CHAPTER 1

Lena feels him before she sees him—the slow roll of the wave's hip rising behind her, towering over her, propelling her forward. Heart pounding, she paddles furiously to keep him within her grasp, then pops-up in a low crouch on her surfboard, arms wide as she pulls in and out of the wave.

He's everywhere, everything at once now—beneath her, above her, around her. Wave, body, board—all one slow motion as his arms wrap around her. She slips into the shimmering blue grotto of his body, thrilling at the sight, her fingers trailing his trembling flesh. He melts at her touch. She shivers with delight while dancing in and out of his reach and dissolving into one liquid moment of bliss. When the ride ends and wave, body, board, separate into their several selves, Lena kicks her board around and paddles out to start over.

Some see the ocean as a feminine presence, but Lena never has. How could she? All that power and restless energy, the sheer weight and bulk of it. Something in the sea's dark, hypnotic presence, its great heaving muscles and ceaseless motion, calls to her. Calls to a restless yearning, a heated passion, stirring just below the surface of her skin.

Stars were still shivering in the cold, moist air when Lonny, her surfing buddy and best friend, picked her up in his van, eager to test the huge waves thundering up the coast from a hurricane blowing off Baja. He gave up after two wipe-outs, but Lena wasn't ready to come in. When he beckons her to come ashore now, she holds up two fingers. Two more dances with the sea's wanton waves, then she'll come.

Her dad taught her to surf when she was six years old, one year after her mother left. One year after she almost lost him to the grief and sickness that followed. Surfing was the way they grew stronger together and closer without her. The way they learned they didn't need her after all. They had each other.

At first, they surfed tandem, her lying prone in front as he paddled out on his longboard. By the time Lena turned ten she had her own board, lighter and shorter. She learned to brace herself against the biting cold of the breakers' fiercely grinning teeth, to be as stubborn and fierce as the waves themselves. And once she was past them, she learned how to patiently await the perfect wave to ride, how to recognize the heft and weight of it rising behind her. She learned how strong and powerful she could become by surrendering to it as it surrendered to her. How to become one.

Lena heaves her board beneath her arm and trots toward Lonny where he sits waiting for her on their beach blanket. He watches her closely, admiringly, as she nears—her faithful surf buddy who'd like to be so much more. Her breasts loosely clad in her bikini sway in rhythm with her gait. She slows to a walk and then drops down, cold and exhausted, onto the blanket beside him. "That was wild!" she says.

"You're wild," he murmurs, his voice seductive and wistful at the same time. His finger traces a trail of water down her arm. She shivers and slaps it away with a laugh.

"I'm so cold I can't feel my nose or toes. Let's go to Pappy's to warm up. I'm starving!" She starts to rise, but he grabs her arm.

"I'll warm you up." He pulls her down on top of him and rolls to wrap the blanket around them, a warm cocoon. She lets him rub his warm hands over her cold skin and likes the feel of it. Likes being tucked away like this under the blanket, the soft glow of the sun shining through the loose weave. Likes the feel of the heat rising from him, the sound of his quickened breath. His hands slide down her arms, over her hips, along her thighs and then up again. She grows still, attentive, listening to how her body responds to his touch, the little ripples of pleasure, the way her breath hitches, and how the place below her belly button contracts and liquefies. She likes the strangeness and thrill of it.

But when his finger tests the elastic on her bikini bottom—tentatively, as if waiting for permission to advance beyond the boundaries of their long friendship and slide beneath—she tenses and rolls away, stumbling to her feet. He snatches at her ankle, but she twists free and grabs her board.

"Race you to the van," she says and starts running. She glances back and gives him a cheeky grin while he scrambles for the towels, blanket, and his own board. He passes her halfway up the steep slope and turns, trotting backward as he thumbs his nose, grinning in triumph. She sticks out her tongue.

Such a child, she thinks. Affectionately. He's had a crush on her since kindergarten. But she thinks of him more as a brother or kissing cousin, someone you might flirt with because he's cute and fun and you love him, but knowing it's not that kind of love. She's only had one real crush in her life: Mario Savio when she heard him speak at a protest rally when she was thirteen. In the seven years since, she's had little use for boyfriends or crushes. Her interests and passion lie elsewhere.

Lena's father didn't just take her surfing after her mother left. He took her into his classroom where he taught history and philosophy at UCSB, the same university she now attends. At first, she sat at the back of the classroom drawing, but as she grew older she leaned forward on her elbows, enraptured as history came alive in her imagination. She was there with General George Washington, crossing the icy Delaware during the American Revolution. There with Harriet Tubman spying on the Confederates for the Union army. There with the suffragettes in their white petticoats chaining themselves to the steps of city hall. Her father was teaching how the history of the United States is one long lesson in civil disobedience and self-sacrifice in the fight for freedom, justice and human rights. Lena wants to be part of that, following in her father's footsteps. He practiced what he preached and taught his daughter to do likewise, taking her to town hall meetings and protest rallies.

That's how Lena fell in love with Mario, up there on the stage with his wild curly hair speaking fervently about his experiences as a Freedom Fighter, teaching summer school to the children of sharecroppers and helping their parents register to vote. It was his passion that excited her and his devotion to a worthy cause that earned her respect. She memorized Mario's famous speech given at Sproul Hall in 1964 and recited it in her eighth grade Social Studies class, much to the chagrin of her teacher.

There's a time when the operation of the machine becomes so odious, makes you so sick at heart, that you can't take part; you can't even passively take part, and you've got to put your bodies upon the gears and . . . make it stop!

The "bodies on gears" image still gives her chills. It's what inspired her to join SDS, Students for a Democratic Society, organizing protest marches against the Vietnam war and participating in a three-day sit-in on the steps to the Chancellor's office when he banned political activity on campus. When the cops came and she refused to leave, they hauled her away, grabbing her by the arms and dragging her down the cement steps, bruising her arms and legs. Her heart was so hyper she thought it was going to burst from her ribcage. But in the end, she was released from jail with a warning while the policy she was protesting stayed in place.

She had more success interning for the *Santa Barbara Chronicle* where she wrote a series of stories about the plight of low wage service workers who fueled the city's booming tourist economy but couldn't afford to live there. A photograph she took of the striking workers made the front page of the *Chronicle*. She was proud of how the publicity helped the workers gain a modest pay raise and better working conditions. But when the editor moved her to the sports beat after that, thinking her talents lay in photographing action shots, she felt deflated. She wants to do something important and meaningful with her life, and that's not it. She graduates in three weeks with majors in art and journalism and still doesn't know what career she wants to pursue.

It's late morning by the time they leave Pappy's restaurant and Lonny drops Lena off at home, a huge modern structure of steel and cement built in the fifties. It's set on a bluff overlooking the ocean in Hope Ranch, one of Santa Barbara's most exclusive neighborhoods. Her grandfather bought this property and much more back in the forties before real estate values sky-rocketed. Now Santa Barbara is known as America's Riviera, where the rich and famous hang out. As well as surfers and sailors, tourists and hippies, and others who want to enjoy the warm weather and beautiful coastline. Even the homeless have staked out their piece of paradise on State Street where they entertain shoppers, earning coins in return for their guitar serenades and sidewalk chalk drawings, keeping body and soul together in a mean world splashed with sunshine.

Lena's father and aunt, David and Margo Landon, inherited their parents' property when they died in a plane crash before Lena was born. It's how her father could afford to build this house for his new bride, a budding artist and foreign-exchange student from San Balanque, a tiny country in Central America. Lena inherited her social conscience and love of surfing from her father, but her love of art from her mother.

Their home is still filled with Mom's huge abstracts, daring splashes of red, purple, and gold. She was part of the Color Field movement, along with Helen Frankenthaler and other avant-garde women artists who rose to prominence in the forties and fifties. That's why her father built her such a huge studio. She liked to immerse herself into her art, spreading cotton canvases across the floor and crawling on top of them with big buckets of pigment.

Sometimes when Lena was little, her mother would take her into the studio as she worked. One painting on the dining room wall has Lena's tiny handprints stamped all over it, blue on gold, red on orange. She squirmed with excitement as she kneeled beside her mother, trying to decide which bucket of pretty paint to dip her hands into first before pressing her palms onto the canvas. She couldn't have been more than four.

"That's it," her mother said. "You're a natural artist. You know just where to put your hands. The painting tells you where, doesn't it?"

Her dad has a photo of Mom sitting in the middle of one great canvas, her arms wrapped around a knee, surrounded by all that spilled paint. She's barefoot, dressed in paint-splattered black tights and an oversized white T-shirt, her dark hair cascading over one shoulder, her head cocked prettily with a Mona Lisa smile. It's still displayed in his office, not prominently now, but on a side shelf among other family photos.

After showering, Lena finds her father at the dining room table, lingering over a late breakfast of green melon and cinnamon toast. "Good morning, Daddy," she says, dropping a kiss on top of his freckled head, just where his fair hair is beginning to thin. Her own hair is a damp tangle of long dark-blond waves spilling over her shoulders.

"It *is* a good morning," he says cheerily, nodding toward the Sunday edition of the *New York Times* spread across the table. "Forty-thousand protesters showed up for that May Day march in Washington I told you about. Nixon had two thousand arrested. Most were let go, but still . . .. Kinda wish I'd gone now."

"Why? So you could be locked up too?"

"Wouldn't be the first time. Still, the tide's turning. Polls show sixty percent against the war now. But enough of that." He pulls her around to face him, holding her hands. "How are you doing? Your light was on way past midnight."

"Finals, you know."

"Have you decided which graduate program you're going to accept?"

Her body tenses. "Not yet," she says, hoping he doesn't pursue the subject. She pulls away and pours a cup of coffee from the carafe on the dining room table.

"Don't you want breakfast to go with that? Maria left a jug of fresh orange juice and plate of quiche in the fridge last night before she went home."

"That was sweet of her, but I already had breakfast with Lonny." Lena dips her head one last time to kiss him.

"So where are you off to now?"

"The studio. That collage I'm working on is due tomorrow."

Lena pulls on an old ratty sweater she keeps in the studio for chilly mornings and stands before a wall of glass with her coffee cup warming her hands. She looks out over the bluff where scattered whitecaps ruffle the sea's surface.

The studio is huge and mostly empty now, although three of her mother's large canvasses, unfinished, still hang on one wall. In the far corner is Lena's studio. A studio within a studio: A stack of photographic equipment, a worktable, three easels, two bean bag chairs, a turntable, and a stack of LPs.

She pulls out Cali Michaels' iconic anti-war album and drops it onto the spindle. Before long she's immersed in her own artwork, gluing tiny bits of feathers, colored string, and sea glass onto a gesso-backed board. She chose collage instead of photography for her senior art project and is working on a triptych. She's already finished "Earth" and "Sky." This is "Sea," which she saved for last. Lena does little, not large, unlike her mother. She likes the intimacy of smaller works and the intricacy and texture of collage.

When her favorite song "Back to the Garden" comes on, she sings along, imitating Cali's airy bell-like voice:

We must return to the Garden of Eden
To the innocence we once understood:
Where destroyers become dolphins
And bullets butterflies
And Serpents sing sermons of good.

CHAPTER 2

Lena's hard at work when Aunt Margo sails through the door, her colorful kaftan swirling around her ankles. She enters the studio with a careless sense of entitlement like she always does, as if she owns the room and everything in it simply by being there. Yet, at the same time, she exudes warm enthusiasm, as though she's wrapping up everyone and everything around her in an affectionate hug—the way Lena remembers her mother doing. So much of her aunt reminds Lena of her mother that she wonders if she's substituted one for the other in her memories, her aunt having been as close to a mother as she's had all these years.

"Look at you! Cramped up in that tiny corner when you have so much *r-o-o-m* to spread out!" Margo says by way of greeting, twirling in the middle of the room, arms wide, gown flowing, as if to illustrate her point.

"I don't *n-e-e-d* all that room. I'm fine right where I am. I'm not my mother, you know."

"I know that, Darling. Nor should you be. But you're much more like her than you want to believe."

"Stop it," Lena says. Her aunt is forever trying to reconcile the two. But Lena wants nothing to do with her mother. Why should she? The memory of the night her mother left still haunts her. She was only five when her mother slipped into her room and woke her to say goodbye.

"Malenque Mia," her mother whispered in her ear, using her given name, the one only she used, instead of Lena. "Wake up, my sleepy girl. I'm leaving for a little while. But I'll be back soon to get you and take you away with me."

It was so dark Lena could barely see as her mother knelt beside the bed, brushing her hair from her face. "Take me where?" Lena yawned. Her mother didn't answer as she continued smoothing back her hair, her hand warm and comforting. "Is Daddy coming too?"

"No, Darling, Daddy can't come. It will just be the two of us."

Lena frowned. While her mother read to her at night and brought her into the studio to paint, most of the time she was too busy and preoccupied to be with Lena. But her father was always there, listening closely to everything she said, even when she was chattering away aimlessly or being silly or demanding. He always had time for her.

"Why can't Daddy come?"

"He just can't. That's all."

Lena clutched the sides of her mother's face as she often did when she wanted to hold her attention and felt it slipping away. "Don't go. Stay here with us."

Her mother's face was wet beneath Lena's fingers as she pulled back to swipe at the tears. "I can't. But I'll be back to get you, I promise." She kissed Lena's forehead one more time before leaving, her shadowy figure swallowed by darkness.

Lena still remembers the feel of her mother's soft, round body slipping from her grasp. All the warmth of her flowery scent, gone. All those tiny, tickly, kisses covering her face, gone. She remembers too how she felt afterwards. Angry that her mother left her and fearful she'd return and take her away as promised, leaving her father behind, alone, like she was then. She steeled her heart against her mother and wound it ever more tightly around her father.

Her mother came back several times those first few years to see Lena, but it never went well. Lena would panic and push against her, thinking she was coming to take her away. And her mother would retreat from her fury like a small, wounded animal.

Lena was ten years old the last time her mother came to visit. She was on the softball field, wearing her white shorts and red jersey, clutching her catcher's mitt. Her team won the game, and her aunt came onto the field to hug and congratulate her. "Look! Your mother's here! She's so proud of you."

Lena looked across the field and there she was, dressed in dark capris and a flowery blouse side-tied across her hips. She looked so beautiful. For a moment Lena felt her heart catch, as if snagged by something long buried being brought to the surface, a grief and despair too dangerous to acknowledge. She pushed that feeling down where it belonged. When she looked again at her mother, it was like looking at a stranger. Lena didn't want to dredge up old memories or make new ones, to go through all that again. She shook her head.

"I'm done with her," she told her aunt matter-of-factly. And she was. No love, no hate, no fear, no regret. It was as if her mother didn't exist. Then she ran off to be with her jubilant teammates, joining them as they jumped up and down and patted each other's backs. It was the last time she saw her mother.

Margo looks across the studio at Lena now like she wants to say more, wants Lena to forgive her mother like she and her father did long ago. But instead, her aunt changes the subject.

"Will you be staying for dinner tonight? Maria's making her fabulous paella. I invited a few friends." Margo took full advantage of her brother's home and hospitality for entertaining, including their cook and housekeeper. Maria was a refugee from Guatemala her mother hired who stayed on after she left, keeping up the Spanish lessons for Lena that her mother started.

"You remember Geoff. We dated years ago, and now he's back—we're back! And Coco? No one can forget her! She's bringing someone new. A starlet, it appears. Only I don't think you call young male actors starlets. What do you call them? Starlings?" She laughs at her joke.

"I wish I could come," Lena says, looking away, not wishing that at all. "But I have to head back to Isla Vista tonight. I have an early class tomorrow morning."

Isla Vista is where she lives during the school week, a small but lively enclave off campus, notorious, according to the local rags, for its wild parties, sex, and drugs. Lena's not much into any of that. She rarely drinks and her experiments with drugs have been few, sharing a joint a time or two with her roommates and once taking the tiny white pill that helped her survive an all-night study jam. Her sex life is nil. By choice.

Still, it was exciting when she first came to live there. It made her realize how sheltered her life had been at home with her dad. Now, though, she prefers spending weekends back at home where she can study in peace and let her roommates and their boyfriends have the apartment to themselves.

"And more studying tonight, I graduate in three weeks!" Lena adds, wanting to change the subject.

"I know, I'm so proud of you, but you can't study all the time. All work and no play, you know what they say . . .." She gets a funny look on her face.

"What?"

"W-e-l-l, I shouldn't. Your father would kill me, but . . .."

"But, what?"

"I have a little something that could help you with those long nights studying, to stay awake and keep focused. I use it sometimes, it's perfectly harmless."

"Speed, you mean," Lena says.

"It's not dangerous! I mean, when used in moderation."

Lena laughs. "Stop. It's okay. But no thanks. If I needed it, I would, but I don't."

Margo looks sideways at her. "You've tried it then?"

Lena cocks her head warily, wondering where this is leading. "Once. It was fine. But not for me."

"And other things?" Her aunt suggests. When Lena frowns, she counters, "I'm just curious, I'm not prying!"

"You are prying! And I don't have time for this! I've got work to do. Now go!"

Her aunt grimaces, then leans in to give her niece a loud smooch on the cheek. "You are your father's daughter, too!"

"What's that supposed to mean?"

"True blue and straight as an arrow!" Then Margo's gone, pouring out the door in her flowing gown.

Lena watches her go with amused and exasperated affection. But the longer she watches, the more her chest tightens. Margo took care of her when her mother left. Her father was so devastated he could barely function and eventually came down with pneumonia. She and her aunt would visit him as he was recuperating, looking small and fragile in the big bed he once shared with her mother. He smiled at her through his broken face, wanting to reassure her that all was well. But tears would leak out and she would hug him fiercely, her anger at her mother refreshed.

When her father recovered, he took over caring for Lena, and Margo went back to being what she'd been before. Having a fun aunt who spoiled her was so much better than having a mother. Why would she need a mother when she had her father and he was everything to her?

"I'm so-o-o not an arrow," Lena tells Lonny three weeks later, her head lolling on his shoulder as they stumble down the street. It's past midnight in Isla Vista on graduation night.

"What?" he says, laughing at her.

"Am I? Do you think? True blue and straight as an arrow?"

"Well, not right now, that's for sure!"

Most of the partying has spilled outdoors. Streetlights throw dark shadows at the feet of students strolling down the middle of the road, arms locked, singing and shouting congratulations. Some kids squirt wine from bota bags into each other's mouths. Others smoke pot, blowing the sweet, grassy scent into the air. Several couples are wrapped in each other's arms, making out. And Lena in the midst of it, soaking up all that exuberance.

Lonny is so loving this new Lena and taking full advantage. But she hardly notices. She's just taking it all in, all the emotion pulsing around and through her. One of his hands has slipped beneath her blouse and is kneading her breasts, sending shivers of excitement through her body. She melts against him, hearing him groan in her ear, until she realizes: This is Lonny! Lonny's hands fondling her breasts. He whom she loves like a brother. She pushes him away, breaking the spell.

"I'm too drunk for this and you know it, sweetie, don't you?" she tells him in a voice that surprises her with its looseness, with the way her words blur and blend. "Be a good boy and take me home. Okay? I wouldn't trust anyone but you to drive me home right now. You know that."

And so, having smoothed over his disappointment with flattery, he drives her home like the good boy he is. "Some woman will be so lucky to have you someday, Lonny," she tells him, her head rolling back against the car seat as they drive through the dark hillsides.

"Sure, whatever," he says, surly now.

"I mean that!" She sits up to look at him. "You're going to have a wonderful life. We all are," she says, leaning back again. "Aren't we wonderful? We're all so fucking awesome, don't you think?"

He laughs now. "You are so fucking drunk, girl." He pulls up in her driveway and leans over to open her door. "Can you get to the door on your own? Or do I have to carry you?"

"I'm good," she assures him as she stumbles out the door and then leans back in to blow him kisses. "I love you Lonny Sanders, I do!"

"I love you too. More than you know. That's the problem."

"No, no!" She shakes her finger at him. "No problems, no worries . . . nothing but . . . stardust," she says as she strolls across the damp lawn, gazing up at the immense darkness of a sky swirling with pricks of light. Getting dizzier, she sinks to the grass. She lays there, reaching toward the stars until the porchlight comes on, spilling a misty trail across the lawn where her father finds her and helps her into the house.

The next morning Lena wakes with the worst headache. She tries remembering what all went on last night—how drunk she and Lonny were as they strolled down the middle of the street; how good she felt, all boneless and loose-limbed; how Lonny put his hand . . ..

"Oh my God!" She groans and cringes. It will be so awkward seeing him again. Maybe she should pretend she doesn't remember what he did. Or maybe she should let him have his way with her. Get it out of his system. She can't stay a virgin forever. Someone's got to be the first. Why not Lonny? At least he loves her.

It's not like she's saving herself for marriage, or anything. Or that she doesn't have urges. It's just that she hasn't met anyone who makes her want to explore his body the way he wants to explore hers. No one who makes her feel the way the sea does when it rises behind her and sweeps her away. She wants that sense of excitement and urgency. Surely that isn't too much to ask. Or maybe it is. Look at her parents. They were head-over-heels in love once. Then her mother ran off.

Lena looks up at the ceiling, still covered with glittery constellations of stars that glow in the dark. Her mother painted them when she was three years old. The rest of the room looks pretty much as it was in high school, the posters she hung then still on the walls: A bare-chested Jim Morrison from *The Doors* with his dark mane and sultry stare, Janis Joplin wailing her little heart out, Einstein sticking out his tongue at the world. A large poster of Georgia O'Keefe's sexually suggestive *Blue Flower* hangs behind her bed.

Her bookshelves are filled with memories of her childhood: a stack of MAD magazines and a row of Trixie Beldon books. Then there's that series of Juan Bobo books that her mother used to teach her to speak and read Spanish. Thanks to her and Maria, Lena now speaks Spanish fluently. She's always wanted to visit San Balanque and learn more about her mother's mysterious homeland, learn more about her heritage. Maybe now is the time to visit.

The truth is she really isn't ready to start graduate school. That's why she could never decide which program to accept. She needs to get out of her comfort zone to figure out what she wants to do with her life. She's looking for something momentous and irresistible to give her life purpose and direction. Maybe she'll find that in San Balanque.

There's a whole unexplored part of herself she knows nothing about. That inner fire and restlessness, that stubbornness and passion, didn't come from her cool, collected, and tender-hearted father. Nor did her name.

"You were named after a Mayan goddess," her mother told her. "Malenque was beautiful and brave, like you. She saved her kingdom from the horrible tyrant Vucub, the Demon Sea-Dragon who ruled the underworld."

"Tell me," Lena said, and so she did, reading from a beautifully illustrated book about Malenque and her brother Balanque, the legendary Hero Twins. They were the patron saints of San Balanque, the heart of its origin story. Lena carries the name as well as the blood of a heritage she knows little about.

She pulls the large book with its glossy dust jacket from her bookcase. A dark maroon background frames a vividly colored image that looks like something Gauguin could have painted, capturing the dream-like, primitive feel of his South Pacific paintings. A beautiful woman, Malenque, is sprawled against a lush hillside, her dark hair and limbs twined with flowers and vines and waterfalls, her eyes closed as if asleep. Balanque kneels at her side, a fierce warrior with a feathered headdress and round shield. In his raised hand is a sword poised to slash down on the head of a ferocious sea dragon rising from the frothy waves.

Something in this image makes Lena shiver and her heart heave. As a child she always felt that she wasn't just named after Malenque, but she was her in another time and place. As she reads the story, she's seized with a deep sense of déjà vu, as if what she's reading is more memory than myth. It's the tale of twins, sired of two gods, whose flesh at birth was joined at the hip. They were tasked by their parents—the lovely mermaid Xite and the golden god Hun—with a sacred mission: To create a land bridge between the two Americas, which were then separated by a tumultuous sea. Not only would this unite that which was divided, but it would block Vucub, that ferocious sea demon, from chasing Xite from one sea to another in his quest to claim her for himself.

When their land bridge was completed, the twins lay down to rest and fell fast asleep. From their dreams rose all the flora and fauna that now adorns and inhabits the lush isthmus. From Malenque's soft curves and flowing hair, her hips and breasts, came the flowing rivers and waterfalls, the tangling vines of the jungle, the hills and mountains and fertile valleys. From her rosebud lips, blooming cheeks, and dancing eyes came the wild orchids and sweet mangos, the trilling songbirds and darting butterflies. Balanque's dreams were full of jaguars and howling monkeys that sprung from his powerful thighs and grasping arms. Red and yellow macaws flew out of his mouth, and great sensuous snakes slithered from his muscled calves.

But when Vucub discovered he could no longer swim freely between the two continents to pursue Xite, he grew wild with fury. With his great forearms grabbing the edge of the isthmus and his serpent tail and mighty wings thrashing the sea, he created an army of waves to destroy the land bridge and drown all the flora and fauna that flourished there.

Now the howls of the monkeys and the roars of the jaguars woke the sleeping twins, but they were still so drunken with dreams and heavy-limbed in their drowsiness they could not rise to defend their creation. Balanque struggled to his knees, but Malenque was entangled in the vines and tree roots of the great jungled forests and could rise only to her elbows.

Malenque begs her brother to slash down with his mighty sword and part their bodies so he can rise to fight Vucub. But Balanque, who loves his sister more than his own life, fears doing so will slay her. Seeing that their sacred mission is doomed to failure because of her brother's love of her, Malenque knows what must be done. She grabs his sword and strikes down with all her might between them, severing his hip from hers, and freeing him to fight. As blood spills from her dying body, with a screech of grief and rage, Balanque grabs his sword and slays the Demon Sea-Dragon, severing its head from its thrashing body.

When Balanque's father, the god Hun, ruler of the now united Americas, crowns him with Vucub's head, he takes no pleasure from it, for his beloved Malenque is no longer at his side. Her body has been reclaimed by the land. Now when Balanque walks there, he sees and hears her everywhere, her laughter in the rushing waterfalls, her whispers in the swaying trees, her wide eyes in the orchids, and her graceful arms in the jungle vines. His grief at her loss is so fierce the deluge of his tears become great lakes, and his cries shake the earth and topple boulders. His wrath rises in fiery volcanoes that spill memories of Malenque's blood sacrifice across the land.

And so, even today, the beautiful isthmus that Balanque and Malenque created together to join two great continents—this slender thread, this graceful waist that unites them—is riven with the tremors and terrors of Balanque's great grief, even as it sings with the beauty of Malenque's great sacrifice, and the Hero Twins' everlasting love.

Lena's eyes are filled with tears when she finishes reading, as if for people she's loved and lost. She's moved by the siblings' innocent love and devotion to each other, by the way Malenque is all tangled up in the beauty spilling out of her, and by her willingness to sacrifice herself to save her brother and the land they love.

Her desire to know more about this mysterious homeland that birthed her mother and gave Lena her name deepens. She doesn't yet know what she wants to do for the rest of her life, but she knows what she wants to do and where she wants to go now.

CHAPTER 3

"Your mother will be so happy!" Aunt Margo grabs Lena's hands, smiling ecstatically, when learning Lena is going to San Balanque.

Lena stares at her in horror and pulls away. "You cannot tell her I'm coming!"

At her aunt's look of confusion and dismay, Lena adds emphatically, "I'm not going there for *her*. I'm going there for *me*, and she's not part of that. I don't want to see her. Is that understood?"

"Well, of course," her aunt says, perplexed. "But I don't know why—"

"If you tell her, it would be such a betrayal I don't know if I could forgive you any more than I could forgive her for leaving. Do you understand how serious I am?"

Her aunt stares at her with the seriousness Lena is hoping to inspire. "I see that now," she says tartly. "I don't understand how you could go and not see her. But—!" she holds up her hand when Lena is about to interrupt "—I understand how serious you are, and I will not betray your trust." She gives Lena a stern look. "There! Does that make you happy?"

Lena sighs, relieved. "It does. Thank you." She hugs her aunt and then looks at her with a wry smile. "I wouldn't want to ever lose you. It would be like cutting out my own heart. I did that once already. I couldn't survive it a second time."

Margo makes a face, looking somewhat placated. "I know, dear," she says, and then adds, drily. "None of us could survive that."

Sometimes it strikes Lena as strange, this indifference she feels for her mother. So many who lose parents through divorce or adoption go to extraordinary lengths to find them. Yet she wants nothing to do with her mother. Whenever she thinks of her, she feels a hardening of her heart, a sharp-edged defensiveness, a dark distaste that sours her mouth. It's as if her whole body goes into battle mode to protect some soft, sloshy part that threatens to spill over. She must not let it. The harder her heart, the more dismissive her demeanor, the safer she feels. More contained.

Last year Lena overheard her father and aunt discussing her mother. He was seated at the dining room table reading aloud to Margo from the *New York Times*. "Marcos Machado, former ambassador to the United States, was appointed vice-president of San Balanque by President Viktor Ortiz after the prior vice president died under mysterious circumstances. While President Ortiz holds tight reins over his government, Machado is seen by many as his righthand man."

He put the paper down and removed his reading glasses. "Good God! I can't believe Dolly is married to someone like that! At first, I thought Machado might be a good influence on Ortiz. But now it appears Dolly's husband is right in the thick of all the abuse and corruption going on."

"W-e-l-l," said Margo, skeptically, "perhaps he's trying to change things from the inside. All I know is, he wasn't like that when they first married. Anyway, Dolly was never political. She probably doesn't know what he's up to. She's all into her art, you know that."

Lena turned away. She didn't need to hear more. Just hearing them use their pet name for her mother—Dolly instead of Dolores—she found extremely irritating. Their conversation confirmed all the negative feelings she had about her mother, which were bad enough already. But only a week later, a jubilant Margo sailed triumphantly into their living room with a copy of *Artforum International*. She leaned over the back of the couch where Lena and her father were sitting, showing them how she was right about Dolly. She was all about her art, not politics.

"Look, Lena!" she said. "Your mother's on the cover."

A dark haired, dark-eyed beauty stood in an opulent living room next to a painting she just unveiled, the dusty rose cloth still draped gracefully over the corner of its gilded frame. It wasn't one of her mother's abstracts. This was totally different. It was a richly detailed oil painting of a woman in a long rose-colored gown, her bare arms luminous, her face flushed and triumphant, black hair piled high on her head, eyes flashing. What was so amazing to Lena were the colors, so luminous they shone. Her silk dress, her pale flesh, the satin upholstery, the elaborately carved arms of the chair were all hyper-realistic, while the rest of the painting was muted, surreal: the stone fireplace, brocaded walls, and Turkish rug wavering as if beneath a sea.

What made it even more surreal was that the woman in eighteenth century garb was a self-portrait of the woman unveiling it in modern dress: A painting of Lena's mother sitting in the same room in which the painting was being unveiled.

"Isn't it marvelous?" cooed Margo. "Dolly's all the rage. Everyone wants her to paint their portrait. Princess Grace commissioned her, as well as Eva Gabor. Even Elvis Presley! Can you imagine?"

Lena took the magazine into her room to read later that night. According to the *Artforum,* her mother's art evolved in a radical way when she was confined to bed, recovering from a car accident. They dubbed her art as "a new kind of magical realism, or hyper-surrealism, placing contemporary personages into historical scenes with lush ethereal backgrounds that serve as a foil to the highly detailed super-real figures, setting them like shining jewels into a soft abstracted casing."

One portrait featured a child who looked unnervingly like Lena. She was running on the beach wearing a long light blue dress streaming ribbons and lace, her dark blond curls flying out behind her, her skirts hitched up in her fists, billowing out in the breeze. Her face was full of a wild exuberance. The sand and sea and cloud-filled sky behind her blurred as if seen through a train window. But the girl was frozen in flight as if preserved in amber. It was stunning.

"Dolores Machado," the article went on to say, "is a quiet, reticent artist who is loath to speak about her past." There was no mention of a former husband or any children.

That's good, Lena thinks now, remembering. When she visits San Balanque no one will suspect she's the daughter of Dolores Machado, the wife of Ortiz's right-arm man, because no one knows she had a child.

Lena dives into her preparations for the trip, getting her passport and visa, her anti-malaria tablets, and typhoid and cholera immunizations. She'll take her surfboard, of course. And the Nikon camera she bought for her photography classes. She doesn't want to be a tourist. She wants to do something useful while she's there.

She talks with Ron, the editor of *The Santa Barbara Chronicle* where she's been interning, about freelancing for him while she's abroad.

"I could write surfing articles for the travel section," she tells him. "Or, with all the turmoil in the region—the civil war in Guatemala and rebel uprisings in Nicaragua and El Salvador—I could check out the political situation in San Balanque. I heard there's lots of corruption and abuse going on there."

"You'd be getting in over your head going political," Ron says. "Stick with surfing and travel. And take lots of photos. You're good at that. No promises, but I'll look at whatever you send." He gives her a press pass and then leans back in his chair. "I hear Daniel Weatherly is down in Balanque. You remember him? He was still here when you came onboard. He's with the Associated Press now."

"I remember. Glasses. Sandy hair falling in his eyes. Kinda shy?"

He smiles. "Shy around you, I'm sure. Not much of a ladies' man. But not so shy in the field. A bulldog with a bone when he's on a good story. He did that series about the shenanigans at City Hall that got the manager fired. You should look him up while you're there."

When Lena returns home, she finds her father seated behind his desk in his study, a notebook open and pen in hand when she sits down in the round-backed leather chair facing his desk. Her father was surprisingly supportive of her decision to travel to San Balanque before starting graduate school. When she tells him about her conversation with Ron, he puts his pen down and nods.

"I was Daniel's thesis advisor when he was writing about the Cuban revolution. I didn't know he was down there, but if he is, he's working the rebel angle. I'll see if I can reach him, let him know you're coming."

"So, there's rebels there too? How did you know?"

He is quiet.

"Daddy?" She watches his face. "No-o-o! Mother? You keep in touch? You never told me!"

"Don't worry, I won't let her know you're coming. I wouldn't want you to cut me off, like you threatened Margo," he says, half-joking.

"She told you."

"You can't keep cutting people out of your life just because they disappoint you."

"You think that's what I did to mother?"

He doesn't answer.

"She threatened to take me away from you!"

"Yes, she shouldn't have done that. But I never would have let you go."

"How would I have known that? You let *her* go! Why not let her take me too?"

His head shoots back. "That's what you thought?"

"That's what I know. You loved her so much and yet you let her go. If you couldn't stop her the first time, how would you do it when she came for me?"

"Oh, my dear girl, is that what you feared? All these years?"

She crosses her arms, her face flushed and frowning. "What's done is done. I don't want to rehash that now. And I don't want to see her when I'm in San Balanque, or for her to even know I'm there."

"All right, but you will be careful, won't you, and stay out of trouble? Steer clear of politics and you should be safe enough. Apparently, the rebels are sticking to the hills. They're mostly bandits, your mother told me. And no," he adds when she gives him an alarmed look, "I haven't spoken to her recently. I probably won't get my next call until well after you return. But remember, if for some reason you need help, you can still count on her. She's your mother and she loves you."

CHAPTER 4

A week later Lena peers through the window of the 747 jet as it lifts above the yellow LA smog into a bank of clouds and through that to blue skies above. It's July first, the beginning of a new adventure. Saying goodbye to her father and aunt at the airport was a wrenching experience. She rarely spent time away from either, and both looked as anxious and weepy as she felt.

Her last visit with Lonny was bittersweet. They'd hardly seen each other since graduation, her getting ready for her trip, him getting ready to move to San Francisco where he'd be starting a paid internship with a new tech company. When they met for one last surf together, both were uncharacteristically quiet, as if not knowing what to say to each other. Or perhaps knowing so much still needed saying that neither wanted to bring up. In the end, they agreed it was probably best they were both moving on, going in different directions. Made the parting easier that way. They agreed to stay in touch, but as she watched Lonny pick up his board and head out alone as she was leaving, something in the set of his shoulders, in the wry smile he gave her, made her think he was saying goodbye for good.

Lena's eyes smart, remembering. Hoping to dissolve the raw emotion she's feeling, she pulls from her backpack one of the three books her father gave her as she was preparing for her trip. The first was a history of San Balanque, which he said was like so many countries in Latin America.

"And this one tells you why," he said, handing her a hefty volume titled *Open Veins of Latin America: Five Centuries of the Pillage of a Continent.* "It's quite ambitious," he continued. "It starts with the Spanish

Conquistadors and ends with the United Fruit Company's assault on the economy, which ignited the Guatemalan Civil War that's still ongoing. The veins in the title refer to all the riches drained away by European colonists, the gold and silver and the land itself, huge tracts bought up by foreign corporations for their coffee and banana plantations." He gave her a wry smile. "Not light reading, but it provides context to the struggles still going on."

Then he handed her a slim hardbound book. "Ramon Fernandez was San Balanque's foremost poet and one of your mother's favorites. Quite good, and I'm not much of a poetry lover like you and your mother. He's considered the Walt Whitman of Central America, renowned for capturing the beauty of the land and the spirit of the people. Your mother and I used to read it in bed together."

He laughed when Lena gave him a pained look. "Too much information, I take it. All right. But poets are revered in Latin America. Every street vender and the most jaded politician can wax poetic reciting long passages. Familiarity with their premier poet will endear you to them."

Lena runs her fingers over the poetry book's dusty rose cover and puts it aside. Instead, she begins reading the history of San Balanque. Like her father said, it's a micro version of "Open Veins," which she'd been skimming through over the past few weeks. As she reads, she sees it all play out in her mind's eye as if she's watching a movie through the lens of all the great artists who captured such scenes on canvas.

She sees the Mayas gathered on the beach watching the great ships approach, their eyes filled with wonder and dread. She imagines Malenque and Balanque among them, standing shoulder to shoulder with their swords and shields, hands clasped between them. Waiting, waiting, with the great tangled wall of jungle behind them, the frothy waves crashing ashore before them, and the ships with their tall white sails like exotic birds resting at sea. Longboats with long-legged paddles are filled with helmeted warriors rowing toward them.

Two whole civilizations were slaughtered. The Aztecs and Mayas, which had persisted for over three thousand years, were completely decimated, to be seen no more. Or do their hearts still beat on in this land through their ancestors, in the volcanos and rainforests nourished by their myths? The hearts of Malenque and Balanque must still inspire new generations. How could such powerful mythmaking be lost forever?

Lena is shaken awake and grasps the history book sliding off her lap. She peers out the window, the earth reeling beneath her as the plane approaches Mexico City. She leans closer, taking it all in, the deep greens and purples of the forested mountains, the sharp clefts and soft contours that shape them. Foothills falling away in sensuous folds, ribbons of rivers shimmering in the sun. All growing larger and more distinct as they descend. Images she wishes she could capture on film or in collage.

Finally, the great metropolis of Mexico City takes shape. There she will have a short layover before boarding a small commuter plane to San Balanque.

It's not the politics she's come here for. Nor the sordid history. It's the land, the people, the culture. It's to learn more about her heritage, her other half, this hidden part of her and who she might become.

It's hot and sticky outside the terminal when Lena leaves to catch her next flight. She lifts her hair from her back, allowing the breeze generated by the airport shuttle to cool her neck. The acrid smell of hot tar and gasoline fumes fills the air.

"It's a Douglas DC-3, an old cargo and troop plane left over from World War Two," says the distinguished looking gentleman sitting next to her. He nods admiringly at the commuter plane waiting for them on the tarmac. "You don't see them much these days, at least in the States. They're common down here though. Good little planes. They got the job done they were commissioned for during World War Two."

She studies him while he talks. Ex-military, she decides, noting his tan face and gray buzz haircut, plus the way he sits so straight and tall with a starched white collar even in this melting heat. She wonders if they are "getting the job done" in Vietnam too.

"It does look old," Lena concedes, noting the twin propellers and dull gray fuselage with its handful of round windows.

He grins at her and winks. "Wait till you see inside." Then he gives her an appraising look. "You're American. From California. College kid, right?"

"How could you tell?"

He gives her a sly smile and shrugs. "So, what brings you to San Balanque, business or pleasure?"

She hesitates before answering. "A bit of both. And you?"

"Same," he says as the shuttle slows. He stands and glances down at her. "Take my advice, honey, and stick to the touristy areas. Things can go south fast down here." Then he darts off toward the plane before she has a chance to ask what he means.

He's not wrong about the plane, Lena thinks as she boards. The rows of passenger seats look like they were borrowed from an old school bus. Some vinyl seats are cracked with white stuffing showing beneath. Flooring that looks like worn kitchen linoleum runs down the aisle. Tiny orange curtains hang on rods over the windows.

Lena snags another window seat and pulls from her backpack that book of poetry she put aside earlier. Something to get lost in or put her asleep, and it does both by equal measure in the miles and hours that follow.

Ramon Fernandez, according to the introduction, is someone who "captures the history of the land and lays its bare bones and beating heart at our feet. The music of San Balanque's seas and forests, the yearning of its people, the eroticism of its primal past, and the ecstasy of its soaring spirit are all woven into his elegiac verses."

As Lena turns the pages, the chatter around her and the rumble of the engines fall away. She becomes immersed in the vivid imagery and waves of emotion rising from black print moving across white pages in a steady, relentless, intoxicating stream.

The first poem she reads, "This Sea Within All Things," opens with refrains that echoes so much of Lena's own sense of restless yearning.

This sea that lies within, without, all things,
All bodies, minds, and soaring hearts and grasping hands,

This ceaseless stirring, this Siren's call, these turbulent thoughts
And tireless rhythms that know no end.
This urgent quest.

It goes on from there, stanza after stanza, showing how the sea "throws itself upon our shores, heaving boulders and breaking cliffs, leaving in its wake the detritus of humanity and small broken things." And then, when the storm passes, how the "sea unbroken in its vastness spreads out like a calm, comforting blanket, safe as sand."

Its lacy traces washing our feet,
Seducing us with dreams of endless pleasure.
Its tender kisses everywhere,
Its mesmerizing music everywhere.

This is how the sea "lures and soothes" us before lashing out again, "breaking whole continents apart" with "its endless cycles of peace and plunder, plunder and peace." But the final stanzas tell the reader not to despair.

O drowning heart, O vale of tears
O lovers lost, sons and daughters,
Be not dismayed.
As ceaseless as the sea's turmoil is the spirit that rides upon it
And survives to rise again.
Savor those sweet kisses and balmy breezes.
Even when the drowning seas rise up and crash down,
Do not despair.
Tis the way of weather,
And weathered hearts, and leathered minds,
And grasping hands, and the sons of man.
We lay our lives and histories
Upon such shores as storms do rage
And retreating bare all to see
Such luster still in the strong arms and stalwart hearts
Of souls long lost.
Where all that's left of mighty ships' splintered rails
And torn sails sink below and wait to rise
Once more. Once more.

Lena puts the open book face-down in her lap and lets the melancholy refrains and images wash through her. It reflects so much of what she's been reading all morning, the constant warfare and clash of civilizations. But it's distilled in a way that doesn't leave her feeling desolate or hopeless, as the histories did. Instead, she feels stronger, more measured, more capable of withstanding whatever struggles come her way.

She reads another poem and another, each sweet and sorrowful, sensual and strong. Lena finds she's drifting in and out of sleep as she reads, enveloped by a dreamlike drowsiness when she wakes and a poetic landscape when she slumbers. It's like she's in some weird fever-dream. And she doesn't know whether the images and words that rise in her mind come from her reading or her dreams.

The runway flashes by her in a blur as they land. Something momentous is about to happen. She feels it. She's been whisked away from her old life and is about to be dropped into something explosive, overwhelming, surreal. She struggles to find strands of her old self to hold onto as she steps off the plane, even while, at the same time, she wants to become undone and remade anew.

CHAPTER 5

The heat hits Lena like a slap in the face as she steps off the plane and looks out at San Balanque for the first time. The sunlight is so dazzling she must shade her eyes. Stretching out before her is a black wavering field splotched with rain puddles reflecting the cloud-dappled sky. It's so magical, she wants to paint it. She's sure she's seen this exact sky in one of Monet's paintings.

She stumbles down the ramp with her heavy backpack, still feeling under the influence of her heady reading, and walks rather unsteadily with the other passengers toward the terminal, a low squat rectangle shimmering in the distance. She's never experienced this intensity of heat and humidity, like she's wading through a steam bath as the tarmac melts beneath her feet. With each step the backpack strapped across her shoulders grows heavier. The terminal wavering in the steamy atmosphere seems further away than ever.

"Lena Landon!"

Lena looks past the backs of passengers in front of her and sees a young man emerging from the crowd like a fish swimming upstream, his hand held high.

"Daniel!" she cries. After her father told Daniel Weatherly when she was arriving, he offered to pick her up and show her around. He even recommended a boardinghouse where she could stay.

By the time he reaches her she feels a giddy pleasure, as if she's been rescued—not just from the heaviness of the heat and backpack that's been weighing her down, but from the dream-fever of her sky-borne reading. All that history and poetry, that sense of being swept into something cataclysmic and other-worldly, even that ex-military man's dire warnings about things going south, shatter at the sight of Daniel, and she's just Lena again. She laughs in delight and relief at this boy-man she remembers from before, who connects her with her father and Ron and the university—her whole former life comes sweeping back on his coattails, or so it seems, and she hugs him as if he's a dear lost friend.

He looks surprised by her enthusiastic embrace.

"Thank God you came! I needed to see a familiar face. You are real, aren't you?" She touches his cheek, then laughs at herself. "Never mind me. The heat's made me giddy. Is it always like this? I'm dying here!" She swipes at her wet forehead.

"I'm afraid it is," he tells her. "But you'll get used to it. In the meantime, beware of heatstroke. It's not uncommon for newcomers."

"Heatstroke! Maybe that's why I feel so strange." He's just as she remembered, the same shy grin and that hank of sandy hair falling over his glasses. She likes his wide-open face and fair, faintly freckled complexion, a bit pink around the edges. The heat, no doubt. She's probably pretty rosy herself. She rummages through her backpack and pulls out a leather clip to secure her hair into a messy topknot. Then she slips on her yellow-tinted sunglasses.

"Wow! I can see without squinting!" The sky is a sunny turquoise now and those popcorn clouds buttered gold.

He offers to take her backpack, and she gratefully accepts. "I kinda feel like a damp rag right now. I don't know what I would have done if you hadn't shown up. Soldiered on, I suppose."

"Did you have a good trip?"

"Oh, yes! What an experience on that old DC," she says, showing off her newfound knowledge of aircraft. "I thought I saw oil dripping from a wing when we first boarded. Quite disturbing. But when I told the steward, he said to let him know if it stops dripping, then we're in trouble." She laughs, and so does Daniel. "I think he was teasing me, don't you? Although I have to say, it was hard not to keep my eye on that drip after that."

"They're all like that—the commuter planes, I mean. They look like they're ready to fall apart, but they're quite reliable."

She's fanning herself with her left-over ticket but it's as damp as she is and produces little relief. Inside the terminal, she sits while Daniel goes to get her water but comes back with orange soda pop. "That's all they have," he apologizes.

She chugs it down and feels better by the time they reach the luggage carrousel. She retrieves her suitcase and her surfboard in its long gray bag. Daniel helps with her large duffle bag.

"Watch out, it's a monster," she warns.

"What do you have in here? Bricks?"

"Close enough. Books!" She laughs at the face he gives her. "And hiking boots. I don't remember what else. More than I need, I'm sure. Not quite the experienced backpacker, am I?"

"Oh! And water!" she remembers. "A large thermos. My aunt insisted. Until I get acclimatized. You know what they say about the water down here."

He gives her another funny look.

"I know, what a gringo, right?" She grins at him.

The look Daniel gives her now is more appraising, and then approving. Even admiring— which makes her unexpectedly shy. Neither talk as they trudge with all the luggage toward the parking lot and a small dull red Fiat.

"Whoops!" Lena says, looking at the car and then her surfboard. "Looks like I should have found room for one more thing. Racks! What was I thinking?"

Fortunately, the Fiat's rear door lifts and they are able to squeeze everything in, with only the surfboard's tail sticking out. The car has no air conditioning, but the hot breeze blowing through the open windows when they take off provides welcome relief.

The airport lies fifteen miles outside Curico, the capital of San Balanque, on swampland reclaimed from the sea, Daniel tells her. "Geologists warned against building an airport here, and environmentalists claimed it would endanger important ecological resources, but those who paid unnamed government officials huge bribes to approve it insisted this was only wasteland waiting to be rescued for some practical purpose."

The estuaries are rife with wildlife: flocks of geese, a few pink flamingos and blue herons, their elegant necks shaped like question marks, legs bent like broken twigs. Daniel stops so Lena can start a photo-log of her journey for Ron to publish back in Santa Barbara. The slanting sun turns tiny streams into threads of silver woven through fields of golden reeds. She breathes in the earthy scent of saltwater and swampland and watches two white egrets lift into the sky, their long dark legs trailing behind them like streamers, their wings beating the air in slow motion.

Daniel watches her snapping shots with her camera while continuing his narrative about the airport. "President Ortiz's uncle owned the swampland—this was when Ortiz was still the commander of the military. The government bought the land at inflated prices and contracted the development to a close friend of the commander. Some claim the whole airport will eventually be swallowed up by the swamps. In the meantime, land on the other side of the city has been purchased to build a new airport. I'm working on that story, to see who owns that land and how it financially benefits President Ortiz."

"So, the corruption I've read about is true," Lena says as she puts her camera away and slides back into the car.

"Triple what you've read and you're getting close."

"And there's nothing anyone can do?"

He shrugs. "Not much. Outraged editorials, a few protests, that's about it."

"No rebels in the hillsides ready to descend?"

He looks at her. "Well, yes, that too."

"So, it's true. Do they have any chance?"

He's silent for a moment. "They're gaining momentum. People are sick of the cronyism and corruption, the worsening poverty. Some fear another big purge is coming like they had back in the fifties, rounding up and imprisoning dissidents and opposition leaders. But how big the opposition is to date, how much of a real threat? No one knows for sure. That's what we're trying to discover."

"Meaning reporters like you?"

He nods. "Not to mention the Federales."

"I was warned about trouble brewing here."

"Already? By who?"

"Some guy on the plane. He looked ex-military."

"Lots of those guys down here, helping Ortiz stay in power. What'd he say?"

"Just that I should stick to the touristy areas as things could go south here fast. Why? Do you think he knows something we don't?"

"If he's here working for Ortiz, he might. I'll see if I can get the plane manifest, find out who he is. I have a friend working the CIA-Ortiz angle."

Soon they enter the outskirts of the city: factories and warehouses with shantytowns tucked between, makeshift homes with corrugated tin roofs and laundry strung beneath. That gives way to a decaying version of the modern industrial streets in the States: crumbling roadways crisscrossed by electric wires, abandoned buildings, trash dumped along curbs. As they near the center of the city the buildings are less dilapidated and the traffic more tangled.

"I'm taking you to an older, prettier part of town with an Old European feel." He's right. This area resembles travel posters of Spain and Italy—cobblestone paving, round plazas with fountains, colorful sidewalk cafés, wrought-iron balconies full of ferns and flower baskets.

Daniel turns up a narrow side street and pulls the car halfway up the sidewalk to park. He points to a building across the way with faux balconies on the upper two stories, a few with flowering vines growing across the iron gratings.

"Your new home, La Rosaleda," he tells her. "It's the boardinghouse I told your dad about, mostly university students and a few pensioners. Mostly empty now since the university is closed for the summer. Mrs. Henson eagerly awaits your arrival. She's Dutch, originally, but has been here forever. Friendly enough in her own way, but not nosy, and not too many rules as long as no one gives her trouble. Then they get the broom, and after that the boot." He grins at her.

"Don't tell me . . . you were one of those who got evicted?"

He laughs. "Not me, a friend. Now he's at my new residence up the street."

"Why didn't you put me there?"

He gives her a look she can't decipher. "We're mostly journalists, a few artists. Mostly male. Very noisy. Rowdy. People coming and going all times of day and night. A nasty bunch." He gives her a jaunty grin. "Not a good fit for a lovely demure lady like you, I'm sure."

She raises an eyebrow. "So, I'm too demure for the likes of you and your friends, am I?" she teases.

"Let's just say, when I told your father where I was staying, he said, in no uncertain terms, 'Not there.'"

Lena likes the landlady, an older woman with a soft face and soft body but a brusque, businesslike manner. She likes her room even more, which is on the third floor beneath the eaves where doves are cooing. While hot and stuffy, it's facing east so at least the afternoon sun won't sneak in. Mrs. Henson makes a second trip up the stairs to bring Lena a portable fan. "To be used only as needed," she says sternly. "Electricity is very expensive here, you know!"

"Thank you!" Lena says, taking it joyfully and looking for a plug.

"Thank Mr. Weatherly. He insisted. Till you get 'acclimatized,' he said." She leaves before Lena has a chance to say she'll gladly pay to cover the extra cost of electricity.

The room is small, a single bed with a brass headboard and white chenille bedspread embroidered with tiny roses and green vines. A dresser and mirror, tall chest of drawers, writing table and cane-seated chair complete the furnishings.

What she loves most are the tall, narrow French doors that open onto the faux balcony. But when she opens the doors, she discovers it's not quite faux. A narrow ledge is enclosed by wrought iron. Will it hold her weight? She gingerly steps out and is delighted to find it does.

Below her is a courtyard surrounded by apartment buildings, some with proper balconies filled with patio furniture and potted ferns. A young woman steps onto the balcony across from her with a small crying child in her arms. She rocks him back and forth and pats his back a few times, then retreats into the dark room again.

Lena is about to go inside when a man appears on the same balcony stark naked. He leans his arms on the railing, smoking his cigarette, lazily surveying the world. The full-frontal view showing clearly between the iron bars is enough to cause Lena to freeze. He looks up and sees her. She flushes in embarrassment and takes a hasty step back, but the man doesn't seem to mind. He nonchalantly half-raises a hand in greeting, then continues the slow survey of his surroundings as he lifts his cigarette to his lips.

She's glad she didn't dart away. *How cosmopolitan*, she thinks, feeling a renewed enthusiasm for her adventure here in San Balanque, where life is so different from anything she's experienced.

CHAPTER 6

Lena's first mission the next morning is to find something lighter and looser to wear. Her wardrobe is woefully inadequate for this kind of weather. Her little cotton rompers, cut-offs and crop-tops, and skimpy miniskirts are inappropriate for daytime city wear, and her jeans and slacks too heavy. She only has one sundress, which she's now wearing.

Mrs. Henson gives her directions to a nearby plaza with an assortment of shops. "You never have to go into town. Everything you could ever desire is within walking distance. Grocer, butcher, dry goods—"

"Dress shops?"

"Of course! Shoes, jewelry, whatever you need. All here for you!" She looks pleased with herself, as if she alone brought all these conveniences nearby for guests to enjoy.

The narrow streets at mid-morning are steeped in deep shade. As Lena walks, a breath of cool air rises from the cobblestones. But as soon as she turns onto a wider sunny thoroughfare, the damp heat hits her. After only a short block, perspiration pools between her breasts and thighs, glazing her face with its fine sheen. She digs her sunglasses from her bag to help with the sun's glare. The relief is immediate. And she likes what she sees.

She's entered a small round plaza surrounded by brick and stucco buildings, their balconies festooned with flowerpots and drying laundry. At its center, a green-stained statue of a monk in flowing robes rises above a fountain where a young boy with skinned knees sits, his fingers stirring the water. A gray-haired woman rides by on an old-fashioned bicycle, its basket full of plantains and papayas.

She looks up when a bell starts ringing, slow and sonorous. A spired golden dome rises above the rooftops, glinting in the sunlight. *I could live here forever,* Lena thinks. She gets out her camera to chronicle her adventure: A pot of red geraniums peeking through a lacy wrought iron balcony. A display of jewel-like candies in the window of a confectioner's shop. Two men sitting on a bench conversing animatedly, the elder smoking a pipe, the younger with a cigarette in a tapered holder.

Then she snaps a reflection of herself in a shop window, holding her camera beside a mannequin wearing a pair of wide, loose pantaloons—what her aunt calls harem pants. She steps inside and comes out with two pairs of pantaloons, a white cotton shirt with long tails, a wide-brimmed felt sombrero, and two swirling sundresses.

"Do I look like a gaucho?" Lena asks gaily when Daniel picks her up at the boardinghouse for lunch. She's wearing her new emerald-green pantaloons, the white shirt tied at her waist, and the tan sombrero.

"Like no gaucho I've ever seen," he says, his eyes lighting up, "and yet, decidedly so, it seems." She laughs at his answer, which tells her exactly nothing.

They drive toward the center of town, down wide busy streets with roundabouts large enough for four cars to traverse side-by-side, and tall department stores displaying the latest fashions. City buses spew plumes of exhaust, and crowds of people gather at stoplights. Daniel points to a magnificent palace-like structure with wide stone steps leading to the entrance.

"That's the Museo de Bellas Artes. Your father told me you majored in art."

"I did," she says, turning in her seat to gaze at the museum as they pass by. "But also in journalism," she adds, turning back. "I couldn't decide which to pursue so I decided to travel instead." Which isn't exactly true. She's come here to learn more about her heritage. And possibly herself.

But she doesn't want him to start asking questions about her mother. No one must know who she is.

"Sounds sensible. Although pursuing either isn't going to earn you much of a living. So, I'd say, go with your passion."

"But what if I'm passionate about both?"

"Then combine them. Photojournalism."

"Yes! I was thinking the same thing this morning. I've been taking loads of photos already. Now I need something to write about. Maybe you can help me with that."

He laughs. "Don't worry. There's plenty to write about, so much culture and art and history, not to mention all the natural beauty and tourism."

"But what if I want to write about something more . . . important?"

"Like what?"

She wants to say politics but realizes how naïve she'd sound after being in the county for what, not quite 24 hours? So, instead, she says, mysteriously, "We'll see."

They park on a side street and walk half a block to an arched stone entrance leading to a large courtyard filled with dining tables fronting an assortment of restaurants. They stop at one restaurant for wine and an appetizer of empanadas, another for what Daniel proclaims is the best paella in the city, and a third for demi-cups of the pure, rich coffee San Balanque is known for.

"It was wonderful!" Lena says, patting her stomach. "I've never been so full!"

"Ah, then, it's time for siesta. This is when everything closes until around ten tonight, when it all wakes up again." Already the restaurants are clearing tables and vendors closing shutters on their carts.

"Well, when you eat like this, I see why a siesta is needed. A break from the heat too."

"It's always like this," Daniel says, an edge of resignation in his voice. "People in full tilt, charging recklessly ahead, or blown out, listless, irresolute." She watches his face, his eyes seeming to look far away at something troubling coming their way. Then he turns back to her with a wistful smile. "There's no middle way."

"And there are rebels in the hills," Lena says, wondering if that's the cause of his anxiety.

"Yes, and scoundrels in the capital. And exploitation in the mines and plantations . . .." He looks at her like he's going to add more, but instead says, "And vast beauty in the people and the countryside. You should get out of the city and see it."

"You're sad," she says. "So, you agree with that man at the airport about how things could go south any minute. Tell me about that."

He looks at her earnestly for a moment, then shakes his head and looks down, that hank of hair falling over his glasses. When he looks up, he gives her another wan smile. "I'm being cynical. It comes with the job. I don't want to spoil this trip for you. You'll be fine, and there's so much to enjoy here, like this," he adds, waving toward the quaint, secluded enclave. "You must get out into the countryside though, up into the mountains and cloud forests, see the volcanos, and take that surfboard of yours to one of San Balanque's many pristine beaches."

"Now you sound like a tour guide," says Lena. "I want to see more than that." She leans forward eagerly, pinning him with her gaze. "I want to know everything! That's why I've come here. To learn what San Balanque is all about. The good, the bad, the in-between."

He smiles at her enthusiasm. "I'm sure you'll learn all that on your own," he tells her, which Lena takes as a dismissal of the subject. She's sure she'll learn all that too. And she's determined Daniel, eventually, will help her.

Daniel leaves for a few days on a story, so Mrs. Henson gives Lena a map with a bus schedule so she can explore the city on her own. She rides the bus to various parts and then gets out and walks, taking photos before re-boarding. Her press pass hangs on a cord around her neck in case anyone questions her about the photos or she wants to interview someone.

One area looks like a war zone with collapsed buildings and rubble swept to the roadside. An older woman sitting next to her tells Lena there was an earthquake years ago, people here too poor to rebuild and the government refused to do so. Everything looks so bleak: people dredging along with bent heads, trash blown up against fences. Listless teens leaning against boarded storefronts, smoking cigarettes.

Everywhere she goes, large posters are plastered on walls, some looking as if they'd been torn away, then pasted back. All feature a man with a mane of dark wavy hair, large dark eyes, and full sensuous lips. He reminds her of Jim Morrison in *The Doors* poster she has at home. Or Che Guevara in those new posters. For like Che, this man is dressed in fatigues with a bandolier slung over his shoulder.

"Who's that on the poster?" Lena asks the young woman next to her on the bus.

"Ah, that is Raoul, leader of the Aguileros." When Lena looks puzzled, she explains, "Leader of the freedom fighters."

"The rebels hiding in the hills?"

She shrugs. "The hills, the villages, the city—as you can see. He's what you Norte-Americanos might call a Robin Hood, who takes from the rich and gives to the poor. The people love him!"

"And do you?"

She grins. "But of course! He's so handsome. All the girls swoon. But," she adds, her grin disappearing, "his days are numbered. It's regrettable, but what can you do?" She turns from Lena to scold the little boy sitting on her lap, slapping his hand as he reaches into her satchel to pull out a bun.

Lena looks again at the poster before they drive away, noticing the name Raoul in big block letters below the image. The artwork reminds her of Andy Warhol's Marilyn Monroe, an idealized image silkscreened in three colors. This one's in orange, gold and maroon—the colors of San Balanque's flag. He is strikingly handsome, she concedes—too handsome to be taken seriously. Those large dark eyes are like Christ's on the cross. They've already made him into a martyr! He's just a figurehead, someone to rally around, she decides. He looks like a model made up to look like a rebel. Sexy and sultry, but certainly not dangerous. He needs a beard or mustache, at least. Or a cocky beret. The bandolier helps, but it's not enough. She sees why they chose this face though—all the women half in love with him, all the men wanting to look like him. He's like a movie star, larger than life. All their hopes and dreams pinned on his pretty face. But the real power behind these Aguileros, if there's any at all, lies elsewhere. She's sure of it.

"So, tell me about Raoul and the Aguileros," Lena says when Daniel returns two days later. They've met at the café in the plaza where she shopped that first day. The air is heavy and damp from the rain early this morning. More rain is expected tonight.

Daniel looks surprised. "How did you . . .?"

"The posters. They're everywhere." She leans forward, eager to test her theory. "The face of the rebels, but not the power behind them, right?"

He raises an eyebrow. "What makes you think that?"

"He's too pretty to be the leader of hard-core guerrilla fighters."

"What about Che? Some think he was quite handsome."

"Which proves my point. Unlikely to happen twice. So-o-o, am I right?"

He thinks it over. "Maybe. Of the three Aguilero brothers, Tomás is said to be the fiercest fighter. When their mother sent them away to boarding school in the States, Tomás dropped out and went to Cuba to be trained in guerilla warfare. Raoul stayed and graduated from Berkeley—in political science, I heard."

"Berkeley! That's impressive. What about the other Aguilero brother?"

"Pepe. He's much younger than the other two."

"And the rebels are named after these brothers?"

"Not exactly. The Aguileros are named after their great uncle, Eduardo Aguilero. He died a hero in 1907 on the sixth of August, which they now celebrate as Martyr's Day."

Lena nods. "I read about him. Something about a stand-off in the mountains?"

"Yes, Eduardo Aguilero was extremely critical of President Armando Ruiz, another U.S. backed dictator. When the Federales burned down his publishing firm, he set up a smaller press in the mountains and continued fueling the fire for rebellion. There was a stand-off when the military surrounded the compound where Aguilero and other freedom fighters were dug in. They were outgunned and killed, of course. From the photos I've seen, Eduardo looked very much like Raoul. Perhaps that's why his face is on the posters.

"Eduardo's death galvanized the people," Daniel continues. "Ruiz was defeated in the next election, and a new democratically elected government replaced his in 1916. One of the few times of peace and prosperity for the country. It only lasted thirty-four years. That's when the Great Banana Strikes spread through the region. The United Fruit Company lobbied the U.S for regime change, and a new pro-business military dictatorship was installed in San Balanque and other Central American countries."

"But how did this new group of Aguileros get started?" Lena asks.

He takes a deep breath and blows out. "Well, that was the infamous purge of 1954. Ortiz had taken over by then and was imprisoning leaders of any pro-democracy forces left in San Balanque, including prominent professors like Raoul's father. He was considered especially dangerous because of his name and reputation. He died shortly after his release from prison."

"No wonder they want to overthrow Ortiz."

"And so, history repeats itself," Daniel says with a sigh. "When Raoul and Tomás returned to San Balanque, they banded with other dissidents and idealists, calling themselves the Freedom and Prosperity Front. But the people call them the Aguileros, remembering how their great uncle's death ushered in the only real democracy the county ever knew. They hope these new freedom fighters will do the same."

Lena sits quietly for a moment, taking it all in. "And what do you think? Can they succeed?"

"Given the history of Central America, it's unlikely. But the Aguileros are not alone. There's widespread dissatisfaction with the government. And a powerful group that lives in the shadows, so it appears, is fueling that dissatisfaction, made up of liberal-minded elites and intellectuals and artists. Whether these two groups are affiliated, we don't know. But it's likely that at some point they'll join forces."

"So, trouble is brewing, like that guy said?"

"No doubt. I have my finger in the air and can't tell which direction the wind is blowing right now. But will there be a storm eventually? I feel certain about that."

"But tell me this, why do they let the rebels put up all those posters, if Ortiz fears insurrection?"

He grins. "They go up faster than they can tear them away. They're looking everywhere for the artist who created them and those who hang them up. There must be a small army of them." He stops and looks at her, as if hesitant to say more.

"What?" she asks.

"I have a lead on the poster's artist. We've set up a meeting for next week. My third try. He didn't show the first two times. It's like he's testing me. Maybe watching, following me. This time I'm supposed to be at a café downtown."

"Can I come?" Lena asks eagerly.

Daniel opens his mouth as if to say no, but then stops. His forehead wrinkles. "You know, that might not be a bad idea. If I'm sitting at a café table with a lovely woman beside me, I may seem more approachable, less like a spy or informant. I'm sure he worries about the Federales following a journalist like me, although I doubt it. I'm not a big fish in the media pool. All the same, the next time he calls, I'll suggest he bring someone too, as if we're just two couples, friends, meeting for lunch."

CHAPTER 7

The interview with the rebel artist is just what Lena has been hoping to cover while down here. More and more, she's convinced photojournalism is the profession she wants to pursue. She puts a new roll of film in her camera and takes off, catching a bus to where she last saw the posters. She wants close-ups to study before meeting with the artist. But when she gets there—a semi-commercial district—the posters are gone. All that's left are torn corners and white residue from the glue.

Disappointed, she heads back to the bus stop. Walking ahead of her is a trio of college students wearing backpacks, two boys and a girl. She still thinks of young people her age that way: boys, girls, not fully grown. She thinks of herself that way too—not quite an adult. What's the magic ingredient that turns the young into full-fledged adults?

The students are talking anxiously among themselves, glancing over their shoulders and down alleys, as if scouting out trouble. What are they afraid of? When they turn down a side street, Lena stops and peers around the corner of a brick building to see what's up. They are pulling from their backpacks long boxes, big white jars, and paint rollers. They're re-hanging Raoul's posters!

Lena can't believe her luck. She feels like a spy, heart hammering as she grabs her camera. Then she hears shouts. Three policemen sprint toward the students. One boy takes off, pushing past Lena and knocking her against the wall. The others are stuffing everything back into their packs. The girl looks up and starts running when the police are almost on top of them. One grabs her by the hair and throws her to the ground. The other boy is already on the ground, two policemen kicking him in the ribs and head.

Lena is too shocked to move. She watches in horror as the scene unfolds. The girl screams when the policeman stomps on her wrist to keep her down. She kicks him, and he punches her in the face. The boy being beaten is curled in a ball, blood pouring from his head.

"Stop!" Lena cries out. "You're going to kill them!

That gets their attention. A policeman charges toward her. "Journalist, American journalist!" she shouts, holding up her press pass. He rips it from her neck and throws it on the ground. Then he goes for her camera.

"Wait! Wait!" She twists away so she can tear out the unused roll of film. "Here! This is what you want." She thrusts it into his hands.

"You took photos of them hanging posters?"

"Yes, yes, lots," she lies.

He looks her over, eyes narrowed. Then he shoves her against the building, her head crashing against the bricks. "Get out of here before I take you in too!"

The handcuffed students are dragged away to a waiting police car. The girl glances Lena's way before she's pushed inside. Their eyes lock. "I'm so, so sorry!" Lena mouths silently. Then she picks up her press pass and runs to the bus stop.

Lena is still shaking when she arrives back at La Rosaleda. The back of her head is matted with blood, her fingers sticky and trembling as she tries to wash it away. A sour bile rises to her throat, thinking of those kids, bloody and beaten. What will they do to them in jail? She could have been arrested too. What would she have done then? Call her father? Her mother?

Her mother! She thinks contemptuously. She's the cause of all this, she and her husband and Ortiz. And the United States too, for supporting a dictator. She's more determined than ever to do this interview, to let people know what's going on down here.

Two days later Daniel calls and tells her to meet him in front of her boardinghouse in half an hour. She debates telling him about what happened, worried that if she does, he might not take her with him to meet the artist, thinking it's too dangerous. And now it does seem dangerous. Not the lark she imagined.

He's sitting in his car smoking and startles when she opens the passenger door.

"I didn't know you smoked," Lena says, waving away the fumes.

"Usually I don't." He puts out his cigarette, his forehead creasing. "Are you sure you still want to do this?"

Lena hesitates. Daniel looks so edgy with his pinched eyebrows and clenched jaw it makes her heartbeat quicken. Does she want to do this? "Absolutely," she says, despite her misgivings, knowing they both need shoring up.

The café where they are to meet stands on the corner of a busy boulevard, a dozen tables scattered in front. They drive past and park, as instructed, walking the rest of the way.

"We're supposed to sit at a table near the entrance," Daniel says as they make their way back to the cafe. "They'll arrive soon after."

"How will they know us? Or we them?"

"I'm sure they already know what I look like. They're probably watching us already." Lena glances around to see if anyone is looking their way. "We won't know them until they introduce themselves. The plan is I do all the talking and you sit there looking demure and lovely."

"Yeah, right. You don't know me very well, do you?"

"Seriously, let me do the talking, except for the polite chit-chat before the interview."

"But I can help! I'm an artist too. I can relate to him on that level, show we understand the power of art, how it moves and inspires people. Build empathy."

"Okay but take your cues from me. I'll kick you if I want you to clam up."

"Yes, master," she says demurely. "Just don't kick too hard. I kick back."

He stops and grabs her arm "You're being way too flippant. These people are not to be trifled with. Do you understand?"

"I get it," she says, removing his hand.

"We have to protect ourselves and our source," Daniel continues. "Anything that happens today must stay between us. You can't share the details of this meeting with anyone. I thought you understood what you're getting into, what would be expected of you. Do you?"

"I do. I promise," she assures him. He stares at her sternly. Then, seeming satisfied, he turns toward the restaurant again. Lena lets out the breath she was holding and follows, glancing sideways around her. "I wonder what they thought of all that, if they're watching," she says.

He's quiet and then gives her a strange look. "Lovers' spat, I suppose."

She makes a face. "Now look who's being flippant."

He picks up her hand and holds it snugly in his.

"What are you doing?"

He looks at her nervously. "We're posing as lovers, you know."

"Are you kidding?"

He gives her a quick glance as he leads her through the sidewalk tables and then says, "I'm not, actually."

"Whose idea was that?"

"Here we are. This should do." He takes a seat at a patio table next to the front door.

"You didn't answer my question," she reminds him as they sit facing the street. "Daniel?" she asks again.

"I may have led them to believe we are very *close* friends. Is that a problem? At the time, it seemed strategic. They'll see you as someone close to me who I wouldn't bring into harm's way if I was planning anything nefarious."

"Okay, no problem. But maybe I should be told these things. Is there anything else I should know?"

He gives her a sheepish grin. "If there is, I've forgotten."

The waiter comes and they both order coffee, hers iced and sweet. His hot and black.

"I can't see how you can drink hot coffee in this heat," she says.

"That doesn't seem as odd as putting ice in yours."

"Well then, we can have another lovers' spat about that, I suppose."

She smiles and he grins back. She's happy he's looking more relaxed than earlier. Wanting to keep the light banter going, she says, glancing around again, "I wonder which way they'll come. Do you think that's them?" She nods toward an older couple, the man with a large paunch and plaid shorts, the woman wearing a floppy hat and too-red lipstick. They look like tourists. Daniel laughs.

"Well, they could be in disguise," she says. "I'd never guess they were rebels."

"Nor would I. But here's a more likely couple. See those two men in hard hats heading this way?"

"But there's no woman!"

"Exactly! Now that would be a proper disguise."

She laughs. "Okay, you win."

They are still laughing when a couple exits the restaurant and pauses at their table. They look up, disconcerted, then realizing who it is, Lena and Daniel rise to greet them.

The man is scruffy with dark blond dreadlocks, cargo shorts, and a Hawaiian shirt. A skateboard is tucked beneath his arm. The woman is pretty with short dark hair and bangs. Her silky sleeveless blouse shows off slender but amazingly well-toned arms.

"Daniel?" asks the skateboarder, sticking out a hand.

He takes it. "Yes, and you?"

"Call me Marley." He grins, fingering his dreadlocks.

"I'm Lena." Marley looks surprised when she sticks out her hand, as if reluctant to take it. Lena glances at Daniel. Has she done something wrong already?

"Carla," the woman says, reaching across Marley to take Lena's hand. Her smile looks more appraising than welcoming.

"Nice to meet you," Lena says, smiling back in the same way. The woman doesn't look like Marley's type. Definitely not a couple.

Daniel waves his hand at the chairs across from them. "Sit, please. Can I order you anything?"

Carla smiles sweetly at him. "Would you mind trading places? I feel claustrophobic staring at a wall." She has a distinctive, gravelly, voice. A slight accent. Eastern European, Lena guesses.

Daniel looks surprised at her request, but quickly recovers. "Of course!"

He and Lena exchange glances as they gather their drinks and napkins and move to the other side of the table. Now Marley and Carla have a street view and Lena and Daniel are staring at a wall. When they are all situated again, Daniel catches the eye of a passing waiter. Marley orders a cherry coke, lots of ice. Carla, water, no ice.

"So where do you skate?" Lena asks Marley. "I've not seen many skateboarders in town."

"Yeah, it hasn't caught on here yet," he tells her. "It's how I get around. More transportation than sport. Although I get in my licks when I want." His Spanish has a decidedly Aussie accent. The nervousness she saw earlier disappears as he grins at her. "And you, do you skate?"

"I did years ago. Now I stick to surfing. Fewer broken bones."

His eyes light up. "No way, mate! Me too! Have you been to Aqua Verde? Bitchin' waves. Smooth as glass. Curl so deep you can get lost in it."

"I haven't, but I can't wait to go."

He leans forward. "You could come with us. A group will be heading that way soon . . . I mean—" his eyes flicker to Daniel and then Carla "—if it's cool?" Carla does not look encouraging.

"I'd love that!" Lena says.

Daniel kicks her under the table, then turns toward Marley. "Tell me more about your poster of Raoul. What inspired you to make it?"

"Well," Marley says, looking hesitantly at Carla, "everyone's heard of the Aguileros, but they got no face, man. And Raoul, well, he does. So, I thought . . . maybe . . .." He falters, not sure where to take this.

Lena breaks in. "It's brilliant! Reminds me of what Warhol does, idealizing Marilyn that way. But even more what Fitzpatrick did with Che's iconic photo. I mean, wow! The power of reducing the image to black and red with that bit of gold on his beret. And then he mass-produced it and gave it away! No profit motive. Just pure passion for the cause. Was it that way for you?"

Daniel gives her a curious but encouraging look. Carla's is more appraising. Marley gives her two thumbs up. "Right on, dude! You got it." He smiles broadly.

Daniel takes over. "So, was it your idea to make the poster, or the Aguileros?"

"They called me. Wanted a photo-shoot."

"They commissioned you? Why'd they choose you?"

"Well, they saw the stuff I made back home in Oz. I had a gig creating LP covers for Australian rock and surf bands—Easy Beats, The Twilights, Pipeliners. They wanted something similar. I mean, at first, I thought they were some rock band!" He laughs.

Lena's eyes light up. "They want to brand and market themselves!" She shoots Daniel a bright I-told-you-so look.

Daniel ignores her and takes over. "Did you meet with Raoul by himself? Or were others there?"

Marley shoots a questioning look at Carla, who seems to give him the go ahead. "I met with all three brothers. But I can't tell you where." He gives Daniel a defiant look. "I was blindfolded, anyway, and we drove for hours, so I couldn't tell you anything even if I wanted. And I don't."

"That's understandable. So, what happened when they took the blindfold off?"

"Well, we were somewhere out in the jungle. They wanted photos of them to turn into a poster. Part of a propaganda campaign, I figured. Which was cool with me. I don't like those bloody Federales. So anyway, they were all dressed in their fatigues, like they were ready to go to battle, you know, bandoliers, machine guns. It was awesome. But they were wearing those baseball type caps, you know, which were hiding half their face, so I told them the hats had to go."

"Then why is the poster of Raoul by himself?" Lena thinks she knows the answer, but she wants to hear him say it.

"Well, I started with the three brothers like Tomás wanted, but even when I reduced the image to its most basic form, wiping out most of the detail, it was still too busy. These kinds of graphics need a single, simple image. So, I showed them one of Raoul alone. I cut him away from the original and blew it up so they could see for themselves what I meant about a single, powerful image. They got it and agreed to go with that."

"But why put Raoul's name on the poster? Why not The Aguileros?" Lena asks. "Whose idea was that?"

"Mine," he says proudly. "Everyone knows who the Aguileros are. But with the single image, they need a single name to brand them—like Elvis or Che or Fidel."

"So, Raoul, then. That was clever." Lena is impressed.

"I thought so," he says, grinning.

Lena leans forward. "It sounds like Tomás is the leader, right? He's the one you had to convince to go with the single image." She flashes a smug smile at Daniel, as if to say, here it comes, my theory corroborated.

"I don't know about that. No one said anything about a leader."

"But surely you could tell," Lena insisted.

Daniel puts his hand on her arm. "Just tell us what they were like, from your perspective, what you saw."

Marley glances at Carla. "Well, Tomás is the oldest brother, and he acts like it. Very macho, you know. Fierce. Built strong too. Husky. The other soldiers, they seem—"

"Wait!" Lena breaks in, "You mean others beside the brothers were there?"

"Of course. We were at one of their camps."

"Okay, go on." Daniel says, giving Lena another stern look. "What about Tomás and the other men?"

"They were very respectful of him. Even fearful, I'd say. They didn't want to piss the guy off, you know?"

"And the other brothers?"

"Well, Pepe was like everyone's favorite younger brother, full of jokes and fun. Patted him on the head, pulled his cap over his eyes, stuff like that."

"And Raoul?" Lena asks.

He licks his lips again and gives Carla a sideways glance.

"It's all right," Carla tells him.

"Raoul was quiet, watching everything going on all around him. It was clear to me this photo-shoot was his idea, part of a larger plan, I figured. Like he had a grand strategy going on in his head, everything mapped out like clockwork." Marley sits back and seems to think a moment. "Raoul, I figure, is the strategist. Tomás, because he's so fierce and feared, and bragged about training with Fidel, he's the commander, leads in the field, is my guess. But I get the impression Raoul is the one pulling the strings." He looks defiantly at Carla. "You told me to go on."

"It's all right," she assures him.

Lena frowns, her grand theory collapsing about Raoul being a fig-urehead, not the group's leader. "So then how do the men feel about Raoul?"

"They like him. They respect him. They look up to him and do what he says." Marley stops and leans forward. "But they don't fear him like they do Tomás or love him like they do Pepe." He pauses a moment. "They revere him."

"Revere?" Lena asks skeptically, thinking he got the word wrong.

"Revere," he says solemnly, decidedly.

Lena's eyes light up. "And that's why you wanted *his* face, *his* name, on the poster."

"You got it," he answers. "I lifted his head and shoulders out of the group, showed them how much more powerful he looks, alone. And *kapow*! A star was born. History in the making."

CHAPTER 8

"So, what did you think of Carla?" Lena asks Daniel. "Was she Marley's handler, or what?" They are sitting in Daniel's car near the Museo de Bellas Artes where he's dropping her off before heading back to type up his notes.

He nods. "It would seem so. Although I wonder if Marley is legit. The man I've been talking with to set up the interview didn't have an Australian accent."

"No kidding? I wonder if it was Raoul. I think Marley is legit though. He's so squirrelly, surely they could have found someone else to pretend to be the artist if they wanted."

"You're probably right. Which explains the handler. Without her, we could have gotten more material from him."

"What Marley is doing here—or, what it appears Raoul is doing—is brilliant," Lena says. "Creating a brand, a powerful visual symbol for people to rally around, rather than just a name like the Freedom and Prosperity Front, or even the Aguileros." She pauses, an idea brewing. "You know, you could do a smaller story on protest art—art used for political purposes. How it's being used here and to what effect. Maybe a brief history on how it's been used elsewhere." She looks hopefully at him.

"Not a bad idea. But art's not my beat. Why don't you write the story? I could look it over, add anything relevant I've discovered."

"I'd love that!"

"Here's a great place to start," Daniel says, nodding toward the museum. "I don't know what political art they may have, but we'd want to find out if there's any local precedent for what Raoul is doing."

"I'd also like to check out the local art scene. Do you know where artists or the local literati hang out? Some pub or club?"

"I'll ask around and let you know."

Lena fairly flies up the flight of stone steps toward an expansive terrace fronting the museum. Inside, a long spacious corridor lined with marble statues leads to side rooms full of paintings. Above her head, a forty-foot ceiling reveals a second and third floor, each with more rooms branching off. She'll need more than one afternoon to see everything.

A brochure map shows where the different collections are found. One catches her eye: "Fantasy Extraordinaire: San Balanque's own Dolores Machado." One whole room devoted exclusively to her mother's work! She's tempted to go there, but then she sees a special exhibit of Francisco Goya's paintings on loan from the Prado, featuring his *Third of May, 1808* "Executioners of the Defender of Madrid." Talk about protest art! This is where it all began. And this is where she heads now, working her way through the surrounding throng until she's close enough to view the entire painting unhindered. It's stunning!

Eleven feet long and nine feet tall, its impact is shocking. A row of soldiers point rifles at a kneeling prisoner. His arms are held high and wide. His blazingly white shirt forms a triumphant V for victory in stark contrast against the black night arching over him and the pile of bloody bodies at his feet. Yet, it's the man's face that arrests her—the raised eyebrows over wide, anguished eyes, waiting for everything he's fought for to drain away with his last breath. It's almost too much to bear. Yet she can't look away.

When she finally does, another Goya piece captures her gaze, a small sepia-toned etching entitled "And They Are Fierce." Women in long dresses are fighting armed soldiers. One heaves a heavy rock over her head. Another clasps a naked child protectively behind her back as she drives a spear into a soldier's belly. The desperation of these women's plight is matched only by the fierceness of their faces. Their courage and determination are heart-breaking and heroic.

Yet, as powerful as this image is, Lena's mind keeps returning to that man in Goya's masterpiece with his raised arms and raised eyebrows. Does it always end like this for these freedom fighters going against armies with so much more power and resources? Apparently so, according to the histories she's read. Her spirits, so high before, are now flagging. She forces herself to wander through two more rooms, but her heart's not in it.

That night, a note arrives from Daniel, telling Lena he's leaving for a while to follow a lead on another story. He gives her a list of artist hangouts, but says to wait for him, not to go out alone at night. She slumps down on her bed. She was looking forward to lively music and art-talk to lift her spirits. And she's eager to do more research for her protest art story. If she's going to be a photojournalist, she can't wait for someone to hold her hand. Daniel is off working on *his* story, and so must she.

Tomorrow.

Upon entering *El Barrio,* Lena pauses to get her bearings, listening to the sexy strains of Santana's "Black Magic Woman" pulsing through the room. She's never gone to a pub alone before, and even then, nothing like this. Santa Barbara, for all its culture and art, is more provincial than cosmopolitan when it comes to a lively night life. Most college kids she hung out with partied at each other's homes, or bonfires on the beach, or yachts in the marina. But maybe Lena just didn't run with the fast crowd.

She weaves her way through an assortment of tall tables and stools surrounding a dance floor where two couples sway and cling. A long bar stretches across one wall. Servers with trays of drinks dart here and there. As she passes one table, she overhears a name she recognizes:

"Dolores Machado." She freezes and glances back to where two women are discussing her mother's art.

One sits on a high stool with a long-tapered cigarette holder held between two fingertips. A pale pink shift falls loosely from her bare shoulders. A glittering tiara crowns her raven-dark hair, a sharp wing-tip curving onto her creamy cheek. Her long white legs, crossed, dazzle with their tiny silver-strapped heels. She looks like a flapper from the Roaring Twenties.

The other woman leans against the high tabletop, flamboyantly dressed in men's clothing—striped hip-huggers and a fuzzy neon-green vest over a pink shirt and black tie. Her oversized clothes fall from her slender body as if from a hanger. A tan fedora crowns her platinum blond hair cut razor sharp to fall straight as a pin to her shoulders. Her skin is as dark as her friend's is dazzling white. Both look as if they're dressed for a masquerade party, but then so do half the people meandering through the pub, with their tiaras or berets, kaftans and Nehru shirts. It seems no style is unstylish here. Even so, Lena feels conspicuously unhip and underdressed in her bell-bottoms and peasant blouse.

"She's taking her subjects back to the time and garb of Colonialism! As if that was the golden age," says the woman in the tiara.

"No," says the other woman, "Dolores Machado is showing us how to survive in a brutal world, to dress ourselves in the most beautiful clothing we can imagine and surround ourselves in a world of wonder."

"But that's escapism in the extreme, avoiding the dark realities of life, refusing to engage with them."

"She's showing us how to buoy ourselves in the maelstrom, how to recreate ourselves into something that can survive the worst life throws at us."

"Let them eat cake! That's how I see it." The tiara woman haughtily puffs on her tapered cigarette holder.

"But you are a cynic, not a dreamer. And a cynic cannot see past her own nose."

"A cynic is a realist, and a dreamer is delusional. But that, my dear, is why we love each other so much, opposites attract . . . And look, we have an audience." She cocks her head toward Lena.

Lena flushes and turns toward them. "You found me out. I'm blushing."

"So you are. How charming," says the tiara woman. But her look is warm and inviting.

"It's just that I overheard you discussing Machado's art," Lena says, wishing now she'd visited her mother's art at the museum. "I was curious to hear your opinions."

"And what did you think? Which of us has the right view of it?"

Lena laughs. "I'm not foolish enough to be reeled into that battle."

"But you must have an opinion. What do you think of her artwork?"

Lena struggles to organize her thoughts, remembering the paintings in the *Artforum* magazine, the self-portrait and girl running, as well as all the abstracts on the walls back home.

"I find them breathtakingly beautiful," she answers honestly, "mysterious and masterful. I'm a bit in awe. Frankly, I'm not interested in the artist or why she painted them. Can't they be appreciated simply for what they are, not what they mean?"

Tiara lady lifts her eyebrows. "Art for art's sake? Well, my dear, they can be anything you want them to be, even that. Come sit with us. Our twosome enjoys the company of a threesome, especially one as beautiful and articulate as you. Charlie, pull out a stool for her." The woman in the vest does as she was asked and holds out her hand, inviting Lena to join them.

Lena reads the double meaning and laughs. "I would not dare intrude! I know when I'm in over my head. But thank you for the invitation."

Charlie pushes the stool under the table again. "A shame," she says.

"Yes," the other agrees. "A pity." Then they turn away and resume their conversation.

Lena wanders toward the bar where she orders a glass of Chablis.

"I see you've met Charlie and Marilyn." A man who has been sitting farther down the bar approaches her. He's slightly taller than Lena, lean, attractive, maybe in his thirties, dressed in flared jeans and a long-sleeved striped shirt that shows off the dark curls on his chest. He leans against the bar as she does, looking out. "So, what did you think?" he asks, sounding amused.

"Of what?"

"Our colorful twosome." He nods toward the couple she had been with.

She laughs. "I never kiss and tell."

He smiles. "I'm happy to hear that." He holds out his hand. "Francisco Romero, at your service."

"Lena Landon," she says taking his hand. He holds it a moment longer than needed.

"Sit," he says, pulling out a bar stool. "Please."

She does and he sits too. Now they are facing the bar with its colorful array of liquor bottles, the mirror behind it reflecting the room behind them. She takes another sip of wine. He swirls the amber liquor in his glass.

"You're new here," Francisco tells her, but whether he means new to the pub or San Balanque isn't clear.

"Yes, fresh from the States. And you? Are you new or old?"

He laughs. "I'm so old, I'm like a ghost, I haunt this pub so much. But tell me, what do you think of San Balanque so far?"

"Well, I'm still getting my bearings, but . . . I think I'm falling fast in love with this country of yours."

"She is easy to love. But she will break your heart."

"Why do you say that?"

"Ah, what do I know? I'm just a poet. It seems I feel too deeply for my own good."

"I heard everyone in San Balanque is a poet."

He laughs. "This is true, but there are two kinds. One who writes poems to hand down to his progeny. And one who publishes them. I am of the latter."

"I'm impressed. Can you recite something for me?"

"Hmmm. Let me think. All right." He takes on a new voice and demeanor as he speaks. "And the wasted land lies like a lover that's been abandoned by all she loves. The mountains and hills cry out, the streams and rivers weep, and there's nothing left in all her world but tears."

"That's beautiful!"

Francisco puts his hand on his heart in gratitude. "Not quite the poem for this moment, but it's what came to mind on sudden notice."

"Do many poets and artists hang out here?"

"A few." He cocks his head. "You are interested in these things?"

"Yes. Art especially. I was just at the Museo's amazing Goya exhibit. But I'm even more interested in meeting local artists."

"You are an artist then."

She laughs. "I'm a work in progress."

"Aren't we all."

"I've been fascinated by those Raoul posters plastered all over town. What do you know about them?"

"Ah, Raoul! The rock star of the Aguileros."

"The Aguileros?" she asks, pretending not to know, to see what he'll say.

"The freedom fighters. Those that oppose the current administration."

"Is it so bad?"

He gives her a keen look, then glances away. "I stay out of politics. It's bad for one's health. And one's career."

"I see," Lena says, remembering the students being beaten. She gulps the last of her wine, feeling slightly buzzed, then watches while Francisco has the bartender pour her another Chablis and refill his glass.

"Thank you," she says, raising her glass. "I'm still interested in those posters, though. Do you know the artist who made them?"

He shakes his head. "No one knows. But since you are so keen on this subject, I did meet Raoul once."

Her eyes widen as she leans in. "What's he like? These guerilla fighters, Latin rebels, are all the rage back home. Che, Fidel. Is Raoul like them?"

"I couldn't say, having not met the others. It was years ago I met Raoul. At *La Respuesta*. That's where the Aguileros may have been born. There are so many different rooms, salons they are called, where people of different persuasions and interests gather. I wandered among them to get a taste of it all. One room was political, loud and angry. Raoul was there among them. It was not long after he'd returned from the States, I believe. His brother Tomás was there too. Neither talked much at first. I may not have noticed them, but the young woman on my arm who was more political than me pointed them out and told me all about them. 'Watch him,' she said, indicating Raoul. 'He's the power behind this group. He will be famous someday. Wait and see.'

"It was true what she said. Raoul seemed to be absorbing everything going on, all the conversations, like a magnet drawing in all the room's energy. The eyes of those speaking were drawn to him as well. Then, while I was watching, he began to speak. For one who had been so silent to take over the room the way he did, speaking in a low voice that forced everyone to be still so they could hear, was astonishing. They all turned toward him, his words pouring out in long eloquent paragraphs, fully formed. Words of power and passion about the history of San Balanque and our common heritage, about the land and the people who work it, about freedom and injustice, sacrifice and courage. It was mesmerizing. Even I, who have no interest in politics, was moved. Soon the crowd was banging cups against the tables and raising their voices: 'Aguileros! Aguileros!'

"A rebel leader and movement were born that day, or so it seemed to me, although my friend said this had been going on for a while. Till the Federales arrived."

"They raided while you were there!?"

"No. That was days later. But I heard they arrested many people. I don't know if Raoul or Tomás were among them that night. I think not. But that's when the brothers went underground."

"And eventually, into the hills, I heard."

He cocks an eyebrow at her. "So, you have heard of them." He smiles when she doesn't answer. "And now you know everything I do about the Aguileros, and why politics is bad for the health here in San Balanque."

"Thank you for sharing that. What was the name of the club where they were meeting? Is it still open?"

"Oh, yes. *La Respuesta*. Still an artist and dissident haven, but more lowkey. I could take you there if you like." He looks hopefully at her.

She smiles, touching his arm. "Thank you. I'll think about that," she says as she slides from her stool.

"Can I have your number before you go?" he asks, seeing she's getting ready to leave.

"I'm sorry, I don't have one. But I'll be back here again. Do you come often?"

"I will now," he tells her.

"It was nice to meet you, Francisco. Your poetry truly is beautiful. I'd like to read more someday."

"I would be pleased," he says, taking the hand she offers him. Then she excuses herself to call a taxi.

CHAPTER 9

Lena wakes the next morning with disturbing images in her mind: wisps of a dream she tries to gather before they drift away. She sees Raoul, the rebel from the poster with his dark eyes and lush mouth. He's not the quiet man Francisco described. He speaks to Lena with wild animation, flinging his hands into the air, his voice loud and passionate. They are arguing heatedly in a long, narrow hallway. She's angry, hurt. She can't remember why. But when he disappears, she panics and searches for him everywhere, in and out of so many crowded rooms. When she finds him, he's kneeling in front of a wall, hands held high and wide. His face is nothing like the man being executed in Goya's painting—it's shining with pride and defiance. She cries out, but he can't hear her. That's when she wakes.

The dream is so disturbing she cannot shake it. She goes into the courtyard, thinking to sketch the tiny finches splashing in the birdbath. Like surfing, drawing helps clear her mind. But it's not going well. The air is heavy. The heat suffocating.

"It's going to storm," Mrs. Henson tells her sagely. But there are no clouds in the sky.

Lena feels pensive all day, puttering about, waiting for evening. Yesterday she was eager to visit *La Respuesta*. But now as she dresses to go, she's tense. Maybe she should wait for Daniel. *Wait!* She mutters disgustedly. No, she needs to be doing something—working on her story, finding out more about what's happening here. *More about Raoul.*

In the taxi, the driver tells her a hurricane is blowing in the Caribbean. It already hit Haiti and is headed toward the Gulf Coast. "They get all the wind," complains the driver. "All we get is the wet, the heat, and humidity."

"I suppose that's better than wind," she says. "Do you get many hurricanes here?"

"Not as many as you might think. About on par with the earthquakes and volcano eruptions." He looks back at her with a grin. She smiles too, realizing he's teasing her.

"We get the monsoons though. That's just as bad," he says. No grin this time.

When she exits the taxi, she stops to gaze at a bank of angry clouds crushed together on the horizon, smeared in streaks of scarlet and purple. It looks and feels ominous. The suffocating humidity wraps its heavy folds around her like a wet towel. She takes a moment to breathe in the metallic scent of rain before entering the club, wondering if she's made a mistake coming here. Too late now.

La Respuesta is larger than *El Barrio*. It has a different vibe too. Quieter but more intense, more exclusive. Lena stops at the bar on her way in and orders a glass of Chablis, her go-to drink. The dance floor is empty, but three musicians are setting up their equipment in the corner. Music, smoke, and laughter drift toward her from the back of the club. She follows the energy into the hallway and through a labyrinth of rooms, one flowing into the next. She has the disconcerting feeling she's entering last night's dreamscape.

Most rooms have couches and armchairs, low coffee tables, stacks of books on side tables, posters and other artwork lining the walls. Music plays in all of them. The sultry strains of Nina Simone flow through several doorways she passes. Cigarette smoke and the smell of marijuana drift through.

Few people pay attention to Lena, aside from an occasional male gaze, showing appreciation, no doubt, for the miniskirt she's wearing tonight, the platform heels and slinky top. A step up from the casual look she wore at *El Barrio*. She put on mascara and shadow and a smear of pink gloss this time too, and exchanged her large hemp bag for a tiny, beaded clutch.

A woman's husky laugh arrests her. That voice. She's heard it before. Carla. She stops and looks around but doesn't see the petite woman with short black hair and bangs from the café. When she hears the voice again, it's coming from a woman with a long, light brown braid hanging down her back, no bangs, but she has Carla's toned arms.

"Carla?" Lena says, coming up behind her.

The woman turns and gives Lena an icy look. "Pardon?"

"We met at that café with Marley?"

"You must be mistaken." It's obviously her: same build, eyes, voice, arms.

"It appears I am," Lena says, willing to play along. Then she sticks out her hand. "I'm Lena."

The woman glances down at Lena's hand but does not take it. "So you are," she says and turns her back.

Lena is less affronted by the snub than thrilled at the knowledge she was right. Not only is this Carla, but the Carla she met was in disguise.

"So sorry!" Lena says rather gleefully to the woman's back.

She weaves her way through various rooms heading back to the front bar. After that run-in with Carla, she needs a celebratory drink. Something stronger than Chablis. She's never been much for hard liquor, but she once tried a Tequila Sunrise that was surprisingly tasty, so she orders that. A jazz trio is playing now. Piano, sax, and bass. Two couples on the dance floor are swaying to Miles Davis's *Blue in Green*, one of her father's favorites. She stands with a few others, watching the trio play.

"So, this Carla you mistake me for is a friend of yours?"

Lena turns to face the woman. "No. Someone I met during an interview."

"With whom?"

"An artist. Juan Baptiste," she says, making up a name to continue the pretense they've never met. "A sculptor. Carla was his lover. They were hanging all over each other. Very pretty woman, but stern. Forbidding. Nothing like you, I can see now."

Carla's mouth quirks in amusement. "No. I'm so warm and fuzzy."

"Exactly," Lena says.

They stare in silence at each other for a moment, and then the woman asks, "So, you're a journalist then?"

"Yes. Sometimes."

"And what brings you to San Balanque?"

Lena shrugs. "The usual. Adventure, romance, surfing. Practice my Spanish. My friend Daniel was here and invited me."

"He's your lover?"

"He would like to be," Lena says, remembering how they posed as lovers at the cafe.

They study each other again.

"And you. What do you do?" Lena asks.

She hesitates, then says, "I'm a boxer. I manage a gym."

Lena raises her eyebrows in surprise, then realizes how that makes sense. She has the fluid gait of an athlete, the wiry build and toned body. The pugnacious attitude. "I've always wanted to learn to box."

Carla cocks her head. "You should visit my gym. It's on Clancy Street, in the Creole District." Then she turns away before Lena has a chance to ask her name.

The storm that Mrs. Henson predicted finally comes. In spades. Lena never knew clouds could hold so much rain or the earth absorb so much water. Apparently, it can't. The streets become rushing rivers, the boardinghouse's courtyard a lake. The steady drum of rain on leaky roof tiles and constant pinging of raindrops in buckets create a wild cacophony in her small room. Which seems smaller than ever now she's stuck inside, swaddled in a humidity she could drown in, she writes in a letter to her father. But at least the heat has lessened.

Lena loves feeling the cool air gusting through the balcony doors she cracks open. Loves the scent too, like nothing she's ever known. A primal, earthy, sweet-dank scent, she tells her father in the letter. An exciting scent, like danger, adventure, romance, she tells herself. Isn't that what she told Carla, why she came here? Although she was being flippant with Carla and it's not why she came, now that she's here, she's loving this wild weather, this stormy adventure that tastes like the high seas. That conjures up images of pirates and rebels and Latin lovers, mixed with a heavy dose of mystery.

She sleeps with the doors ajar to better smell the rain, to feel the cool air moving luxuriously, wantonly, over her body as she lays dreaming of other wanton things. She wakes feeling refreshed and energized, then restless and frustrated because she's still stuck in this room. Thankfully, a few days before the monsoon broke, she picked up several library books to research for her protest art piece, so she works on that.

A week goes by. Then three more days. Finally, the torrents of rain that fell like a solid curtain thin into sheer veils and part with the breeze, revealing glimpses of blue. The melting away of rain leaves behind rich wet scents that Lena drinks in like heady wine. She disappears out of doors and down the street, dodging puddles and jumping over the streams that still course through the gutters.

California never had so much rain in a decade, let alone ten days! Everything is so clean and sparkling now. All the windows along the street flung wide open. All the faces she passes shining. A lightheaded giddiness bubbles through her.

"I have so much to tell you!" Lena tells Daniel when they meet later that week at a nearby café. She plops down in a chair across from him. Her hair is pulled into a sloppy ponytail, and she's wearing cut-off shorts and a clingy tank top, no make-up. She knows she looks twelve years old dressed like this, but she doesn't care.

Daniel stood to greet her but sits back down again, seeing the excited state she's in.

"Hi to you too!" he says with an amused smile.

"Oh, sorry!" She half-rises and leans across the little table to hug him. They meet in the middle for a quick, awkward greeting.

"I have exciting news too," he tells her. "But you go first, before you burst."

She tells him everything Francisco said about Raoul, and then about running into Carla at *La Respuesta*, her being in disguise and telling Lena where she works. She says all this in a rush and jumble. Then she sits back, excitedly awaiting his response.

"So, you completely ignored my warnings about going to the clubs alone."

"What! Is that all you have to say? Of course I couldn't wait. But that's not the point! We cracked the Carla code. We know who she is now. Well, not her real name, but where to find her if needed. And Raoul and the salon and the raid. Can't you use that in the piece you're writing?" She slumps back in her chair. "I couldn't wait to tell you, and you're not a bit interested."

"I am! Good work, Lena." He sounds far from enthusiastic, yet his eyes are shining.

"So. Your news trumps mine," she says, wondering what could top cracking the Carla code. She leans forward again. "Okay, let's hear it before *you* burst."

"I have an interview set up with the Aguilero brothers."

Her eyes bug out and she grabs his arm, fingernails digging in. "You have to take me!"

He looks startled. "I thought you'd say that, just not so vehemently."

"So? What do you say?" She's still grabbing his arm.

He pulls away, gently, and then puts his hands on hers. He looks sympathetic. "That's not a good idea. This will be far riskier than meeting with Marley and Carla. Besides, I don't think the Aguileros will allow it. I can only bring a photographer."

"I'm a photographer!"

He laughs. "Since when?"

"One of my photos of striking workers was on the front page of the *Chronicle* when I interned there. And look at these." She pulls from her bag several envelopes full of photos from her excursions around the city. She was so pleased when she picked them up at the shop this morning.

She sits back, nervously watching as Daniel looks through them one by one.

"Yes, very nice. Artistic. But photojournalism isn't the same."

"Who told you that? What are the most famous photos taken by journalists? Tell me."

He just looks at her.

"All right, I'll tell you. The most recent being that photo by Margaret Bourke-White of the naked Vietnamese girl running for her life, and Marc Riboud's photo of the flower child with those rifles pointed at her. Then there's Dorothea Lange's iconic photo of the migrant woman and her children. What makes them so memorable? You need an artist's eye to capture the drama of the moment, to reveal what's important, what might be missed if you don't have an eye to see. And I have one," she says boldly, pinning his eyes with hers.

He looks taken aback. "I dare say you do. And the passion too. But it's still too dangerous."

"I'm not as young as I look, you know. I'd be perfect for this job. They already know and trust me. Carla didn't have to come back and talk to me, didn't have to reveal where she works. But she did. If she trusts me, why can't you?"

His eyebrows are pinched, as if weighing his options or fighting against his own instincts. "It's true, they already know you, but . . .." He shakes his head.

"Please! This is what I want to do with my life, be a photojournalist. Surely you can see how important this is to me!"

He looks up at her through that hank of hair falling over his eyes, shakes his head, and sighs. "I hope I don't come to regret this."

She leans across the table, takes his hands and kisses them.

CHAPTER 10

Lena and Daniel meet often while he awaits a call from the Aguileros about the interview. Daniel tells her everything he knows about them, and she shares drafts of her protest art piece. He's sweet and encouraging and she learns much, not only about the rebels but about being a journalist.

He reminds her of Lonny—not with a sibling vibe, but with his basic goodness, his trustworthiness. Even when Lonny made unwanted advances, she felt safe with him. The way Daniel looks at her sometimes suggests that he, like Lonny, would like there to be more between them.

Lena could feel more than friendship for him too. While Daniel isn't handsome, he's attractive in a wholesome way. She admires his intellect, his dedication to journalism. He's four years her senior, but often seems even older, more worldly. Other times, when he's bashful or unsure how to take her, he appears as young and inexperienced as Lena. She likes that vulnerability. She finds it endearing the way that hank of fair hair is forever falling over his eyes. She's tempted to brush it back. When she does, their eyes meet in a way that makes him swallow and her breath catch. But neither follows up.

Daniel isn't the one she dreams about: that dark, irresistible force rising like the sea to carry her away. But possibly he could be her first. She'd like her first to be someone like him, someone she admires and trusts.

The call from the Aguileros finally comes. "They want to meet in one week," Daniel tells Lena after showing up unexpectedly at La Rosaleda.

Lena feels a surge of excitement. "That's great! Then I have time to go surfing. I've been fantasizing about hitting the waves all week, but afraid I'd miss the call. I need to release some of this pent-up energy about meeting the notorious Aguilero brothers." She laughs at herself. "The beach is only an hour away by bus."

"No, I'll drive you," Daniel says.

"Really? You sure?"

"I could use some down time too before we go."

When they arrive at the beach—a tender curve of white sand lined with nodding palms—Lena stands there, drinking it all in, the briny scent of salt and seaweed, the rumble of tumbling waves, the cool caress of a breeze lifting her hair from her shoulders, molding her long peasant dress against her body. It feels like she's home again. The waves beckon to her like friends, calling her name. She strips while Daniel spreads a blanket on the sand, pulls off his shirt and takes a seat. He blushes when he looks up to see her half-naked in her bikini.

She laughs. *Yes, he'll be my first.*

"Come with me," she says, leaning down to take his hand. He's wearing a pair of madras shorts, his bare chest as pale as his legs. A bit of a roll shows above his shorts. She thinks it's cute. "I'll teach you to surf."

"I can barely swim. I'll just wait and watch."

Like Lonny, she thinks. Only this time, watching him watch her turns Lena on in a way that Lonny's gaze never did. When she catches her last wave and turns toward shore, she wonders if Daniel will make the first move or if she'll have to.

"You put the local boys to shame," Daniel says admiringly as she wrings out her hair and drops down beside him.

"Flatterer! You know that's not true. But I can hold my own," she says, lifting her chin.

"You're good at everything you do: surfing, photography, writing. Is there nothing you can't do well?"

"That remains to be seen. I haven't tried *everything*," she says with a saucy grin, rubbing her bare foot against his. Then she sobers. "The thing is, I'm good at some things but excel at none. I'll never be a great artist like—" She stops before saying, *my mother.* "Like Dolores Machado. Or a great surfer like Margo Oberg. Or journalist, like you," she adds coyly.

"Don't sell yourself short. You have plenty of time to excel." He looks at his watch. "Are you ready to go? I'm starving. We could stop at that little restaurant we passed." He rises to his feet.

"All right, I guess," she says, trying to hide her disappointment. Maybe he's not into her after all. Here she decided to grant him the privilege of being her first, and he's not a bit interested! She laughs.

"What?" he asks, looking down at her.

"Nothing," she says. Then she jumps up, grabs her board, and gives him a gleeful look. "Race you to the car," she says and starts running, soft sand flying.

A week later, the danger Daniel warned Lena about hits her full force when a black hood is pulled over her head. She and Daniel were given convoluted directions to their pick-up spot, travelling by bus to Thirty-fourth Street, catching the next bus to Fourteenth, then walking five blocks to a bodega where they went inside and out the back to an alley.

The man waiting for them is built like a bulldog and about as friendly. His dark eyes are dull and menacing as he grunts at them to get into the back seat of a green sedan. Lena takes an instant dislike to him even before he brings out the black hood and reaches toward her.

"What? Wait!" she says, panic rising through her. The hood comes down regardless, enveloping her in a suffocating darkness.

"For your protection, and ours," he growls.

"It's okay," Daniel reassures her, reaching over to pat her leg. "They did this to Marley too, remember?"

She reaches out blindly for Daniel's hand.

"You alright?" he asks. She nods and then realizes he can't see. He's hooded too.

The car's motion makes their bodies sway and Lena puts her hand on the vinyl seat to keep from sliding. The heat is stifling. She wishes she'd worn something cooler than these khaki slacks and clingy blouse. She's sure the sweat pooling between her thighs and under her arms is already staining her clothes. Her feet—stuffed in new, unbroken Doc Marten boots—feel cramped and swollen from the heat.

They drive for hours, and Lena drifts in and out of an uneasy sleep. Occasionally Daniel reaches over and squeezes her arm or leg, startling her. "You okay?" he asks.

The radio is playing, but it goes in and out, turning to static, then back again. Eventually the static wins, and someone turns it off. The two men in front occasionally murmur to each other, but she can't understand what they say. Hot humid air breezes in through the windows, giving some relief. She rolls up her hood far enough to uncover her nose and half her ears, focusing like a blind person on her other senses: the scent of diesel fuel and sound of heavy trucks grinding by, a factory whistle, and once, the distinct sound and feel of going over train tracks.

Eventually the oily, acrid scents of hot asphalt and city streets give way to a whiff of salt and sage, then a rich loamy scent, like wet grass and decaying leaves. The road is bumpy now, and she hears the trill and chatter of bird calls. A flowery scent wafts in with the breeze.

When Lena wakes from the squeak of the vehicle's emergency brake, she realizes she's been drowsing. A slamming door startles her. Then her car door opens, her hood is yanked off. She blinks in the light. The bulldog who greeted them in the alley laughs, not kindly. Lena scoots out, feeling wobbly, her feet half-asleep. She wants to stretch her body but won't give the man the satisfaction of seeing her do so. She discreetly pulls at the damp blouse plastered to her skin.

"Wait there," says the man, pointing to a log at the edge of a large encampment. Tents and lean-tos of assorted sizes are scattered about, along with men and women dressed in green fatigues. A few glance curiously at them, then turn away.

She and Daniel sit on the log.

A young man approaches, his arms held wide and a big grin on his handsome face. "Welcome to Camp Plantain!" He sticks out his hand and they each shake it. "I'm Pepe," he tells them as if expecting they already know who he is. "Sorry for the hoods and all that, but it's for your own protection."

"Of course," Daniel says.

Pepe looks at Lena. "We weren't expecting a girl."

"I'm the photographer," she says, patting the camera bag she brought with the lenses and tripod.

"Really! Can you take my photo? People say I'm very photogenic."

This must be the youngest Aguilero brother, the one Marley said everyone loves. She feels his good humor working to erase her earlier panic. "Of course," she says, smiling up at him. Then, as he strikes a pose, sticking out a foot and turning his face sideways with a fierce look, she adds, "You mean now?"

"Pepe!" someone calls loudly from across the camp. They all turn to look. The bulldog who brought them here beckons to Pepe.

"Who's that?" Lena asks, her eyes narrowing in distaste.

"Tomás, my brother," he says, ignoring him. Then there's a loud whistle: Tomás again.

Pepe groans and turns toward his brother with an exasperated shrug, hands held out as if asking, what now? He sighs and shakes his head. "Please excuse me, the commander calls. Wait here till someone comes for you." He saunters off toward his brother.

In a few minutes, a soldier who looks too young to have a rifle slung over his shoulder hands them two canteens of water. Lena takes a long chug, then splashes water on her neck. The bun she wore this morning has come loose and she can't find the clip. Long, hot tangles fall over her shoulders. She wishes there was a way to contain it.

Daniel looks at his watch. "Three hours here and now another—"

As he's speaking, a soldier comes striding forward and escorts them to a large tent. Tomás stands behind a table, looking at a chart which he rolls up when they enter.

"Not her," he says pointedly, frowning at Lena. The soldier grabs Lena's arm as if to escort her out.

"Wait!" she says, pulling free. "I'm the photographer!"

Tomás waves her away. "We just need the journalist for the interview."

She turns to Daniel for help, but he only offers an apologetic shrug. When the soldier tries to take her arm again, she snaps, "I know where the door is."

She returns to her log, fuming at being sidelined. She closes her eyes and tries to still herself the way her father taught her when she's feeling out of sorts, breathing in the sounds and scents of her surroundings. A slight breeze whispers through the banyan trees behind her. A whiff of honeysuckle. A sound like wild laughter. Monkeys? And something else. Rushing water. She's tempted to get up and explore, but will they let her?

Across the way a female soldier is mending a large green tarp pulled halfway into her lap. Her hair is drawn back into a long braid. Maybe she has a spare band Lena can borrow to pull back her hair.

When Lena approaches, the woman frowns. So instead, she wanders to the edge of the encampment, looking at the dense jungle wall surrounding them. She sees a slight opening. A trail, perhaps, leading down to the rushing water she hears in the ravine below. She glances back to see if anyone is watching. Then Lena parts the jungle wall and steps through.

CHAPTER 11

The trail is soft and spongy, cushioned by countless layers of decaying leaves, now slick from rain. And steep. Lena grabs hold of branches and digs her heels into tree roots to keep from slipping as she moves through a dark green tunnel toward the light below.

She steps into a grassy clearing. Her breath catches as she takes in the scene before her. Fingers of light slant through trees and dapple the grass with patches of gold. Dragonflies with translucent turquoise wings chase each other across the clearing. A honeysuckle vine winds its tender arms around the trunk of a tree, its scent so heavy in the warm air she closes her eyes to drink it in. She feels she's been transported into the mythical landscape she read about, the one created from Malenque's body as she lay dreaming. This is the San Balanque she's longed to find. A sense of wonder rushes through her.

The sound of gushing water draws her toward the stream. A swish and swirl of whitewater cascades softly into a wide deep pool, its surface reflecting the lacy branches above. At the far end, deep green shadows lurk, murky and mysterious, drawing her closer. It looks so inviting she wishes she could slip through those cool waters. But as she watches, a rippling motion stirs the stillness. Her breath catches. Something deep beneath the surface rises. A dark head. A flash of arms. Swimming toward her.

She gasps and steps back into the shadow of the trees. A man rises slowly from the pool, water streaming from his naked body. He runs his hands over his face and hair that falls in dark waves to his shoulders. He moves gracefully, leisurely, like a panther with his smooth lean muscles, the slow roll of hips, long arms loose and languid as he steps ashore.

He doesn't seem naked at all. He seems natural and at ease, at one with his surroundings. He seems like what a man was meant to be. He is beautifully and powerfully built. Wide shoulders bracket a chest lightly matted with damp hair. Torso narrows toward slim hips and a mass of curls between strong thighs. An unsettling heat rises through Lena, making it hard to breathe. She steps deeper into the shadows, then freezes when his eyes find hers.

The moment grows and grows. He's like nothing she's ever seen. Not just the power of his body, but the intensity of his gaze. She cannot look away. His lips part into a slow smile, as if he knows something she doesn't. He slowly moves toward her. His dark eyes are heavy-lidded, his mouth wide, lips full. He's looking at her as if she's as naked as he is and he's having his fill of her, but it's not nearly enough. He moves toward her as if he wants more.

She steps back. He stops and reaches for the fatigues lying in the grass. His eyes never leave hers as he steps into a pair of loose, wide-legged trousers, pulling them up over his slender hips, buttoning them halfway up, the waist left open. She's mesmerized by the dark cavern of his belly button and feels the pull of it on her fingers.

"So. You must be the journalist," he says as he shrugs into his shirt, leaving it unbuttoned.

It's his voice that undoes her—so low and intimate, casual and intense at the same time. He touches the light scattering of dark hair that lies so soft and inviting against his brown chest. She gazes at his hand and feels the warm flesh beneath.

All her senses are heightened, experiencing everything in slow, sensuous motion. *I'm in some sort of trance*, she thinks. She shakes her head, as if to cast off this spell.

"No? Not the journalist?" he says, mistaking her head shake.

"No. I mean, yes," she says confusingly. "I mean, I *am* a journalist, but not today. I'm here to take photos."

He nods sagely at her. He picks up his bandolier and slips it over his head and chest. Picks up his rifle and slings it over his shoulder. His eyes never leave her face.

"And your mother, what does she call you?"

"Malenque," she says, breathlessly. Then shakes herself. "I mean, Malenque is my given name, but Lena is what everyone calls me."

He nods slowly again, as if absorbing this new sobering information. "Then I shall call you Malenque." He looks closely at her. "So. Your mother is San Balanquan?"

"Yes."

"Then you must know Malenque is the mother of all you see here. These flowers at your feet, these trees and vines, the river behind me and its deep pools, the very pool I bathe in each day—they all grew from her body." His dark gaze grazes slowly over Lena's body, as if caressing every hill and vale, every curve and swell.

She shivers and is still speechless, having no idea how to respond. With his intense gaze roving shamelessly, intimately, over her body, she feels shy and apprehensive.

"Lena!" She startles at the sound, then feels immense relief. It's Daniel calling.

"I must go," she tells him.

He cocks his head. "Do you always come when he calls?"

Her eyes flash. "Of course not!"

"You are not his woman?"

"I am no man's woman!" she says, lifting her chin.

He smiles, white teeth gleaming against dark skin, dark eyes sparkling.

"Then go to him, 'No Man's Woman'," he says flippantly. His gaze is light, teasing.

She opens her mouth, then snaps it shut and turns. She stumbles up the steep path, grabbing onto vines and roots to keep from sliding back down the incline. She feels his warm eyes on her as she climbs. Hears his soft mellow laughter rising after her.

"Where have you been?" Daniel says, looking frantic as he watches Lena emerge from the path. "I've been looking everywhere for you!"

She's breathing hard and stops to catch her breath. "I got tired of waiting and decided to explore." She glances nervously down the path, heart pounding.

"I warned you about that. It's not safe to wander off. There are poisonous snakes, wild animals."

"I know," she says, and almost laughs, remembering the panther-like way he walked toward her. "I'm sorry," she says, flustered. "I'm fine."

But her heart is still racing, and she's drenched in sweat. She feels like she's woken from a fever dream. Her hands sting, her palms scratched and dirty from grabbing rough vines as she climbed. One hand is bleeding.

"Look what I've done!" She holds up her hand to show Daniel.

He pulls a red bandanna from his back pocket and dabs at the blood. "Here, hold this while I find some water." A moment later he washes the mud from her hands, covering her bleeding palm with his bandanna. "Press down. It will stop soon."

She hears someone coming up the steep embankment behind her in long, easy strides.

As he takes the final leap up, he looks surprised, and then pleased to see her standing there. He's fully dressed now, pants and shirt buttoned, boots tied. Then he sees Daniel holding her hand and his gaze darkens. He says nothing and strides away.

"Do you know who that was?" Daniel whispers excitedly.

"Raoul," she says, looking after him. His stride falters for an instant when Lena utters his name.

"We've been waiting so I could interview him too," says Daniel.

Raoul disappears into the tent. A moment later, Tomás comes out and motions for them to come. But as Lena follows, he once again shuts her out. "Photos later," he tells her.

This time as Lena waits by the log, all she can think about is Raoul, the way he looked rising from the pool, the way he moved toward her, the way her body responded to his. The sound of his voice like a soft caress she feels even now remembering it. The way his eyes moved over her felt more intimate than a mere undressing. Like he knew—and knew she knew—something that could not be undone was happening between them.

She's never felt that magnetic pull toward anyone before and doesn't know what to make of it. He seemed as mesmerized by her as she was by him. But that's crazy. *Don't be a fool,* she tells herself. It's the heat, it's the excitement of coming to a rebel camp. It's the allure of meeting this great revered hero, this rebel rock-star. You're just starstruck. *Surely, he can't feel the same about me.*

But she cannot stop thinking about him, even as she could not stop staring at him. It's like some madness has taken over. She thinks, crazily, of *The Godfather,* a film she watched with Lonny, the way Michael Corleone chanced upon Apolonia while walking through the Sicilian hills. How they stared at each other in such a way that one of his soldiers said they were "struck by the thunderbolt." That very afternoon Michael tells Apolonia's father he wants to marry her. And they hadn't even spoken to each other yet!

Afterward, she and Lonny laughed at such craziness. Only in the movies, right?

Yet, this feels like that. And this isn't the movies. It's something else. Surely it will pass. But still, it's disconcerting, feeling this way. All she wants is to see him again. Maybe then she can be rid of this crazy feeling. But no. That's not why she wants to see him again. Not to get rid of this feeling. Or even to confirm it. But just to *see* him. See him.

She paces in front of the log as these thoughts and emotions swirl through her. Back and forth she walks, head down, hands fisted.

"Lena?" Daniel says. The men have exited the tent. "Are you alright? Did something happen?"

Raoul stands behind Daniel, closely watching. Their eyes seem to melt into each other. Daniel looks over his shoulder to see what she's staring at. When he looks back, she answers his question. "No. Nothing happened. I'm fine."

Raoul's mouth widens into a slow smile, as if he knows better.

"They're ready for the photos," Daniel says, looking unsure at her. "Where do you want them?"

She is speechless. Where does she want them? Want him? She must look stunned, confused, for Raoul takes over.

"A group photo, here, in front of this log would be good, don't you think, Malenque?"

She doesn't trust herself to answer or look his way. The sound of his voice saying her name, her most private name, the name no one calls her, flusters her. She fumbles through her camera bag and takes out her Nikon. A dozen soldiers distribute themselves around the log, several with rifles and bandoliers, some wearing green caps or floppy safari hats. Raoul has tied his wild hair back into a low ponytail and is wearing a cap.

"Maybe," Lena begins, then stops to clear her throat. "Maybe a few should sit on the log."

Tomás waves Raoul toward the log and heads to the back. Raoul sits with his knees spread wide, his rifle butt planted on the ground between, leaning forward, forearms on legs, staring straight at Lena. Looking both relaxed and intense at once.

Lena's breath catches. She's finding it difficult to breathe.

"Lena, what's wrong?" Daniel whispers, leaning toward her.

"I don't know," she says truthfully.

"You look ill. Maybe you're having heatstroke. Here, let me do this. Go get some water, sit in the shade."

She nods wordlessly and passes the camera to him. Maybe he's right. She does feel ill. Maybe that's all this is, heatstroke. But then she glances at Raoul, sees his cocky grin, as if he knows what his presence is doing to her.

He's enjoying this, his effect on me! She glares at him and takes back the camera.

"No," she says. "I can do this."

She looks Raoul in the eye and starts snapping photos from different angles. Some with him in it, some not. When she's done and packing away the camera, Raoul calls Daniel over to where he and Tomás are standing and begins a lively conversation.

Daniel, he summons. Not her. All the men are deliberately excluding her. Again.

She's furious with the whole lot: Raoul, Tomás, even Daniel, the whole male race. But mostly Raoul. She hates how he flustered her, and now how he's ignoring her. He's been playing with her emotions all along, knowing his effect on women. Half the female population already in love with him! Well, not her.

When he glances her way, she gives him a look so dark she hopes it turns him into stone. Then she deliberately turns her back on him and wonders what to do next. Certainly she's not going to just stand here and wait for them to conclude their discussion.

She looks around, sees that opening in the jungle and decides, just for spite, she's going down there again—thorny vines, poisonous snakes, infuriating panthers, be damned.

She half slides down the path, not caring about her hands. Not caring about anything. She goes to the river and squats, rinsing mud and new blood from her hands. She's glad it stings. It should sting. She splashes cool water onto her face, letting it drip down her neck, into her blouse. She looks at the water in her cupped hands and wonders if it's safe to drink. It smells good, sweet.

It smells like him, some infuriating voice in her head tells her. She decides it's not worth tasting and stands.

When she turns around, she sees him half-sliding down the path in the same hasty and careless way she did. She's not surprised. She knew he would come. She realizes that's why she came here: to confront him. She puts her fists on her hips and defiantly stares him down. If he thinks she's going to shrivel into a puddle, he's wrong.

He takes a few steps toward her, then stops.

Her glare melts at his look. Her fists fall from her hips.

His grin is gone. She's never seen a face look so open, so vulnerable. He looks stricken. He looks as lost and confused and helpless as she feels.

"I must see you again," he tells her. "We're leaving soon, so you cannot stay. But I'll send word when you can come. When it's safe." He continues staring at her, his rifle still slung over his shoulder. He's lost his cap, and his wild hair is loose. He's almost grim the way he stares and stares, as if he cannot rip his eyes away. Then, abruptly, he turns and is gone.

Daniel is excited when she sees him again. He can barely contain his glee until they are in the car and driving away. No one has bothered to hood them. Tomás is not in the car now. It's only the driver, a younger soldier who has turned on the radio. Daniel leans in to tell Lena the good news in a hushed voice.

"They want to meet again. A second interview. They insist you come, you be part of it next time. They'll send word when they're ready."

She does not answer. Her breath has not quite returned.

"Are you okay?" he asks, looking closely at her. "You still look pale. Are you sick?"

She can't answer. Her heart is beating in a new way, and she's afraid if she looks at Daniel, the joy and triumph she's feeling will light up her face and he'll see everything that passed between her and Raoul. She keeps her head down while twisting her hands in her lap.

Daniel mistakes her agitation and strokes her arm. "There's nothing to be frightened of. I know I was worried before, but this Raoul is okay. Very friendly. He likes journalists. They need us to tell their story, and he wants to give us an exclusive. They'll ensure our safety. He promised."

CHAPTER 12

Over the next few days, Lena cannot sit still with her thoughts. She wanders the streets of Curico, her path taking her from one Raoul poster to another. His face haunts her. Every time she sees it, she's shaken to the core, as if her former life has been forever upended

She spends her evenings remembering every detail of their time together: the way his dark eyes lit up when he saw her, the way they half-closed when he walked toward her. His mouth, those lips. She sees things she doesn't remember seeing. Scars on his arms, a black bruise on his thigh. That furry darkness at his center. She remembers how lost and vulnerable he looked after following her down the trail to the pool. The naked need she saw. The same need she feels now.

Days go by. Never have so many days gone by so slowly. Lena anxiously scans newspaper headlines and listens to talk on the streets, in the cafes, desperate to hear news about the Aguileros. What is happening on the frontlines of this struggle? Who is being ambushed, gunned down, imprisoned? Never has the political turmoil in San Balanque felt so real to her, so fraught with danger, so horribly, horribly wrong.

If something happens to Raoul, if she cannot see him again . . .. No, impossible. Nothing will stop her from seeing him again.

She returns to the museum to see her mother's paintings. The Goya exhibit, thank God, has moved on to Peru in its Latin American tour. She never wants to see again the painting of the rebel on his knees being executed and tries desperately to erase it from her mind. But since meeting Raoul, since telling him her given name, Malenque, then hearing it in his voice—she has this urgent need to discover more about her mother and why she named her Malenque.

At her mother's exhibit, she moves slowly around the room. The large abstracts are carefree, full of light with a feminine playfulness. But her more recent, richly detailed paintings set like exquisite jewels along the wall are not playful at all, despite their dreamlike, fantastical quality. They were painted with extreme care, not abandon. Every eyelash just so. Every lace-fringe meticulously detailed. Lena doesn't know what to think of them, or what they say about her mother, why she would go from one extreme to the other in her painting style.

In some strange way they remind her of her meeting with Raoul, the surreal sense of him rising from that pool of water, his slow panther-like movements, his mesmerizing eyes. Even that fairyland-like vale she entered before seeing him, the dancing dragonflies, the perfumed honeysuckle. The whole effect was dreamlike. Intoxicating. Something of that feeling is in her mother's paintings. Once you enter them, you cannot tear your eyes away.

The next day Lena takes a bus to the library to see what more she can discover about her mother. The periodical room is filled with newspapers going back the last year or two. The oldest have been copied on microfiche. That's where she finds a photo of her mother's Quinceañera, celebrating her fifteenth birthday. She's wearing a white diaphanous dress, her dark hair curled in ringlets, her still-childish face round, innocent, full of promise. A pretty girl standing between her proud, protective parents. Her father has wide grey sideburns, a goatee and mustache. A long straight nose and lively eyes. The mother is barely taller than her daughter, barely older. A May-November marriage? Lena's grandmother is darker than the others, her features rounder, wider, fuller. She looks like the Malenque in the book her mother gave her.

Lena discovers her grandparents died in a car accident a year after the photo was taken. Ricardo Morales was a prosperous, well-respected mine owner. He had two sons from a previous marriage, Simon and Gilbert, whose mother died in childbirth. Ricardo was fifty-two when he died. Her grandmother only thirty-three. Her name was Malenque too. Lena was named after her grandmother. She lets that fact settle like a pebble sinking slowly to the bottom of a pond.

A newspaper from a year ago shows a photo of her mother and her husband, Marcos Machado, at a gala. They are standing with President Ortiz and his wife. The men in tuxes, the women in ball gowns. All look relaxed, happy. *Except for Mother*, Lena thinks, looking closer. Her mother's smile is not as full-hearted as the others. Her eyes seem guarded. She's thinner too. She'd always been curvy like her aunt, but here she's almost svelte. The man beside her with her arm tucked into his is handsome, a full head of dark hair with gray at the temples, and a small, neatly trimmed mustache, giving him a distinguished look like Lena's grandfather.

Was Marcos worth it? Lena wonders of her mother. The sacrifice she made to have him? Her mother's arm looks stiff in his, like he forced her to take it. Or is Lena only imagining this? Does she *want* her mother to be unhappy, to regret her choice?

No! It makes Lena sad to think so. No one who gave up so much to have someone else should come to regret it. Life is too short. *Let her be happy.* There's enough sadness in the world.

She turns away from the photo and thinks of Raoul, remembering his face, those eyes, that smile. Her heart squeezes with a kind of pain never felt before. This yearning for him has nothing to do with happiness. It's something that makes happiness, right or wrong, irrelevant. *The heart wants what the heart wants.* She never understood that saying before. She always thought it meant something selfish or stubborn or greedy. It's none of that. Feeling so choice-less is quite terrifying.

Did her mother once feel that way? For the first time since she was a child Lena feels something like . . . not love, but sympathy for her mother. If she left Lena because she, too, felt that terrifying choiceless need, then let her not regret that.

Let me not regret it. Let her be happy. Let me be, she whispers to whatever there is in this world that hears and answers such prayers.

"Juan Costello was arrested yesterday," Daniel tells Lena. They are sitting in his Fiat in front of La Rosaleda. He looks as nervous now as when they went to meet Marley and Carla. She hasn't seen him since they left camp, ten days ago. "Juan's the one I told you about working on the CIA-Ortiz connection. They're accusing him of being an Aguilero because of the sympathetic stories he's written."

Lena's stomach twists. "That's horrible! Are you in danger too?"

"I don't think so since I'm American and working for the Associated Press. Still, we've got to be careful. Especially after my story comes out. I hoped *La Palabra* in San Balanque would print it, but since Juan's arrest they're being more cautious. Instead, it will be out tomorrow in *El Norte*, Mexico's main newspaper, which is widely read here."

"I didn't use your name in the story," Daniel continues, "not even for the photo caption. It's safer for you that way. You'll still have bragging rights when you put together your resume." He pauses. "Lena, you shouldn't come to the next interview. I can find another photographer."

"No! I want to come. They wanted me there too, didn't they?"

"Yes, but—"

"Well, then, it must be important to them. You can leave my name out again . . . but I need to be there."

The next morning Lena picks up *El Norte* and brings it back into her room to read. Daniel's story is short with only one photo: the group shot with Raoul sitting on the log, staring at her with that cocky grin. Seeing him like that again makes her stomach squirm and her heartbeat quicken. What is it about this man that does this to her? It's like a sickness. A drug.

The story is titled "A New Revolutionary Force Rises in Central America" and quotes Raoul at length: "Our movement is a massive coalition of the people who make up this great country. The heart and soul of San Balanque. We come from the mountains and rainforests, the seacoasts and islands, the cities, villages and tribal lands.

"We are a richly diverse and talented people. With all our natural resources we should be leading the world in our prosperity. And yet our land is being drained of its riches and poured into the pockets of foreign corporations and corrupt politicians. The spirit of our people is being crushed in poverty, our children illiterate, our drinking water polluted, our roads washed away every monsoon season. We want a government that puts the welfare of the common people before the interests of the wealthy few."

The article quotes an official in the Ortiz administration dismissing the Aguileros as a ragtag group of dissidents, outlaws, and malcontents, riding on the coattails of the Cuban revolution and the Sandinistas in Nicaragua. "They're a pesky mosquito to be squashed. Their noble ideals are nothing but propaganda to fool the people. Their real aim is to bring Communism to our shores like Fidel did in Cuba."

Yet the people in the villages and cities tell a different story, Daniel writes. The Aguileros are their friends, helping build schools and bridges, digging wells and organizing workers. "They care about us, the people, unlike Ortiz," insists a laborer at a coffee plantation. "Do you see this?" He points to his son's wheelchair. "Raoul bought this for us out of his own pocket when he saw my son dragging himself by his hands across the field to join us. This is how true leaders behave, by example, by serving those they would lead."

The manager of the coffee plantation has a different take on the Aguileros. When they are mentioned, he spits on the ground. "Nothing but bandits, thieves, and murderers." Hearing about the wheelchair, he laughs. "This is the mentality we must deal with! They buy a kid a wheelchair and suddenly they're saints? Saviors? A cheap propaganda trick if you ask me."

And yet, writes Daniel, acts of dissent are spreading: striking farmworkers, protests in the shantytowns for lack of clean water, a sit-in at the university demanding free speech for students. There are rumors of dissidents being thrown in prison on trumped-up charges, and a well-respected journalist was arrested and accused of espionage.

Daniel's story ends with an interview of a brother and his sister, asking them why the posters of Raoul are being replaced as fast as the authorities tear them down. "Because he stands for the people. He stands for freedom," the brother says. "This is true," his sister agrees. "He stands for us, our hopes and dreams. The future of San Balanque."

CHAPTER 13

After reading Daniel's story, Lena feels calmer, reassured. Raoul is who she hoped he was, a leader of intelligence and integrity, dedicated to a righteous cause. The rebels are not alone. The people are with them, a huge movement working behind the scenes. It's not a hopeless cause.

After learning about her own family's history and seeing photos of her mother and grandparents, she feels a deeper connection with San Balanque and its people. They're her people too. Her mother was born here, her grandparents. Her half-uncles live here still. Other relatives perhaps she knows nothing about. If she'd been born here, gone to school here, she would have marched against Ortiz instead of the Vietnam War. She would have written stories about the shantytowns with no sanitation. She would have joined the Aguileros by now, and it would have nothing to do with Raoul, but because that's who she is. Where her passion lies.

She doesn't know what will happen when she sees Raoul again, but it doesn't worry her now. Her fever dream has passed. The thought of him is as strong as ever but is anchored in reality. Not enchantment. Or romantic fantasy. She wants to know everything about him, this man, this rebel, this leader. His movement and his people. *Her people*. It's her San Balanque too.

This wave that's risen so unexpectedly behind her, lifting her to her feet—she's ready for whatever unfolds. Whichever way this wave breaks, she will ride it.

Two days later Daniel calls. "Tomorrow," he says. "They want us to arrive separately at the pick-up spot, me first, then you if everything looks safe. So they gave me two sets of directions. I'll drop off your instructions at La Rosaleda"

Mrs. Henson brings them up later that afternoon, along with a letter from Lena's aunt. She reads the letter first. It's short and breezy, full of exclamations points, like all her letters.

Hello Darling,

Well, your father's off again! On another sabbatical. Japan this time. A Zen Monastery, no less! Research for a new class, he says. But we know better, don't we dear? Your father is becoming a mendicant. It wouldn't surprise me if he shaved his head into a tonsure and joined the Jesuits next. The dear poor fool. He was always like this. Mother thought he'd go into the priesthood or ministry if we'd ever been a church-going family. Then your mother came along and cured him of that for a while.

Well, I hope you're having the time of your life among all those hot-blooded Latin Romeos. But don't stay too long! With your father gone, I'm feeling skittish. I have Geoffrey, of course. But he's part of the problem, wanting to tie me down! Hah! We know better, don't we? We're sailing to Catalina tomorrow. I may well have a ring on my finger by the time you get home. I'm kidding, of course. But anything is possible!

I love you madly, you know, and miss your pouty little face. Yes, dear, you do pout at me quite a bit. But if you didn't, I'd know something was wrong—with you, or me, more likely! Hah!

Kisses,

Auntie Margo

Lena smiles as she puts the letter away. She doubts Margo will ever marry, she's too flighty for that, too full of herself. But she wouldn't mind seeing her and Geoffrey make a go of it, as friends and partners. She needs that devoted companionship. Her father, not so much. He's happy when he's deep into his books or in front of a classroom or sitting cross-legged on his cushion. Each in their own way—her aunt, so exuberant and carefree; her father, so intellectually curious, ever ready to serve a higher purpose—is living on the edge, unrestrained. Nothing holds them back. It's how they've taught her to be, by example. To find worthy causes and pursue them was her father's legacy. Her aunt's, to live joyfully, fully, without regret.

The instructions from the Aguileros after her aunt's breezy letter sound so terse and grim: Catch Bus #3 on Linden Street at 8:30 am. Get off at Ninth Street, walk one block north to the Mendez Pharmacia. Go inside, buy something, pay in cash. Then cross the street and board Bus #20 going south. Get off two blocks later and keep walking south, pretending to window shop until someone contacts you.

Her aunt's letter and the instructions could not be more different in tone and intent, yet they point her in the same direction. Pursue passion without regret.

Lena frowns when it's Tomás instead of Raoul who picks them up. Where is he? If he's so anxious to see her, why didn't he escort her to camp? Why send Tomás, who clearly dislikes her? Or maybe she's the one who clearly dislikes him. At least this time she and Daniel are given masks—the kind day-sleepers use—instead of hoods to wear. Thanks to Raoul, Tomás tells them.

After another long, sweaty ride, Lena steps out into a clearing with an assortment of tents and lean-tos scattered about like last time. Around them looms the tightly tangled green walls of the jungle, the humid air thick with the buzz of insects. The earthy-sweet aroma of beans and bacon wafts toward her from a makeshift kitchen.

Then she sees Raoul striding toward her. And her breath catches.

He wears fatigues, but no rifle, no bandolier. His smile is confident and welcoming. It's a brand new, unfamiliar, Raoul she's looking at now. Not the naked man rising like a Greek god from the pool. Not the cocky soldier with his rifle planted between his knees and that infuriating grin planted on his face. Not the confused, grim-faced man sliding down the steep path and looking so bewildered, so needy. No. The man striding toward them now is the calm, cool commander of a rebel force, the charismatic leader of a populist movement, the beloved champion of the people. In command of himself and everyone around him. She feels that force.

He thanks them for coming, holding out his hand first to Daniel, then to Lena, as if this meeting is nothing more than an agreement among professionals to do business with each other. Only the fact that his hand lingers in Lena's, his thumb pressing the middle of her palm as his gaze grows darker and more intense, keeps her from believing that's all this is: a second interview.

He's a charming and attentive host, introducing them to the two lieutenants standing on either side of him, offering Daniel and her cold Coca Colas from a portable propane-fueled fridge. The small, green-tinted bottle, slick with condensation, feels good in Lena's hand, the sweet syrupy liquid so lovely on her parched throat. But neither Raoul nor his men take one. Apparently, this is a luxury reserved for guests.

Raoul shows them around the camp like the proud owner of an estate. He directs most of his remarks to Daniel while sliding soft, warm glances her way. She feels his interest but also his determination to keep her at a distance, as if his purpose now is merely to watch her and learn, and allow her to watch him and learn, to test for themselves whether what they felt for each other before was real.

This new Raoul is a man she can wrap her mind around. He makes her feel more at ease, more in control of her feelings, more trusting of his intentions. And all this makes her want him even more. There's no doubt in her mind that this is real.

He leads them to a remote corner of the camp where they sit at a table for the interview. Daniel takes out his tape recorder. Lena opens her notebook, happy she took shorthand in high school.

Daniel starts with a few softball questions. "I notice this camp, like your last one, is rather small, a hundred soldiers or less. Are they all like that?"

"By necessity our many camps are small, well-hidden, and move continually. In guerilla warfare there are few big camps. Our numbers remain the mystery that we want them to be. I'm sure you can understand the reason for this."

Daniel nods and then leans in. "Ortiz claims you're a Marxist like Che and Fidel, that you want to turn San Balanque into a Communist country."

"Unlike Che, Fidel was not a Marxist at the beginning," Raoul answers, "He became one when the U.S refused to buy his sugar and closed their ports to him. Fidel had no choice but to seek other trade partners. The Soviet Union was happy to comply, to win a convert so close to the shores of its enemy. You could say U.S foreign policy is what pushed Fidel into Khrushchev's arms. As it has pushed so many opposed to corrupt dictators toward Communism.

"Regardless, I'm not a Marxist. Although some in our faction lean that way. I tell them, Capitalism and Communism are two sides of the same coin, the coin that always goes into the purse of a privileged few and not the pockets of the workers who produce that wealth.

"We seek is a third way. Our people want to own their own businesses and work their own land. They want to be in control of what they produce. But they also want a government that allows them to negotiate for better wages and working conditions, that provides a safety net when they fall on bad times. Capitalism and socialism are good when they coexist and serve to rein in each other. That's what I want. A Social Democracy."

The interview concludes shortly after that. Daniel turns off the tape recorder and excuses himself to use the latrine before they head back, leaving Lena alone with Raoul.

"So, what do you think?" He leans back in his camp chair, tilted on two legs.

Lena pretends not to know what he really means. "I think you are dedicated to your cause. I admire that."

He looks away, as if waiting for her to respond to his real question.

She tries again. "I think we have enough information and photos for a good story. I don't think you'll be disappointed."

His chair comes down sharply on all four legs as he leans his forearms on the table, peering into her eyes. "So, I won't be disappointed? You've learned what you came here to learn about me? This is good. But perhaps you need more time here, a day or two to be sure. Is that true?" His eyes are so intense, she blushes.

He smiles. "You are right. I am not disappointed, nor shall you be."

Her heart is beating so fast now she can't think clearly and has no idea what to say. She doesn't have time to consider further for she hears Daniel returning. They all stand.

Daniel is smiling. He holds out his hand to Raoul and thanks him for the interview.

"You're most welcome," Raoul says. "Pepe is bringing the car around. He'll take you home."

Daniel looks at Lena and lifts his eyebrow, waiting for her to thank Raoul so they can go.

She gives Raoul an anxious, bewildered look. He moves closer to her.

"I've invited Ms. Landon to remain here in camp a few more days as a photojournalist, to get a broader feel for who we are and what we're doing. And she's accepted my invitation." Raoul looks intently at Lena. "Unless I've misread you, or you've changed your mind? It would be understandable."

She stares back just as intently and lets two deep breaths come and go as Daniel emphatically says, "That is out of the question." Then, turning to her, "Lena?"

"No, I haven't changed my mind," she answers, looking at Raoul. "I'd like to stay and learn more." His eyes warm at her words.

Daniel looks shocked. "Lena, may I have a few words with you? In private." He cocks his head toward the car and starts to move that direction.

She grabs his arm. "Please, Daniel, I want this. It's important to me. Don't be alarmed. I'll be safe here."

"You can count on that," Raoul tells him.

Daniel reels back and stares open-mouthed at Lena. "You can't be serious. This is crazy." Then he turns to Raoul. "We have enough material without her staying here. We can always come back later if we need more." He looks at Lena again and, seeing her determination, turns back to Raoul. "Look, I'll come back and stay if that's what you want."

"But she's the photojournalist, not you. And she's already agreed. There are other women here. And I can assure you—and her—that she will be safe in my care."

Daniel looks back and forth between the two as if trying to figure out what's going on.

Lena takes his hand and squeezes. "I know what I'm doing. I'll be fine. I feel safe. And grateful for this opportunity. Surely you understand what this means for my career?"

"Your career, huh?" Daniel looks at her with such disdain it makes her flinch. "Fine!" he says, snatching back his hand and holding it up like a stop sign. "But if you're not back in three days . . .." He looks menacingly at both.

"She will be. I promise," Raoul says, holding out his hand.

Daniel looks at it, as if he's not going to take it. Then he gives his hand a hard shake while sternly staring into Raoul's eyes. "She better be!"

He gives Lena a withering look, shakes his head, and turns toward the waiting car. Pepe, who has been standing by watching all this, hops into the driver's seat, and then they are gone.

Lena watches them go, wishing they had parted on better terms.

"Thank you," Raoul tells Lena. His gaze lingers warmly on her face, and then he beckons to a female soldier. "Bianca will show you to your tent. We can talk more later." He turns and strides away.

Bianca regards Lena with as much skepticism as Daniel did, then shrugs, leading her to a tent at the edge of camp. Apparently, Raoul prepared for her stay in advance of her arrival. That realization makes Lena's stomach somersault in the most delicious way.

CHAPTER 14

Lena stoops to enter the small tent prepared for her. There's a cot with bedding and a mosquito net. A stool with a chipped porcelain bowl on top. A towel and bar of soap. A three-gallon jug stands next to that for washing, Bianca tells her. Then she points to the small suitcase tucked beneath the cot. "My sister brought you clothes. She's about your size."

"Please thank her for me," Lena says, wondering what in the world Raoul told people about why he prepared all this for her.

What if I hadn't agreed to stay? But he knew I would.

Another thrilling somersault whirls through her.

When Bianca leaves, Lena opens the suitcase and finds a pair of loose brown slacks and a long-sleeved lightweight tunic, two pairs of socks, a toothbrush and can of tooth powder, a stick of insect repellant, and a hairbrush. No bra or panties. An oversight? Or did Raoul notice she doesn't wear a bra, and he expects her to go without panties too, commando-style, like so many soldiers do in Vietnam to keep from getting jungle rot? The thought of Raoul walking around commando in those baggy trousers sends a delicious feeling pulsing through her lower extremities.

She snaps the suitcase shut. The tent is too hot, too confining. She grabs her camera and heads outside. The smell of bacon and beans grows stronger as she approaches the center of camp.

"Food is the most essential ingredient for the success of any campaign," Raoul told them on the tour as he showed them the cooking hut. "It feeds not only our bodies, but our spirits and sense of community. With the breaking of bread, we come to know each other, tell our stories, hear each other's hearts. These rituals are important in our training camps because out in the field we eat on the run what we carry in our rucksacks, mostly dried meat or fish and hard tack. So, we are fortunate to have Bosco and his wife Manuela here with us now, who not only cook our food but coordinate its acquisition."

The cooks are busy working now. Lena greets them and begins taking photos, avoiding their faces as instructed: Manuela's thick hips and legs as she stirs a huge iron kettle set on a tripod over smoldering embers, Bosco's hairy arms pulling out the pan of rolls from an oven built of stones and pieces of metal. Inside a lean-to, Lena photographs bags of pinto and coffee beans, wheels of cheese, a tub of root vegetables, and a net full of mangos, papayas, and plantains. The Aguileros are being well fed—for now at least. "We feast, so we can ration later." Raoul told them.

"There you are!" Bianca says, handing her a small bag filled with eating utensils. "For your meals." As she turns away, Lena touches her arm.

"If you have a minute, I'd like to ask you a few questions. It's the reason Raoul brought me here, to hear your stories, why you became Aguileros."

Bianca's face clouds. "Fine," she says begrudgingly, "but you'll have to join me as I work."

Lena follows her into the jungle where she walks quickly, purpose-fully, toward a stream. She's shorter and leaner than Lena, more tautly built. Her braid hangs down her back to her waist like a dark rope. Lena sneaks shots of Bianca gathering clothes draped over bushes and tree limbs. Apparently, Bianca is the laundress for the day. Lena helps gather the clothes while asking questions about camp. She learns how different it is from when they are in the field, training, or on a mission. Then they sleep in hammocks strung between trees and carry everything on their backs.

"Like turtles," Bianca says with a hint of a grin as she grabs the last piece of clothing and turns toward camp.

"Wait. Can we sit a moment? Please? I'd like to know how you came to be an Aguilero."

Bianca shifts her armload of clothes from one hip to the other. "It's simple. When the mine killed my father, the manager turned me and my sister out of our home. We were starving in the forest when the Aguileros found us. They fed us and brought us to a friendly village that took us in. When I was old enough, they allowed me to join them. It is a great honor."

"Is your sister an Aguilero too?"

"But of course."

"She's a soldier like you?"

"She's a student. She helps in other ways."

"Like loaning clothes to journalists?" Lena smiles at her.

"She does whatever is needed, as long as it doesn't interfere with her education. Mostly, she's a courier, delivering messages, packages." She shrugs. "Whatever's needed."

"How long have you been Aguileros?"

"In our hearts, since the day they rescued us. In terms of service, when we turned fifteen. That was two years ago for me, only four months for Marta."

"So, you're seventeen now?"

She lifts her chin. "I'll be eighteen next month."

"In September?" Lena asks enthusiastically. "Me too. I'll be twenty-one."

Bianca looks her over skeptically. "You look younger."

That dampens Lena's enthusiasm. When they return to camp, Bianca adds Lena's armful of clothes to hers and turns away. Lena watches her go, this taciturn warrior woman, three years younger than she is.

She wonders how old Raoul is. If he graduated five years ago, like she and Daniel guessed, he must be twenty-six or seven. So young to be leading a revolution. Then again, look at Bianca: fifteen when she took up arms. Lena feels like a child next to her and the others. She has no experiences to compare with theirs. The only reason she's here is because of this strong attraction between her and Raoul. *No, that's not true.* She wanted to interview the rebels before she ever met Raoul.

Lena returns to her tent to get a new roll of film. When she comes out, a jeep is approaching camp. Raoul and Tomás hop out, along with the two lieutenants she was introduced to earlier, Carlos and Bernard. Carlos is slimmer and taller than Raoul, with slightly stooped shoulders and a receding hairline. For all his soldierly attire, he looks more like a doctor or civil servant than a freedom fighter. But Bernard looks every inch a warrior. He's the same height as Raoul, but even more muscular, almost burly. His features are flatter, wider, his skin darker, his bushy hair a dark halo around his head. Tomás is the shortest, but the powerful way he moves, like a bulldog, makes him seem as formidable as the others. His dark hair is short and straight, unlike Raoul's wavy locks. All four men stride off together, while the rest of the camp lines up at the kitchen hut. Lena joins them.

Bosco scoops beans with fat chunks of bacon into their dishes as Manuela pours coffee into their cups. Everyone helps themselves to hot rolls. Lena follows the others as they huddle around a campfire, some sitting on camp chairs, stools, or logs. Others hunker down on their haunches. Pepe waves her over to the log where he's perched.

"So, what do you think of our accommodations?" he asks.

"More luxurious than I imagined."

He laughs. "Wait until we take you out into the field. Fifteen-hour hikes, carrying thirty-pound rucksacks, plus guns and ammunition. You won't find that so luxurious."

"This is your base camp then?"

"You could call it that. But it moves too. Every few weeks or so."

He looks closely at her. "You're from California, right? A Surfer?"

"How'd you guess?"

He slaps his knee. "I knew it! You look like those California girls the Pipeliners sing about. You know the song, Surfer Girls, right?" He grins and then begins singing.

"We've travelled all around these U.S. towns
And kissed all kinds of girls,
From the City Slickers with their trendy knickers
To the Southern Dolls with their sexy drawls.
But none out there can ever compare
With the gals we find back home."

By now, others nearby are egging him on, so he gets up to milk the crowd, leaning into a pretend microphone.

"With their sun-kissed hair and tan limbs bare,
These wild Wahinis in their French bikinis
Put all the rest to shame.
Why can't they all be surfer girls."

He points his thumb over his shoulder at Lena as he sings the chorus, "Why can't they all be surfer girls?"

By the time he's finished, all are clapping, and Lena is blushing. "Stop it! You're embarrassing me." Pepe plops down beside her again. "You seemed to enjoy that."

"Immensely," he agrees, grinning. "Maybe you can teach Raoul to surf. He always said he regretted not learning when he was in California."

"And why do you suppose he didn't?"

"Too studious for his own good." He gives her a knowing look. "I'm hoping that will change now."

She doesn't know what to say to that, if it means what she thinks.

"He wants to send me to the U.S. too," Pepe continues. "To study. But I won't go. My place is here with my brothers."

"He wants to protect you."

"He wants to protect everyone. But he can't fight to free people and protect everyone at the same time. It must be each person's choice: to fight or be safe." He looks at her closely. "Like you. You must make that choice too."

"But I've made that choice already, being here rather than safe in the city." He looks skeptical. "What? There's more than one way to fight for a cause, Pepe. Sometimes with arms. Sometimes with words. The pen is mightier than the sword, they say."

"So says Raoul." Pepe lifts his chin, looking across the way. She follows his glance and sees Raoul. Somewhere in the middle of this, he's gotten his dinner and is hunkered down on his haunches with Tomás and his lieutenants.

Their gazes lock. Then Raoul puts aside his bowl and moves toward the campfire around which soldiers are seated. As they look up expectantly at him, a hush falls.

"Now we've had our entertainment and our stomachs are full, I have something to say." Raoul looks at Lena and gestures for her to join him.

She freezes, unsure what's happening, but then she puts down her plate and moves beside him. To her surprise, he takes her hand.

"Comrades, I want to introduce you to our guest. Her mother is from San Balanque and named her Malenque, after the Hero Twins who drew this land from the sea and protected it against those who would destroy it. She's a photojournalist who has come to learn about us—who we are and what we are fighting for. To share with the world the righteousness of our cause, our determination to free our people and bring them the peace, prosperity, and dignity they deserve. This is the San Balanque of our hearts, the San Balanque we fight and die for. So say we all!"

"So say we all!" rises a chorus of voices and beating of utensils on tin bowls.

When it's quiet, he turns to Lena and lifts their entwined hands above their heads as he looks back at the people gathered before him. "And so we welcome Malenque, for she will tell our stories to the world, and this will hearten the people and solicit support for our cause."

He looks down at her. "Feel free to wander where you may, speak to people and take photographs. For we all welcome you here and will make you feel at home." His gaze moves slowly around the camp, as if extracting a promise from each person. His eyes linger at last on Tomás, then he turns back to Lena with an encouraging smile.

"Thank you," she says to him, then looks out to the crowd. "Many thanks to all of you."

"So," says Raoul, letting go of Lena's hand at last, "if anyone wishes to share their story while our bellies are full and our hearts are warm, feel free to do so."

And many do. Night drops quickly, like a black cloak falling around their shoulders. But the campfire grows brighter in the darkness and sends sparks like fireflies fluttering toward the treetops. The faces of the people who rise to tell their stories flicker with a warm, orange glow. In the background is a chorus of night sounds: the thrum of insects, the settling of logs in the fire, the creaks and rustles of tree limbs and small creatures moving through the brush.

On her log again, Lena sits entranced, listening to all the stories and jotting down notes in shorthand on the small tablet she pulls from her pocket. Tales of land owned for generations stolen from them, of brothers disappearing in the dead of night, uncles held for years in prisons for so-called political crimes. Union organizers found dead in their beds with slit throats, workers being maimed and mutilated in factories and mines from faulty equipment.

It's a heart-wrenching recital, but the faces of the people who tell these stories, while sometimes wrenched in pain, also glow with pride and determination. Because now they are Aguileros, and there is renewed hope for their families, hope for their country.

When the talking finally dies down, people wash their dishes in the buckets of water prepared for them, and start moving off toward tents, or they retire into smaller groups to talk more. As the tips of cigarettes and pipes glow in the dark, Lena rinses her dishes and heads toward her tent, the night around her dimly lit by firelight and a few glowing lamps.

She turns when she hears a sound behind her. All she sees is his dark silhouette, but she knows who it is. The hairs on her arms rise and she shivers.

"May I have a word before you retire for the night?" asks Raoul.

He leads her deep into the dark where they are alone. The light from the dying campfire and lanterns throws long shifting shadows at their feet. Their faces are half lost in darkness as they face each other.

"You know why I brought you here, why I asked you to stay?"

She knows. But with him standing so close that she smells the strong masculine scent of his body, the saltiness of his sweat-dried fatigues, the muskiness of his skin, she cannot answer. All she wants is to drink up the heady scent of him. She wants so much to touch him she curls her fingers into fists to keep from doing so.

He nods, as if confirming from the way she's looking at him that he knows. "You must say it, Malenque. I must hear."

She takes a shaky breath. "You want me to learn about the Aguileros, about you, about . . . us." A blush rises to her face which she hopes he can't see.

"Yes. I am strongly attracted to you, as you must know, and you appear to feel the same for me. But is that all this is—a strong mutual attraction—or something more? We must find out. We must look at each other with clear eyes. You must see me as I am, as I must be, here and now. I don't have time for . . . the formalities of courtship, or to be involved with someone who doesn't accept who I am or what it means if we become involved. I want you. I think you want the same thing, but . . . important decisions must be made with a clear head."

Lena swallows hard. "I understand."

"In the meantime, we each have important work that cannot wait. Tomorrow we will do our jobs. You can tour the camp, photograph, interview, and write our stories, remembering not to use anyone's real name or reveal details that could identify them."

"I'll remember. But if that's my job tomorrow, what will yours be?"

He steps closer and brushes the back of his fingers against her cheek. The touch is so light and soft, she wants to press her face against it.

"My job is to keep you safe. To keep all of us safe. To do whatever is needed to free this country and overthrow Ortiz. That's my job."

"All that just for tomorrow?" she teases. "And the day after tomorrow? What will our jobs be then?"

His gaze is now on her mouth, and he looks so intense she's not sure he heard her.

She sees him swallow and watches his jaw clench. He looks up into her eyes.

"The day after tomorrow . . . we shall see."

CHAPTER 15

Lena sleeps fitfully that night with only a sheet pulled over her naked body as she twists and turns beneath the mosquito netting hanging over her narrow cot. She replays all Raoul revealed about his feelings for her. The word courtship startled and thrilled her. Does it mean what she thinks—the promise of a future together? They barely know each other! And yet, that's what she wants too, something lasting and momentous. She's always been impetuous this way, going after things she wants full tilt. And now she wants Raoul, wants him to be hers in all the ways that matter. It seems crazy how fast it's moving. But it's what they both want—not just her. Somehow that makes it seem less crazy.

And yet, if he's looking for long-term commitment, what does that mean? Not returning to California? What will her father and aunt say about her staying here, being with him? She can't think of that. One step at a time.

Lena spends the next morning writing up stories she heard at the campfire last night. She leans against a large fig tree, its huge roots like octopus arms rising around her, creating a little nest. Her trouser cuffs are tucked into her boots to keep out crawly things. Even so, she feels scratchy and slaps at pesky flies, despite having covered herself with insect repellant. A powerful story is taking shape in her mind, highlighting the strength and dignity she saw in those faces last night, the vulnerability and defiance that comes when people band together, determined to stand and fight whatever the cost.

She tries not to think of Raoul, but she senses his presence everywhere as she wanders the camp, taking photos and gathering stories. She sees him in the faces of his comrades, in the determined way they go about the business of camp life, in the ever-present jungle that crouches, beautifully and dangerously, just outside the encampment. But in person, she sees him nowhere at all, and when she asks Bianca, she's told he's on a reconnaissance mission.

She snaps photos of trainees learning to take apart and reassemble their rifles. They also learn how to make Molotov cocktails, deploy and throw grenades, and engage in hand-to-hand combat.

When Pepe joins her, he says, "These are the basics. Later they will learn how to ambush and sabotage, how to gather intelligence, what to do if they are caught, and other strategies, depending on their mission, whether soldier, spy, courier, recruiter. . .."

"Where is all the fighting taking place? I've read so little about the Aguileros in the newspapers."

"Guerrilla warfare is small-scale, fast-moving. We hide and strike. Retreat, regroup, and strike again. Few see us come and go, and it's quickly over. There are no reporters in the field to write about how many weapon caches we've confiscated, supply routes disrupted, units demoralized from constant harassment. We're like the French Resistance in World War Two."

"But do you win a war that way?"

"We triumph by winning the people's hearts and minds—so says Raoul. We'll never have the military advantage to defeat Ortiz. But we have the psychological advantage, and that is more deadly. At a critical point we'll rise up with the people beside us and take back our country."

Lena looks at Pepe in a new way. There's more to him than she first thought with all his silly songs and photo-posing. He's still young—no older than Bianca, she guesses. Perhaps that's why both are still stationed here at the training camp instead of being in the field.

"And what is your job as a soldier?" she asks. His brow lowers and jaw clenches. *He wants to be in the field*, Lena thinks, *not here in camp*.

"I do as I'm ordered. For the moment, my job is to keep an eye on you."

"What? You think I'm a spy?"

He gives her Raoul's slow mocking smile, revealing a glimpse of what Raoul must have looked like when younger. "It's not what I think that matters. It's what Raoul thinks."

"And what does Raoul think about me?"

He gives her Raoul's smirk, the way he looked sitting with his rifle between his legs. Then Pepe looks away and says mysteriously, "Many things."

With that, he's gone, striding away as Raoul so often does. But Lena is glad of it, her mind tightly wound around his words: the "many things" Raoul might be thinking about her. The many wanton things she's trying not to think about him.

Raoul doesn't return until well after dark when Lena has retired to her tent. She hears excited voices outside when his team arrives, his among them. Then it grows quiet again. She waits, thinking he'll come to her now. How could they spend a whole day here and not see each other? He will come. She knows it and she's ready for him. She's brushed out her braid into waves that fall halfway down her back. She's washed beneath her arms and between her thighs, in those places that light up when she thinks about him touching her there. She's brushed her teeth and tested her breath in her cupped hand. Then she lies down on her cot to wait.

No perfume to dab. No candles to light. No music to play. But the stage is lit, the script ready, one player stretched out on the stage awaiting the other's entrance.

But Raoul does not come. One moment leaks into the next, and on and on, and still he does not come. An hour goes by as she lays in the dark waiting for him, then another begins its slow round.

What is he waiting for? Will he come at all? Will she be waiting like this all night? We're supposed to be getting to know each other, testing this strong attraction to see where it leads. *If he won't come to me, I'll go to him,* she tells herself in a fury, while another more sensible part of her rises in alarm to stop this madness. She paces, trying to decide whether to wait or go. *I don't care what he might think. I'm done waiting.*

She's a swirl of heavy-heated motion as she yanks on her boots, too impatient to bother tying them, and pulls her borrowed tunic over her naked body where it hangs halfway to her knees. She grabs her lantern, turning it low, then pushes past the tent flap into the night.

A formidable darkness crouches beyond her pool of light. The contrast too harsh, too blinding. She tries turning the lantern lower, but it goes out. Darkness swallows her. It's a physical thing, how whole it is, how she can disappear into its void. She allows her eyes to adjust. A few low gleams of lantern light can be discerned in the distance. A trickle of moonlight filters through the trees. She moves cautiously forward in the direction where she knows his tent is. The night is full of mysterious stirrings, rustles, whispers.

She freezes when she sees a warm glow ahead bobbing through the trees, dipping and disappearing, growing larger as it nears. Someone is coming. Suddenly she's self-conscious that she's wearing only her tunic and boots and realizes how ridiculous she must look. What was she thinking? Coming here like this!

What if it's Raoul? Her heart beats faster now in anticipation and fear, full of misgivings. Just then something cold touches her ankle and slithers upward. She screams and kicks her leg. Her boot flies off. The approaching light stills, then dashes toward her all at once, stopping several feet away. She freezes, balancing stork-like on one leg.

Raoul's low laugh, a sound like honey, sweet and soothing, pours over her. He comes closer, his lantern held high, a look of astonished amusement on his face. "Whatever are you doing?"

A flush of embarrassment floods her face, knowing how foolish she looks. Feeling the need to defend herself, she lifts her chin. "What did you think? That I would wait forever for you to come?"

"So you come dressed like this!"

"Why would you care how I'm dressed?"

He throws back his head and laughs. Then he scoops her up. Her remaining boot falls off, and her tunic rides up to expose her bare bottom.

"What do you think you're doing?"

"Saving you from yourself, from getting your legs covered with ticks and leeches."

"You're kidding!"

He laughs again as he turns away toward his tent. "I wish I were."

He carries her inside and puts her down. While Raoul closes the tent flap behind him, she backs further into the tent where a lantern glows. Now that they are alone, now that she's standing nearly naked in his tent, she is nervous. More than nervous, scared. She can't catch her breath. Her heart is pounding erratically, her mouth so dry, she licks her lips. He turns back toward her and freezes, staring as she stands with the light shining through her tunic.

"I can see right through that, you know." His voice is thick and heavy.

She runs her hands down her sides as if to erase her silhouette.

"And what do you see?" she asks, swallowing hard.

"Everything," he says slowly, reverently, staring at her as if she's everything he's ever wanted. Slowly, he moves toward her. She steps back, still breathing hard. But when he touches her gently on the shoulders, she stills. He lifts her tunic over her head and steps back, as if to marvel at what he's uncovered. She stands before him as naked as he was that first day she saw him. His gaze drinks her up and she lets him, thrilling at the shivers surging through her.

He pulls her close, his hands sliding down her back, over the swell of her hips and buttocks, molding her against his body. The roughness of his shirt brushes her breasts, the hardness of his groin presses against her stomach, his strong hands move possessively over her body as if he owns it already. He picks her up again and carries her to his cot, lays her down. His gaze grazes the whole of her, and his fingers follow, lightly tracing her face and trailing down her neck, around each breast, over her stomach, along her thighs.

"I can't believe how unbelievably beautiful you are."

She closes her eyes and luxuriates in the exquisite feel of his fingers and the way it makes her body quiver with delight and anticipation. She doesn't know what he will do next. She just wants to soak up all she's feeling. Now he's caressing her feet with firm fingers, his thumb rubbing the tender arch. She lets out a soft moan. Then he's gone.

She opens her eyes in alarm at the absence of his touch. He turns off the lantern and disappears into the darkness. She hears him removing clothes, kicking off boots. Then he lies down beside her on the narrow cot. He holds her lightly in his arms, his hands stroking her, feeling her all over. He's kissing her deeply, possessively, opening her mouth and entering, his tongue hungry and fierce.

She's expecting him to make love to her. It's what she wants. She feels how hard he is, the throb against her thighs. But apparently, he's in no hurry. They kiss and pet each other. He rubs his chin against her hair, and she nestles her face against his neck and damp chest, smelling and tasting through her pores the salt of him, his musky scent, the warmth of his skin. His arms and legs pull her tight. She's wrapped within the cocoon of his body and wants to stay there forever. She hears herself purr against him and his low growl in response.

"I will cherish you forever," he whispers huskily. "Now sleep. There's much to do in the morning."

She lies on the cot, drinking up the feel and scent of him. She never wants to let go. It's like she's found her place in the world, the only place she ever wants to be. Slowly her ecstatic thoughts dissolve into a drowsy bliss.

CHAPTER 16

Long, melodic trills and hoots, exotic and haunting, break through Lena's slumber as she slowly wakes. Next, she feels the heat like a warm blanket wrapped around her. When she opens her eyes, light is glowing through the green canvas tent. Then she feels a feathery tickling on her cheek, soft breathing in her ear. That low sexy voice.

"I thought you'd never wake," Raoul tells her. She hears his smile. Feels her back pressed against his chest. He's tickling her with a curl of her own hair. She wriggles back against him.

"I don't want to wake," she says. "Let's stay here like this forever."

He laughs softly as she turns toward him. His thumb traces her lips.

She studies his face, then brushes the tender skin beneath his dark eyes and runs her finger over a pale scar that dissects one of his eyebrows. "You know, I've been collecting everyone's stories about how they became Aguileros, but I haven't heard yours."

"Surely you must know by now."

"But I haven't heard it from you. I want to know everything."

Much of what he tells her she knows already until he gets to his mother's story, how when Ortiz came to power he undertook a major land-grab, evicting private farmers and estate owners from their land, claiming they owed back taxes. The only way they could pay was to sell off large chunks of their properties for a pittance to the United Fruit Company.

"That's how my mother's family lost their estate and why she hates Ortiz almost more than my father did. For him, it was academic, a wrong that needed righting. For her, it was personal, visceral. As a girl she'd gone from being the daughter of a prosperous landowner living on a fine estate to being almost penniless, the daughter of a shopkeeper living upstairs. Half the reason she fell in love with my father, I'm convinced, was because she saw him as a champion of her father and Ortiz's enemy. She encouraged him when he spoke against the regime, even though she knew how dangerous it was. She thought he was destined to overthrow Ortiz.

"My father was a healthy, robust man when he went to prison. When he returned, he was a shell of himself, thin, stooped, broken in mind and body, suffering from internal injuries from many beatings. He died two weeks later."

"I'm so sorry, Raoul." She caresses his cheek, but his eyes are far away. She tries to bring them back. "So that's when your mother sent you to the States, to keep you safe?"

"Partly, no doubt. She knew my older brother Tomás was a hothead and wanted revenge. But he was too young and would end up dead like my father if he stayed, so there was that. But she also wanted her sons to grow strong enough to return and take down Ortiz. To succeed where our father failed."

"Is that what you wanted too?"

"Yes, in a way. I was close to my father. I wanted to be a scholar like him, believing more in the power of the pen than the sword. But after his death, I knew both were needed. I was happy to go to the States. I learned much there studying the history of your revolution, how your leaders fought with both pen and sword to great effect."

"Did you join SDS while you were at Berkeley?"

"No, but I studied their strategies and admired their speeches. What about you? Did you go to university?"

"Yes, in Santa Barbara, studying art and journalism. I joined SDS and helped organize anti-war protests. I was even arrested at a sit-in."

"So, you were an activist!" He looks admiringly at her. "What inspired you to become involved?"

"My father. He was a professor like yours, history and philosophy. He took me to rallies and protests when I was still very young."

"And your mother? What was she like?"

Lena tenses. Her mother? How did she forget about her! What will he think when he learns she's married to his enemy? She turns her face away to hide her dismay. Her stomach clenches. Someday she'll have to tell him. But not yet. Not while their relationship is still so new and fragile.

"Malenque, are you alright?" He touches her face and brings it back toward him.

She lets out a ragged breath. "It's just that I never really knew my mother . . . I was so young . . . and then she was gone."

"We both have known tragedy in our lives."

"But mine was nothing compared to yours! Losing your father that way."

"It doesn't matter how we lose our parents, it's still a tragedy that shapes us in ways we may never fully understand."

Lena nods, looking up into his face, relieved he's not pressing to learn more about her mother. He's so close she sees the curl of each dark eyelash, the intricate whorl of an ear, and one luscious earlobe. She takes the plumb flesh between her thumb and forefinger. His eyes half-close. *So soft, so fat and juicy*, she thinks, taking it into her mouth, sucking and teasing with her teeth. His low groan vibrates through her. When she pulls away, his eyes are closed, his brows clenched as if in pain. He opens his eyes and kisses the back of her fingers and the middle of her palm. Then he rolls away and rises, looking down at her as she gazes up at him. The sight of him standing there makes her breath catch and her stomach dissolve.

She reaches up to bring him down again. He leans in and takes her mouth. Only their mouths touch. Hungry lips and greedy tongues. Then he breaks away again.

"Why are you leaving?" she asks, missing the lips she was enjoying so much. Wanting more. Wanting all of him. "Don't you want me?"

A painful look fills his face. "How can you ask? You must know how much I want you."

Her eyebrows furrow. "Then why...?"

"Because once I start, once I taste you that way, I'll never be able to stop."

"Then don't stop! I don't want you to stop."

He shakes his head and reaches for his trousers. "We must wait. To be sure."

Lena sits up on the cot, one leg curled beneath, her eyes clouded and confused. "Sure of what?" Her face darkens. "You mean . . . .." Her voice catches. "You mean you're not sure about what you feel for me?"

"Oh, I am sure. For me there's no doubt. But for you?"

"What makes you think I'm not sure too?"

"You may think so, but thinking so is not enough to be sure. For that we need time and space."

"I don't understand," she says, hearing the sob in her voice, feeling the fear and heat and heartbreak of it.

He grabs her shoulders and pulls her up into his arms, crushing her to his chest. He holds her so tightly and for so long she thinks he's not going to answer. And when he does, his voice is so full of feeling, she cannot doubt him.

"There's no going back for me when it comes to you, what I feel for you. I felt it the first day I saw you. When you looked at me the way you did. When you told me your name and said you were no man's woman, I knew we were meant to meet. To be together. You felt it too. I saw it in your face."

Pushing her back and looking into her eyes, he says, "Unfortunately, there's more than you and me to consider. I do important work. And if we want to be together, you need to be part of that. Or we must wait until this war is done. Then I'll come find you. That's what we must be sure of. Whether to be together now or later. And you need time alone to think this through and decide."

I don't need time! she wants to tell him. But seeing how serious he is, she says, "Okay, if you insist. But know this, I want you now and that's not going to change. In the meantime," she looks down at her bare legs, "I'll need more than this tunic before I go outside."

He laughs, his eyes shining. "As much as I love looking at you like this, I don't want anyone else to."

When Raoul returns with her trousers and boots, Lena dresses and returns to her tent to wash up. But when she goes outside to take more photographs, she feels the eyes of everyone she meets slide over her in a new way. Apparently, word has gotten out about their sleeping together last night. Some appear amused or curious. Others feign indifference or ignorance. A few leer or show open disapproval.

At first it stings and shames her—their knowing. Then she pulls herself together. If she's to be with Raoul, she must act like she belongs there. Act like him. Strong and confident, warm and reassuring. Commanding respect. What helps this effort is remembering how he feels about her, how it so perfectly matches how she feels about him. If they were meant to be together, then it must be a perfect fit, not just for them, but for the cause he serves, for these soldiers under his command who revere him.

Moving through the camp, she greets people with confidence, staring down the leers and looks of disapproval, chatting with those nearby as they eat breakfast, learning more of their stories and taking more photos. The longer she does this, the more natural it feels. *I can do this.*

She sees Manuela lifting a heavy sack of flour and helps her carry it to the table where she's making bread. She watches Manuela fill a large plastic bin with flour, throws in a handful of dry yeast and sugar, a pinch of salt and water. Watches while she digs her fingers into the dough and begins kneading.

As she watches, Lena interviews Manuela, discovering how she and Bosco were once the owner-chefs of a popular restaurant in Cordoba. But Bosco had a falling out with the Federales who demanded protection money. When he refused to pay, their restaurant burned down. They returned to the mountain village where Manuela grew up and left their three children with her mother while they joined the Aguileros. Their children would have no future with Ortiz and his bandits in power.

"As you can see, we are back in the restaurant business, doing the work we love while serving a greater cause."

"Tell me about your children. Do you see them often?"

"We visit as often as we can. Benito is the oldest, almost twelve, although he acts as if he's older, lording it over his sisters and grandmother, as if he's the man of the house. He wants nothing more than to become an Aguilero. Our twin daughters are little angels, six years old, sweet and full of giggles, holding hands and whispering into each other's ears." Manuela smiles as she kneads, her strong hands growing more vigorous. "I miss them terribly. But I know they're safe with my mother."

While they are talking, Tomás walks by and slows to watch them, his dark eyes menacing. Lena looks after him as he passes.

"I don't think he likes me," she tells Manuela, who makes a dismissive shrug.

"Pay him no attention. If you're not a soldier, you're not important, not a real Aguilero in his eyes. You're useful, necessary, no doubt, but somewhat suspect. I suppose he sees you that way too. As well as a threat, I imagine."

"A threat?" That surprises Lena.

"A rival for Raoul's attention. The brothers are close. He may not like you being in the mix. But then, what do I know? I'm only the cook." She gives Lena a small grin.

Lena hesitates, and then asks. "So . . . me and Raoul. What do you all know about that, my coming here, I mean?"

Manuela cocks her head. "The rumor is Raoul fell hard for you and brought you here to see how it goes, I suppose." She eyes Lena curiously. "Is this true? It's so unlike Raoul. He's never brought a woman to camp, never had a woman as far as we know. So, we're all a bit nonplussed."

She stops kneading and looks up. "Speaking of our intrepid leader, here comes Raoul." Manuela wipes floury hands on her apron and goes inside the lean-to, emerging moments later with a small package that she hands to Raoul.

"Here's what you asked for, rolls and cheese and fruit," she tells him, then nods at Lena. "Take care of her, Raoul. She will do you good."

His eyes shine when he answers. "I will."

He takes Lena's hand and leads her to the jeep he just arrived in. "We have the whole afternoon to ourselves, and I have something to show you."

CHAPTER 17

The wind blows back Lena's hair as the jeep careens along the rutted road. A thick green canopy forms a leafy arbor over their heads. Whip-thin branches reach out to brush them as they pass. She steals glances at Raoul driving with one strong hand on the wheel, one holding hers. It's almost painful how her heart swells. *Can this beautiful man be mine?* Everything around her—the balmy breeze from the jeep's motion, the earthy scent of the forest, the dazzle of light spilling down through the green arbor—sings, yes!

It's like she's out on her surfboard again feeling that dark green swell rise, lifting her to her feet, claiming her as she claims it. Together they are surging forward to who knows where without a care. She squeezes his hand. He looks at her with that tangle of jungle flashing behind him, the breeze parting his waves, that radiant smile on his face, and she knows she will remember this look, this moment, this feeling, forever.

When the ride ends, silence falls over them like the hush in a cathedral. He takes her hand and leads her down a narrow leafy path. The sound of water grows as they walk. Finally, the path opens onto a large pool fed by a slender waterfall. It cascades down a splay of fern-laced rock and splashes into the pool, scattering ripples of light across its surface.

She turns toward him, a look of wonder on her face. "This is what you wanted to show me. It's beautiful!"

He grins. "I thought you'd like it."

She lifts her tunic and takes it off, exposing her breasts. She leans against a tree and lifts a booted foot toward him. "Help me with these. I want to go swimming." He unties the laces and pulls it off, pulls off her sock. She lifts the other boot, and he does the same. She pulls down her slacks and steps out. He looks at her, heavy-lidded and silent, his chest moving with each breath. She starts to unbutton his shirt, but he stops her.

She cocks her head. "Don't you want to come in too?"

"No, I want to watch you the way you watched me that first day. I want to see you rise naked and wet from the pool walking toward me."

"And then," she says, taunting him, "will you take me and make me yours?"

He laughs, pulling her against him. "You already are, whether I take you here and now or later."

"Why wait?"

"I already told you."

"But—"

He puts his thumb on her mouth to hush her. "Now, go! Let me see you as you saw me."

"All right," she says and slow-walks to the pool's edge, hips swaying, remembering how the slow-roll of his hips excited her. She wades through the cool silky pool up to her knees before bending to splash water over her shoulders. She hears his groan and glances back, giving him a naughty grin before diving in, swimming lazily toward the falls.

She clambers up slippery rocks toward a ledge hidden behind a veil of water, then dives into the pool and swims toward him. As she rises, she runs her fingers through her hair the way he did. She walks slowly toward him with a sultry smile.

He comes to her, unbuttoning his shirt, removing it. Once she's in his arms and they are kissing, he uses his shirt to dry her with the warm fabric that smells of him, slowly, tenderly, neglecting none of her parts, but paying meticulous attention to each swollen, tender place. She quivers in his arms. Is it possible to have an orgasm while someone dries you? And then she knows as she shudders around his fingers and pushes against him. He's murmuring sweet words into her ear, but she hasn't the capacity to decipher them. When she's done, she wilts against him as his arms close around her.

"That's not fair," she murmurs, rubbing her face against his shoulder. "Why can you do that to me, and I can't to you?" He's more in control of his emotions and desires than she is of hers, she realizes. He has to be, she supposes. Otherwise, he couldn't do what he's doing, be the leader of this movement. It makes her feel young and inexperienced.

"Believe me, what you do to me when I'm holding you in my arms is equal to everything you just experienced."

She laughs. "Liar! I'm not as gullible as that, you know." She pulls away from him. "And I'm feeling at a terrible disadvantage here, naked while you're still clothed."

He helps her dress, then spreads out a blanket where they can eat the food Manuela prepared: rolls stuffed with cheese and sweet peppers and slices of mango. They sit chatting, as if they just met on a date, talking about music and movies. He tells her why he loves *Santana*; she tells him about Cali Michael's vocal acrobatics. She loved *Doctor Zhivago*; he thought *Lawrence of Arabia* was better. Neither was crazy about *Dr. Strangelove*.

"I did enjoy *The Pink Panther*, though," he says.

"You were living in the States then, weren't you? I wish we could have met then."

"If we had, I'm not sure I would have made quite the same impression on you."

She laughs. "True! Rising naked from that pool would be hard to top." Then she sobers. "You don't suppose that's all this is, what's happening here, do you? Us meeting in such a dramatic way, at such a momentous time in our lives?"

He seems to think about this. "Perhaps it's the times that drew us together. In such a dramatic way," he adds with a smile, drawing her hand to his lips. "Perhaps our meeting and being together was inevitable."

The sun has drifted low and the jungle is streaked with dark purple shadows when they drive back to camp. "This will be our last night together," Raoul says, reaching to take her hand.

"Pepe will drive you to Curico tomorrow and I'll come to you in two weeks so you can tell me what you've decided."

"But I've already decided. Why won't you believe me?"

"I do believe you. But it's not merely a matter of having *me, being with me,* now. It's having everything I stand for, everything I'm doing, and being a part of it. Being an Aguilero. Taking an oath. Not to me, but to our cause." His eyebrows furrow, his voice hardens. "It's training. It's playing a part in all this. It's understanding how dangerous it is. I will do everything I can to protect you, to keep you safe, but there are no guarantees."

She hears the fear behind his terse words, the caution he's so seriously trying to communicate. He wants her to convince him she's thought it all through, knows the risks, what it will cost her, and, despite all that, decides this is what she wants: To commit wholeheartedly not only to him, but to his cause, and to make it hers. But she doesn't need two weeks to think it through. She wants him now. All of him and all that comes with it.

"Do you understand?" The crease between his eyebrows deepens, and his voice grows sharp. "If I'm the one who chooses when we'll be together, I choose later. It's safer for you. Do you want me to make that choice for you? Because I will!"

"No!" she says, alarmed by the threat in his voice.

"Then take this seriously and consider all I've told you."

"I will."

He sighs with relief, and takes her hand again, squeezes.

"So," he says, lighter now, "in two weeks you can tell me then what's best for you. And remember, what's best for you will be best for us."

He smiles at her. A reassuring smile. A smile that fills her from the inside out. She smiles back at him. A reassuring smile. A smile that melts away the worry from his face. Then she lays her head against his shoulder. She can wait two weeks.

Their last night together is sweet. Lena sleeps in Raoul's tent, wrapped in his arms, where they talk long into the night about their childhoods. He tells her about the dog he raised from a pup and how they loved exploring the forests behind his home. She tells him how her father taught her to surf, taking her tandem when she was young.

"Back then, I wanted to marry my father," she confesses.

"You loved him that much?"

"I wanted to marry him because I thought no one could care for him the way I did, and I didn't want him to be lonely. He was so sad after we lost mother."

He strokes her hair, her head nestled in his shoulder. "So did you two stay close, even as you grew older?"

"Yes, he's the person I admire most in the world. He and Gandhi and Martin Luther King."

Raoul leans away to look down into her face. "Is that right? Gandhi is one of mine too. He and Che Guevara."

She laughs. "Strange combination. How do you figure?"

"Well, Che for his brilliance in guerrilla warfare, but also because he fought for the freedom of all Latin America, fighting for Cuba, even though he was from Argentina. He fought in Guatemala and died fighting in Bolivia. That unselfishness makes him a hero for freedom fighters everywhere."

He's silent a moment, absently stroking Lena's arm. "I admire Gandhi for championing the Untouchables, the poorest and most oppressed people in his country, and for his commitment to non-violence. I wish that strategy would work where dictators rule, but the values he espoused do work. Freedom movements must be firmly rooted in the ideals of the people and steered by clear eyes and a steel will."

"And yet," Lena says, "sadly, Che did not free Guatemala or Bolivia, nor Gandhi the Untouchables. They are as oppressed today as they ever were."

"Yet, they tried. Who else can say that? We may not overthrow Ortiz. But we will try. That's the least, and sometimes the most, we can do."

PART TWO

Hour Up in Arms

September – December 1971

How like the sea, the myriad-minded sea,
Is this large love of ours: so vast, so deep,
So full of mysteries!
—Ella Wheeler Wilcox, from "How Like the Sea"

It does not take a majority to prevail . . . but rather an irate, tireless
minority, keen on setting brushfires of freedom in the minds of men.
—Samuel Adams

CHAPTER 18

As promised, Lena calls Daniel as soon as she returns to Curico.

"Thank God!" he says when he hears her voice. "I can't tell you how worried I was. What happened out there?"

"Nothing," she says, wanting to reassure him. Then, feeling deliriously happy, she adds a bit breathlessly, drawing out the word, "E-v-e-r-y-thing . . . ."

The phone goes quiet.

"Oh, God . . . don't tell me," he says at last, his voice tired, disillusioned.

She stays silent.

"Meet me tomorrow for lunch. Better yet, I'll pick you up."

"Why?" she asks warily.

"Debriefing."

She laughs. "Well, okay. For that. I have tons of notes and photos. Three rolls. Can you get them developed for me? Safely? Faces will need to be blurred so you can't identify them. Do you know someone who can do that?"

"Yeah, I know someone."

"Tell him he can take credit for the photos if he wants. You too if you want to help me put this altogether. In fact, you can have the whole byline. It might be safer that way. I'll be going dark here in a while."

More silence.

"I'll pick you up twelve sharp." The phone slams down.

Daniel doesn't even try to hide his displeasure when he picks up Lena. He screeches away from the curb and gives her a withering look. "So, what's this about 'going dark'?"

"Hello to you too," she says, squaring on her lap the portfolio filled with her notes and film, feeling like a schoolgirl in a principal's office.

"Tell me," he insists between tight lips.

"What! What do you want to know?"

"E-v-e-r-y-thing," he tells her, drawing out the word.

"Well, that may take some time."

"I have all day. Start with the 'going dark' part."

Starting there at least will skip the parts she doesn't want to share. "In two weeks, I'll be joining the Aguileros."

He gapes at her, then jerks the wheel to the curb, pulling up on the sidewalk, letting honking cars pass.

"Please tell me you're kidding!" He looks more sick than angry now.

"I'm not. I believe in their cause. I think I can help."

He stares at her. "Did something happen between you and Raoul?"

"Like what?" she asks, trying to buy time and furious she didn't think through more carefully what she'd reveal.

"Like did he fuck you?"

"That's none of your damn business!"

He shakes his head wearily. "So, he did."

"He didn't, in fact!" she says, not adding she wished he had.

He searches her face. "I don't believe you," he says calmly.

"Fuck you!" she says, and jerks open the car door. He grabs her arm.

"Don't go! Please. We need to talk. And . . . I'm sorry. I shouldn't have. . . ." He looks at her, his face full of regret. He lets go of her arm and leans his head back against the seat, eyes closed. When he opens them, he looks at her again. "Let's just go have lunch like we planned, okay?" She still has one hand on the open door. "Please," he adds.

He takes her to the plaza where they first had lunch and leads her to a table in the middle. "What would you like?"

"I'm not hungry," she tells him, holding her portfolio tightly against her chest.

"Then I'll get us coffee, okay?"

Daniel is reacting just like Lonny would have. Only worse. But can she blame him? So much has changed so quickly. For the first time she wonders if she should back up a bit, give herself more time to think this through, like Raoul wanted.

Raoul! Now Daniel! What about what she wants? What does she want? To be with Raoul. To become an Aguilero. *Oh, God*, she thinks, as her father's face surfaces in her mind. *What will he think*? Suddenly everything is so much messier than it was back in camp.

By the time Daniel returns with a tray full of coffee and cream, she feels a bit chagrined, even contrite. He sets the tray down on the table.

"Thank you." She takes a cup and pours in the cream. He pulls sugar packets from his shirt pocket and hands them to her.

She smiles. "You remembered."

"Can we start over?" he asks. She nods. "Tell me whatever you were going to tell me when we agreed to have lunch together."

"Okay," she says and takes a deep breath. "Let's start here. I interviewed so many people with incredibly powerful stories about why they became Aguileros. This will make a great story and help their cause, which I believe in. But I need your help to get it published. I don't want a byline; I'd rather stay anonymous."

She makes a self-deprecating face. "*Dark*. That sounded rather ominous, didn't it? I hadn't meant to alarm you. But I want to go back and get more material. What do they call it when reporters live inside a camp and report from there? *Embedded*, that's it. That's what I mean when I say I'm going dark."

He puts his hand on her arm. "That's very noble of you. But being embedded isn't the same as joining the Aguileros. So, which is it?"

She just looks at him and chews her lip.

"Aside from the cause, which I understand why you'd support, is there anything else making you want to go back to their camp?"

She leans back in her chair. "And if there was? Would it matter?"

"I don't know. I want to understand. Is it just for the story?" He's looking steadily, calmly, at her now, and she knows he deserves a straight answer.

"Yes, there's more."

He waits, giving her the space to explain. But what can she say that will make sense to anyone other than her and Raoul? That it was love at first sight? That they understand each other and want the same things? That she wants this more than anything she's ever wanted in her life? She glowers at Daniel, knowing how crazy this will sound if she tells him. He's looking at her with studied patience, as if she's a child he's trying to make confess some transgression. As if he already knows what's she's going to say, and already made up his mind what he thinks about it. So, she says nothing.

"Lena, please, tell me." He looks almost sorry for her now. Like she's lost her mind and he's got to walk her back from the cliff. Well, he's getting nothing.

She lifts her chin and stares him down. "Do you want to help with this story or not? Because I don't need to explain anything. My reasons are my own."

He gives her a pained look, shaking his head, then looks away. "You think you're in love with him." He says this as matter-of-factly as he can, but she can hear the contempt—and regret.

"I don't think so, I know I am," she answers in the same pragmatic way, but then she rushes ahead, more passionately, "And I know what you're going to say, and I don't care. It is what it is."

"Lena—" he tries again, pleadingly.

She leans in. "I know how it sounds. But it's so much more. Something I can't even explain, something I wouldn't even have known existed and never would have believed if I'd not felt it for myself."

"I see," he says, leaning back in his chair.

"So now what? Are you going to help me, or not?"

"I can't be part of this, Lena."

"What do you mean? You're a journalist. This is a great story. How could you turn it down?"

He just shakes his head.

"Tell me this, if it was anyone else asking for help on this story, another journalist, Marley or Carla, anyone else, would you help them, or turn your nose up at it?"

"I care about you, Lena."

"So, it's personal, not professional." She waits to hear his response, then leans forward. "Look, Daniel. I'll do this with you or without you. I've made my choice. And you! Supposedly you're a journalist. Since when do you let your personal feelings—whether attachment or animosity—keep you from a good story?"

He makes a pained face. "Your father asked me to look after you."

She lurches back. "My father! What's he got to do with this?" Her mind reels in alarm.

Will Daniel tell him about Raoul before she gets a chance to? She wants to beg him not to tell, but then she'll sound like the child he already thinks she is. Instead, keeping her voice steady, she says, "You're going to tell him, aren't you?"

He sighs, and then, as if he's as disgusted with himself as her, says brusquely, "No. I won't tell him. I made it clear when he called that I would pick you up at the airport, show you around, be a friend, but that I wouldn't be your babysitter or his spy."

She sighs with relief. "Thank you," she says softly, humbly, her eyes filling despite herself.

"But Jesus, Lena! I care about you. I don't want anything to happen to you. You're in way over your head. And I blame myself for getting you involved." He looks at her with such anguish and frustration. "I wish I could tie you up and throw you into the trunk of my car, drive you to the airport, and send you home!"

She wants to laugh at the ridiculous image but resists the impulse. Instead, she touches his hand. "Please don't worry about me. I know what I'm doing. And Raoul will keep me safe."

He looks like he wants to tear his hair out, then he visibly tries to calm himself.

"Raoul will keep you safe," he repeats in a low dangerous voice, nodding. "Raoul will keep you safe. Jesus, Lena! Will you listen to yourself? Raoul is a hunted man, a rebel with a target on his back. He will take care of you? If he wanted to keep you safe, he'd tell you to get the hell out of here and have nothing more to do with him."

Lena's eyes narrow. Daniel has gone too far now. He knows nothing about Raoul, what's between them, or the fact that if it was Raoul's choice, he would send her home. But it's not his choice. It's hers. Raoul understands this. Daniel doesn't.

She pushes back her chair. "I didn't come here to be lectured or mocked. I came to offer you a story we could collaborate on and, failing that, to let you know I'd be leaving soon so you wouldn't . . ." she falters, realizing what she's about to say.

"Wouldn't what? Worry about you? Seriously. That didn't quite work out, did it?"

"I guess there's nothing more to say . . .."

He is silent.

"So, I'll be going." She rises and moves toward him, as if to give him a hug, but he puts up his hand to stop her. "Just go," he says, sounding so weary and defeated, it breaks her heart.

She starts to leave, then turns back, not wanting it to end like this. "Just so you know, I care about you too."

Lena grabs a bus back to the boardinghouse. It's crowded, so she's standing, holding on to the back of a seat as the bus sways through the streets. She can't stop thinking about Daniel, the sorrow she's feeling at losing his confidence and trust—perhaps even his friendship. While she's sure about the rightness of being with Raoul—that he's the one she's been waiting for, she doesn't want to lose Daniel either.

He's important to me. He's important to the cause as well, a trusted journalist to turn to when needed. She must win him back, both as a friend and a colleague who can help the Aguileros.

Meanwhile, she has a story to write, photos to develop, and she's on her own. She hops off the bus with renewed determination and an eagerness to start writing. She has two weeks to get this done.

CHAPTER 19

Lena calls Daniel several times over the next week and leaves messages, but he doesn't call back. He can't be *that* angry! Surely he's had time to cool off. She knows a big part of this is jealousy. He's disappointed in her, in himself, she gets it. But he's also her friend. He can't just disown her, can he? If he won't return her calls, she'll go to him.

Daniel's boardinghouse is an impressive two-story Colonial that once housed an American ambassador. Now it's owned by an "adult film star" who fancies himself a friend of western-style journalism and rents it out to writers, artists, and other free-speech advocates.

Lena hesitates before mounting the steps to the door. As she's lifting the brass knocker, someone comes charging out and slams against her.

"Oh, sorry!" He catches her elbow. "Are you okay?"

She gives him a shaky smile as she regathers her jostled portfolio. "I'm fine, thanks. I was looking for Daniel Weatherly. Do you know him? Is he in?"

The man is slim with dark hair and a trim mustache. He raises his eyebrows as he looks her over. "The journalist, right?" She nods. "No, he's been gone a couple of days. Off on a story about the Aguileros, no doubt. He's obsessed with them."

"The Aguileros? Are you sure? I thought . . . .." She frowns. Why would he be doing that after turning her down?

"Don't be alarmed. I'm sure he's fine. Maybe I can help you instead."

"I don't think so. But thanks anyway." She turns to go.

"Wait!" he says, "You're Paula, right? You went with him to that interview, didn't you?"

"Yes, but I'm not—"

"Please, come in! I've heard all about you." He looks at her excitedly. "I'll ring a friend, see if I can find Daniel for you."

"I thought you were leaving?"

"Nothing that can't wait. I'm Deke, by the way. I own the place," he adds as he ushers her inside.

"Oh! Then you're the . . .." She blushes, realizing what she was about to say.

He grins. "Yes, the porn star. But back in the day I was a journalist, only there's no money in it. Now I'm a patron of the arts!" He gives her a wide, disarming smile. "Sit! I'll make that call, see if we can find him."

As Deke disappears down the hallway, Lena sits on the couch, feeling confused and uncomfortable. Daniel's working on another Aguilero story without her? When she had so much to share with him? It makes no sense.

Deke comes back a few minutes later, sliding his fingers through his short curly locks as he approaches. "No luck, but we can try again later." He eyes her portfolio. "Is that what you're working on now? A story about the Aguileros?"

"Yes, I wanted advice on editing and where a story like this might be published."

"I could help with that. Editing was my specialty. May I?" He reaches for the portfolio.

She hesitates, reluctant to turn it over to a stranger. But she came here for help. How could it hurt? She takes out the story and hands it to him.

He leans back against the couch, looking pleased with himself. Lena watches him read. He's rather good looking in a glib, movie-star kind of way. Lean angular face, lean body, long elegant-looking hands, perfect white teeth with a roguish smile to go with it. He reads three pages and skims the rest.

"This is great stuff. Very passionate. These stories about the soldiers are powerful and the scenes you paint about camp life, vivid, memorable."

Lena thrills at the compliment.

"But no legitimate news source would publish it."

She blinks, confused. "Why not?"

"It's clear you sympathize with the Aguileros, if not outright support them. There's no balance, nothing from Ortiz's point of view about the atrocities the Aguileros committed. Nothing to show these stories are true. Do you have any corroborating witnesses or secondary sources?"

Lena frowns. "There's no role in journalism for reporting why a people might rebel against their government? Or for those who sympathize with their plight to write about it?"

"Of course. But not by any unbiased news source. You'll have to find a publisher who sympathizes with your point of view."

"Like a *Mother Jones* or *The Nation*?"

"Exactly. If you leave this with me, I could give it my professional edit. Like here," he holds up her manuscript. "You have nine words when five would do. And there, moving this around would make your point clearer." She looks over his shoulder, fascinated.

She's tempted, but what she really wants is Daniel's help.

"That's kind of you. But I better wait for Daniel." She glances around the room, realizing how quiet it is. "Where is everyone? Daniel always said how busy it was here, people coming and going all day and night."

Deke glances around the room too, as if just noticing this himself. Then he shrugs. "Sometimes it's busy, sometimes not. Did you have photographs too? Daniel said you were a photographer."

"I am . . . but . . .." Lena stops and frowns. Didn't he think her name was Paula earlier? Did he simply misremember? Or did Daniel give him a pseudonym to protect her? She looks closely at Deke. His eyes flicker to the front window, as if expecting someone.

"We have a darkroom in the back. If you have film with you that needs developing, we could start that now."

"No, but thanks," she says, sliding her story back into her portfolio.

"It would be no trouble at all. You could wait here for it, or better yet, come with me to watch it being developed."

"That's very kind, but I really must go."

There's a flash of irritation in his face as she rises, but he quickly hides it and follows her to the door. "It was a pleasure meeting you. If you change your mind on that offer . . .." He smiles charmingly at Lena, but something in his eyes doesn't match the warmth he's trying so hard to convey.

Lena leaves, feeling unsettled. On the short walk back to her boardinghouse, she keeps glancing over her shoulder, as if someone might be watching her. When she arrives at La Rosaleda, the tall, narrow brick building that seemed so safe before—her home away from home these past two months—now looks more forbidding than comforting, as if it's slipped behind a gray shadow.

She hurries up to her room. Everything is in order. But there's a chill in the air, or maybe it's just in her. Everything seems darker than before. The grandmotherly furnishings so lovingly arranged by Mrs. Henson should be reassuring. Instead, she's hugging her arms, feeling cold. She peeks through the French doors into the courtyard. But, of course, no one's there.

She sits on the edge of her bed sorting through these ominous feelings. It centers on the way Deke latched onto her when he thought she was the one who had gone with Daniel to meet the Aguileros. The way he disappeared to make that phone call, supposedly to locate Daniel. His irritation when she wouldn't leave her story or film.

It might be nothing. But even the chance that it could be something makes her anxious. Raoul's face floats up in her mind.

It's not safe here any longer. She must move. Before Raoul comes to get her.

"But why are you leaving, my dear? I thought you liked it here." Mrs. Henson's gray eyes are wide with surprise and concern. Lena stands in the foyer surrounded by her packed bags, awaiting the taxi she called.

"Oh, I do, so much. You've been great and I'll miss you. Perhaps I'll come back later. But for now, I must leave."

"Where are you going?"

"I don't know yet."

"Now I'm worried." She bites her lip.

Lena hugs her. "Please don't be. I'm fine. I know it's all so mysterious and I'm sorry for that. I wish I could say more."

They kiss each other's cheeks when they hear the taxi honk.

Lena looks out the back window and down side streets as the taxi pulls away, worried she's being watched, followed. But by whom? The Federales? Deke? It's nonsense, of course. But she can't shake it.

She doesn't know how to get hold of Raoul. The only Aguilero in Curico she knows is Carla. Or rather, the woman pretending to be Carla. She'll have to get a message to Raoul through her somehow. But not yet.

The taxi drops her off at the train station where she buys a ticket for Tegucigalpa in Honduras. A decoy. Then she stuffs a few clothes and toiletries, her portfolio and some books in her backpack, and leaves her suitcase and duffle bag behind in a large locker. She catches a bus, getting on and off at intervals, creating the kind of circuitous route she took when meeting the Aguileros. When she's sure she hasn't been followed, she ducks into a shoddy-looking hotel and pays cash with a fake name for two nights.

Is this all in her head? Is she getting carried away having watched too many spy movies? Or is it just the sense of danger that comes from being involved with a rebel leader? One with a target on his back as Daniel pointed out. She cannot sit still and paces the hotel room, her hands pulling at each other. Whether she's being foolish or not, at least she's taking every precaution to protect the man she loves.

The man she loves.

She sinks down on the narrow bed. Yes. Love him she does. She can hardly think of him without feeling him, the way he looks at her, his hands, his laugh, his growl. His naked body. She squeezes her knees together, then jumps up. She must warn Raoul not to go to the boardinghouse.

Downstairs the clerk points her to a payphone at the end of the hallway. She looks up the number for the gym on Clancy Street where Carla said she works. A man answers.

"No Carla works here. But leave me a message. If a Carla shows up, I'll give it to her."

This is weird, Lena thinks. But maybe it's part of the whole espionage bit. Should she leave a message? Is it safe? But what choice does she have?

"Okay," she says, her stomach twisting, "If a Carla comes, tell her to call Lena at this number." She recites the number on the payphone. "Tell her it's important. Tell her . . . the man Marley photographed will want to hear what I have to say."

She asks the hotel clerk to let her know if someone calls asking for Lena. As she's walking slowly up the stairs, feeling disappointed and thinking this is all so crazy, the payphone starts ringing. She runs down to answer it.

"Hello," she says, breathlessly.

"Is this Lena?"

"Yes, is this Carla?"

"This is Carla's friend, Fiona. You have a message for someone, I hear."

"Yes. Please tell him the answer is *now*. *Now*, you understand? But it's not safe where I used to live, so we'll have to meet somewhere else."

There's silence on the other end.

"Do you understand what I'm telling you?" Lena asks.

"I do," the woman named Fiona says in Carla's husky, clipped voice. "I'll get the message to him. But Carla has been asking about you. She misses you. You should drop by and see her tonight."

"Where will I find her?"

"Where you found her last time."

When they hang up, Lena stands there a moment, letting it soak in. Tonight. At *La Respuesta*. A wave of relief and joy flows through her. Carla, or Fiona, whoever she is, will know what to do. And Raoul will come get her. It's already been ten days. It's too late for waiting. She dashes up the stairs, spurred by a surge of adrenaline. A tingle of fear and excitement shoots through her.

It's already crowded when the taxi drops off Lena at *La Respuesta*. The jazz trio includes a sax this time, the player leaning back with his eyes closed, his mouth and fingers doing wicked things to his instrument that fills the room with lust and longing. She waits a moment by the front door, looking for Carla, then heads toward the back rooms. But as soon as she rounds a corner someone grabs her arm and hustles her through a back passageway toward a side door that opens onto an alley. A car is waiting.

"Get in!" The woman Lena knows as Carla pushes her into the back seat. She slides in beside her.

"Go!" she tells the driver, then rips off her wig, letting her braid fall free. Lights from the street flicker over her face, like strobe lights on a dance floor. "So, what's this all about?"

Lena looks at her, feeling rushed and unsettled. She doesn't like the way she's been manhandled. "What shall I call you now, Fiona or Carla?" she asks with an accusatory tone.

The woman with the flickering face smiles. "You may call me Fiona now."

"Did you get my message to Raoul?"

"I got the message to my contact, and he will get it to Raoul." Her voice is smooth and sultry. She gives Lena a slight, mysterious smile and says in a mocking tone, "So the rumors are true. Our Raoul has fallen for you."

Lena decides it's none of Fiona's business and ignores the comment. She doesn't like the way Fiona says "our Raoul" either. Although it is disconcerting to discover that word about them being together has spread this far.

"I think someone may be following me and don't feel safe at the boardinghouse anymore."

Fiona gives one of her dry laughs. "It's true you were being followed, or so I'm told, but by one of us. Apparently, you're good at this. You ditched him."

"One of us? Not the Federales?"

"Why would you think they were following you?"

She tells her about Deke, his interest in the story and photos, how empty the house was even though Daniel said it's always swarming with people.

"Interesting." She pats Lena's knee. "You did good. We can't be too cautious. I'll check into it, see if anything is going on there we should know about."

"Can you find out about Daniel too? I thought he wasn't returning my calls because he was angry, but now I'm wondering if he's in trouble."

"I'll see what I can discover. Where are you staying?"

Lena gives her the hotel address. Fiona grimaces in distaste when her driver pulls up in front. "We can do better than this for you. I'll make calls and get you moved to a safehouse."

"No need. This won't be for long."

"No? Where will you be going?"

"Someone will be coming for me soon."

Fiona lifts an eyebrow. "Raoul?" A look of amazement passes over her face.

Lena nods and jumps out of the car before Fiona can say anything else.

CHAPTER 20

R aoul doesn't come the next day as Lena hoped. Nor the day after that. Or the next. She's been holed up in this crappy hotel room for five days now! She knows it's unreasonable to expect him to drop everything and come as soon as he finds out about the trouble. Unreasonable, yes. But when has anything about the two of them ever been reasonable?

Her stomach tightens as she moves between window and door, past the unmade bed and TV console, her only companion for the past five days. All the soapy telenovelas she's been watching to divert her have only heightened her longing for Raoul and her annoyance he's taking so long to claim her. He said he'd come in two weeks. It's been fifteen days.

That afternoon Fiona unexpectedly shows up. Lena hasn't heard from her since the night at La Respuesta. "Pack your bags. You're moving," she says in her exasperatingly clipped, no-nonsense way.

"What? Why?"

"Raoul's orders."

"You've heard from him? Where is he?" Lena begins gathering her clothes and books scattered around the small room and stuffing them into her backpack. Fiona ignores her questions and leans against a wall, her arms folded across her chest, looking smug or bored or both. As if she's been taken away from more important work to deal with a minor, irksome matter.

"Where are you taking me?" Lena asks crossly as she crams in more stuff.

"To a safehouse to wait."

"Wait for what?"

Fiona lifts an eyebrow. "What do I know? I just take orders."

The driver that brought her here now drives her to the "safehouse." Pablo, he calls himself as he affably shakes her hand. He's a chubby guy, mid-thirties with a scruffy dark beard, but his eyes are lively, as if greatly amused by all that's going on.

The safehouse, set in a quiet suburb outside Curico, is small and sparsely furnished. A lumpy couch and fake-wood coffee table, a tiny dinette pushed against the wall in the kitchen, two bedrooms and bath in between.

"There's food in the cupboards and fridge," Fiona tells her. "And a coffeemaker beneath the sink. Pablo here will check in daily to see if you need anything else."

Lena stands in the living room and looks around. Not even a TV. She isn't going to be stuck here like she was at the hotel with nothing to do. She wants to get back to her writing. "Could you get me a typewriter? I left the one I borrowed at the boardinghouse."

"A typewriter! Whatever for?"

What is it about this woman that irks Lena so, making her feel like she must defend herself? She lifts her chin. "I'm a journalist. I'm working on a story about the Aguileros and need to finish it. What do you think I was doing at the camp?"

Fiona raises her eyebrows with a smirk.

Lena's face heats up. "Never mind. I'll get my own typewriter."

Fiona shakes her head. "No, until we know what's going on with Deke, Raoul wants you to stay off the streets. I'll get the typewriter. Anything else you need?"

"Yes. I need someone to develop film. Someone we can trust."

"We?" Fiona gives her a funny look.

"Yes, we. Do you have a problem with that?"

She laughs. "No, ma'am! I'll see what I can do."

"And—" Lena starts and bites her lip. She really is asking a lot of these people who do not know her at all "—can you get the rest of my luggage? I left it at the train station in a locker. And there's my surfboard still at the boardinghouse." She digs the locker key out of her bag. "Look, you don't have to do any of this. I can grab a taxi and get this stuff myself."

"I'll get them," Pablo says, taking her key. He gives her a friendly salute before leaving. Lena's glad he'll be looking after her and fervently hopes never to see Fiona again.

But it's Fiona who returns the next day with a typewriter and bulky rucksack. She sets it on the floor next to the coffee table as Pablo brings in Lena's luggage and surfboard.

"You were right," Fiona tells Lena. "The secret police raided the journalists' house. Everyone gathered up, questioned. That's why no one was there but Deke. He was spying for them. Probably stayed behind to gather up anyone who was out when the raid happened."

"What about Daniel?" Lena asks in a panic. "Was he taken? Or is he out on assignment like Deke said?"

"We don't know. We'll try to find out."

"Thank you," Lena says, feeling a bit warmer toward her.

Fiona gives her a clipped nod. "I've asked Billy about developing your film. He says he knows someone we can trust."

"Billy?"

Fiona smiles and leans back against the door jamb. "You know him as Marley. Actually, he's Billy Flynn. Part of our communications arm."

"And what's this?" Lena nods toward the rucksack.

"Homework," says Fiona.

Lena kneels beside the bag and opens it. It's full of books.

"Education is an important part of our movement. You can't be an Aguilero without knowing what you're becoming part of—our history, doctrines, philosophy."

Lena pulls out a dog-eared copy of Frantz Fanon's *The Wretched Earth*, Che's *Guerrilla Warfare* and the history of San Balanque she read on the plane.

"I've already read this one," she says and pulls out more books. "Also, Karl Marx and Thomas Paine, both in high school, and what's this? *Leaves of Grass*? What's Whitman's poetry doing here? And Paine for that matter?"

"I suppose Raoul wants you to see what we are doing through the lens of your own country's revolutionary writings."

"Raoul packed these books?"

"Some are from his own library. Others he asked me to add."

Lena pulls out a spiral-bound book that looks like it was printed up at Kinko's—*Doctrines of the Freedom and Prosperity Movement: The Credo of the Aguileros*. The next book is thick and heavy. "*Open Veins!*" She laughs. "My father gave me this. You mean I didn't need to lug my copy all the way from California?"

Fiona looks surprised. "You've read it?"

"Skimmed mostly. Do all recruits have to read this?"

"Not just read. But study, absorb, discuss."

"You have study groups?"

"Of course. It's essential not only to have a meeting of minds, but the ability to question, to push against what we read, to create our own personal revolutionary theology. We are pledging our lives to something greater than ourselves. We need to thoroughly understand what we're willing to die for."

Die for. That gives Lena pause.

"Check the front pocket," Fiona says. "Raoul not only left instructions for your care and education, as he called it, but a letter."

Lena's eyes widen. She's tempted to snatch it up right then to read but waits until Fiona leaves. Then, with trembling fingers, she pulls out Raoul's letter. Just the sight of her name, Malenque, handwritten across the envelope, knowing it was Raoul's hand that wrote it, the hand that touched her so intimately, makes it hard to breathe. She sits on the couch, takes a deep breath, and slides her finger through the seal.

Malenque Mia,

It is a hard thing putting words on paper when all I want to do is reach out and touch you. I wish I could hold you on my lap and stroke your hair and tell you how strong and brave you are, how wise and resourceful. Tell you how proud I am of you, the keen insight that kept you from harm's way and led you to safety. How humble and grateful I am, knowing I have your trust and that you choose to be with me now, to stand by my side in this, our great cause. I want to lace my fingers with yours and never let go. But I feel our hands are already so entwined.

Wait for me to come to you a little longer. Use this time to continue your work writing our stories and learning more about this cause you have committed yourself to. I've given instructions to Fiona and others on how to care for you in my absence, and to aid you in the important work you are doing for us already. Trust them and learn from them. Remember, though, while you are new to this, you are also their equal in every way. From the moment I saw you and heard your name I knew you were not only the one meant for me personally, but also the one who, uniting with us, would help bring to fruition my hopes and desires for San Balanque.

Stay strong, my sweet. Work hard. I will be with you as soon as it's safe and my duties allow.

Your Raoul

Lena presses the pages to her breast as if to soak up the words. She sits for a few moments reveling in the memory of him and the promise of their life together, then shakes herself loose.

He's right. She has work to do. And it's thrilling work.

A great wave of change is rising behind them and pushing them forward. She is riding that wave with Raoul and Fiona, Pablo and Pepe, Bianca and Billy, and all the Aguileros. There's no stopping what has been put into motion. They will ride this wave to wherever it takes them.

CHAPTER 21

Lena starts meeting with a study group twice a week. Most gatherings are small, six to ten people, all using aliases to protect each other. Among them are a mechanic and his daughter, a university student; a butcher and bookseller; a doctor and the secretary of a large law firm. Some identified as communists, others as socialists. Most claimed all ideology is beside the point. Getting rid of Ortiz was the one point they all agreed upon. And that Raoul and the Aguileros would help them do that.

When reading the Aguilero founding documents, Lena discovers the movement is larger than she imagined. Supporters include well-known politicians, soccer stars, labor leaders, rock bands, renowned poets, and TV stars. This surprises Lena, and feels somewhat overwhelming, knowing that her Raoul is the leader of all this.

The problem, as she sees it, is how to keep all these people with their divergent beliefs and priorities united in a single cohesive movement that can turn the tide and overthrow a government. This is where publicity is so important. Raoul's posters have been a huge uniting tool, helping to draw interest in their cause and giving people a face to rally around. But they need more of that. She hopes her stories will help.

Meanwhile, Ortiz's Federales and secret police are doing all they can to root out whatever resistance they find. But all they have is brute force and fear. No one to inspire them, no cause to champion, nothing to endear them to the people.

Fiona agrees. They are in the kitchen putting away the groceries she delivered to the safe house. "They have no one like Raoul. Ortiz is feared but not loved, not admired. The closest his regime has in the way of a rock star or cultural icon is Dolores Machado. She has the prestige and mysterious aura that appeal to the populace. They are proud of her. But even she doesn't inspire people like Raoul does."

Lena freezes at the mention of her mother's name. The fear of telling Raoul about her roils her stomach like a swarm of angry bees. What will he think, what will they all think, when she tells them?

"Her renown brings honor to San Balanque and helps Ortiz's regime seem more civilized," Fiona continues. "People think the horror stories about government brutality must be fabricated. Otherwise, how would someone so refined and sensitive tolerate being part of that? But then, no one knows much about her. Her past is a mystery. That's part of her mystique."

"How do you know all this?"

"It's my job to know these things. Everything we learn about Ortiz and his administration is potentially useful. This will be your job too. Raoul is assigning you to the Publicity and Propaganda arm of the organization. Humberto Rodrigues heads it and will be able to help you with your stories. He also owns a publishing firm. Talk to him. We're going to one of their meetings tonight."

Lena stands awkwardly at the back of the crowded room. The meeting is hosted by a wealthy couple in a manor at the edge of town. Ornate carpets cover the tiled floors, and gilded paintings adorn the walls. Eloquently dressed people congregate in small groups or gather for intimate conversation on the overstuffed sofas and armchairs. This group is much larger and more sophisticated than the other groups she's attended. All here are seasoned Aguileros who have taken its oath—therefore, aliases aren't used. They are the ones who create news stories and opinion pieces for various media outlets and recruit friendly journalists, artists, and celebrities to spread revolutionary theology to the "masses." They also produce the internal documents, including educational materials for other arms of the organization, like those that secure and distribute supplies, or gather intelligence, or train recruits. Lena is amazed at how well-organized the movement is.

Fortunately, President Ortiz and his minions have no idea. They assume the Aguileros are a ragtag militia operating in the jungles. Or maybe that's what they want the people of San Balanque to believe.

When they first arrive, Fiona introduces Lena to a few key people, then disappears. Everyone looks at Lena with keen interest, perhaps because they want to make new members feel welcomed. But some seem almost gleeful to meet her, others more "honored" than they should be. Has word of her being with Raoul traveled this widely?

The group leader tonight is a young woman named Mariam who appears not much older than Lena. Her dark hair is pulled back into a severe bun and she's wearing over-sized glasses, as if to seem older or more assured. But her attempts to keep the group on topic when discussing Marxism are failing since most don't want to crush Capitalism but reform it.

"Poor Mariam. It always gets like this when so many show up."

Lena turns to see Humberto Rodrigues, who she met earlier, holding a cocktail glass with an olive floating in the clear liquid. "I want to jump in and bring things back to order," he says, "but then I would deprive her the opportunity to learn and grow as a leader."

Lena looks him over, a tall, robust man, a bit on the fleshy side, but exuding such humor and confidence, he seems unaware of that fact, and is quite attractive with his dark curly hair, thick mustache, and rosy complexion.

"This study group is different from the others I've attended," Lena says.

"Well, that's because, technically, we aren't a study group. So even while we have these kinds of philosophical discussions periodically to keep our radical roots watered, they often break down this way." He looks at her with an amused smile and swirls the liquid in his glass before taking another drink.

She's not quite sure what to make of him, but he's the one Fiona said could help with her stories. So, despite her reservations, she plunges forward, telling him all about her interviews with the Aguileros and what

Deke said after reading an early draft. Humberto gazes at her with great interest, but in a way she finds disconcerting. His glance lingers a little too long on her mouth, then wanders down to her chest and back again, all with an amused glint in his eye. She's wishing she hadn't turned to him for help, but when she's done speaking, his look turns serious and encouraging.

"I'm honored you've entrusted me to help you. Do you have the manuscript with you?" She pulls it from her bag. "This won't take long, I'm a fast reader," he says. "May I take it to read now?"

"But of course. Thank you." Humberto gives her a polite bow and takes it to a far corner to read. He turns on a lamp by an armchair and pulls reading glasses from his shirt pocket. He settles into the chair, legs crossed, shoulders slightly hunched, to read.

Lena remains with the others but glances at him now and then. He takes his time with the first few pages, then skims the rest. He puts his glasses back into his pocket and looks toward her with an encouraging smile. Then he turns off the lamp and comes to her, drawing her aside.

"Your friend Deke was right."

She frowns. "He's not my friend."

"Nevertheless, he's right. No one in the mainstream media will pick up this story."

Her frown deepens into confusion. "So, I should send it to some left-leaning rags?"

"Maybe. But that's not who you wrote these stories for. The sympathetic way you portray the people makes it clear you side with them or are even one of them."

"And that's not good journalism," she concludes.

"Good journalism!" He scoffs. "We don't give a crap about good journalism. We care about good stories. Why do you suppose Raoul invited you to his camp to interview his soldiers? To give an objective account about who they are to jaundiced minds? Or to get their stories out to sympathetic ears to solicit support, as well as inspire recruits?"

She looks at him, confused. "So . . .?"

"So, these stories are not meant for mainstream publications, far less left-wing rags. It's not the elite but the common people who are your audience—people like those whose stories you tell: laborers who have lost their land, owners of mom-and-pop stores, farmer's wives and miner's children. People stuck in dead-end jobs whose existence consists of much drudgery and few rewards. These stories tug at the heartstrings of humanity and elicit righteous anger. You need to get these published in the popular tabloids. You know, the ones you see at grocery counters with the photos of flying saucers and babies with two heads."

"You're kidding!"

"I'm serious. People love this stuff. They want stories that make them laugh and cry. To be moved, to be outraged, to be inspired. They want to hear about others like them who have overcome great obstacles, who have suffered the same kinds of humiliations and exploitation—but who, unlike them, have stood up and fought back. They want heroes to admire and saviors to worship. To inspire them to become part of something greater than themselves. And that's what we want too. For them to become Aguileros and support our cause or, at the very least, to be sympathetic toward what we are doing. That's your audience. That's where you want to get these published. Your work will reach far more people that way and may well fly under the radar of Ortiz's cronies who, like others, scorn these kinds of publications." He smiles broadly at Lena, then moves to the center of the room.

"Listen, comrades, I have good news to share!" he says in his booming, jovial way. After he tells them about the stories Lena has written and shares their discussion about where they should be published, a general discussion unfolds. Should the various pieces be published all at once, or come out slowly as a series for more impact and outreach? They decide the latter. Should Lena publish under her real name? When it's determined she shouldn't, the question becomes what name to use.

Several ideas are thrown out before Lena shyly raises her hand, suggesting they publish under the name Malenque. No one besides Raoul and those he introduced her to at camp know that it's Lena's real given name. No one who reads the stories would associate it with Lena Landon.

"Just the one name, nothing else," she adds.

"Perfecto!" says Humberto. "Everyone knows the legendary Malenque and will associate these stories with her love and self-sacrifice for her brother and San Balanque. This is genius, Lena!" He regards her with immense pride and affection, then turns back to the others.

"We already have the posters with the name San Balanque emblazoned above the rock-star image of Raoul, who is recognized by all as the leader of the Aguileros. Now we have his counterpart, Malenque, fighting for the same cause in a different way.

"We need another poster to match the first, one with both of these beautiful people. To capitalize on the love affair between these two Aguileros. Their willingness to sacrifice themselves for this great country, as the legendary twin heroes did. They will be seen as the people's champions, the saviors of San Balanque."

Lena blushes furiously. So, they all *do* know about her and Raoul!

Humberto sees her face and laughs, then speaks quietly in her ear. "Did you think this was a secret? If Raoul wanted it so, none would know. But he took no precautions to hide it. Perhaps for this reason. Raoul is forward thinking. A brilliant strategist. No one understands the heart of the people and what inspires them better than Raoul."

This revelation is even more astounding to Lena than the one before. She tries wrapping her mind around it. Is their so-called love affair a manipulation, part of a pre-ordained plan to rally the troops? It troubles her they want to make her out to be a savior-figure when she's nothing of the sort. And having her face on a poster, wouldn't that make her a target too? Never mind the fact her mother might recognize her. Who knows when her father last shared a photo of her?

"Don't worry," Humberto says when she shares some of those concerns. "We'll make sure Billy alters your features so no one recognizes you. As far as making you into some kind of savior-figure, think of it more as mythmaking. All great movements are based on great myths, making their leaders larger-than-life. And as for Raoul, he would not use your love for him, or pretend love for you, simply to advance some propaganda plan. If there was not strength and truth behind what you two have together, it could backfire spectacularly, and Raoul would not risk that. I know him well."

"You've talked to him? He's told you about me?"

"No, but I've heard the rumors from camp, how Raoul was thunderstruck by this beautiful journalist from the United States. How she stole his heart and then captured the hearts of the soldiers who told her their stories." He laughs. "They love this stuff. There's even some crazy nonsense about how the two of you were so eager to make love you flew into each other's arms beneath a full moon and there on the jungle floor made wild passionate love that woke up the camp. Your boots and clothes were left behind for all to find the next day."

She blushes, and he throws back his head in laughter. "So, it's true! That part at least." He looks at her with amused admiration, and a glint of lust. "Our Raoul is a lucky man."

"It wasn't like that at all," she says primly.

"What can I say, they like to embellish. Trust me, this will not be the end of rumors." He turns back to the others whose discussions have gone on without them.

"This is premature," Fiona says in that tone of voice meant to tamp things down. "The people in these posters should be the faces of our soldiers, not legendary siblings, let alone a love affair between two people."

"No, you are wrong." Humberto says. "Myth and magic, tragic heroes, and a passionate love affair between rebel leaders will gain us huge interest, a huge following. Just as Raoul's poster did. We want the Aguileros to rise in the minds of San Balanquans as heroic figures with a sacred mission. The people must take possession of this cause, and this gives them something to wrap their collective minds and hearts around. A real-life telenovela that gets everyone talking, waiting to see what happens next. This will win sympathy and support, especially when wrapped in the righteous cause of freedom and democracy. This we must do. Billy must produce a new poster for us."

Fiona's objection is overridden in the general enthusiasm for this strategy. The meeting breaks up soon after that.

On the ride back to the safehouse, Lena turns to Fiona, curious about her opposition to Humberto's plan. "There was more to it than what you said, wasn't there?"

Fiona is quiet for a moment, then says, "Raoul is too important to the cause to have his image trifled with or diluted. Too important to become distracted by . . . Don't misunderstand me. I'm happy he's found someone to love and comfort him. As long as . . .."

"What? I don't distract him?" Lena gives her a searing look. "You are wrong about him. About us. Raoul cannot be distracted. It's who he is. Who I commit myself to, the whole of him. All he stands for. This cause and everyone involved, including you, and everyone in that room tonight, and all those at camp. I'm not happy about the poster idea, either. But I'm here to play my part, to do whatever I can to help the cause."

Passing lights flicker over Fiona's face like darting fish in a dark pond as she listens. A slow soft smile gathers in the gloom.

"I'm happy to hear that," she tells Lena in her low gravelly voice. Then, unexpectedly, she reaches for Lena's hand and gives it a quick squeeze before looking away.

CHAPTER 22

"**M**arley!" Lena cries out in joy when Fiona brings him into the safehouse. She feels such an unexpected rush of affection for this fellow artist, fellow surfer, fellow Aguilero outsider, that she jumps up and hugs him. Then she pushes him back to look at his freckled face and dirty-blond dreadlocks. So Californian. He looks like home.

"I know your name's Billy, but I like calling you Marley," Lena says, fingering the Australian's matted locks. He seems surprised but pleased at her affectionate outburst.

Fiona too looks surprised. "I assumed you'd be happy to see him, since he's helping get your film developed, but not quite this happy!"

"The film! I almost forgot." Lena's face lights up as she turns back to Billy. "You know someone we can trust?"

"I know just the guy."

Pablo drives them to a small photo shop where they meet with Jorge, a short stocky man with a Fu-Manchu mustache. He runs the film through the automatic printer in the back of the shop. Most show the Aguileros in training, or mending, cooking, eating, sleeping. The scenes are powerful in their ordinariness. These aren't people to fear, not rabid dogs or murderers like the Federales depict them. They could be your brother or sister, people you might meet anywhere on the street, in a store, driving a taxi or a tractor.

"I wish I could show these to Daniel," Lena says wistfully and turns to Fiona. "Have you found out anything more about him?"

Billy starts speaking but Fiona cuts him off. "He's fine. I'll tell you more later."

When they leave, Billy stays behind to help Jorge with the photos, and Fiona climbs into the back seat with Lena, as she always does, leaving Pablo in the front by himself.

Lena looks anxiously at Fiona. "What couldn't you say in front of Jorge?"

"Don't worry. This is good news. Daniel was off on a story when they raided. He'll be questioned eventually, but we gave him a cover story to use so it won't lead back to you."

"Well, that *is* good news. How's he doing? Did he ask about me?"

Fiona's eyes slide away from her. "Billy was the one who talked to him."

"What did he say?"

"Do you really want to know?"

"Of course!" He couldn't possibly still be mad at her, could he?

Fiona shrugs. "He said little about you. A lot about Raoul. He thinks Raoul has cast some spell over you, playing with your emotions and deliberately putting you into danger. He thinks Raoul is using you."

Lena's face burns with anger and embarrassment.

"I didn't think you really wanted to know," Fiona says with a wry smile. "But there's more. You were right about the phone call Deke made. It was to the secret police. He was an informant. He followed you to the boardinghouse and saw you leave in a taxi. The next day police questioned Mrs. Henson. But since she knew nothing, she wasn't helpful. She said she didn't know any Paula. She was savvy enough not to give you away when they asked if anyone recently left in a taxi."

"Poor Mrs. Henson! That must have been terrifying. I hope they don't find another Paula and blame her, thinking she's me."

"They won't be looking for her anymore. When the secret police went back to Deke to follow up, it appeared he left in haste, leaving behind incriminating evidence showing he was one of ours working as a double agent. So, any info he gave them about some Paula will be worthless."

"I'm confused. He was working for us?"

"No, but that's what they believe now."

"You mean *you* left incriminating evidence! But what will happen to Deke when they find him?"

"They won't find him."

"How can you be sure?"

Fiona cocks her head. "How do you think?"

Lena frowns. "I have no idea." Then her eyes widen. "You have him?"

"We did. No longer."

"And so?" Lena prods, watching Fiona closely. Then her face goes white. "You don't mean . . .."

"It was quick and clean."

Lena's stomach lurches. "No! You didn't."

"We are at war. You know this, do you not? Sometimes this is necessary, but we don't torture, as they do."

"But we assassinate? No trial, no jury?"

"Deke knew the risk he was taking when he agreed to work for them. If they found you, Lena, you would have been tortured. If we let him live, they would have continued searching for you. Your landlady would have been taken in for a deeper interrogation, and then she would have told them it was you who left in a taxi. A bounty would have been put on your head. The risk was too great."

Lena's mind reels. This is the danger Daniel warned her about, that being with Raoul put her in.

"But the good news is that no one is looking for you now," Fiona continues. "You could even return to Mrs. Henson's if you want. No more looking over your shoulder. We'll keep a tail on you a while longer to be sure, but so far there's been nothing to indicate you're in any danger."

Lena stares at her, too shocked and queasy to think straight.

When they drop her off at the safehouse, she rushes to the bathroom and empties her stomach. Then she sits beside the toilet on the cold tiles shivering. *Good news*, Fiona told her. She's safe because someone else was murdered. She sees Deke's handsome face, the wide eyes, the encouraging smile as he sat beside her critiquing her story. She pictures a blade coming from behind, crossing his throat. It's as if it's her own hand committed the act. If she hadn't gone there that day. If she hadn't told on him . . ..

Her head jerks up. Told on him? *Listen to me, talking like a child!* Deke was not only putting her in danger, but Daniel and Raoul and all the Aguileros, threatening all they were fighting for!

What about non-violence, she asks herself? Her heroes. Gandhi, Martin Luther King? But how could non-violence work against a brutal dictator where there's no rule of law but his? Non-violence would no more work here than against Hitler. Or King George. Even during the American Revolution, they hung spies.

She picks herself up from the floor and crawls into bed, trying to convince herself that Deke's death was a justified killing. Soft, silent tears fall until a hazy fog wraps around her.

Lena wakes the next morning feeling jittery and edgy. She pulls her hair into a ponytail and slips on jogging shorts. She hates jogging but running fast and furious is just what she needs to staunch the sense of grief and guilt she still feels for being party to someone's death, however deserved that death might be.

She runs through the neighborhood, past tiny squat houses like the one she's staying in, until she's panting so hard she must stop. Putting hands on knees, she hangs her head. She's dripping wet, so hot she thinks she's going to faint. Then she pulls herself up and starts running again.

The following day Fiona enters the house just as Lena is rolling out of bed. Lena pads silently past her in her panties and t-shirt, heading toward the kitchen where she starts the percolator, desperate for coffee. She feels drained and angry. It's been four weeks since she left camp where Raoul promised he'd come to her in two weeks. Was he the one who ordered Deke's assassination? The thought that he might be sickens her.

Fiona watches her from the doorway. "Are you all right?"

"No." Lena drums her fingers on the kitchen counter, waiting for the coffee. She decides she's waited long enough and pours some out before the cycle has completed. She doesn't bother adding cream and sugar.

Bitter is good. She takes a big gulp, letting it burn her throat. Just what she needs.

"Pablo says you've taken up running."

"I *tried* running. It didn't work. Too damn hot. What I really need is to go surfing. It's the only thing that will clear my head."

"If it's a good workout you need, I can give you that. You told me you wanted to learn to box. And Raoul wants me to start training you in self-defense."

"Raoul!" Lena scoffs. "He talks to you more than me. If Raoul wants something, let him come here and tell me in person."

Fiona's lips quirk. "Military training, too, he said. In good time."

She's enjoying this. She'd like to see me walk away.

From the start, Lena felt this tension between them. A silent questioning, distrust. A competitive vibe. On both sides. She's certain Fiona and Raoul were once lovers. And that Fiona still cares for him and resents Lena coming into his life. Not because she's taking him away from her—Lena gets the impression their relationship was in the past. But while Fiona may have accepted that Raoul has moved on, Lena doesn't think Fiona has. Given that, why would Raoul put Fiona in charge of her? And can she really trust Fiona?

Lena realizes she resents Fiona as much as Fiona seems to resent her. Getting into the boxing ring with her probably isn't a good idea.

On second thought, maybe it's just what they need. To clear the air.

Lena takes another sip of bitter coffee, then slams the cup down on the tile. She looks Fiona square in the eye. "All right then. I'm ready. Let's go."

"To the gym?"

"Where else? I need a good workout."

CHAPTER 23

"**E**lbows in! Chin down!" Fiona shouts above the noise of Lena's punches. They've been training for nearly two hours. Sweat drips down Lena's face, her once-high ponytail droops around her shoulders, loose strands hang in her face. She blows them back. Holding a boxer's stance, her gloved fists punch against the heavy bag that Fiona holds steady. *One, two, three!* A jolt passes through her body each time she strikes the leather.

"Look forward through the furrow of your brows. Punch straight out like the pistons on an engine. It's all connected—eyes, chin, elbows, hands. Keep your core tight. That's where your power is," Fiona tells her. "Boxing, like most things, is more mental than physical. Be what you want to become, and your body will obey."

Lena tightens her core and furrows her brow. Her punches become pistons. She's no longer Lena. She's the pure power of her striking fists.

A shout comes from across the room. "Fiona! That's enough. Give the girl a break!" It's Manuel, the gym's co-owner standing with his arms crossed at the edge of a small group of men who stopped their own practice to watch her.

Fiona pulls the bag away. "He's right. Let's rest."

Lena collapses into a folding chair against the wall and Fiona helps remove Lena's gloves. "You did good," Fiona says, handing her a water bottle. "You're in better shape than I thought."

Lena gratefully guzzles the water and takes the towel Fiona hands her to wipe sweat from her face and chest. "I can't feel my arms."

Fiona laughs in that dark, husky way she has. "Oh, you'll feel them tomorrow."

"That's what I'm afraid of."

They sit quietly, Lena still trying to catch her breath, Fiona leaning back against her chair, head tipped against the wall, eyes closed. "Raoul will be proud of you," she says unexpectedly.

Lena studies Fiona. Her skin is pale, like someone who doesn't see the sun much. Her mouth is a faint thin line. Her neck stretched long and taut. Two beauty marks spaced slantwise on the left side become a source of fascination for Lena. Had it been so for Raoul?

The thought makes her stomach lurch. But how can she be jealous now that he's hers? She almost feels sorry for Fiona, to lose someone like him. In a way it makes them sisters, sharing this familiarity. She wants everyone to love her Raoul.

Fiona senses Lena gaze and opens her eyes. "What?"

Lena looks away, then back again. "Are you in love with Raoul?"

Fiona shuts her eyes. "I thought I was once. Now it's something else. Not tangled up with lust and possessiveness like before." She opens her eyes and looks at Lena. "Now it's . . . cleaner, purer. More like . . . .." She pauses as if reaching for the right word.

"Reverence?" Lena guesses, remembering what Billy said.

"Perhaps," Fiona says, leaning back again, eyes closed. "I would die for him," she says matter-of-factly. "Make of it what you will."

That startles Lena. *Would I do the same?* The memory of Malenque slashing down with that sword to save Balanque flashes through her mind.

After a few seconds, Fiona sits up and slaps Lena's knee. "Get up. We have more work to do."

"But I'm exhausted! I can't lift my arms."

Fiona gives her a mysterious grin. "Not that kind of work. Clubbing. Do you really think we Aguileros are all work and no play? Raoul told me to take care of you. Not turn you into a drone."

She calls out to Pablo. "Take Lena home so she can shower and change. Then put on your dancing shoes. We're going to show Lena the seamier side of Curico."

"I thought we were going someplace new?" Lena says when Pablo parks in front of *La Respuesta*.

"We will," Fiona tells her. "But first we have work to do, while you're still sober."

Lena laughs. "You're expecting to get me drunk?"

"I am," Fiona says with a sly smile. "But later. I want to introduce you to people sympathetic to our cause, who we may want to recruit eventually. So much of what we do is networking, making friends, cultivating alliances, listening to gossip that may help us. Memorize the names and faces of people you meet. You will be coming back here on your own and creating your own circle of friends and confidants."

"So, you were lying when you said Aguileros aren't all work and no play."

Fiona smiles. "Work and play are often mixed. Tonight we start with work then shift to play. You'll see." She takes Lena's hand and leads her through the crowds in the back rooms, stopping to introduce Lena as a good friend from the States who's come to stay a while. Being introduced by Fiona seems to gain Lena a certain cache and a mysterious regard. She can almost hear people's thoughts as they size her up, or welcome her in, or admire her as if she's some exotic prize.

"Do they know we're Aguileros?" Lena whispers as Fiona escorts her deeper into the labyrinth.

"Some do, some wonder, most couldn't care less. Others assume you are my new lover," Fiona adds with a sly backward glance. Seeing Lena's startled face, she laughs. "Yes, I lean both ways. But don't worry—I know to whom you belong. He entrusted me with your care, and I do not take that lightly."

After an hour of mingling and two more glasses of wine, Fiona says, "Enough work. Let's find Pablo. It's time to play."

A thundering soundwave of disco washes over Lena when they enter the club. She grabs Fiona's arm to keep from stumbling. By the time they've reached the bar, Pablo has peeled away to the dance floor. Lena glimpses him through the crowd, his shiny white Nehru jacket catching the multicolored strobe lights that bounce off dancers, making them look like rainbow puppets pulled on strings.

Fiona orders two shots of tequila. "San Balanque's finest!" she says, clinking her glass against Lena's. "To us!" She throws back her head and downs it in one swallow.

Lena gives her drink a strong sniff, which sends her reeling from the fumes. "You know, if I was still in California, they wouldn't be allowed to serve me this. Technically, I'm still under-age."

"You're kidding! How old do you have to be?"

"Twenty-one. Which means I shouldn't be drinking this until tomorrow, September 28."

Her first birthday without her father and aunt. She hasn't heard from either since writing that she was joining the Aguileros. While she's nervous about that and misses them, she's glad she's here. Her life in California seems so far away. It's been three months since she left, yet it feels like a lifetime.

"Then we must celebrate tonight. So, drink up!"

Lena looks at the golden liquid in the shot glass and takes a tiny sip. It burns all the way down to her belly. She shakes her body like a wet dog. When Fiona laughs, Lena laughs back.

"Oh, you think that's funny?" asks Lena. "Watch this." She throws back her head like Fiona did, downing the rest in one gulp . . . and nearly passes out. Fiona grabs her arm as Lena lurches.

"That is god-awful stuff!" Lena says. But she likes the ways it makes her feel, warm and woozy, like graduation night with Lonny. So much has happened since then. She hardly feels like the same person. The music pounds through her and the strobe lights make her hand holding her drink seem like a stranger's. Even Fiona looks like someone else. Like a sultry siren with the tight-fitting mini and those sexy boots. *I want boots like that*, Lena thinks, then catches Fiona's glance.

The way her cool eyes slide over Lena's tight tube top and loose pantaloons riding below her bellybutton feels seductive. She hastily lifts her glass to her lips again, only to remember she's already gulped it down.

"Two more," Fiona tells the bartender.

"Oh, no! I shouldn't."

Fiona pays her no attention. She's scanning the crowd and then grabs Lena's shoulder. "Look there! It's Humberto and Mariam."

"That's Mariam?" Lena hardly recognizes the bookish woman with her tight bun and pencil skirt as this woman in a red mini dress stretched tight around her thighs. The laces of her high strappy heels are wound around her calves, her hips swaying, her dark hair a mass of loose curls. Nor is Humberto the suave intellectual he seemed before. His face is flushed and glistening, his soft belly jiggling beneath the loose shirt that rides up as he too sways his hips. His hands play over Mariam's back and buttocks, squeezing her close.

"They're lovers!" Lena gasps. "I thought he was married."

"He is. You're surprised? Don't be. Humberto has always had women on the side. This is common in San Balanque. Is it not in the States?"

"I suppose it is, it's just . . .," she starts, then stops. Just what? That she's been sheltered her whole life? That she's barely been part of the adult world outside her family and the university? Lena feels hopelessly naïve and somehow vulnerable, watching Mariam and Humberto making love to each other on the dance floor, with no one caring he has a wife at home, or that Mariam is half his age—or his protégé, for God's sake! It feels dangerous to Lena. Is she the only one who feels this way?

"And Raoul?" she asks with a catch in her throat. "Is he like Humberto?"

Fiona gives her a sharp look. "Raoul is nothing like Humberto, except in their passion for the cause."

"So, he hasn't had a string of—"

"If Raoul had lovers before or after me, I wouldn't know. He's discreet. Hardly anyone knew when we were together. Which is why his being so open about you is surprising."

Lena only half-hears this. She is swaying inside her head. And maybe outside too from the way Fiona is looking at her now, highly amused. "You want to dance?"

She does.

She doesn't remember much after that, and what she does remember comes in flashes: Dancing with her fingers snapping over her head the way everyone else seems to do. People buying her drinks and toasting her birthday. Slipping on the dance floor and having to be righted. She remembers hands sliding down her arms and cupping her buttocks. She remembers Fiona pushing the man aside, taking his place on the dance floor, smiling at Lena with amused affection. She remembers the lights over her head beginning to blur and being led from the dance floor. She doesn't remember being taken home or tucked into bed.

When she wakes the next morning, she's still swaying.

Lena spends the next week training in boxing and self-defense and visiting the clubs under Pablo's care to create her own circle of friends and potential recruits. In the afternoons, she puts the final touches on her stories with Humberto's help. They decide to submit them to *The Weekly Star*, similar to the *National Enquirer* in the States.

Then one morning, five weeks and four days after Lena last saw Raoul, Fiona arrives at the safehouse and says crisply, "Pack your bags. You're moving."

"What?" Lena finally feels like she has a life again, a routine she enjoys, a place where she belongs and fits in. Is it going to change all over again? "Isn't it safe to stay here any longer? I don't want to move."

Fiona gives her a wry smile. "I think you'll like where you're going next."

"How can you be sure?"

Fiona smiles mysteriously.

"You mean?"

"Yes. Raoul wants you."

CHAPTER 24

In some ways Raoul has become this phantom lover in Lena's mind. Although she reads his letter every night and lies in bed remembering those tender nights together, it's only memories holding them together. Now that the time for being together in person has arrived again, she's nervous. It's been nearly six weeks. What if they don't feel the same about each other? What if she disappoints him? What if she misses her work here and wants to return?

Cold feet, her aunt would tell her. The jitters. That's all this is, she tells herself as she finishes packing her clothes. She picks up her silky panties and pictures Raoul sliding them down her body, touching the parts they cover. Her insides melt. Yes, she will go to him, if only for this, to feel what their lovemaking might be without restraints. *I want this. I want him. I do,* she whispers.

Raoul has never seen her in anything but trousers, so she slips on a floral sundress with spaghetti straps and a tight bodice, the full skirt skimming her knees. She steps into high platform sandals that make her long legs look longer. When she emerges from the bedroom, Fiona's gaze slides down her body.

"This should please him," she says with an amused smirk.

Lena stands on the front stoop with her packed bags at her feet, waiting for the taxi driver—another Aguilero, she's told. Pablo will drive Fiona back to the gym after Lena leaves.

"I'll miss you, Pablo!" Lena says, hugging him. "Thank you for watching over me and driving me all over the place."

"Of course, my pleasure," he says. But he doesn't say he'll miss her too. And it stings. She's not sure what she expected. She was just a job to him, nothing more. So why is she feeling so misty-eyed? Her damn sentimentality. She always gets too attached to people, places. Pablo was a friendly face, if not a friend. A driver, a bodyguard. She tried to draw him out, discover more about his life, but the most she learned was that he's married with five children.

"It's best we do not know too much about each other," he said. "If we're arrested, we won't be able to give away too much, you see."

Lena did see. But it was still sad. She didn't even know if Pablo was his real name.

Her feelings for Fiona are even more complicated. The woman annoys her to pieces sometimes. But Lena also admires her street smarts and calm reticence. The way she never gets ruffled. Lena wishes she was more like her: less sentimental, less emotional. Fiona is a role model and mentor of sorts. And Lena feels for her—her loss of Raoul, her continuing love for him, having to take care of his new lover. Sometimes Lena feels—what? A kind of love. Like she might have for an older, bossy, mean sister who looks after her despite all that. She would have liked to have been friends with her. And she feels a sense of loss because they hadn't been.

A taxi pulls up to the house. *So, this is it*, Lena thinks, swallowing hard. She looks at Fiona and wants to hug her goodbye, but Fiona's arms are folded defensively across her body. Instead, Lena sticks out her hand and Fiona takes it. For a moment, Lena thinks Fiona is going to pull her in, but then she returns to her former position, arms crossed, fingers tucked into armpits.

It feels strange to leave with only a cold handshake between them. "Will I see you again?"

Fiona lifts her chin. "I wouldn't be surprised. You still need more training in self-defense. Although Raoul may take that over now."

"Well, then . . .," Lena says.

"Wait! I almost forgot." Fiona dashes inside and returns with two letters. "I picked these up from the P.O. box this morning." Lena recognizes her father's handwriting on one, her aunt's on the other.

As the taxi pulls away Fiona is still standing by the front door, her arms wrapped around her body. But now her crossed arms don't look like she was trying to keep Lena away. Now it looks like she's crossed her arms to hold herself together. They may not have been friends, but there was a bond between them. Pablo may not miss Lena, but she suspects Fiona will. At least a tiny bit.

Lena watches the city she knows so well now, that feels like home, flashing past her window. She put down roots in Curico, established a history of sorts—with Mrs. Henson and Daniel, then Fiona and Pablo, Billy and Humberto. And now she's being uprooted from all that. Tender as those roots might have been, she still feels that tug.

These damn tears! She brushes them away, hoping the driver doesn't see. What an Aguilero she's going to make!

When she looks at the letters waiting in her lap, her stomach tightens. She dreads reading their response to her letters about Raoul and the Aguileros. She's surprised they didn't hop on a plane to retrieve her from this madness. But if they had, they wouldn't have found her since she wasn't at La Rosaleda anymore. No one knows where she's been.

She reads through both letters quickly and then holds them side-by-side, marveling. She thought her aunt would be excited for her, having found this great love, and her father would be telling her to come home. But it was Aunt Margot begging her to return. *Fighting is foolishness,* she wrote. *Bring him too! If he truly loves you, he will. I couldn't bear it if anything happened to you.*

It was her father who understood the depth of her feelings for Raoul and the calling she felt to support his cause. Perhaps because he felt that same irresistible love for her mother, which he never regretted and treasured still. Or because he believed in great causes and sacred callings. In fighting for what's right despite all odds. Or because he was still at that monastery, feeling that Zen-like calm and acceptance. Regardless, his letter was full of tender love and trust in her. Reading it again, she feels his kiss on her forehead as he lets her go with his blessing on the journey she's chosen.

"Where are we going?" Lena asks when the vehicle turns north. She's never been this way before.

The driver glances at her through the rearview mirror. "La Casa de Amor."

"The house of love? You've got to be kidding!"

"No," he tells her seriously. "It's a beautiful hacienda in the mountains. San Balanque's first governor built it for his dying wife. It's like the Taj Mahal of San Balanque—only now it's owned by a couple from New York sympathetic to our cause. They rarely come."

So, it's another safehouse, one Raoul chose especially for their reunion. She smiles at the thought. As nervous as she was to see Raoul before, she feels a kind of peace wash over her now. If her father trusts her to know her own mind, then she should too. Into Raoul's arms is where she needs to go, where she will plant her roots, starting in this Casa de Amor.

A few miles farther they pass Cordoba, the oldest city in the country and, according to the guidebook, the most beautiful with all its colonial architecture, including the Presidential Palace. According to the newspapers, it's where her mother lives too.

Then they drive past a place that turns Lena's stomach cold.

"Debayle Prison," the driver tells her. "This is where the government keeps their political prisoners, where Raoul's father was tortured."

A sickly sense of dread shudders though her as she looks back at the thick walls topped with barbed wire, the armed watchtowers, and rows and rows of tiny, barred windows.

Eventually they turn onto a narrow road winding up through the rainforest. "One more hour," the driver tells her.

One hour till she sees Raoul again. She presses her fingernails into her palms and tries to still her breath. One hour. Till she sees him. The view outside her window blurs with all the emotions surging inside.

At last, they arrive at a gate with an armed Guard. A soldier exchanges words with the driver, then leans in to look at Lena. He smiles as they drive through. A narrow path burrows tunnel-like through dark green foliage. When they emerge, the bright sun spotlights the walls of a large hacienda sprawling gracefully across the hills like a white cat on a green couch. From the driveway, a wide stone stairway winds up toward the front door.

At the top of the stairs stands Raoul. But not Raoul in his green fatigues with a rifle slung over his shoulder. Not like any Raoul she's ever seen. Instead, he looks like he's stepped out of a Gucci ad. His wavy hair is pulled back tight at the nape of his neck, the wide planes of his face sharp and clean, no scruff. His eyes are darker than she remembers, his eyebrows thicker, his mouth redder. His white shirt, a simple cotton tunic open at the neck, is dazzling against his dark skin. He's wearing stonewashed blue jeans and leather sandals. His eyes are ecstatic. He nearly leaps down the stone stairway toward her.

Lena waits breathlessly on the gravel driveway in her heels and sundress. Her hand rises to her chest as if to still her leaping heart.

When he reaches the bottom step, he stills and looks at her, as if searing into his mind the image of her standing there. She does the same with him, this new, shiny, suave Raoul that she barely knows. She's so stunned by his beauty she feels faint—from anxiety or anticipation or sheer exhilaration—she cannot unpack all she's feeling.

He comes to her, lifting her hands to his lips, his soft mouth on her fingertips, his hot breath on her face. Then she's in his arms, pressed against his chest, clutching him tightly. His broad, warm back feels like a rock, a fortress, a haven. A homecoming. The misgivings she felt this morning dissolve with his body pressed around her. She never wants to leave the circle of his arms. This is where she's meant to be.

"You came," he says, as if he still can't believe it. He takes her by the hand and leads her up steps to a wide terrace overlooking the valley. Rows of forested hills fade away into the distance.

"It's so beautiful!" Lena says gazing out across the wide expanse. Then she looks behind her where a table is set beneath the veranda. "And what have we here?"

"I made you lunch. Are you hungry? Come, sit." He pulls out a rattan chair. She is so full of feeling, she doesn't think she can eat a bite—but when she sees what he's prepared, she realizes she's ravenous. Blue ceramic platters are full of sliced papaya and pineapple. White bowls hold orange persimmons and ruby red pomegranates. Crystal glasses sparkle with white wine. A basket is filled with round rolls. Wide soup bowls hold what looks like pumpkin soup drizzled with green-gold olive oil.

"Gazpacho," Raoul tells her. "One of my grandmother's recipes. Extra-virgin olive oil made here in San Balanque makes all the difference. Too little and the soup loses its richness, too much and it sits heavy on your stomach. But just right it melts in your mouth and warms your belly and makes it glow."

"So, you're a chef too?"

"Only the gazpacho I made," he says. "Antonio baked the rolls this morning at my direction."

"Your direction?"

"Yes," he says, a wicked gleam in his eye. "I told him they must be soft and plump and sweet, like my love's breasts."

She chokes in surprise. "You did not say that!"

"I did," he says. "Now, eat."

She lifts a spoonful of the cold soup to her mouth, letting the rich creaminess slide down her throat to warm her belly.

CHAPTER 25

After lunch Raoul takes Lena's hand and shows her the hacienda, making grand gestures as he highlights its finer points. Parts of Casa de Amor are over two hundred years old, he tells her, pointing out the two-foot-thick adobe walls and the worn passageways along the terracotta tiled floors from centuries of foot traffic. The small arched windows were positioned for light, not the magnificent views beyond. But the newer wings feature wide wooden beams across the ceilings and walls of plate glass looking out over the mountains and valleys below.

"And this," Raoul says, flinging open a pair of ornately carved doors at the end of a wide corridor, "is our room." It's an elegantly furnished corner suite with wide glass doors looking onto the balcony and beyond. A four-poster bed of dark mahogany sits in the center of the room, its tall posts crowned with carved pineapples. A pure white fur-like spread covers the bed. Lena can't help but stroke the plush pile. It feels like the fur of a Persian kitten.

"So soft," she says, smiling beguilingly at Raoul as she sits on the edge, leaning back on her hands. "A long way from that soldier's cot we shared." She watches him swallow hard as he gazes back at her.

How will it happen, she wonders, watching him stand so still, backlit against the bright windows behind him. Here and now, in broad daylight as they look across the room at each other, or later after a candle-lit dinner? Will it be a slow and languid coming together, or a furious, torrid coupling? Will he undress her? Will she undress him? She asks all this with her eyes as they stare at each other.

Slowly he answers her unspoken questions.

Here and now, he says, pulling his tunic over his head and letting it drop to the floor. Slow and languid, as he slips off one sandal and then the other. He pulls out the leather thong restraining his wild wavy mane. He's all lion now, his dark predatory eyes fastened on hers. Slowly he unbuttons his jeans and slips them off. Fully naked he moves toward her with cat-like grace and power.

Her eyes widen, her breath catches. Something dark and wild roils through her as she gazes at him. He is so beautiful and so dangerous in his beauty. She sits up in alarm as something that feels like fear, like anticipation, like desire all rolled into one shudders through her.

He kneels before her, seeming to sense her unease, and gently strokes her bare arms with his warm hands, moving from shoulders to fingertips so lightly it makes her shiver. Then he slips the thin straps from her shoulders and leans in to kiss the curve of her neck with delicate softness, one side and then the other. He unzips the back of her dress and pulls it down to puddle at her waist. His breath catches when he sees her bare breasts. He lifts them in his rough hands as if savoring their weight. Then he buries his face between them.

As he suckles one nipple, then the other, the feeling grows so intense she must stop him. She pushes him back so she can see his face. It is transformed again. This is not Raoul. This is some ravenous animal, hungry with need.

He scoops her up and tosses her onto the soft fur, stripping away her dress and panties and staring down at her nakedness with such ferocious desire it scares her. His hands are twisting through her hair now, his tongue filling her mouth with an urgent fire that surges through her whole body. His mouth is everywhere, kissing her eyelids, behind her ears, the hollow of her neck, visiting each tender part as it travels down her body. He rubs his face in the soft curls at the center of her, breathing in her scent. His fingers slip between her thighs, touching a part of her that swells and makes her whole body light up. Then he buries his face between her thighs.

The ecstasy of his mouth devouring her is almost too much to bear. And yet she never wants it to end. The exquisite pleasure mounts and pulses through her with such intensity she thinks she can't take it anymore. It's too much. She clamps down with her knees. He pushes them back and continues to devour her, this wild man, fierce with hunger, lapping her up. Her head thrashes back and forth as something breaks loose inside and spills over. She cries out and fists his hair as she bucks against him. Again and again.

When the fierce sensations ease, he moves up her body to cover her face with kisses. He pets her hair and whispers into her ear as her body continues to pulse and quiver. "It's all right, I have you. Shh, I have you," he says, cuddling her in his arms like she's a child and whispering endearments. "Mi caro, Malenque Mia."

His nestles her neck and then rumbles into her ear, "Are you on the pill?"

At first, she's not sure what he's asking. Then she almost laughs. How could he think to ask that in the heat of passion! He's so much more in control of himself, even now, than she is.

"I am," she tells him, thankful her aunt insisted when she turned eighteen, just in case.

She tries not to wince when he enters her, watching his face as he burrows deeper with each thrust, melting in the ecstasy of being inside her. But she doesn't enjoy this part so much. The further he pushes, the more uncomfortable it feels. Yet he's so clearly enjoying himself she doesn't want to stop him. She wants to give him the same pleasure he gave her. She wills herself to open around him, to go wider. She bites back the pain when he pushes further. But on the next thrust, a small cry escapes.

He stops and looks at her in alarm. "What's wrong? Are you alright?"

She bites her lip. "It's okay. I want this."

"*It's okay*? What do you mean? You're not enjoying this? You seemed so ready, so eager."

"I am! It's just that . . . you know . . . sometimes they say, the first time . . .."

He stares at her, wide-eyed and open mouthed. "The first time! You mean...?"

She gives him a sheepish grin.

He shakes his head at her in wonder. "My God. Why didn't you tell me?"

"I'm sorry. I didn't think I needed to. I didn't think you'd mind."

He lets out a choked laugh. "Of course, I don't mind . . . but had I known, I would have gone slower, made sure you were ready. That you wanted this." He starts to pull out. She wraps her legs fiercely around him, holding him there.

"But I do, I do! Please don't leave. I've wanted this since the first moment I saw you."

He's looking at her strangely, amused and amazed, concerned and confused, in the most tender way. "You wanted me even then?"

"I want you now. In me, filling me up. Every inch. Please."

"My God, you're amazing. You break my heart, you tear me in two. There's nothing I would not do for you."

"Then do it. Now."

"Yes, but softer, sweeter." He covers her face with tender kisses and starts over more slowly than before until a warm, glowing sensation takes hold. Her attention moves there now, the feel of his fullness inside growing as he moves in and out, back and forth. As he pushes further, she opens for him, loving the new sensations, the hot friction that melts her inner walls. His thrusts become faster, more urgent. Then he plunges one more time, crying out in a mighty roar. She feels him shuddering, throbbing inside her. She pets him like he did her when she came.

He murmurs soft, husky endearments in her ear as he peppers her face with kisses. "Malenque Mia . . . mi alma . . . mi carina." Finally, he slides off and rolls her up in his arms. *We are the same now*, she thinks, nestled within his body. His arm her arm, her leg his leg, his lips her lips. She has all of him and he has all of her.

His forehead touches hers as he looks into her eyes. "So, it's true? I was your first?"

"Yes," she tells him, smiling sleepily, eyes half-closed.

"And only. Promise me this. First and only, now and forever." His eyes look so serious, almost painful. She feels his whole body stiffen beside her as he awaits her answer. She's sure he's stopped breathing. And she's amazed, humbled, terrified of the pull she has on him, he has on her.

She touches his face, her finger moving across the wide strong brow, between those dark riveting eyes, down the bridge of his nose, tracing that plump mouth she loves to kiss.

"First and only, now and forever. I promise."

CHAPTER 26

Lena wakes from a deep sleep with the feel of something warm and precious slipping from her. She grabs hold of Raoul's arm.

"It's all right, Mi Amor," Raoul tells her as he slips from her grasp. "It's only Antonio at the door. He's brought us something to eat."

Lena pulls the covers over her chest as he walks naked to the door and speaks in a hushed voice with Antonio. He turns, holding a tray of food. She can't help staring at the dark weight hanging between his thighs as he comes toward her. She squeezes her own thighs together in response to the puddling feeling growing there. She realizes she's not hungry, at least not for food.

She pushes the tray away when he tries to pass it to her, and pulls back the spread instead, inviting him in. "I'm not hungry, I just want you."

He laughs, sets the tray on the nightstand and climbs in beside her. She doesn't pull the covers back over him. "What? No covers for me?" he asks playfully.

"I want to look at you. Explore you. Every part. Will you let me?"

His reply is a low moan and half-lidded look. She starts with her hands in his hair, then his face, the wide forehead and dark brow. She traces the length of his nose, his lush lips.

"Why is it I can't get enough looking at you?" she asks. Her finger traces a scar across his left eyebrow. "What is this?"

"Oh, that. A love tap. Cain and Abel style."

"Tomás did this?"

"We were children playing, wrestling in a field. I was getting the upper hand so he grabbed the first thing he could find, a sharp rock. He does not like to lose. Especially to me."

"You fought a lot when you were young?"

"Not so much as you might think. We revered our father who disdained physical violence. We would do anything to please him. That's where the trouble started, for he seemed more pleased with what I could bring him than Tomás. As it was with Cain and Abel. Papa actually lectured us about not being like them, not seeing his part in the problem, thinking he treated us equally. But it was clear to everyone he favored me."

"Why was that?" she asks, her fingers playing with the curls on his chest.

"Because I was more like him. I loved school and could express myself easily—my feelings and ideas—unlike Tomás, who holds everything inside. He hated school and thought his teachers treated him unfairly. Often he fought on the playground, so he was always getting into trouble at school and being lectured at home. I pitied Tomás, knowing well how it felt to displease our father. But we also earned his praise when we pleased him. That praise, unfortunately for Tomás, fell more on me than him."

Raoul leans against the pillows, one arm behind his head, the other wrapped around Lena. She's nestled into the crook of his arm, loving the low rumble of his voice vibrating against her hand on his chest.

"I tried to console him by reminding him how mother favored him. As the eldest, she doted on Tomás and defended him, excusing his aggression, even seeming to admire the way he pushed back against authority or people who slighted him. She was that way herself. She felt slighted by our father. He didn't pay enough attention to her—or to us, she thought. He was away too often. And when he was home, he spent too much time in his study."

"So, she was unhappy with him, with their marriage," Lena surmises.

"No, far from it. She was devoted to him. He was the man. The head of the family. She was proud when he stood up against President Ortiz who humiliated her family, wrested away its land and wealth. Mama was proud of his accomplishments, his prestige in the community. People looked up to him, sought him out, deferred to him. He had that rare quality: strength in dignity. So, while our mother complained, she was totally devoted to him."

How different our two cultures are, Lena thinks. Or maybe it's a generational gap. Certainly, Raoul's mother was no feminist, but no doubt she resented her limited ability to exert power and influence in society. She favored the son who was like her, relishing his rebellion against authority. But now Raoul is the authority figure to whom Tomás must yield. Surely, he must resent that.

"So, is it still that way between you and Tomás?" Lena thinks she knows the answer.

"No, we've come to an understanding." He looks closely at her. "You mustn't worry about me or Tomás. All brothers fight. It's nothing to concern yourself with. Besides, this talk is making me hungry. Don't you want to see what Antonio prepared for us?" He pulls the tray onto their laps.

Lena lifts one silver cover, revealing a dish of paella full of fat pink shrimp and black olives. "Mm!" she says, breathing in its rich, spicy aroma. "This smells divine. Did Antonio make this at your direction as well?"

"But of course. I take these things seriously. Feeding my woman. We also have a carafe of hot coffee made the way you like, sweet with plenty of cream."

"What? No wine?"

He grins. "I've heard you're not so good holding your liquor, and I don't want you falling asleep on me this early in the evening."

"How did you know that? Also, the way I like my coffee?" she asks, then raises a sharp eyebrow. "Oh, right. Fiona." His last lover. She looks down at the paella and stabs a small pink shrimp. "It appears you communicated with her far more than you did with me while we were apart." She chews it mercilessly.

"What? Could this be jealousy I'm hearing?"

"I don't understand how you could put me under the care of your former lover! Then have her report to you about me."

He looks alarmed. "Malenque Mia—" he starts.

"That was cruel!"

He looks truly baffled, and she wonders how he could be so dense.

"She told you this about us?" he asks.

"No. I figured it out on my own."

"I'm surprised. Fiona's not an easy read."

"When it comes to you, she's an open book."

He gives a doubtful laugh. "Really? Fiona? Many people would be surprised to learn that."

"That's beside the point. How could you put your ex-lover in charge of your new one?"

He looks at her with amazement. "You say that as if there's some equivalency between my feelings for the two of you. I care deeply for Fiona. I have great respect for her. And when I was with her, I felt great tenderness too. But that was long ago. And it was nothing like what I feel for you. I put Fiona in charge of you because there's no one I trust more to protect you and train you. I trust her with my life and with the life of anyone I care about."

Lena thinks about this. Perhaps he never realized the depth of Fiona's feelings for him. "She said she would die for you."

"This I believe. But it's not so much for me as what I stand for."

"She worships you. You know that don't you?"

He shakes his head. "No. It's something else—loyalty, devotion, perhaps. She sees me as the last bulwark against all she hates. If I fail, all she loves fails, all we've been fighting for fails."

Lena considers what he's said. "We think alike, me and Fiona," she says, pushing aside her food and turning toward him as if she has much more to say on this subject.

"Do you, now?" His gaze moves from her face to her bare breasts. "Do you know what I think?" He gives her that slow, smoldering smile. "I think I'm done thinking about Fiona."

Looking at that smile, all thoughts of Fiona vanish as a wave of heat washes over Lena. "And what are you thinking of now?"

"All the many ways I want to take you."

"Take me!" Somehow that alarms and excites her at the same time.

"Remember what we promised earlier today? First and only?"

She swallows hard. "I remember."

"I want to deepen that promise, add a new dimension: Always and in all ways."

"Always and in all ways," she repeats slowly, sensing a catch.

"Do you know what this means?"

"I'm not sure."

"It means I don't want you just in my bed, I want you by my side, as a partner, a comrade, a friend and confidante," he says, cupping her face in his hands. "I want you young, I want you old, I want you all the places in-between . . . Is this too much? Am I being too demanding? Tell me, and I will stop. For the last thing I want is to scare you or make you jealous or angry or . . . want to leave me, for any reason. You understand?"

She nods, unable to speak, overcome by what he's telling her.

"And you want this too?'

"I do," she tells him. Her heart is heaving and singing at the same time. She feels so full, as if his words are helium and she's about to levitate. "I do."

He smiles at her in a way that makes her realize he's not done. "But it also means when you are in my bed, I want you in all ways too. In every way I can think of making love to you."

Her eyebrows lift. "How many ways of making love can there be?"

He gives her that lion's smile. "Here, let me show you."

Then he proceeds to make love to her in ways she never imagined possible, and each time, despite initial trepidation, she feels her pleasure mount and soar. As they explore each other's bodies, the sky outside their window turns pink, then purple, finally deepening until their bodies dissolve into dusky shadows. When they are done, both deeply sated, they lay in each other's arms.

I could die here and now and have no regrets, Lena thinks, her body still pulsing with the pleasure of his touch. *No regrets,* she murmurs, as her mind drifts into some deep, contented world of wonder where Raoul's nearness laps against her like gentle waves, and she's nothing but the purr of sand beneath him.

CHAPTER 27

The next morning Lena wakes ravenous. "I didn't know rice could be such a wonderful breakfast dish," she says as she sits with Raoul on the terrace eating the left-over paella Antonio reheated for them. She stabs another pink shrimp with gusto this time.

"Rice Atole made with milk and cinnamon was my favorite breakfast as a boy," Raoul tells her.

"I wish I could have known you then. Sometimes I see a younger you in Pepe. But I don't see any of you in Tomás." She pauses a moment, putting down her fork. "You know, you never answered my question about you and Tomás. Doesn't he resent the fact you're in command and he's second fiddle, so to speak?"

He laughs, pushing away his empty plate and leaning back in his chair. "Tomás would be surprised to hear you say that. It's not the way I see it either. He's my most trusted advisor and commander of our troops."

She frowns. "Then why was he sent to escort me and Daniel to camp?"

"He chose to do so. He had concerns about bringing journalists into camp and wanted to oversee the operation. We complement each other that way. He fears I am too trusting, and I fear he is too distrustful, so we strike a balance. We are stronger together than we would be on our own. Tomás is a well-respected and feared commander in the field. He is fierce and ruthless as he must be. I wouldn't do as well in that capacity. And he knows I know this.

"But he also recognizes I'm better at leading and growing the movement, strategizing our next moves, rallying support, firing up the troops, creating coalitions. He trusts me that way. We are both learning as we go and adjusting as needed in our strategies and operations."

"What do you mean?" Lena asks, thinking Raoul's not clearly seeing his brother at all. Doesn't he see the simmering resentment behind his deference? She hopes she's wrong and it's only her own dislike of Tomás and his apparent dislike of her that's stirring up all these fears. But she needs persuading.

"Well, for instance, at the beginning his skirmishes with the Feds and others were too vicious and merciless, in my mind. He didn't plan how to decrease collateral damage to property or the people we want to win over and recruit, not alienate. I convinced him that our struggle was more *for* the people than *against* the government or Federales. It's the people of San Balanque we are championing. We must protect them and their interests as much as we want to protect our own soldiers. Tomás got it. And while his methods are not always the ones I would choose, I respect them."

"Bianca said he was the one who found her family starving in the forest and saved them," Lena says, trying to give Tomás the benefit of a doubt.

"Yes, he brought them under our protection. And he exacted retribution for their cruelty. He raided the mining camp and confronted the manager who evicted them. He made it clear that the miners and their families in that camp were under our protection. We won many recruits and support that day.

"In another early incident, his squad ambushed a United Fruit Company payroll convoy along a mountain road. But as the gunfire began, a wagon rounded the corner with a father and son. The eleven-year-old boy was shot in the head. No one knew who fired that shot. But after the mercenaries hired to protect the convoy were captured, Tomás pushed one to his knees and told the father, 'This is the man who shot your son, and this is what we do to those who murder children.' Tomás shot him."

Lena gasps, but Raoul looks at her with a fiery pride in his eyes—pride for his brother. "The father, who was suffering for the needless death of his boy, now had his revenge and a sense of justice. Tomás told him we would pay for his son's funeral and all Aguileros would mourn his death. The ambush to gain resources was turned into an operation to avenge the death of one of our sons. For all San Balanquan sons are our sons. We won new recruits and much goodwill.

"The truth is," Raoul continues, "had I been there, I would not have shot the mercenary. For all we know, it could have been Tomás' bullet that killed the boy. But those who hired the mercenaries are the same who exploit the people and keep them poor and struggling while they grow rich. And the government that protects and supports those who exploit its people is no less guilty of that needless death. I praised Tomás for his righteous and ruthless act and used it as a lesson on why we need to always protect the people and give them the dignity and honor that Ortiz and his corporate cronies deny them. This is what we are fighting for."

Lena has stopped eating, the rice sitting heavy on her stomach. No doubt Raoul sees how troubled she feels for he pulls up a chair beside her and takes her hands into his.

"I know you don't want to hear this, Malenque, but yes, innocents sometimes will die needlessly in this battle. But they will be honored in death by us as they never were in life by Ortiz. And we will give the brothers and sisters of these martyred innocents a chance to live free and dignified lives. Without us doing this work, there is no hope for us or our people. This is why sometimes we must be ruthless, even while, were we not at war, we never would imagine doing these things. You understand what I'm saying?"

Lena nods. "You're saying this because of Deke, aren't you?"

"I am," he says, squeezing her hands. "I heard it upset you. I never want to cause you pain. But I cannot promise that everything we do to protect our people or overthrow Ortiz will not cause you anguish. Deke chose the wrong side in this battle. He could have had you arrested, tortured. I do not regret what we had to do to keep you safe from him. You understand?"

"I do."

"I tell you all this so you understand I care deeply for my brother and trust him with my life. You don't have to worry that because we fought as children he's a danger to me now. You understand?"

"I do," she says. But she doesn't. Tomás troubles her. And that Raoul trusts him so explicitly makes her fearful for him too.

Over the next several days Lena and Raoul spend their time, in bed and out, exploring each other's bodies. She's continually amazed by the ways touch and tongue can elicit such an exquisite range of sensations, like notes played in a symphony—ecstatic trills, slow steady drumbeats, a burst of trumpets, the soaring strains of a violin.

"How could such a thing be?" she asks Raoul, her voice full of wonder. "This capacity for extreme pleasure lay hidden inside me all this time, and I may never have known if it hadn't been for you, taking me the way you did. It was like you were the key that unlocked all that—your mouth, your tongue, your lust . . . .."

". . . my love, my longing," he adds, curling a tendril of her hair around a finger.

"Sometimes I felt like I shouldn't let you do the things you were doing, and yet when I opened myself up to you that way, the excitement and pleasure I felt overcame all sense of modesty . . . you know?"

He nods. "It's a great mystery, how the world was created to be so dependent upon, and greedy for, such intimate couplings. Is the flower ashamed when it opens its petals fully to the sun's gaze and welcomes the probing tongues of bees and butterflies? Are bees to be blamed for being drawn to such beauty, craving its sweet nectar? It's how we are made, to delight in each other as we bury ourselves so deeply, so intimately, within. It's how the world rejuvenates itself. There's no shame in this reveling. It's what was wanted when we were made this way."

They revel in and explore their surroundings as deeply as they do each other, hiking up a steep trail where they stand breathless on a ridge overlooking a sea of trees that rise and fall like waves across the slopes and valleys below. They wander into glades where the undergrowth is so deep and spongy Lena's boots sink to her ankles. She gapes in wonder at a cathedral of treetops with the glint of sun piercing the mosaic of leaves like light through stained glass. They clamber over boulders and felled trees following streams to discover a series of waterfalls, some mere trickles that tumble over lichen-splashed rocks; others rushing freefall from great heights, like daredevils in frothy white robes diving headlong into dark streams.

Lena feels like she's walking through a dreamscape, her surroundings so lush and exotic they couldn't possibly be real. Flocks of parakeets fly overhead like trailing kite strings, or weave through the lacy treetops like fish through kelp beds. Howler monkeys cry out at the invasion of their privacy, throwing fruit and feces their way. As they pass, an exotic-looking lizard with brilliant turquoise flanks and a spiked headdress stares at them with regal disdain.

Twice Raoul grabs her arm and puts a finger to his lips as he raises his rifle. Some lethal beast is nearby—leopard or jaguar. Often Raoul's machete is needed to hack through the thickets. Lena loves watching his wide back and heaving shoulders as he carves a path through the entangling vines for her to follow. She will follow him forever, wherever he goes.

Along the way she gathers treasures: colorful stones and leaves, seedpods and feathers. She uses them for collages, which she works on when their reveries are interrupted by missives from the field. Couriers arrive at all hours and soldiers with urgent messages come and go, the strained looks upon their somber faces causing Lena's stomach to twist. Raoul disappears with them into the library.

Antonio the chef, she learns, is one of Raoul's bodyguards. And Raoul's lieutenants are his eyes and ears in the field while he's away, sending him dispatches as needed. Lena never questions Raoul about these. Despite Raoul's insistence that he wants her to be a comrade and confidante, she's not that—not yet. And Raoul never volunteers information. He only apologizes for leaving her so long and puts his arms around her waist and touches his forehead to hers.

"Unfortunately, I cannot take a holiday from our struggle," Raoul tells her. "But I did manage this romantic retreat for us."

"How long will we have here together?"

"Until I am needed elsewhere."

CHAPTER 28

A week later Lena sits cross-legged on the cotton blanket spread in a leafy glen by a pond, a favorite picnic spot a short hike from the Casa. She's reading a book about sun signs found in the Casa library. Her aunt Margo loved astrology, often exclaiming how accurate the sun signs were.

"Guess what I am?" she once asked Lena. "Aries, the Ram! Don't you love it? Always charging ahead, energetic and outgoing. And you, my dear, are a perfect Libra: the Scales. Always weighing things, looking for that perfect balance—harmony, justice, world peace, you know."

It does seem uncanny how their signs seem to fit. Lena laughs when she learns Raoul's sign is Leo, the Lion.

"Wouldn't you know it!" she says, eyeing Raoul who is stretched out on his side across from her. "According to this, you are a good-hearted lion, compassionate and self-assured. A natural leader, ambitious and determined. Charming and seductive." She gives him a smug *don't I know it* look.

Raoul eyes her lazily. "You look very pleased with yourself," he says. "Somehow, I find that oddly seductive."

She purses her lips and continues. "'You're a loyal friend, a just but powerful enemy, and a fierce protector of those under your care.'" She skims down the page. "Listen to this! 'Leo's are as playful as they are arrogant, often at the same time, which is why they get away with murder.' Ha! That's you to a tee."

Raoul gives her a sly, idle smile. "Go on, I want to hear more about how you see me."

"There it is! That lazy predatory look! The book's got that right too. It says that Leos often resemble lions with their wild mane of hair and proud, smooth gait."

"So, you see me as a lion. I like that. Then you must be my plaything, the little mouse caught between my powerful paws." He reaches for her leg and tries to pull her toward him. She snatches it away.

"Not so fast. There's more: 'Leos are extremely passionate about the things they love and life itself.'" She puts down the book and looks at him. He's practically purring with pleasure. "You're eating this up, aren't you? They've got that part right too. Leos love to be flattered."

He grabs at her again, but this time it's for the book. "Okay, let's see what they have to say about you, little Libra. Here it is." His eyes dart over the pages as he skims, then stops. He laughs and looks at her with a gleam in his eyes. "This truly is uncanny. 'Libras may appear as sweet and innocent as a kitten but beware their sharp claws and teeth. They are as stubborn as they are passionate, seeking beauty and balance. They are famously indecisive, weighing everything endlessly.' And here's my favorite part, 'Libras almost always have ample dimples—as you do. And they are prone to plumpness.'" He closes the book.

"I am not!" She slaps his arm.

"You are quite fond of slapping, I've noticed. Could Libras be prone to violence as well?"

She resists the urge to slap him again. "You're awful! Were you like this as a child? I don't know how your mother put up with you."

"My mother paid little attention to me. I was, after all, the middle child. But she was devoted to Tomás and Pepe. And our sister."

"Your sister! I didn't know you had one."

"Angelica." A fond, sad smile shapes his lips. "She was born soon after father was imprisoned. Mother said she knew from the womb Angelica would be a special child in need of protection."

"Special? How?"

"Mentally she's still a child. While her body bloomed—Angelica's a beautiful girl—her mind stays innocent. She spends her days playing with dolls, singing, and drawing. She has a lovely, lilting voice and her drawings are quite remarkable. She may be precocious that way."

"Do you see her and your mother often?"

"No. The Federales watch their home, hoping to catch us. Tomás occasionally sneaks in. Or he meets them secretly when they go to mass."

"I would love to meet them someday."

"Someday," he says. "You will love my sister. My mother, not so much, perhaps." He stands and stretches, looking down at Lena sitting at his feet and holds out his hand. "This lion is ready for a swim."

They strip and swim through the cool shallow pool. He washes himself, scrubbing under his arms, as if he has soap. She laughs at him, and he roars for her. He chases her around the pool and grabs her by the waist, pulling her in for a soft, deep kiss. He grows hard against her. She touches him there and looks down at that tangle of dark hair and those strange male organs. So different from the rest of his body. Here, at his center, he is soft and vulnerable, so sensitive. Heat in her body rises as his cock swells and grows harder. She drops to her knees.

He pulls her up. "What are you doing?"

"You know what I'm doing."

"But you've never done this before?"

"No." She's surprised he's stopping her. "Don't you want me to?" she asks, feeling strangely hurt and confused.

"It's not that I don't. It's that this isn't necessary for now. We have plenty of time for that."

"But what about our promise 'always and in all ways'?"

He looks at her strangely, a crease deepening between his eyebrows. "You want this? It will give you pleasure?"

Will it? How would she know? But then she does know, for everything about him gives her pleasure. "Yes," she says. "This will give me immense pleasure."

And it does. Heat pools between her thighs as she explores his most erotic parts with her hands and mouth and tongue. His head is thrown back, his long muscular throat stretched taut, his buttocks clenched, as he takes in all the sensations she elicits. His hands press the sides of her head as if to keep her there, as if he couldn't bear it if she stopped. An immense sense of power and pride and protectiveness toward him surges through her. A deep almost primal sense of possessiveness. *He's mine. All of him.* Even these most sensitive and vulnerable parts. Raoul is hers to do with whatever she wants. She's the one making him groan, making him stiff and swollen. He's putty in her hands as she is in his.

I did this. He's mine.

His whole body begins to shudder and then he pulls her up roughly into his arms, hefting her onto his hips. He's thrusting inside her now, deep and long, long and deep, faster, faster as they cling to each other. His roar is so loud, a flock of yellow finches rises noisily into the air. Just like the lion he is and always will be.

His hands are on the sides of her face again and he's kissing her all over, murmuring endearments. "Mi tesora. Where did I get such a treasure? How are you mine?" He wraps his arms around her with the same fierce possessiveness she feels and rocks her in his arms. His kiss is now soft and tender as she melts against him.

They are walking back to the Casa together, swinging their hands between them, when Raoul freezes. He pushes her behind him and raises his rifle. Someone is running up the trail toward them. But it's only a young soldier from the Casa.

"What's wrong, Alphonso?"

"Your brother, Commander Aguilero, just arrived, sir. He says it's urgent."

Raoul looks at Lena, his eyebrows furrowed.

"Go," she says. "I'll catch up later." She watches him sprint away. Her stomach clenches. If it's urgent and it's Tomás, this can't be good.

Lena is in the atrium, trying to divert herself with a collage, while Raoul and Tomás talk in the study behind closed doors. An hour later, Raoul enters the atrium in full military garb, a bandolier strapped across his chest and a machine gun at his side. His hair is drawn back, and his green cap pulled over his forehead. Raoul, the grim-faced commander, is back.

"No-o-o," Lena says, shaking her head.

He lays his gun aside and draws her into his arms. "I must leave for a while," he says, his chin on her head, his breath in her hair. She pulls back to look him in the face.

"What is it? What happened?"

He looks away, his face fierce, jaw clenched. An informant led the Federales to the village where Manuela's and Bosco's children live, hoping to find them there too. Their son tried to escape, and his young sisters ran after him. The Federales turned their rifles on them. The two young girls were killed.

"Oh God, please, no!" Lena cries, remembering Manuela's radiant smile when she spoke of her twin daughters. Those angels, she called them.

"Benito got away. But no one knows where the boy is. We must find him. And we must make sure this never happens again."

"Please take me too!" She clutches his arms.

He shakes his head. "This is a military operation, Lena. You cannot go."

"Then let me go to Manuela. I can't stay here. I must do something."

"I'm sorry, it's impossible."

She pushes away from him. "When will I become an Aguilero? When will I be able to go with you?"

His eyes close and then open with a sad smile. "Malenque Mia. Not every Aguilero fights. You have important work, telling our stories—"

"It's not enough! Not when something like this happens. I want to be with you, at your side, always. You said that."

"And so you will be, but not when I'm fighting." He lifts her chin. "You must be strong." He crushes her against him, then turns abruptly.

She follows him to the front door and watches him climb into the jeep beside Tomás. *I will not cry,* she tells herself as they disappear from her sight. She pushes the hot wash of rising tears down into her throat and chest, where it joins the hard knot twisting in her stomach.

CHAPTER 29

The next nine days are torture. How do people do this? Lena wonders. How do they send loved ones into harm's way? The families of soldiers, police officers, firefighters and so many others. It's excruciating. Or maybe you get used to it. Maybe it's a hard knot that never leaves but stays contained. Her tears are contained. But the fear? No. If anything happens to him . . . well, she won't even think about it. She can't.

She pores over newspapers brought by couriers. One report says a band of Aguileros held up a government payroll shipment a week ago. Three guards were killed. A gruesome photo shows bloody men splayed in a jeep. Another paper says the corpses of two butchered men were found in a ditch, their feet and heads cut off. According to the report, cutting off the feet means the killers want to stop their "movement"—which is why they suspect the victims were Aguileros. Lena remembers the students she saw arrested. Fiona told her the girl was eventually released, but the boy had gone missing. Was he in a ditch?

When she sees that a story about a group of protesting students was written by Daniel Weatherly, she smiles with relief. He's still in San Balanque, still working, still bringing attention to the unrest spilling across the land. A photo with the story shows students carrying signs reading "Ortiz Thugs" and "Students United for Justice," while the city streets are lined with police brandishing firearms. Daniel reports that this time no shots were fired, but last month police responded to rock-throwing with live rounds, killing one student and maiming a dozen others.

So much violence. Does her father hear of this? Her mother surely has. How could she still support Ortiz? Lena is glad she never told Raoul she's related to someone like that.

She sees now what her role must be. Not just to write for the tabloids, but to tell the world about the plight of San Balanquans and the Aguileros' fight for freedom. To throw light on this vicious cycle of tyranny and abuse that has been going on too long. US policy toward Latin America must be changed before there can be any hope for lasting peace and justice. She knows how difficult that will be. Too many powerful people profit from corruption. Back home journalists are helping turn the tide of public opinion against the Vietnam War. What about cruel, violent dictators in our own backyard?

This is the important work she must do. The knot in her stomach never completely disappears, but the fire in her belly grows.

Lena is in the atrium working on a new story, a personal account of what she's learned about the Ortiz regime, something she hopes Ron will publish in the *Santa Barbara Chronicle*. She's so absorbed in her work she doesn't notice someone enter the room. But then the back of her head tingles, and she knows.

That sweet, salty scent. Raoul!

She turns, and there he is, his face lit with excitement and amused affection all rolled into one. She runs to him and hops into his arms, her legs around his waist. He reels with the impact and drops what he's holding.

She kisses him with such fervor their teeth crunch. "I've been so worried about you!"

He pulls back and laughs, her feet go to the floor. His fingers caress her face. "It warms my heart to be so heartily missed, but you mustn't worry about me."

"How can I not? Impossible!"

"I have something for you." He picks up the package he dropped, then smiles as she rips off its brown paper packaging. "Don't get too excited. It's not every girl's dream gift. But it's something I very much want to see you wearing."

"I can only imagine what you want to see me wearing," Lena says, eager to discover what kind of sexy underwear or naughty nighty he's brought. But then she frowns. "What's this?" She touches the shiny green fabric and shakes it loose. Pants and a shirt, deeply creased from folding. "Fatigues!"

He laughs loudly at her surprise. "My comrade-in-arms standing by my side should look like the warrior woman she is when I introduce her to my troops, don't you think?"

"You're taking me to meet your troops?"

"Yes. And to the villages too. To introduce you as my Malenque, the woman who stands beside me and strengthens me, who like the Malenque of Old will help give birth to a new San Balanque."

He sounds like he's practicing a speech, Lena thinks, and gives him a worried frown.

She's wanted for so long to be a real Aguilero, but she hasn't earned the right to be likened to "the Malenque of Old," even if it's only propaganda, a hook to capture the people's hearts.

"Surely this is too soon," she says.

"Only if you've changed your mind. Otherwise, we have no time to lose. Events are moving quickly." He pulls a rolled-up newspaper from his back pocket. "One more gift for you."

The Weekly Star. On the front cover is Lena's photo of three soldiers lined up with their rifles pointing toward the trees. The caption in big block letters reads: "Aguileros Pledge to Free San Balanque from El Diablo's Iron Clasp." Below is the byline in large letters: "Malenque".

"You got it published!" Lena flips through the pages. Her eyebrows knit together. "Looks like they've done some editing. Purpled it up quite a bit!"

"Well, yes. You're part of a team. We agreed it should appeal to the tastes of this readership. The first printing sold out! More are on the way. It will be distributed across San Balanque to every newsstand and grocery store. As you can see, this is Part One. More stories are queued up for printing over the next few weeks."

He clasps her shoulders. "That's why we need to start visiting the villages, to introduce you—our newest rebel rock-star—to the people. And why we need to get Billy working on those new posters."

Lena has been so excited to see Raoul again, she almost forgot why he left in the first place. Now she's afraid to ask what happened, but since he's in such high spirits, it must be good news. Anxiously she asks, "How are Manuela and Bosco? Did you find their son?" She holds her breath waiting for his answer. His face hardens.

"He was hiding in the forest, scared and hungry. He didn't know his sisters tried to follow and were killed. He blames himself. We took him to his parents." Raoul pauses, nostrils flaring. "Our next story in *The Star* will be about the Federales' brutality, how they gunned down two innocent girls, and how we retaliated. Humberto and Mariam are working on it. But it will come under the name Malenque."

Lena doesn't like the sound of this and wants to object, but he looks so fierce, she hesitates. "I don't know, Raoul . . . capitalizing off their murder for publicity . . . It doesn't seem right." She frowns and looks up at him.

His face freezes in disbelief. Then a cascade of confused emotions washes over it. Hurt. Disappointment. Anger. Disdain. He steps away from her. "You think this of me? Of us? That this is a publicity stunt?"

She's never seen this Raoul before, and it shocks her. She doesn't know how to respond.

His lip curls. "I thought you knew us better than this."

"Raoul . . .," she says, reaching toward him. He pulls away.

"You have much to learn, it seems. This isn't about publicity. It's about accountability. About telling the truth, what the *Federales* did to innocent children. What they are capable of. It's about respect, not allowing these young girls' deaths go unnoticed, un-mourned. They are martyrs to the cause, Lena. They would not have been murdered if their parents and thousands of others didn't feel this rebellion is the only way we can win back our country and make people safe again. It's about allowing everyone who believes in our cause to take these girls into their hearts and mourn their senseless murder as we do. It's to acknowledge Manuela's and Bosco's personal sacrifice. And it's a warning to Ortiz and his Federales that these kinds of deaths will not go unpunished."

Lena's throat is filled with the pain she hears in his voice. "I'm sorry, Raoul," she chokes out. "You're right. I do have much to learn." His face softens, but he does not go toward her. "So, you will punish these people. And rightfully so," she continues.

"It's already done. The informant was found and executed. He was hung from a tree with a sign around his neck so everyone will know him for what he was. And we attacked the *Federale* outpost where the brutes who killed those girls came from. We killed every soldier and hung them in trees too with signs around their necks."

Lena feels like she's been punched in the gut, and her legs start to buckle. Raoul grabs her arms to steady her. But then, looking into her horrified eyes, he lets go and pulls back.

"You disapprove?" His voice is choked in amazement, hurt, and anger. "What kind of war did you think we were fighting? Where no one gets hurt, no one gets killed, no one retaliates in kind against such atrocities?"

The disdain in his voice shocks and angers her. Her chin juts out. "No trial, Raoul? Hanging in trees? That sounds like you're no better than Ortiz! How do you know you got the real informant? Did he confess? Did you torture him? Did you . . . .." She takes a deep breath. "Who shot him, Raoul?"

He looks at her with steel in his eyes. "We do not torture. Witnesses identified him. And yes, I shot him, a single bullet to the back of the head. I am the Commander. It was my responsibility to do so."

The image of the execution from Goya's painting fills Lena's mind. Only now Raoul stands as the executioner rather than the man on his knees, and she doesn't know which is more terrifying.

"He was on his knees? Hands up?" Tears fill her eyes.

Raoul's eyes grow wide in shock, his mouth curls in disgust. "You cry for him? You think we are monsters like Ortiz?"

She wraps her arms around her body, digging her fingers deep into the flesh. She shakes her head. "Don't assume you know what I'm thinking."

"Then tell me." The cold disdain is still there.

She's breathing hard. The trouble is, she's not sure what she's thinking. She's still reeling from all this information, all these images exploding in her mind. She's horrified and outraged at the death of those children, angry at the people who betrayed them. Glad they were avenged. But also sickened by how it was done, hanging people from trees with signs around their necks. It brings up horrific images of what the Klan does to Black people in the South.

"I'm not crying for him. I know you aren't monsters like Ortiz. I don't know what I think. I need time to process this." She turns away toward the door. But as she's doing so, she remembers that story being written in her name and stops. Her mind whirls.

She turns back and faces him.

"This is what I think, Raoul. We must show we're better than Ortiz. What's done is done. But we must be truthful in the telling of it. If my name is going on the story about these two little girls and how the Aguileros avenged their deaths, how we did so in that way to send a clear message to everyone, I want to be part of that writing. No purple prose. Clear, hard facts about what happened and why. The story is horrible and heart-wrenching on its own. And it will be a powerful story and powerful message if done right. Don't underestimate the intelligence of the people who read these stories. They will know when you are trying to milk their sympathy and outrage, when you are embellishing something for their amusement or horror, and when you are telling the simple truth in a powerful way. That's what I think."

As she's speaking, his face changes. A new set of emotions wash over it—surprise, understanding, agreement, pride. And then pure affection. He comes to her and takes her hands, presses them to his lips.

"Malenque Mia. It appears we understand each other after all."

They don't make love that night, but hold each other, talking into the wee hours of the morning. He understands now how certain things will shock her sensibilities and she'll need time to process it. They agree she will tell him when she thinks he's wrong, and he will tell her when he thinks she is. They may not agree about some things. Despite this, they will trust each other, no matter what.

Lena also understands how she's needed by Raoul's side. How a fresh perspective on what the Aguileros are doing can help them. She can breach the gap between an idealist supporting the cause from afar and soldiers in the field who must be ruthless to win a revolution. She cannot remain the innocent. She must learn and adapt from experience what being a true Aguilero is and might require of her.

The next morning, Raoul rises early and tells her they will be leaving soon to visit the troops so he can introduce her as his "Malenque of Old." His warrior-woman, his heartmate.

Lena smiles at him doubtfully. "Am I truly all that to you?"

"All that and more. Now get packing. We have work to do."

Lena lies there, watching him dress. His mind is elsewhere. When he looks back and sees she's still in bed, he leans over and bites her ear. "Up, I say!" And then he's gone.

Raoul's orders, she thinks, remembering how much it rankled when Fiona said that. Instead of getting up, she allows herself time to luxuriate in this bed she's come to love. She fans out her arms and legs over the silken sheets as if making a snow angel, presses the kitten fur spread to her face, burrows her nose into Raoul's warm pillow, breathing in his sweet-salty scent. *Like the sea*, she thinks lazily.

She doesn't want this part of their life to end. The Casa has been a sanctuary for her initiation into the world of lovemaking, for exploring all the pleasure centers of each other's bodies, for coming to know each other from the inside out. It's been their refuge from the torment of war and political strife, from the responsibilities that will resume once they leave. She knows where they're headed will be fraught with dangers beyond anything she's ever experienced or could imagine.

She doesn't want to lose all the Raoul's she's come to know and love so well: The heavy-lidded amorous Raoul, the playful grinning Raoul, the annoying cocky Raoul, the roaring lion, the confident commander, the passionate orator, the fierce warrior. He's so much for so many people and purposes, all wrapped in one. No wonder people love and revere him. *As I do*, Lena thinks as she packs her bags, even while wishing she could pull him back into bed and never leave.

She looks around the Casa, all these rooms, all the places where their lovemaking spilled over. She makes a shrine of it in her mind where she imprints each detail, each moment, each memory. Their time here will be stretched into a never-ending infinity where she can return and relive it all over again, every second she's spent here with Raoul.

CHAPTER 30

The rainforest is a densely tangled wall behind them as Raoul stands on a raised platform at the edge of the encampment, Lena at his side. Before them nearly five hundred soldiers spread out across the clearing.

Raoul looks down at her, as if to ask if she's ready. She's wearing her new green fatigues. The trousers fit snugly around her waist and hips but are loose in the seat and legs. The bottoms are gathered with elastic at her ankles. Her shirt is unbuttoned, sleeves rolled up. She wears it like a jacket over a thin, white tank-top tucked into her trousers. A green cap, like Raoul's, is pulled down over her head, her wavy hair pulled back into a thick braid.

She feels like an imposter up here beside Raoul, the commander they all respect and revere. How could they ever think of her as one of them? As worthy of their leader? She shifts nervously from one foot to the other, then stills herself, trying to stand tall and proud. Trying to be strong and confident like Raoul.

"I have come here today to introduce you to Malenque, who is helping us with our great cause. She is San Balanquan although she grew up in the United States where, as you know, my brother and I were educated, along with our father and great uncle, the martyr Eduardo Aguilero, where this dream of a free and democratic San Balanque was born.

"Malenque came here to learn of her heritage and fell in love with us, the San Balanquan people. She is a journalist who will tell our stories and give our voices the wings they need to reach everyone within our borders and beyond.

"In this woman standing at my side I have found my heartmate, my other half. Just as San Balanque's legendary creators, Balanque and Malenque, were joined at the hip, so shall we, and all gathered here today, be joined. Like the Twin Gods before us who rose up to throw off the Demon God that would destroy them, we today rise up to throw off the brutal grip of the Ortiz Regime, to free our beloved San Balanque.

"I am but one man, and she who stands by my side is but one woman, but together we form a united front. Just as all of you here today are a united front. We train together. We fight together. We live together. And if we must, we die together. And we do all that so we may triumph together, and our sons and daughters may live as free men and women, in peace and prosperity. In a free San Balanque created of the people, by the people and for the people. So say we all!"

He takes Malenque's hand in his and raises them above their heads. And then they join hands with those next to them, Pepe beside Lena, Tomás beside Raoul, as if this had been planned all along and not the organic phenomena it was, inspired by his words and passion.

"So say we all!" he shouts again, and all the people around and before him join in with raised fists.

"One heart, one soul, one voice! One San Balanque!"

Lena looks out on that sea of faces and feels like she's riding the crest of a great wave that has come up behind her and swept her away. Her heart swells with love and pride. She came here only five short months ago looking for something momentous and irresistible to give her life purpose and direction. And she found it in the Aguileros, in the stories she's writing, in the cause they are fighting for. And in Raoul.

She doesn't know what lies in the future. So many have tried and failed to do what they are attempting. What will become of us, she wonders, squeezing Raoul's hand. Whatever their fate, they will face it together. He christened her Malenque of San Balanque. And so she shall be.

PART THREE
Hour of Blood

January – August 1972

I see all that you are
and all that you have become to me.
Your love is a sea,
and I am its trawler—harbored in dreams,
I ride out night's storms;
—Michael R. Burch, from "Floating"

The true revolutionary is guided by great feelings of love. It is impossible to think of a genuine revolutionary lacking this quality.
—Che Guevara, *Socialism and Man in Cuba*

Our cruel and unrelenting enemy leaves us only the choice of a brave resistance, or the most abject submission. We have, therefore, to resolve to conquer or to die.
—George Washington, August 1776

CHAPTER 31

*S**an Balanque is easy to love, but she will break your heart.*

A poet in a pub once told Lena that. This is true, she's learning during her travels with Raoul. They've been touring San Balanque for the past three months. Thanksgiving, Christmas, New Year's Day have come and gone, but she's hardly noticed, they've been so busy: Raoul introducing her to the troops, meeting with local leaders and potential allies; taking photographs and collecting new stories about the atrocities and injustices committed by Ortiz's regime.

It breaks Lena's heart every time she visits a new village and learns how its people have suffered. She weeps in her heart while listening, holding their hands, petting their children, and promising their stories will be told.

But travelling through the countryside also nourishes her spirit. The tropical landscape is so bright and green, it hurts her eyes, and so beautiful it makes her heart sing. White beaches sparkle like spilled sugar. Seas are shifting mosaics in shades of turquoise, teal, and sapphire. Skies are dizzying, dazzling, constantly changing throughout the day: A blue deep enough to swim through will dissolve into powdery trails of mares' tails, while dark-bottom storm clouds build in the distance, slanting rain.

She smells the rain before it arrives—a moist, mineral scent cooling her cheek. Hears the slow distant whooshing growing louder as it nears. A soft rustling as it sweeps through treetops. A slow sizzling as it strikes the sea's surface. A loud rattling as it shakes thatched rooftops. A staccato drumbeat hitting tin roofs. Cloudbursts can last moments, drenching everything in sight before moving on just as quickly, or lasting so long she's breathing in its cool metallic mist long after.

If it weren't for the beauty, the brutality she bears witness to would be too hard to endure. That and the fact they are working to end that brutality. She was told the Aguileros were like Robin Hood, stealing from the rich and giving to the poor. This, she's learning, is true. Robbing those who exploit the poor enables them to provide for the people in practical ways as well as finance their own operations. They help build schools and dig wells. They support orphanages and supply farmers with seed and clinics with medicine.

These gestures of compassion and comradery win hearts and minds. They are the leaven hidden in a pound of meal that will inspire the people to rise with them when the time comes to take down Ortiz for good. That's what they're building toward, one recruit at a time, one gesture of goodwill after another, one shared hope renewed or hungry mouth fed.

Lena slaps at a beetle that lands on her neck and returns to her work. She's typing up the stories she collected from the last village they visited, sitting in the shade of the tent she and Raoul share at a small makeshift camp on the Caribbean coast. The morning sea breeze is long gone, the air now heavy and still. Her cotton tank top is plastered to her skin from humidity and perspiration.

A large swath of San Balanque is already under Aguilero control, Lena has learned in their travels, although you'd never know it from the newspapers or scuttlebutt heard in the pubs and coffee shops in Curico. Their success is the best kept secret in San Balanque. The whole southeast corner of the Caribbean coast, along with several mountainous regions, is loyal to the Aguileros. This includes the Miskit reservations and Huixla Natural Reserve, as well as two small harbors, Aruba and Trujillo, and a chain of islands comprising the Santa Lucia Archipelago.

Along this coast and in the mountains is where their larger and more permanent camps are found.

But most military operations are conducted by small squads of eight to ten guerrilla fighters who are constantly on the move. Each squad is part of a larger platoon, and these are grouped into columns of one hundred or more soldiers. Then, of course, urban guerrillas gather intelligence and sow disinformation, steal valuable equipment, and sabotage Federale infrastructure.

Lena is a small cog in a complex movement, and yet she's been elevated to stand at Raoul's side, to play the role of the Malenque of Old, a warrior woman when she's no warrior at all. But she is needed. She knows that now, even if it's only to provide Raoul a fresh perspective or calming influence, or the physical release and rejuvenation that comes only in the arms of someone you love and trust.

Trust, Lena thinks, feeling a sharp pang near her heart. She still hasn't told Raoul about her mother. That's the last thing he needs, she tells herself. It's what she'd rather forget. Or pretend isn't true. But it weighs on her.

Lena looks up as Raoul approaches, a dark silhouette against the bright sea behind him until he enters the canopy's shade.

"Anything left in there?" She nods at the canteen he's carrying.

He shakes it, takes off the cap and hands it to her. She takes a drink of the warm, stale-tasting water and looks him over. He's bare-chested, stripped to his trousers and boots. She loves seeing him this way. The consummate hard-muscled soldier. The dark hair sprinkled lightly over his chest funnels down to slip beneath his low-hanging trousers. His stomach looks almost concave now. They've both lost weight since leaving the Casa, living on soldier rations.

"Will we be staying here long?" she asks, rolling her shoulders to ease the stiffness from sitting and typing so long.

"Three more days. Then we'll head to Camp Horchata. Billy will be coming to take our photos for our new poster."

She smiles. "It's hard to picture Billy out here in his baggy cargo shorts and Hawaiian shirts. Although he'll be more properly dressed for the climate than we are."

He takes a seat and leans toward her. "Maybe I'll take you skinny dipping tonight." His eyes half-close as he gives her that feral look he has.

"Hah! You've been saying that for two days now. But as soon as your head hits the cot, you're snoring like a rhino."

"Tonight," he promises and lifts her hand to kiss her sweaty palm. She takes a deep breath, wondering if now is a good time to talk to him about something she's been putting off.

"You know, about those posters . . .."

"What about them?"

Her mouth goes dry again, afraid she's walking into a minefield like she did at the Casa when she accused him of using the deaths of those girls for publicity. She takes another drink from his canteen, then rubs his palm with her thumb as she talks. "I'm worried we're setting ourselves up as cult figures, plastering our posters all over San Balanque as if we're some kind of messiahs. Trying to cultivate this cult-like following to support our cause. Isn't it kind of, you know, dishonest? Manipulative?"

He thinks about that and laces his fingers through hers.

"I don't think so. It's not us they'll be drawn to, but what we symbolize: that hope of freedom already burning in their hearts or smoldering beneath a sense of despair. It's not manipulation. It's inspiration. We're fueling their spirits with hope and courage."

She watches his face as he speaks—those dark eyes, the sharp planes and generous mouth. The intelligence. The warmth. The strength. Everything about him excites and inspires her. She wants to pull his head down, open those lips, and drink from that mouth, long and hard.

But he's not done. She almost hears the gears whirling in his mind.

"Besides, cult figures can be for good or ill. Jesus was a kind of cult figure, all those people following him everywhere, when few truly understood who or what he was. But they felt a burning in their hearts. As if his words kindled something dormant within. People strive to be like him because they recognize his spirit—what he represents—lies within them too."

She raises an eyebrow. "You're comparing us to Jesus?"

"That's one example. There's Gandhi too. And Che. It may seem sacrilegious, putting all three together like this. But love for humanity was at the root of each man's quest. The need to lift people up, free them from bondage, from pain and suffering, exploitation and tyranny.

"Sometimes a need grows so strong within the hearts of a people that they themselves draw out the leader among them to meet that need. And because I am my father's son and the great nephew of San Balanque's first hero-martyr, because I carry on their name and mission, they see me as the person needed to lead them. I cannot deny this calling. It comes from the will of a people who are ready to cast off their chains and be free."

"You've thought a lot about this."

He smiles wryly. "Had I been born in another time or place, I would have been a philosopher, or poet."

"Yes. You would have made a great Philosopher King, as Plato called for."

"A part of me still aspires to such. Luckily, another part detests any form of autocracy, even a benevolent one. Democracy is messy, contentious, chaotic at times, and extremely hard to maintain. But it's the only kind of government that rises from the people and allows them to govern themselves. Even so, the hearts of men are unruly. Sometimes they prefer to lean on a strong arm to rule them, benevolent or otherwise, rather than relying on their own wits and reason. We cannot tell how all this will end, Malenque. All we can do is follow our own hearts, our own path. Love for my people and country is what drives me on this quest. I have no choice but to do what I'm doing. And these posters will help in that effort."

He squeezes her hand, now completely entwined with his. The strength and tenderness of his hand overpowers Lena's senses. She wishes she had words to express all she's feeling but cannot find them. Instead, she leans forward to taste those luscious lips, to enter his hot mouth, to feel the ferocious power of his tongue, that most eloquent member, which claims her body and soul.

When Lena and Raoul arrive in Camp Horchata, she's surprised how large it is, nothing like the small, temporary camps she's used to. This one is hidden on tribal land in the rainforests along the Caribbean coast. Few roads go into this area, which makes it easier to control. It's their largest camp, where squads and troops scattered around the country come to train together, strategize and replenish. It's where the most seriously wounded soldiers come to recover. Most camp structures—the barracks, mess hall, bakery, ammunitions factory, hospital, and commander head-quarters—are hidden beneath trees or camouflage nets, as are the fleet of jeeps and transport trucks.

When Billy arrives, he's dressed like Lena suspected, looking out of place among soldiers dressed in fatigues with rifles slung over their shoulders. And now she's one of them.

"Whoa, girl!" he says when he sees her. "You've gone guerrilla on me! Where's those short-shorts and crop-tops you were wearing the last time I saw you?"

She laughs. "The same place as my harem pants and tube tops, I guess. You like?" She twirls, holding out the baggy pant legs.

Raoul, watching this exchange, does not look amused.

"What's wrong?" she asks him.

Billy too notices his sour face and clears his throat nervously. "Well, guess we better get to work. How about you two stand over there next to those trees . . .? Yeah, like that," he adds as Raoul drapes an arm over Lena's shoulder.

After a moment, Billy pulls back. "This isn't working. I can't get you both in the frame the way I want. Raoul is too tall."

"Should he hunch down to my level?" Lena suggests with a smirk at Raoul.

He returns the look. "I have a better way." He grabs a camp chair and pulls her between his spread legs so she's sitting on the chair leaning against his chest. Now her head is slightly lower than his.

"Yeah, yeah, that's it," Billy says. "Now give each other a long smoldering look, then look back at the camera like you own the world." Billy takes a bunch of shots, then lowers the camera. "Damn! I think we struck gold, boys and girls!"

Billy takes the film to the nearest town to develop and then comes back to show Lena and Raoul. He's right. The photos with Lena sitting between Raoul's legs are perfect. His wild mane blends with hers and frames their heads and shoulders. Both look at the camera with pride and confidence.

"You know these will be torn down by the Federales as fast as they go up, don't you?" Billy says. They sit on the front porch of the Commander Headquarters where Raoul and Lena are staying. A little bed in the back makes a cozy nest for them. Lena perches on the porch railing, trying to cool herself with a rattan fan she found inside.

"Of course. But that helps our cause," Raoul answers. "The posters appeal largely to the young, those plugged into the Pop Art scene. The posters being torn down makes them seem like forbidden fruit—and therefore more desired. Everyone wants one. And seeing how popular they are will unnerve the enemy. Another good thing. Fear and uncertainty weaken them. It acts like a virus, spreading through the system, sowing doubt. Most Federale soldiers are conscripts. Others fight because they need the income. So, they ask themselves, whose side am I on? The people who love these Aguileros? Or Ortiz?"

"So, it's a kind of psychological warfare," Billy says. "Cool."

Raoul nods. "Seeing us as symbols of the Twin Heroes who defeated the Demon God sends a powerful message to Ortiz—who is already known as El Diablo." He laughs. "We might need a third poster: Ortiz depicted as Vucub with a sword striking his neck."

"Awesome!" Billy says. "Totally doable."

Holding one photo, Lena frowns. Will her mother know it's her if she saw these? "How are you going to change this so people don't recognize me?"

"No worries. I'll make your cheekbones wider, your mouth fuller, darker. We'll darken your hair too. Then yours and Raoul's will be the same, giving you more of the Twin Gods vibe."

"Put 'San Balanque' in big letters below, like it's a travel poster," Raoul says. "That will make it even more popular. Put 'Raoul and Malenque' arching over our heads. Use those psychedelic fonts found on Santana albums. Know what I mean?"

"Gotcha!" Billy says.

"Make up a few options and give them to Fiona. She'll send them by courier for my approval, okay?"

After Billy takes off, Lena sits beside Raoul on the porch. She leans her head against him. "How long will we be here? Will we be doing any more touring?"

"Not at this point. We're planning a major operation that I'll be leading personally," he says. "So, our time here together is limited."

She hooks her elbow through his and draws him closer, as if to counteract the thought of their parting. "What is this major operation?"

"I'm sorry, I can't tell you the details—safer for everyone that way—but it's about making an appearance on the world stage. Ortiz doesn't know the extent to which we've taken over this part of San Balanque, but he will soon enough, and we need to prepare for that. They've been on the offensive in the mountains and have captured dozens of our fighters. We need to get them released, as well as build up our financial reserves. Meanwhile your stories and these posters will fire up the people, so when things come to a head militarily, the population will rise with us to throw out Ortiz and his cronies."

"When will that be?"

"Hard to say. There's still much work to do. Which means you will need to return to Curico to do your part while I stay here and do mine. But before departing," he adds with a grin, "you have something important to accomplish here in camp."

Lena frowns, knowing what he's about to say. She's been dreading this, which, for some perverse reason, seems to delight him.

His grin widens. "The new recruits have arrived. Your combat training starts tomorrow!"

CHAPTER 32

Lena lies on her stomach on the jungle floor, holding an AK-47. In a training exercise, she and four other recruits are waiting to ambush a jeep convoy consisting of five other recruits from their squad. After they swap positions, she'll be defending herself in the jeep rather than attacking from the jungle. She wipes sweat from her forehead, peering through the thick foliage. The dank smell of decaying leaves makes her want to sneeze. This she represses, along with the terrible urge to scratch her pant leg where she fears a bug has crawled. Part of training is learning to resist distractions and remain still so as not to be detected.

She's hot, hungry, filthy, and exhausted. She hasn't bathed since training began eight days ago or had a full night's sleep—pushed out of their hammocks before dawn and training till well past dark. Two weeks down, one to go. Sergeant Hernandez started them off doing squats and pushups and running along the beach wearing twenty-five-pound backpacks to help get them in shape. They hiked up mountains and through jungles, using machetes to hack the undergrowth. In between that came firearm training, learning to shoot rifles, pistols, and now a machine gun!

Lena's never shot a gun in her life, and she's shocked by how loud they are, how much they bite back when she pulls the trigger. She's sure she has massive bruising on her shoulders. She's also learned how to shoot a mortar and throw grenades. She's learned hand-to-hand combat with a knife, for god's sake! And all this was done on a soldier's ration of dried jerky and hardtack.

Learning how to defend herself is one thing, but learning how to kill? She's a pacifist at heart. This goes against every grain of her being. But all new recruits must get combat training despite their specific assignments—drivers, couriers, medics, cooks, mechanics. Training toughens them and steels their nerves. It fosters a sense of common purpose and comradery. It assures each soldier that every other Aguilero will have their back when needed and can do so.

"Be glad you won't be going on the six-week mountain trainings our foot soldiers do," Raoul told her. She bit back a bitter reply. She chose to be with him now rather than waiting, so she will see it through to the end. *Even if it kills me*, she thinks, lying on the ground in a pool of sweat. *But it bloody well won't stop me from scratching my goddam leg!*

When her three weeks training is up, Lena marches back into camp like a rag doll trying to stand tall. Every part of her body hurts. The whole camp has turned out to welcome them back, clapping as they pass through the parade grounds to the barracks. She feels proud. And emotional, looking at the grinning faces of her fellow trainees. She's come to know them in a way you do at summer camps. Three, besides Lena, are women: Teresa, a secretary for an ad agency, who she met in Curico at a study group. Andrea, a university student who is as intellectually engaged with their cause as Lena was with SDS. The third, Rachel, is a nurse who came with her doctor boyfriend, Leonardo. Lena feels especially close to Rachel after seeing her sobbing in her boyfriend's arms because she hurt so much and didn't think she could finish the training.

One of the trainees is a young priest, Father Herrera. It seemed strange seeing a priest learning how to shoot an AK-47. But many in the clergy support the cause, even their own Archbishop Martinez, an avid disciple of the liberation theology. They practice their faith by aiding the poor and oppressed, which sometimes means by political and even revolutionary means. They serve the cause by teaching liberation theology in their classrooms and recruiting students that way. They also serve as couriers and gather intelligence for the Aguileros. Often they're harassed by the Federales, but this only makes them and their flock more committed to the cause.

Then there are the two shy Miskit brothers, Bernard's nephews, John and James; the forty-year-old mechanic, Diego, who complained of his aching hip; and Simon, a wiry, tight-lipped union organizer who is

Sergeant Hernandez' star pupil. The last one, Jose, is a local boy, only fifteen years old. But he looks as stony-faced and committed as Bianca did. He's the second-best pupil.

They all had their own stories of why they signed up for this, and Lena felt like a sponge, soaking it all up so she could write about it later. She feels a true bond with them now and squeezes Rachel's hand as they walk through the camp. Rachel throws an arm around Lena's shoulder and draws her in for a hug. Her eyes are shining. They are all headed back to the barracks to clean up before the ceremony this evening where they will be sworn in as Aguileros.

Lena searches through the crowd for Raoul. She knows what a dirty ragged bunch they must be as they weave their way through the cheering soldiers. Then she finds him standing on the sidelines. He's clapping too, but with a cocky tilt to his head and, if she's not mistaken, a smirk on his lips. While the rest of the recruits turn toward the barracks, she approaches Raoul and punches him in the stomach.

"What was that for!" he asks, rubbing his belly.

"Your smirk! You're loving the fact you made me do this when I didn't want to, aren't you!"

"What? You can't tell a smile from a smirk? I'm proud of you, Malenque! I knew you could do this. And it's important you did. The soldiers need to see that this woman who stands by my side, who I've boasted about so much, is doing the same kind of training they do."

"Well . . . when you put it like that."

"Aren't you proud of yourself? This isn't easy and everyone knows it."

She lets the last of her ire drain away and then admits, "I am proud. I was tempted at times to quit."

"What kept you going?"

She punches him again, softly this time. "You know what it was."

"I do," he says, letting his forehead touch hers. "Come now, you stink like a soldier, and I want my woman back. I'll wash you myself for you look too weary to hold up your head."

"Don't I have to join the others in the barracks?"

"Your training is done. You're all mine now." He leads her by the hand to the camp headquarters where they've taken up residence. Gently, he disrobes her, groans over every revealed bruise, covers them with kisses, and brings her into the small, dank, dishpan shower where a slow stream of brackish water trickles out. He strips and joins her, soaping her so thoroughly she slips in his arms when he backs her up against the slick wall and enters her with a lusty groan. Lena closes her eyes and despite her aching body relishes the feel of him filling her, reaching the center of her being as he holds her up with his rough hands.

After dinner, Raoul signals the troops to turn out so he can swear in the new recruits as Aguileros. Dressed in a fresh pair of fatigues, Lena joins her fellow recruits. She's one of them now and it feels so good. A warm sense of comradery spreads through the group. Big smiles on so many faces. Claps on backs.

They gather in a large field, Raoul standing on a slight rise so all can see. Nearly a thousand Aguileros are gathered here, more than Lena's seen at one time. Her squad wasn't the only one training in the jungle these past few weeks. Fifty new recruits will be sworn in tonight. Raoul calls each by name and asks them to step forward.

They raise their right hands, repeating the pledge Raoul calls out. A rousing roar of claps and cheers erupts. Raoul calms them with his hands.

"There is something more that needs saying, that all Aguileros must know when they swear their oaths and take it into their hearts." Lena has not heard this speech, although she's heard of it. It comes after every oath-taking when Raoul is in the field. His famous "Love Speech."

"Comrades, we are gathered today to fight for what we love—our families, our farms, our freedom. Our beloved San Balanque. Being a freedom fighter—willing to lay down your life for your country and your compatriots—is the ultimate expression of unselfed love. If we fight with love in our hearts, the killing will be clean and bring us honor. For we are fighting in defense of a cause greater than ourselves.

"So do not let your hatred for Ortiz or the Federales corrupt you. Hate is debilitating. Hate cripples and shames us. Love strengthens us, lifting us above the enemy.

"A Federale who fights for money, fights with shame, fights as a cripple because he has no love to strengthen him, no just cause to inspire him.

He is to be pitied, not hated. He has only to open his heart to the people and renounce his fealty to a tyrant to become one of us, a champion of the people rather than a pawn of El Diablo.

"But be fierce in your love. Do not think of love as a soft thing. You are the ferocious tiger defending its young. You are the roaring lion defending its territory, the falcon defending its freedom. Let love be the clean, fierce sword of righteousness.

"Love is the way, my friends, just as our savior Jesus Christ told us. Am I right, Father Herrera?" Father Herrera lifts his fist into the air, and all those around him cheer. When the noise dies down, Raoul continues.

"'Love your enemies,' Jesus said. I confess, I am not so great a man that I could ever love Ortiz or the Federales—forgive me, Jesus!" He pauses while the troops laugh and cheer. "But I am great enough to know that hatred weakens and defiles me. So, while I cannot love my enemies, I will not hate them. And I will show greater mercy and dignity to Ortiz's wretched soldiers when captured than Ortiz ever showed them or their families in his lifetime. They will be treated with dignity and mercy and swift justice when needed. Our soldiers will not be. They will be beaten and tortured, beheaded and thrown into a ditch. Because our enemy has no honor. That's why we are better than them. That's why the people champion us as we do them.

"Remember this in the heat of battle, so your mind will be clean and clear and deadly with passion and purpose. Love is the way we win. And we will win. Be assured of that. So say we all!"

"So say we all," Lena cries out with the rest of the roaring crowd.

CHAPTER 33

"We should record your 'Love' speech next time," Lena tells Raoul as she sits on a chair and pulls off her boots. It's their last night together before she returns to Curico. "I could transcribe it and get it printed. Or you could air it on the radio station you're setting up. It's a great recruiting tool. Letting people know what our values are. How we are better than them."

He's watching her undress as he lies naked in bed, his hands behind his head. She's not even sure he's listening as she removes her shirt and steps out of her trousers.

He pulls back the mosquito netting to let her in. "Enough talk of politics. I want to sample this new hard body of yours, after all your training."

"The taste you had in the shower this afternoon wasn't enough?"

"Not nearly," he tells her as his hands rove over the muscles in her arms and legs. "So strong! But I'm disappointed," he adds, turning her in his arms. "This plump bottom I love so much is a little less so."

"I knew you were going to say that!"

He leans down to bite her ass. "But still so tasty."

"You're impossible Raoul. Sometimes I think you like my bottom more than my face." She's teasing, but it bothers her, this question of lust versus love. Can you tell them apart? Is one stronger than the other? If Raoul turned out to be a tyrant, would she love him still for how he makes her feel when they make love? But this is something she should sort out on her own, not on their last night together when lusty lovemaking is what she really wants.

"You would make me choose between your face and your fanny?" he says with an amused grin. "Let me set your mind at rest." He takes her face between his hands. "Your beautiful face is forever etched in my heart and elicits nothing but pure love from the part of me that is pure. But this," he says, squeezing her ass again, "elicits nothing but pure lust from the animal in me that remains forever untamed. And knowing this garden of earthly delights down here is attached to your angelic face is heaven on earth."

She makes a face. Is he just telling her what he thinks she wants to hear? "You're quite the poet, aren't you Raoul?" she hedges.

"Indeed, I am. As well as a rutting animal helpless in lust, in love, in worshipping every single inch of you."

She laughs. "You know you're making me horny right now, don't you?"

His eyes smolder. "I was counting on that," he says as his kisses trail down her neck and breasts toward the tender earthly delights below.

Later that night, when she's curled up in his arms, he whispers, "I will miss you so much, Mi Amor. Not only your body and the way I feel when you're lying in my arms, but your lovely face and sweet mouth and the way your mind works, all the clever and surprising things you say. The way you make me laugh, and take me to task, and test my love. Even your little puny, futile slaps and punches . . .. Yes, like that," he says as she slaps at his arms holding her. "I may miss those most of all."

She snuggles further into the well of his chest and arms. "Well, don't miss me too long. I want to be back in these arms again as soon as possible, where I would live forever, if you would only let me."

"I will. Soon," he promises.

A knock at the front door wakes them the next morning. Raoul slides out of bed, still naked, and goes into the next room to answer. He returns carrying a cardboard box. "Billy's sample posters came while you were training. I chose the one I liked best and had five thousand printed." He opens the box and gives one to her. "I have more boxes for you to take to Curico to distribute. What do you think?"

"It's beautiful," she says. "I hardly recognize myself. But I love the look of us together. And all the psychedelic fonts. It does look like the cover of a rock album. And you, so handsome. All the ladies will go gaga over these, just like the last posters."

"What they will go gaga over, as you say, are the two of us together. We are an incredibly romantic people, you know, we Latinos. The women love their romantic telenovelas, which idealize our men as both tender lovers and fierce fighters."

"And pompous asses too. I had lots of time to watch those shows when I was stuck in that hotel in Curico."

He laughs. "Yes, pompous asses too, as you well know. But romantic. We revere women as mothers and wives and idealize sisters and daughters as chaste and pure. But we also know our women to be fierce defenders of their families. Here in this poster we have all that: the warrior woman and the warrior man, as well as the tender lovers, and the chaste siblings of old, all who will sacrifice themselves for the love of their people, their country, and each other."

He takes one poster and tacks it onto the wall. "Now your face is on my wall, and everything else about you is etched into my mind and heart."

She looks at it hanging there. "You know when I first saw your original poster, it reminded me of one I still have hanging in my bedroom back home, Jim Morrison from *The Doors*. I bought it when I was a teenager."

He slips back in bed beside her. "Which was only, what? Three years ago? Sometimes I forget how young and inexperienced you are."

"Oh, and you're so experienced? How old are you, Raoul?"

"I turned twenty-seven last August."

"So worldly," she teases. "And how many lovers have you had?"

He laughs. "Far too many to count."

"You're teasing!"

"Am I? How many men have you been with?"

"You know the answer to that."

"Okay, then," he says. "How many men have you loved before me?"

She laughs. "Men? The romantic partners I had were hardly men. Boys, mostly. Except for my first crush, Mario."

"Tell me about this Mario."

"You knew him. Or so you told Daniel in that interview. Mario Savio? You heard him speak when you were at Berkeley."

"Yes, yes. I remember. The 'bodies in the gears' speech."

"That's it! That's when I fell in love with him. Hearing that speech. I was only thirteen but already fancied myself an activist, following in my father's footsteps. Mario was so passionate. And handsome. All that curly hair!" she adds, ruffling up his curly hair. "What was a poor girl supposed to do? I was swept off my feet!"

She laughs. But Raoul doesn't. He's gone silent. But he's looking at her in a peculiar way. "What is it? Are you jealous?"

"I am. Very. But also excited. Because you saw a bit of me in him, even then, and that's what drew you to him."

"But how could that be? I didn't even know you!"

"But you knew what you wanted. What you saw in him then and what you see in me now, that's what you loved, what drew us together. It was the same for me. I was in love with you before I ever met you. And when I saw you the first time, I recognized you. As if I'd always known you. Always loved you."

She realizes this is true. There was something of Mario in Raoul, she sees it now. Even then, so young, Lena saw him as a kindred spirit. Someone with the passion and purpose to right the wrongs of the world. Someone intelligent and inspiring. Someone she could admire. And yes, revere. It's such a weird word. But that's what she feels for Raoul, what she felt for Mario back then, a kind of reverence.

"I felt that way too when I first saw you. Like I'd always known you. Always loved you."

He is quiet. And when he speaks, it's clear he's given this much thought.

"I think what we admire in others, what draws us to them, is in ourselves too. We're drawn to what we love, and what we love is seeded in ourselves, a part of us already."

He is playing with her hair, wrapping it around his fingers. "We're all tangled up," he says. "You and me, what we love, what we champion, what we see in each other. What you love in me is inside you, and what I love in you is inside me."

"Then we can never be apart."

"No, never."

That afternoon Raoul drives the jeep to the edge of the territory they control. Two guards stand by on the road. A yellow taxi waits with them.

"Jesse is here already," Raoul says as the driver gets out and collects her bags and boxes of posters. He's the one who drove her to Casa de Amor. Much has changed since then.

Sitting in the jeep, Raoul's hands are on her face, his eyes closed, fingers moving lightly over her mouth, her cheeks, her eyes, as if wanting to memorize all he's feeling. She lets him, then pulls him close, clinging so tightly she feels his heartbeat in her body.

When they leave the jeep, she takes his hands and looks him in the eyes. "Don't ever leave me," she tells him, meaning be mine forever.

He seems to understand. "Never, Malenque Mia, heart of my heart."

They kiss. A soft, tender, almost chaste kiss. Not filled with longing, or lust, or regret. But with promise. She's the first to turn away. She wouldn't be able to stand watching him walk away. As she turns to leave, she lets one hand trail behind until their fingers slowly slip apart. The feel of his warm, rough, ever-so-lovely fingers remains on hers long after.

Lena feels like she's transcended time and space as the taxi winds through forests and mountains toward the west coast and Curico. As the jungle wall slides past her window, as she sways when the taxi hits a rough spot on the road, as the breeze lifts her hair—the sweet, salty scent of Raoul, the feel of his long lean muscles beneath her hands as they lay cozily in their warm bed last night are still with her. She remembers how he lifted her hips to his mouth and drank from her long and deep. She remembers how intoxicated she became with all she was feeling, how she pressed herself against him, wanting more. She remembers him deep inside her, his eyes holding hers steady as each long thrust bound them together. She remembers the way her heart felt. Like there was no end to this, like this moment would be seared into her consciousness forever. And so it was. Here on the road, transiting between her past and future, he's with her still. She feels him. And yet he's not here at all. How could this be?

How could it be that those intense, intoxicating moments of love-making were taking place in the middle of a bloody war where people were dying every day? Men were being tortured in prison and dumped in ditches. Families were mourning dead children butchered on the road or gunned down running for freedom. Others were hung in trees. How could these things exist side by side in the same world? It's a mystery. She looks out at the green mountain range rising outside her window and watches a white bird flying across its dark expanse in undulating waves of grace and beauty.

CHAPTER 34

Humberto leans back on the crushed velvet couch with his feet on the coffee table of the furnished apartment he finally approved for Lena. He regards her with amused affection as she sits in her armchair and fills out the lease agreement. He insisted the apartment must have a backdoor exit and several escape routes.

"Being close to a bus stop is good too, since you don't have a car or driver yet," he tells her. "Although one will be assigned soon enough. And a bodyguard."

"A bodyguard! You've got to be kidding. Why would I need one? I don't want to be treated different from any other Aguilero."

Humberto's smirk is as infuriating as Fiona's was. "You are not any Aguilero, my dear. You're the commander-in-chief's lover. You're Malenque of the posters. And while we're trying to conceal your identity, if it becomes known, you'd become a high-value target. This is to protect us as much as it is you."

Raoul assigned Humberto to look after her this time, perhaps mindful of Lena's concern about having his former lover do so. This works out well since she and Humberto must work together anyway as members of the Publicity and Propaganda Arm. But she now finds she prefers Fiona's style of "care" over Humberto's. Fiona was mostly hands off, while Humberto, perhaps in his zeal to please Raoul, is a mother hen. When he comes to check on her, he stays long past his welcome.

While it annoyed Lena how taciturn Fiona was, rarely satisfying her need to know, now it's Humberto's ebullience she finds tiring. Still, he's as brilliant as everyone told her. She's learning a lot about writing and publishing and even more about the Aguilero inner circles and feuding between the old guard and newer members. Raoul, he says, is the glue holding everything together. While members of that circle disagree on so much, they all agree on Raoul's leadership.

Humberto is a horrible gossip though and loves to amuse and horrify Lena with tales she's not sure she should believe. According to him, President Ortiz keeps political prisoners in cages at home where his children can taunt them. He has an alligator pit he feeds with anyone who has offended him. Sometimes he rescues them after an arm or leg is severed. Sometimes not. There are rumors of child-sex trafficking, devil worshipping, orgies, bathtubs made of gold, diamond-studded dog collars, and palaces built for pet goats.

"Outrageous things. Disgusting things. But believable in a regime of excess and corruption," Humberto tells her.

"But they're rumors. You don't know if they're true, right?"

"These sorts of things have been going on for centuries. Absolute power breeds absolute contempt for the lives and dignity of lesser mortals. Ortiz is capable of these things, whether he acts on them or not. And a grain of truth seeds every rumor. Atrocities such as these are uncovered after the fall of every brutal dictator. Look at Hitler's death camps. No one wanted to believe it while it was going on.

"Our job," he continues, "is to reveal the truth about the greed and corruption, the cruelty and abuses. And then ramp it up, build on these rumors to heighten the people's enmity against Ortiz, knowing even the worst could be true. We take pains not to start rumors, but we do not dismiss them."

Lena is skeptical. Surely her mother wouldn't support Ortiz if he had cages in his homes, or alligator pits. The woman her father and aunt loved so much wouldn't tolerate something like that. Would she?

But thinking of her mother makes her feel queasy. She should have told Raoul about her by now. Will he be angry she didn't tell him sooner? But why should she? Her mother means nothing to her. She doesn't even know her, hasn't seen her in ages, and has no plans to see her again. So why would it matter?

It's not long before Lena sees the new posters Billy made being hung all over the city. There's buzz about them in the pubs and cafes. Everyone wants to get their hands on one before the Feds tear them down. No one recognizes Lena as the woman in the poster. Except Daniel.

She runs into him at a cafe near La Rosaleda. She dropped by to visit her old landlady and pick up any mail that might have slipped through the cracks since Fiona had it forwarded to a P.O. box. There are two letters. She takes them to the coffee shop to read. A letter from the executor of the family trust says she can start making monthly withdrawals now she's turned twenty-one. Which means Lena can pay for the apartment she's leasing with her own money rather than her father's.

Her father's letter says he's extending his sabbatical at the Zen monastery and hopes to become ordained. *Daddy, a Zen monk!* Lena can't help laughing as she sits stirring her coffee. That's when she hears Daniel's voice.

"It's you in the new poster, isn't it?"

She startles and looks up. He's the same as always, that sandy hank of hair hanging over his glasses. Her face lights up and she starts to rise to hug him hello—but then she sees the grim line of his mouth and stops. She'd forgotten how they parted.

"Is that how you greet someone after so long?" she asks. "No hi, how are you?"

He makes a face. "You're right. Let's start over. May I have a seat?"

"Of course."

"I've been worried about you, you know, especially after the raid at Deke's. Marley gave me a cover story, a way to deflect attention from you. Has that been working?" He looks closely at her.

Her gaze shifts away, uncomfortable with this questioning. "Yes, I'm in the clear, it seems."

"But you're still with Raoul." His face hardens. "So does your father know by now?"

"He does."

"And he approves?" She can almost hear his teeth grinding.

"Daniel, come on, don't do this."

He leans in, voice lowered. "Raoul kills people, Lena. He murdered men and hung them in trees."

A rush of pain and fury rises through her. The horror of those deaths still stabs, but the need to defend the man she loves fuels her fury.

She leans toward him, her voice low and fierce. "He's a freedom fighter! A soldier! They are at war! Of course, he kills people. That's what soldiers do. That's what we did when we revolted against King George. We killed the sons and brothers of our fellow Englishmen. And for what? What was the great tyranny that justified that war? Taxation without representation! Do you think the Aguileros would be fighting to free this country if Ortiz's only crime was taxation without representation?" She's beside herself with righteous indignation, her fury pouring out like a heat wave.

Danial leans back in his chair as far as he can get. But he has the courtesy of not turning away or interrupting her.

"I'm so sick and disgusted at all the peace-loving moralists who condemn these lawless, unruly, violent revolutionaries, as they sit back in the safety of their homes with all their . . .." Her voice catches, tears sting her eyes. "Their children aren't being gunned down. Their young men aren't arrested and tortured. Their farms aren't being confiscated." She wipes a stray tear from the corner of her eye.

Daniel reaches across the table to take her hand. She pulls it away.

"Lena, I'm sorry. Please don't do this. You're right. What they're fighting for is worth the risk. I just . . . I don't want to see you put at risk, that's all."

Her chest is still heaving, her breath painful gulps. People at nearby tables are staring. She shouldn't have drawn attention to herself or spoken about this in public. But when Daniel called Raoul a killer, the image of his hand with a gun to the head of that man flashed though her mind. It was an execution. Without a trial. Same with Deke. She's one of those peace-loving moralists she's so angry with. Arguing against.

She shakes her head. "I shouldn't let myself get worked up this way."

They sit silently together. When Lena tries to take another sip of coffee, her hand is trembling.

"Look," Daniel says. "Here's what I can promise. I won't mention this again. I don't like seeing you part of this, but if you need help, please know you can count on me. And if I hear anything going down, the feds or secret police about to raid somewhere, or anything that could put you in danger, I'll get word to you. And if you ever need a way out, or a place to lie low, let me know. I care about you Lena. More than you know."

That was a month ago. Lena tries not to think about her conversation with Daniel. She isn't ready to wrestle with her mixed feelings about all the violence. She can't. She's one of them now. She believes in the cause.

She's met with Daniel only once since then. He told her he heard rumors that the Federales recruited a high-level Aguilero informer and a plan involving the air force was in the works. She tells Humberto who will pass it on to Raoul. Two months have passed since Lena last saw him.

In some ways it seems like the time she spent with Raoul was another fever-dream. She wakes at night with the heat of that dream still with her, his hot hand between her legs, his lips parting hers and plundering her mouth with such passion it makes her dizzy. She's only heard from him twice—two romantic love notes. He wrote that things were moving quickly and the operation he told her about would take place soon. She still has no idea what it is. No one does. But the rumor about "something big" going down is being whispered through the ranks.

Lena is hunched over a worktable set up in the corner of the living room of her apartment when Hilda Delgado bursts through the front door.

"They finally did it!" she cries. Hilda is the bodyguard-slash-room-mate-slash-driver Humberto found for Lena soon after she moved in. She excitedly waves a newspaper at Lena, who pushes it away. She's typing up the final draft of a story that Humberto will pick up this evening.

"Hold on! I'm almost done."

"Would you hurry? You're going to love it!" Hilda says.

"One second, two . . . there! Done." She turns to look at Hilda who has spread the newspaper on the coffee table before her.

"Come, see," she says eagerly.

Hilda is two years older than Lena. She's powerfully built, half a head taller with flaming red hair. Dyed. She's been with the Aguileros for four years, a leader in San Balanque's equivalent of SDS, a student organization at the University that is pro-democracy and anti-Ortiz. Her political science major is partly a cover. While the Aguileros have been supported by student organizations over the years, they wanted someone in a leadership position whom they had more control over: Hilda. Humberto thought she'd be a perfect cover for Lena, who, as a journalist, could also work with the group. Hilda could introduce her to the crowd as her roommate. She could drive Lena to pubs and clubs where they did their networking, and, since they were roommates, it wouldn't look suspicious.

So far, it's worked out. She likes Hilda. She even got Hilda to go with her to work out with Fiona at the gym. And if Lena is not mistaken, things are heating up between the two.

"So, what is it you want to show me so badly?" Lena asks as she plops down on the couch next to her. Hilda grins and points to the headline printed in big bold letters across the front page: "Swedish Ambassador and Family Kidnapped by Rebel Bandits!"

"What!" Lena grabs up the paper and begins reading.

In lurid details is a story of how the "rebel bandits" burst into the home of Ambassador Holmstrom at four in the morning. They dragged the ambassador, his wife and young son, age seven, from their beds. They gagged them, hooded them, tied their hands and feet, and then threw them into the back of a waiting van. Shots were heard and blood found in the ambassador's bedroom. Authorities fear at least one family member was shot. No ransom note was found, nor any statements made by the kidnappers.

"What makes them think it was us? I don't believe it. We wouldn't do this. Especially not to the ambassador of Sweden, for God's sake!"

Hilda looks at Lena in stunned silence. "I thought you'd be happy! This is a great coup! It gives us publicity, notoriety, and hopefully will bring in big ransom bucks and new recruits! This says we can do big things. We can get to people. We're not just a bunch of bandits living in the hills like they want everyone to believe!"

"It can't be true!" is all Lena can say. "It's Ortiz propaganda, trying to turn the people against us." She heads for the door. "Come on, we're going to Fiona's and see what she says. She'll know."

Hilda gives her a wary look. "I just came from there, Lena. Fiona is beside herself with joy."

Lena almost chokes trying to contain the outrage that incites. "She's joyful an innocent family has been kidnapped? Terrorized! Listen to yourself. This isn't what we do. We're better than that. Better than them. That's what Raoul always says. This can't be Raoul's doing. He couldn't have approved!"

If the Aguileros did do this, it must be Tomás, not Raoul, Lena thinks as they drive to the gym where she jumps out and barges inside. Manuel and Fiona are there, both beaming, looking in wonderful spirits until they see Lena's face.

"What is it?" Manuel asks.

"Wait," says Fiona taking Lena's arm and leading her to a back room. Hilda and Manuel follow, closing the door behind them. Lena turns on Fiona and shakes the newspaper in her face.

"It's Tomás, isn't it? Raoul would never approve this." She looks each in the eye as she says this, hoping for cues of confirmation.

Hilda makes a face at Fiona and shrugs helplessly. Manuel finds something important at his feet to study. Fiona looks calmly at Lena and says matter-of-factly, "No one does anything without Raoul's approval. From what I've heard they've been planning this for a long time. I thought you knew."

Lena lets her hand with the newspaper drop to her side and fists it tightly. She lifts her chin and stares fiercely, defiantly, at them, as if they're on opposing sides now. "Take me to him! Now! I want to hear him say it himself, that he approved this."

Manuel coughs into his hand and looks like he wishes he hadn't followed them into the room. Hilda is bug-eyed and biting her lower lip. Fiona still has that calm pragmatic look on her face. "Impossible," she says.

Lena takes two steps toward her, so their faces are inches apart. "Make it possible!"

Then she throws down the newspaper and heads for the door. She stops when she gets there and turns to Hilda. "Give me your keys or drive me. I'm going back to my apartment to get ready to see Raoul." She gives Fiona another furious look and bangs out the door.

It's Humberto who shows up to try to calm her. He brings Mariam. She and Lena have become good friends since working together on Lena's stories. No doubt Humberto thinks Lena will be calmer with Mariam here. Hilda disappears when they arrive.

"You're not talking me out of this!" Lena tells them straight up, hands on hips.

Humberto holds up his hands. "Whoa now! No one is trying to talk you out of anything. We're here to help. Fiona was worried about you. Thought you might do something crazy."

Mariam gives him a pained look.

"What?" he asks.

"Crazy!" Lena shouts at him. "Fiona is afraid *I'll* do something crazy! Like kidnap an ambassador?"

Mariam steps forward and brushes Lena's shoulder in a calming way. "That's not how she put it. She's just worried. You were so upset." She gives Humberto an exasperated look. He holds up his hands as if to say, how would I know she'd react this way?

"Why am I the only one upset? That's what I'd like to know."

Mariam and Humberto exchange glances. "May we sit?" she asks, pointing to the couch. "Why don't you sit too."

Lena shakes her head. She's hugging her arms, feeling chilled and shaky. Maybe she's coming down with something. Maybe she should sit. She takes an armchair. "So?" she asks, again in an accusatory tone.

"What?" Humberto says.

Mariam touches his arm. "We're not upset because this is a good thing, Lena. I know it sounds horrible and all, but all of this is horrible. What Ortiz is doing is horrible. The fact we must fight for our freedom is horrible. That our children are getting killed, our soldiers beheaded, protesters gunned down—it's all horrible. That's what war is. But this kidnapping will help us win, and then we can throw out Ortiz and get our normal lives back. That's what we want, right?"

Lena takes two big gulps of air, trying to still her body, to stop the way it wants to shake, the way it wants to jump up and pace, or curl up in a ball. Because she doesn't want this to be true. Doesn't want it to be Raoul who planned this, who made it happen. But if he did, she's got to do something about it.

When she's calm enough to talk again, she looks Humberto in the eye.

"Get a message to Raoul. Tell him I want to interview the family. To assure the world they are being well-cared for. If it's publicity he wants, ransom money and all that," she looks menacingly at him, "Raoul should love this!"

CHAPTER 35

Two days later Jesse's taxi pulls up in front of Lena's apartment. She's packed a bag of clothes and toiletries, not sure how long the interview will last, how long Raoul will allow her to stay. She's brought her notebook for shorthand, her tape recorder and camera. She even has a wig and pair of fake glasses in her bag. She'll be publishing the interview under a pseudonym.

As soon as they get out of town, Jesse pulls into a gas station and takes her to the back where an old blue Rambler is waiting. "Someone else will take you the rest of the way."

Lena's relieved that "someone" turns out to be Carlos. But then he opens the back door instead of the front as she expected. When she slides inside he hands her a black hood.

"What's this?"

He gives her a weak smile. "Raoul wants you to be treated like any journalist would be to make this more authentic."

Lena glares at him as he walks away and gets into the front seat. She's still glaring when their eyes meet in the rearview mirror. He leans back, lights a cigarette, turns on the radio, and waits. He's not going to drive until she's hooded.

"This is ridiculous!" she says, pulling the damn thing over her head. Then she begins composing the riot act she's going to read Raoul when she sees him.

An hour and a half later, the car makes a sharp right turn onto a gravel road up a long steep drive. Finally, the car levels out and slows. She rips off the hood and blinks in the bright sunlight. They are parked in a circular driveway in front of a large stucco home, lavishly landscaped.

Raoul comes down the walkway dressed in fatigues. He opens the back door and slides in next to her. Carlos drives them toward the back of the house and exits, leaving them alone.

So far, they've not said a word to each other.

"You hooded me!" Lena says, punching him in the arm.

"So strong," he says, rubbing his arm. "Yes, for your protection as well as ours."

"That's what you always say."

"Because it's true."

Now that she's with him, some of her ire and everything she planned saying melts away. With the bulk of his body so close—the sweet-musky scent of him filling the car, those dark eyes, that lush mouth—she is overwhelmed. Never have they come together after an absence without falling into each other's arms. Sitting here apart, not touching, seems wrong. How can he not touch her? How can he look at her like that? Like he's patiently waiting for her to berate him. His elbow lies casually on the back of the seat, his hand dangles between them, inches away. But he doesn't touch her. He simply looks at her with those patient eyes. And that alone brings back her outrage.

"You told me you don't kidnap innocents! You don't take those kinds of hostages."

He slowly nods, as if taking in her rebuke, considering it, then brushing it aside. He's not her Raoul now. Her lover. He's Raoul the practical, patient, commander-in-chief giving an interview. His voice is brisk, businesslike, confident and secure.

"This was strategic. We want to let the world know what Ortiz is doing here. Why we are fighting. What better way to assure press coverage than to kidnap a diplomat from a social democracy like Sweden? We want to be self-governed as they are. Like-minded leaders across Europe may be inspired to support our cause once they understand what we are doing and why."

He points toward the house, where she can see a pool and tennis court. "Look where we are keeping them. It's like a vacation. Swimming, tennis, they even have their own chef. Antonio is here."

"And guards!"

"Yes. And guards. They are well protected. No harm will come to them."

"Even if Ortiz refuses to meet your demands?"

"Even so."

She narrows her eyes. "You'll keep them here, unharmed, forever."

"Until our demands are met. Or until Ortiz recaptures them. Or until this war ends. Yes."

"But you kidnapped a child! You dragged them from their beds. Shots were heard. Blood was found. You bound and gagged them, hooded them, like me!"

Raoul's eyes darken. "The ambassador had a gun by his bedside. It was our blood on the floor. We tied their hands but did not gag them, and since they were in the back of a van no hoods were needed. Unlike you."

Lena takes a deep breath, feeling some tension ebb away, along with her outrage. Maybe it wasn't as bad as she thought. Maybe she rushed to judgment.

He seems to see this change, for his face and voice soften. "I understand what you're going through, this struggle in your mind and heart over the morality of war and all it involves. You are being pulled two directions, toward your desire to be a pacifist and your desire to be a freedom fighter. I too struggled with this early on. Even today uncertainties and ambiguities arise within and must be settled.

"I too had concerns about this kidnapping. But two things overcame my resistance: First, I knew no harm would come to them by our hand. Second, having a kidnapped child draws greater publicity and human interest. And yes," he says, holding up a finger when Lena looks ready to object, "while at first it might turn some against us, they will follow the story to see what happens to the child. They will learn he was well-cared for, and they will learn why we did this and why doing so was important. I take no pleasure in it, but I'm bound by my duty, to do all I can to ensure we win this war and free our people. And do so in the most expedient way."

He stops a moment and regards her thoughtfully.

"When I am troubled or confused about my duty, I turn to the story of a great warrior who had similar concerns about morality and duty in times of war, as you do. It's a spiritual allegory found in the *Bhagavadad Gita*, the book Mahatma Gandhi turned to often during his campaign to free his people. It is a great source of comfort and strength to me when I struggle to know the right thing to do. Do you know this book?"

"I know it's an ancient Hindu text. My father quotes from it."

"Reading it moved me greatly, as if speaking to me personally. It's a conversation between a warrior named Arjuna and Krishna, a Hindu god. Arjuna is full of despair. A battle is about to take place, and he wants to throw down his arms because he will be fighting against members of his own family. Killing kin is a great sin and unworthy of him, he says.

"But Krishna tells him fighting this righteous battle is his duty and destiny, his Dharma. He was born a warrior and must do what he was called to do. To do so with wisdom and skill, but also with 'selfless action.' Which meant without regard to his own personal preferences or attachment to the outcome. Therein lay his duty to his God and to his people."

"And you identified with that," Lena says. Her whole body has stilled, absorbing what he's telling her.

"Yes. None of us know why we were born at this particular time and place into the families we were given. Our place is not to question that, but to act in the most honorable way we know, from the place we find ourselves. I was born an Aguilero with a history that points me in this direction. I was born in a time and place that calls for this kind of action. And I feel in my heart this deep, keen desire to free my people from Ortiz's abuses. All of this has led me to where I am today. And while I would prefer not to kidnap or ransom anyone, it is my duty to do so if such an act is done with wisdom and skill for a righteous cause."

He stills for a moment, and then his hand touches her hair, travels the length of a curl. His eyes half-shutter before continuing.

"One must honor one's Dharma, one's destiny, Malenque. What we were put here on Earth to do. We must do so through selfless action, our highest sense of right, and leave the rest in God's hands.

"You too must choose. To work beside me for this righteous cause. Or to choose another path. There is no shame in either if what you choose comes from a pure place. Not simply because you love me and want to be with me. If it is to be a pacifist, honor that. Do it with your whole heart. If it is to be a freedom fighter, honor that, and do it with your whole heart. Only you know what you are called to do. You must decide this for yourself."

He's right, she thinks.

"In the meantime," he continues, "I like your idea for an interview. Perhaps it will reassure you as well as others who feel the same way. You always have good ideas, Malenque. This is why I value you so much—your mind and spirit, even your doubts and fears. You seek always to do what's right and good, as you should. And it's not always easy to know what that is."

A child is laughing gleefully when Lena and Raoul enter the house for the interview. A woman's voice reprimands him. "How could you be so cruel, Erik! To take your mother's home away and put her on the street!"

The double doors leading to the family room are wide open. A Monopoly board is set up on a coffee table where the family is gathered. The boy kneels on the floor, leaning over the board, moving a marker. His mother is curled up on the floor beside him.

The boy's father, sitting on the couch, leans over to ruffle his head. "Way to go, son! Show no mercy!" When he sees them standing in the doorway, he rises. The boy and mother remain where they are, curious but not concerned.

"Hello, Ambassador, I've brought someone who wants to speak with you. This lovely lady is a journalist. Ms. Reynolds, may I introduce you to Ambassador Nils Holstrom, his wife Katrina, and their son, Erik."

Lena steps forward, wearing the wig and glasses. The ambassador takes her hand.

"It's so nice to meet you, Ambassador. And your family. I'm glad to see you all looking well. The world is anxiously waiting to see how you're faring."

"Thank you, Ms. Reynolds. We are happy to see you."

His wife and son stand now too, the mother's hands on her son's shoulders.

"Call me Laura, please. Shall we sit?" Lena takes the armchair across from the couch where the three family members take a seat. Katrina looks elegant with her blond hair swept up in a French roll. But there's a deep crease between her brows. The ambassador is beefy, with dark hair and bushy eyebrows. He's wearing white tennis shorts and a polo shirt. The boy too is in shorts. One of his flip-flops falls to the floor as he climbs onto the couch. He scoops it up and pushes it down firmly between his toes.

"I'll let you have privacy for your interview," Raoul says, backing out the doorway. "We'll be outside if you need anything." He closes the doors as he leaves.

Lena watches him go, then turns toward the family. "I hope you didn't have to wear a hood as I did to get here!"

"No, thank goodness," Katrina tells her.

"But they tied my hands!!" Erik says excitedly, like it was a grand adventure.

"Yes, they did, it was quite scary, wasn't it?" His mother gives him a squeeze. "He was so brave! They did untie us when we got here though, didn't they," she says, as if to reassure her son.

"I heard you were asleep when they entered your home. What did they tell you?"

"We were told to pack clothes and everything we might need for the next two weeks. That we were going on vacation," the ambassador says.

"But they told me I had to bring my schoolbooks! That's not fair."

Eric's mother ruffles his hair. "They didn't want you to get behind in your studies." She turns to Lena. "He's enrolled in a correspondence course."

"But they let us bring games too. And my futball."

Lena smiles. "Then it is kind of like a vacation. You get to swim and play tennis too, don't you?"

"Yes, but I don't like tennis." He frowns at his father. "Papa's trying to teach me."

Lena turns back to his parents. "I heard shots had been fired. Did anyone get hurt?"

"Papa did that! Didn't you?"

"I keep a loaded gun by my bed. I'm not a particularly good aim though, I'm afraid. A good thing under the circumstances. A man was injured in the arm, though not badly."

"A flesh wound, Raoul told us. Nothing to worry about. He's fine now," Katrina adds.

Lena looks surprised. "You call the leader of the Aguileros by his first name?"

She startles and glances at her husband. "That's how he introduced himself! As Raoul. We had no idea. We thought he was just, you know, a soldier following orders."

"I'm surprised he didn't tell you. He's Raoul Aguilero, the Commander-in-Chief. They're named after his great uncle who helped usher in the first real democracy in San Balanque. Unfortunately, it didn't last long."

The ambassador and his wife exchange baffled looks.

"Does that make this worse, knowing he's the leader?" Lena asks.

"I'm not sure," says the ambassador, his dark eyebrows gathering. "It's surprising. He's been so informal. And very genial. Not the devil he's portrayed in the press."

"I suppose it's a good thing," Katrina says. "I worried what the people higher up might do. But if Raoul is at the top, well—" she glances at her son with a reassuring look "—he'll take good care of us. Don't you agree, Nils?"

"Yes, I'm quite sure he'll keep us safe as promised."

Katrina strokes her son's head reassuringly. "Erik, dear, go ask Antonio if he'll let you have a snack. No sweets though. Fruit and cheese."

"*M-o-m*," he says, protesting.

"Go now." She scoots him away and watches until he's out of the room.

"Perhaps the commander wanted to be personally responsible for your safety," Lena suggests. "Have you talked to him at length?"

"We've had several long conversations," said the ambassador. "He's extremely interested in learning all about our country, how our social democracy works. It's what they want here, he says."

Lena glances around the room. "I was surprised to find you have such lovely accommodations. Have you been treated well?"

Katrina nods. "They have a wonderful chef!"

The ambassador leans forward. "What have you heard on the outside? Do you know how long they will keep us?"

"No," Lena says, "I don't even know what the ransom is, or if they've made their ask yet, do you?"

"They want five-hundred-thousand dollars cash," the ambassador says, 'and to have their manifesto printed in major newspapers and read on major radio stations. Both here and in Sweden. And some political prisoners released."

Katrina gives a hopeful frown. "That doesn't seem too difficult, does it? I mean, considering."

"I think our prime minister will go along with these demands. I'm not sure about Ortiz. If he doesn't, it could cause a major incident between the two countries," the ambassador says.

"What if he refuses to go along?" Katrina asks her husband anxiously.

"Enough political pressure will be put on Ortiz to meet those demands, I'm sure" He squeezes his wife's hand. "What I don't want," he adds, turning toward Lena, "is anyone barging in here and trying to free us in the meantime! Please tell your readers that!"

CHAPTER 36

"I'm sorry I doubted you," Lena tells Raoul, her head resting on his shoulder. Carlos is driving them to a safehouse in the next province where Lena can write her piece. "I'm in. All the way. I promise. Although you may need to reassure me from time to time when I begin to doubt—or lend me your Bhagavad Gita," she adds, grinning up at him.

He laughs. "I'd be happy to. Doubting, questioning, these are good things. They help us reassess events as they unfold. Find out the truth and decide for yourself."

She pets the back of his hand. "I wish I could stay here with you. I don't want to go back."

"I was thinking the same thing."

"What? Really?"

"I'd like you to stay on as my secretary, take notes, record conversations, write letters and communiques . . .. Can you do that?"

"Of course! I'd love to."

"I'll be travelling these next few months, and you'll come with me for the most part. Sometimes you'll have to stay behind and wait. You can work on your own articles then or collect more stories to add to the ones you already have." He looks down at her and smiles.

"I'm so happy!" Lena says, hugging his arm.

He laughs at her. "You are so easy to please. This is one of the things I love most about you. Tonight, I promise to do a lot more pleasing."

The new safehouse is a small two-bedroom cottage with a barn in the back. The cottage hasn't been used in a while, so Lena spends the first few hours sweeping and dusting and putting sheets on the beds. Raoul and Carlos explore the grounds, discussing what's needed to make this a safe haven for Lena when Raoul is away.

That night, the first time they've been together after two months apart, Lena explores Raoul's body as if she's never seen it before, as if she hasn't already memorized every inch.

Yes, this two-inch scar on his stomach, a white slash surrounded by darker skin, looking so vulnerable, so innocent, needing so many kisses.

Ah, yes, the feel of his muscled back, the slope of his shoulder blades, that lovely rivulet travelling his spine, and this sweet dip right before the rise of his buttocks, bulging like boulders. *I remember this, all this I love, all him, all mine.*

She turns him over and explores the grassy meadow of his chest, the firm mounds where his dark nipples rise. She teases them with her tongue. He tastes sweet and salty. Her hand reaches toward that wild thicket between his thighs, playing with the lushness she finds there, all those soft, mobile parts, so unlike the rest of his body, till that firmer member rises, strong and hard. Demanding attention. She moves her mouth there and waits to hear the sounds it entices, the hitched breath, the low moan, the dark growl that grows until he flips her over and plays the same game on all her parts. Until finally the two are so aroused, so poised to explode, he enters her with one long thrust, and she melts around him. Soon they are shuddering in each other's arms, praising and stroking and whispering all the endearments she remembers so well.

I never want to forget this, she thinks. *I will play this song, this symphony of our twining bodies and stroking fingers, our sighs and caresses, over and over till time out of mind.*

The next day, Lena and Raoul go about the pretense of being separate beings fulfilling their normal duties and all appears ordinary. Yet, even then, Lena feels every breath she takes is his breath, and she knows from the way his nostrils fill when he looks at her it's the same for him.

But when her piece on the ambassador's family is done, her interview and film sent by courier to Humberto to publish, Raoul takes her to the field behind the barn for target practice.

Lena learned how to shoot a pistol during combat training, so now she shows off what she can do. Raoul stands behind her and praises her, then leans in to spread her legs a little wider, just so. To pull her shoulders back. To wrap his arm around her stomach so he can feel how she's concentrating her breath. To whisper instructions seductively into her ear. Or maybe it only seems seductive because his voice, whether soft or firm or commanding, does something to her insides, as if every cell of her being is hot-wired.

While she's in this highly charged attentive state of mind, he tells her to let go of everything, all thoughts, all intentions. He tells her to breathe deeply, steadily, while letting all thoughts drain away.

"The key is just to be, to wait without purpose. To get yourself, the pistol, the target out of the way, free of all intent. To see all these things as one thing, not separate. It's normal for us to breathe in and out without intention. To blink without intention. Now you aim for the target the same way. You pull the trigger without intent. It happens by itself for no reason at all. In that state of mind, the bullet finds the target effortlessly."

She tries doing as he says and finds her aim steadily improving. The next day, Raoul tests her self-defense skills. He has her walk away from him and grabs her from behind. Has her facing him while he attacks from the front, throws her to the ground and mounts her. She fights back using her hands and knees and elbows the way Fiona taught her, but each time he overcomes her. Before long, his assaults don't seem like training anymore. She becomes angry and frustrated, determined to disable him enough to get away. She does not hold back, but neither does he, and their encounters are painful.

"This isn't fair! You're so much bigger and better trained!"

He cocks his head. "Do you think your attacker will not be?"

"I've had enough of this!" she says and walks away.

He grabs her by the waist, lifting her off the ground. "We're done when I say we are. When I see progress, Malenque. So far, you've shown yourself to be as helpless as a kitten."

That riles her up. Her face turns red, and her claws come out. At the first opening, she scratches him with her nails and tries to gouge his eye.

He laughs and holds her off, but says, "This is good. I wasn't expecting that. Give me more."

She attacks him again and he wrestles her to the ground, pinning down her arms and legs. Her breath comes in painful, angry gasps. She feels so helpless, her eyes smarting, the dreaded tears starting to rise. She twists her face away, hoping he doesn't see. But he does.

He doesn't let her up, but his hold softens. He looks curiously at her. "These tears. Where are they coming from?"

"What do you mean, where are they coming from! My eyes, damn you. Let me go."

"No, we must get to the bottom of this. What are you feeling when they start to rise?"

She thinks. "Helpless. Angry. Frustrated. Ashamed." With that last word, a fresh wave of tears washes through her.

He moves off her then and tries to pull her into his lap, but she pushes away and rises, swiping at the tears. He sits on the grass looking up at her. "Come," he says.

She shakes her head.

"Please," he says, reaching for her.

"You come to me," she says.

He slowly rises, then gently, tentatively, takes her in his arms, resting his chin on her head. "We must work through this because the tears, if they come under attack, will undo you. And they will embolden your attacker."

"But what can I do? They come unbidden."

"It comes when you're feeling angry and helpless, and that brings on a sense of shame, is that it?" Raoul asks. She nods. "Okay, here's what we do. Anger is good when fierce feelings are directed outward, onto your attacker. But if the anger is matched with a sense of helplessness, that's when shame comes, and anger turns inward. You blame yourself because you feel helpless. You need to turn the anger outward again."

"How do I do that?"

"Just knowing what's causing the tears will help redirect your anger outward. But even better would be finding a way to displace the anger. Anger is hard to control. Sometimes it strengthens us. But it can also weaken us, cause us to make poor choices. The imperturbable mind is the secret of warfare, say the samurai. Better than anger is a sense of confidence and calm. That comes with much practice. The more you practice self-defense, the more confidence you build, the more control you feel, and the calmer you become."

"So, more practice, that's what you're saying. And turning my anger outward, not inward." Already she's feeling more hopeful, less helpless.

"Yes, but mental practice is just as important. The most successful battles take place in your mind before you face the enemy. Think, if all these ways I overpowered you today happened in a real confrontation, how could you have done better? What if the enemy pinned you on the ground as I did? What if he raped you? How could you get the upper hand in your mind and heart even if horrendous things are happening to your body? Think on these things. Prepare for them. That's how you will survive. And survival is the ultimate defeat of the enemy." He pushes her back to look into her eyes again.

"When the storm is too strong, the trees that survive are the ones that bend the lowest without breaking. Lay low, knowing this storm will pass. And if it doesn't, if death is the inevitable outcome, how will you face death? Think these things through. Each outcome is less fearful when you do." He stops. The intensity with which he's looking at her is unnerving. His grip on her shoulders sharpens.

"We all die. If it comes in battle, or in prison, how will you do it, Malenque? How did your namesake do it? For love. For love. Let the love which inspired you to become a freedom fighter allow you to die as one. With that love and sense of pride in your heart.

"We are fighting for our liberty, our homes and family, our dignity. This fight is personal, which is a good thing. Making it personal brings us to the battle. But making it impersonal brings us through it. When we fight, it's better to make it impersonal. The enemy becomes what's standing between us and what we love, and therefore it must be defeated. But it's not hate in our hearts, not outrage—it's the calm, unperturbable mind of the warrior: Love, honor, pride. That's what steels our hearts, sharpens our minds, and strengthens our bodies. That's how we win. Even in death."

That night and during the following days as they practice, Lena thinks about these things. And when she does, she feels calmer and more in control, better able to manage her tears and her anger. But she's not sure she'll be able to do any of this if she's fighting for her life, if she's being raped or has a gun to her head. Still it's comforting knowing she has this tool to turn to when needed.

After a week working hard at target practice and self-defense, they hear good news. President Ortiz and Sweden are ready to meet their demands. Archbishop Martinez is recruited to negotiate the ransom for the ambassador's family and oversee the release of fifty Aguilero prisoners.

The *Aguilero Manifesto* is published in major newspapers across Europe and Latin America, including San Balanque. Lena's interview has already been published in many of the same newspapers. The whole operation is a huge success. They gained international recognition for themselves and their cause. They proved their humanity in caring for the hostages and their expertise in gaining the upper hand in negotiations. They replenished their arms and ammunition with the hostage money. And they inspired the people with their prowess and brought in many new recruits and supporters.

"It's time to take a victory lap," Raoul says.

CHAPTER 37

The next six weeks they visit villages and towns that support the Aguileros, as well as smaller military outposts and larger training camps. Women in many towns and villages form sewing groups to supply the Aguileros with camouflage nets and bandages. They collect donations of food, medical supplies, boots, socks, candy, and comic books for the troops.

"In some ways," Raoul tells Lena, "these tours are our most important mission by uniting all those who support us. We help them recognize how essential their contributions are to our success. This way, we maintain a united front with a common cause."

As they travel, Raoul talks to Lena this way, using her as a sounding board, and she learns much in the process, like why the Miskits support them, how they've been oppressed for centuries, and how the Aguileros promised them a place in their government. She also learns about the high-level recruits they have hiding in plain sight: the mistress of one of Ortiz' most trusted generals, the secretary of a cabinet member, the son of a senator.

Lena's main task, however, is taking shorthand at Raoul's meetings with captains and commanders, village and tribal elders, and influential business and labor leaders. She writes dispatches to send by courier to other Aguilero leaders. She and Raoul rise early, work hard all day, and fall into bed exhausted each night.

When they reach the Caribbean again, Raoul takes Lena to a small, isolated resort where long curls of turquoise spill onto sugar-dusted beaches. They were only supposed to stay one night before heading to

Camp Horchata, where Lena had combat training nearly five months ago. But they end up staying three blissful days.

The resort is owned by an Aguilero and consists of five cabanas. It's June, the beginning of the wet season, so most tourists have left. Carlos and Benito, a new lieutenant to replace Bernard who was promoted to commander of Camp Horchata, stay in the cabana next to Lena and Raoul.

On their last morning at the resort, a cool sea breeze finds its way through the cabana's open doors and wakes Lena. Raoul sleeps beside her on his stomach, one splayed hand covering her breast. She gently lifts his hand and slips away, stepping out onto the deck to catch the cooling breeze. It's well past dawn and the humidity is fierce. Islands from the Santa Lucia archipelago float lazily on the sea's misty surface like a distant dream.

She's stepping into her damp shorts to go for a swim when she's startled by urgent banging at the door. Raoul is instantly on his feet, pistol in hand. He glances out the curtain and then opens the door. It's Carlos.

"A courier arrived. Camp Horchata has been bombed."

Bernardo greets Raoul and Lena when they arrive at camp that afternoon. His face is smeared with dirt and his arm in a bloody sling. "It happened before dawn while we were sleeping. The first strike hit the Commander Headquarters, like that was their prime target. The others seemed more haphazard."

Lena stares in horror at the devastation around her, confirming Daniel's intel about a possible air raid. "Thank God you weren't asleep in the headquarters when they attacked!"

Bernard nods. "We expected you and Raoul to arrive two days ago, so I moved into the officers' barracks. But if you had been here . . .."

We wouldn't have survived, Lena realizes, looking at the pile of smoking rubble where she and Raoul made love the last time they were here.

The training field is pitted with craters where bombs missed their target. Some soldier barracks were destroyed, but not the ones protected by camouflage netting, which considerably reduced casualties. The officers' barracks and the ammunitions factory were spared. But the bakery is mostly rubble.

Two platoons left days earlier on a mission and so were spared, along with the new recruits training in the jungle. That included Sergeant Hernandez and Jose, the fifteen-year-old boy Lena trained with who was now assisting him. Bernard's own nephews, John and James, were spared with only light injuries like his own. Still the causalities were devastating. Thirty-one people were killed, their bodies covered with blankets, lined up outside the field hospital. Twice as many were injured, half critically. Inside the small hospital wounded soldiers lie on beds and cots and blankets spread on the floor. Several had limbs blown off. Many were pockmarked with shrapnel but expected to survive. One man lies on a makeshift operating table where Leonardo, who stayed on after training, is stitching up a cavity wound. Rachel attends him.

"Will he live?" Lena asks, looking at the unconscious man, his face bearing the red ugly marks of shrapnel.

"Hard to know," Leonardo says, peeling off his surgical gloves. "We'll scc tomorrow."

"There's hope," Rachel tells her as she tucks a blanket around him.

Several other medics besides Rachel and Leonardo attend the wounded, one of which is Tomás. A bloody-soaked bandage is wrapped around his side. Raoul goes to his brother, kisses him and pulls his head to his. Lena flinches at the dark, flat, almost reptilian look in Tomás' eyes as he gazes at her over Raoul's shoulder. Whether his fierce look is directed at her or the pain he's suffering, or the enemy who did this, is hard to say. Lena leaves them alone to talk.

She finds Diego, the mechanic she trained with, lying on a cot. He too stayed on, assigned to the mechanic pool. She winces when she sees his badly mangled leg, a bloody tourniquet tied above the knee. He is grimacing in pain when she comes to his side and takes his hand. "What can I do? How can I help?"

His face is gray. "They gave me something for the pain, but it hasn't kicked in yet," he says through gritted teeth.

"What did the doctor say?"

"Wait and see. He's hoping to save my leg, but there's others worse off he must help first."

"More medics and doctors are headed this way. You'll get help soon."

He nods, but it's clear he doesn't want to hold a conversation, so she squeezes his hand and whispers in his ear. "You are strong, Diego. You will survive this."

She travels from bed to bed, doing what she can to help and comfort—bringing canteens of water to parched lips, pulling a blanket over someone who is shivering, helping raise the head of another who is not gravely wounded and wants to look around the room. He's chatty and asks questions. What happened? How many killed? How many injured?

"We'll pay them back twice as hard," he swears. And then his eyes tear.

"Angela," he says. "She's gone. We were on guard duty when a bomb exploded nearby. We both fell. I crawled over to her, but a piece of metal went right through her chest. Her eyes were open, but there was no one there. A minute before she was talking about her boyfriend at the University. He was fighting for the cause too, but all he got to do was make protest posters and march, she said, laughing. Her work was much more exciting. That's when they came, two of them flying in like Pterodactyls. I know it's crazy, but that's what they looked like to me, dipping low like that, like they were ready to grab us up in their claws. 'Run,' I told her, but it was too late. She'd been so happy. And then, nothing. Just like that."

His head dips and he's crying. Lena puts her arms around him and brings him close. Holds him until the sobs subside.

Lena and Raoul spend three days helping in the hospital and around camp, awaiting the new medics and reinforcements. Tomás told Raoul he arrived at camp that morning right before they struck. He had a new driver from Aruba whose wife was about to bear their first child. Tomás promised he could leave as soon as he dropped him off so he could be there for the birth. But when they arrived, Tomás asked him to wait, saying he wouldn't be long. The man insisted he must go, which made

Tomás suspicious, but not overly so. Until the planes came. The driver looked at Tomás with terror in his eyes and started running. That's when Tomás said he knew the driver betrayed them. He knew the planes were coming, that's why he wanted to leave. Tomás shot him as he was trying to escape.

Lena frowns when Raoul tells her this. "But why shoot him? Wouldn't Tomás want to find out what he knew?"

Raoul shrugs. "The heat of the moment? Tomás left already for Aruba to find out if the traitor's wife really was ready to give birth, if others knew of his betrayal."

"Raoul," Lena says, shaking her head. "The driver may have been running from the planes, not a traitor at all."

Raoul puts his hand on her arm. "Wait, there's more. Tomás came here to tell me we have intelligence about collaboration between Ortiz and Somoza, the president of Nicaragua, who our Sandinista allies are fighting against. They are spreading disinformation to pit our two guerilla forces against each other. So, I need to meet with the Sandinistas and sort this out. We don't need another enemy on our southern border to contend with."

"You'll be leaving soon?"

"Yes, but I'll take you back to the safehouse first. All this happening at once seems suspicious. Tomás can get to the bottom of what's going on here, while I try to do the same with our Sandinista friends." He takes her hand. "And you will write about what happened here and give it to Humberto to publish. We'll need photographs too."

Lena moves through the camp photographing the devastation she sees: the bombed barracks and headquarters building, the hospital overrun with wounded soldiers, doctors and nurses operating on patients, a blanket pulled over the face of a soldier who died.

A wide-angle shot taken from the hospital doorway looks across the devastation of the bombed field to an immaculate blue sky and brilliant rainforest beyond. The contrast between the striking beauty of what lies in the distance and the brutality of what lies at her feet—the wounded, the dead, the dying—wrenches her heart. She and Raoul would have been among them had they arrived as planned. The horror of that realization is followed by the sting of guilt that she and Raoul survived while others did not. For the first time since she arrived, tears stream down her face.

It's a long five-hour drive back to the cottage safehouse over rugged terrain. Raoul spends much of the time talking about his coming mission, explaining the complicated relationship between the Sandinistas and Aguileros.

"We are natural allies, in some ways blood brothers, sharing a common culture, a common history, a common enemy—dictators propped up by the United States. It's natural to support and encourage each other, to share intelligence and collaborate when it's in our mutual interest. But we are also competitors, seeking to acquire the same limited resources: weapons, ammunition, funding from sympathetic groups beyond our borders. And now Ortiz and Somoza are trying to exploit those fault lines, to drive a wedge between us and cause us to fight among ourselves. I'll be meeting with Carlos Fonseca, the leader of the Sandinistas, to find ways to de-conflict our operations and cement our cooperation and collaboration with each other."

As he speaks, Lena rests her head on his chest, the sound of his voice rumbling against her ear until her eyelids close and his voice becomes the sea crashing on the shores of her dreams.

That night at the safehouse Raoul stays up late, studying maps and taking notes, planning his meeting with Fonseca. When he comes to bed, Lena briefly wakes as his arms pull her close. In the morning their lovemaking is a passionate burst, and then a tender kiss and meeting of foreheads before he slips out of her arms and is gone.

CHAPTER 38

Lena buries herself in work. Missing Raoul is like a painful pinch in her chest. She puts her hand on the spot and rubs it as tears threaten to rise, still raw from the death and destruction she witnessed. Besides the story about the bombing, there's dispatches to write and a new internal document about supply chains to edit—and then there's Bianca.

Since Raoul took Carlos with him, he sent for Bianca to join Benito as Lena's two bodyguards while he's away. Lena worried Bianca would be resentful, as she seemed when assigned to help her last time, but she doesn't appear so now. She's as taciturn and reserved as before, reminding her of a young Fiona. But she also seems eager to prove herself at this new assignment and throws herself into the effort—not only taking turns with night watches and daily patrols around the grounds, but preparing meals, keeping things tidy, and helping Lena compile and staple documents.

If Bianca is a young Fiona, it's a vulnerable and inexperienced Fiona. It's obvious Fiona is highly educated, but Lena doubts Bianca has more than a sixth-grade education. Few village girls do. She's terribly proud of her younger sister, Marta, though, who is attending a small Catholic college while working as a courier for the Aguileros. Bianca now looks at Lena in a way Fiona never did, as if she's transferred some of her reverence for Raoul, her commander, to Lena. Perhaps because Raoul refers to Lena as being "The Malenque of Old," she enjoys an elevated status in Bianca's mind.

Four days after Raoul leaves, a courier drops off mail, including a letter from Aunt Margo dated June 8. That was the date Lena graduated, the night she got so drunk she let Lonny feel her up. It seems impossible that was only a year ago! She feels at least ten years older now. She hasn't heard from Lonny since leaving California, although she sent him several postcards after she first arrived.

Whenever she thinks of Lonny now, she thinks of Daniel. They both occupy a tender spot in her heart. She hasn't seen Daniel since Curico. Everyone seems so far away. Even Raoul. The longer she's been in San Balanque, the more infrequent her aunt's letters have become, although they are filled with the same breezy nonsense as always: her Geoff dilemma—will they or won't they marry—her latest dinner parties, and juiciest local gossip. Lena thinks Margo and chatty Humberto back in Curico would get along fabulously!

Her father's letters, also infrequent, are shorter. He's back in Santa Barbara, not ordained yet, but setting up a Zendo in their art studio where he meditates with other Zen devotees. Lena wrote him about Raoul turning to the *Bhagavad Gita* for moral guidance. That pleased him.

"Are you alright?" Bianca asks, watching Lena's face as she reads.

"I'm fine. Just a little sad, people I miss and haven't seen in a while. Memories of boys I used to know who were sweet on me." She smiles. "Have you ever had a boyfriend? Anyone you're sweet on?"

Bianca blushes. "Not really."

"Aw, that means you have," Lena teases. "Tell me. Is it someone I know? Someone in camp, another Aguilero?" Bianca's blush deepens to a dark flush.

"I'm sorry, I shouldn't pry."

Bianca looks down at her hands as she nervously straightens a pile of papers on the desk. "No, it's all right. I want to tell you." She looks up at Lena with a stricken smile, like she's shocked at what she's about to reveal, but happy to tell someone, finally. "It's Pepe."

Lena's eyes widen. "Pepe! Of course. Does he feel the same about you?"

"Oh, no! And you can't tell him."

"I won't. I promise. But if he knew, perhaps you'd find he likes you too."

Bianca looks down again. "Sometimes I see him looking at me . . . like, you know . . .."

"I do know. That's a good sign."

She smiles shyly at Lena. "I think he might be interested, but now's not a good time. We're too young, and we have other duties. I want to keep things the way they are for now"

"I understand. Still, it's exciting, and I'm glad you told me. Who knows? Perhaps we'll be sisters-in law someday!"

Bianca looks so shocked, Lena has to laugh. *Who knows? Stranger things have happened.*

Three days later, Pepe shows up. Lena watches from the doorway as he jumps out of the jeep with all the enthusiasm and elasticity of youth. He seems like a more carefree version of Raoul, having none of his steadiness and gravitas, but the same arrogant cockiness she saw earlier on.

Pepe smiles widely as he mounts the porch steps to greet Lena with a hug. She needed that. A little touch of Raoul. She looks behind her to see Bianca's big eyes as she comes to the front door. She had been in the kitchen making lunch. Now she serves lemonade and sandwiches to Lena and Pepe as they sit at a table on the front porch.

"Come join us, Bianca," Lena says, patting a chair beside her.

"Yes, Bianca. It's good to see you," Pepe says, stretching out his legs. "We peons at Camp Plantain miss you now that you've ascended to higher places."

Bianca blushes and ducks her head. That's when Benito comes trudging up to the porch with a rifle over his shoulder. It's Bianca's turn to patrol. "There's sandwiches and lemonade in the kitchen," she tells Benito and waves to Pepe's driver to join him. Then she grabs her rifle and heads out the door.

Pepe's gaze follows her. "A shy one, that."

"Not so shy when you spend more time getting to know her."

"Perhaps," he says, sounding so much like Raoul, her heart pings.

"So, what brings you here? Raoul's off on a mission, as you must know."

"Yes, Tomás told me."

"You've seen him since his injury? How's he doing?"

"He's doing well. He was lucky. So were you and Raoul, showing up after the raid instead of before, as planned."

"Yes, we were lucky—" she starts.

"This is what concerns us," Pepe says, "that the raid was timed when both brothers were supposed to be there."

"Has Tomás made progress finding out who betrayed us?"

"He interrogated people in Aruba, but nothing concrete was revealed."

"Did his driver actually have a wife who was giving birth?"

"Yes, his son was born while Tomás was there."

So, he was telling the truth about his wife. Lena cannot speak, thinking of that poor young, widowed mother and the father who never got a chance to see his son, who may not have been the traitor after all.

"But that's not why I'm here. I'm here on my mother's behalf."

Pepe explains that as things have been heating up, the brothers have become increasingly concerned about their mother's and sister's safety. It would be too easy for Ortiz to grab them to use as bait or force them to give up information about the brothers' whereabouts.

"We need to get them out of the country. And Mother's finally agreed to go. But she won't leave until she meets you. So Tomás sent me to bring you to her."

"Me! Whatever for?" Her brow furrows. "Does Raoul know you're getting her out? That she wants to see me?"

"No. I doubt he'd approve, it's too dangerous. Federales watch our home constantly. But we have a plan to help them escape, and you could be part of that—if you agree. Two soldiers dressed as nuns will go with Father Sierra when he makes his weekly visit. Then our mother and sister will put on the habits and leave with him. We'll create a diversion, so the Federales don't check the nuns too closely when they leave. A boat will be waiting to transport them to Mexico.

"But since Mother insists on seeing you before she goes, we thought you and Bianca could be the ones posing as nuns. There's an escape route through the back woods where a car will be waiting." He looks earnestly at her. "Will you help us? You're almost family now. It would be good for you to meet our mother and sister before they leave."

Lena frowns, feeling torn. She would love to meet Raoul's mother and sister and help them escape. But it seems strange this is happening while Raoul is away.

"I don't know," she says. "If Raoul wouldn't approve, how could I?"

Pepe takes a small blue envelope with a red seal from his front pocket and hands it to her. "Mother gave this to Father Sierra to give to you."

"And Tomás, he agrees with all this?"

"He does not. But he cannot get our mother to change her mind. She refuses to leave until she sees you. And the window of opportunity to get them out safely is closing. He knows he'll have to deal with Raoul's wrath when he finds out we've involved you. But it can't be helped. Our mother's safety comes first."

Not my safety, Lena thinks. But knowing Tomás doesn't approve of this plan makes it seem more palatable. She takes the letter inside the house to read in privacy, slips her finger under the seal, and unfolds the letter, revealing a fine and fluid script.

My dear Malenque,

It is my heart's desire before I leave my beloved San Balanque to meet the woman who stands by my son's side, who everyone says is a reincarnation of the Malenque of Old.

My eldest son Tomás stands as firm and strong as a lone pine tree that discourages nearby company because he needs no other. My youngest son Pepe sways like a sapling who will bend whichever way love blows, and I will have my hands full keeping him firmly grounded.

But my middle son Raoul, who is so like his father, is a mystery to me. I fear I have neglected him. I left him to his father's care, and when he died, I sent him away with Tomás to protect them. When Raoul returned, he was a stranger. No longer the bookworm but the charismatic leader who won the hearts of all he met. Yet my own heart could not open to him.

Raoul is like a tree whose roots travel to every part of this country, holding it together. He is so entwined with our people's future that I fear for him. Not that he will be broken by this country like his father was but absorbed into its soil with no life apart. Or so I worried until I heard of his great love for you.

Do you truly fill that place for him that the Malenque of Old did for her brother, a stalwart partner to stand ever at his side? Will you be what he needs to disentangle him from the fate I fear? This I must know.

Please come to me before I leave. And take my heart, and hopefully my blessing, back to Raoul, my middle son, the son of my husband's heart, whom I have neglected too long.

And show this note to no one. Especially Raoul.

Yours,

Eva Carrillo Diaz Aguilero

Lena folds the letter back into the envelope and tucks it into a zippered pocket inside her rucksack. She looks out the window at Pepe, laughing in the bright sunshine with Benito and his driver as if war is not a serious matter, as if smuggling his mother and sister out of the country and asking her to pose as a nun is just how things go sometimes. It's true, he is like that sapling his mother calls him. But Tomás seems less like a lone pine than a lone wolf to her. And Raoul . . . he's no mystery at all to Lena. But his mother is right about him being so rooted to his cause nothing will turn him from it. Lena will always be by his side, and if assuring his mother of this soothes her anxieties about her son, she will go to her. And truly, when Raoul returns, he might be angry she went, but he will understand why she had to.

CHAPTER 39

E va Carrillo Diaz Aguilero has the austere face and regal bearing of a patrician matriarch. Her profile could be stamped on the back of a Roman coin. Wide dark eyes, prominent cheekbones, and a long thin nose. Beneath that is the lush mouth Raoul inherited. But nothing else about her is like him.

Her dark hair is upswept into a pile of imposing waves. Her dark green, long-sleeved dress is simple but elegant, revealing a slim and surprisingly fragile-looking figure, despite her stiff, impassive posture. Lena isn't sure if Eva's demeanor is meant to intimidate her or if it's how she always is. Her smile appears stilted as she moves forward to take Lena's hand and press it between hers, which are dry and cool. But her head is cocked, her eyes curious and appraising. Perhaps there's something of Raoul in that curious, appraising look.

Earlier that morning Pepe drove Lena and her bodyguards, Bianca and Benito, to a rendezvous with Father Sierra, who was waiting a few miles from the entrance to the hacienda. He was a tall thin man with a strong, determined look when he greeted them and thanked them for coming. He was the one who learned the Federales would be coming soon for Eva and Angelica and urged Tomás to smuggle them out of the country. Lena and Bianca donned the two nun's habits Father Sierra brought with him, pulling the black robes over their fatigues and tucking their long braids inside the wide white bandeaus and coifs that fit snuggly across their foreheads and around their necks.

They spent the week since Pepe's arrival at the safehouse preparing for the operation. Benito had been hesitant at first, not sure if he should agree to this operation. It's his responsibility to keep Lena safe. But between Pepe, Lena, and Bianca, and being assured that Tomás, the commander of all the armies, approved this operation, he finally relented.

Pepe went over the plan one last time with everyone before they headed to the hacienda. "As far as we can tell, only two guards are at the gate today. They will question Father Sierra about the visit and may even search his car, but then they'll let you through. You have one hour to visit and exchange habits with my mother and sister. At two p.m. sharp, you should have them in the car ready to drive, Father. We will be creating a diversion—you will hear it—that will draw the guards away from the gate, allowing you to pass through unmolested. But if something goes wrong and a guard stays, the women should keep their heads down, and if anyone attempts to enter the car, put your foot on the gas and plow past them. If they try to follow, we'll be waiting to head them off.

"Lena, when the diversion occurs, you and Bianca should escape out the back door and run as fast as you can to the shelter of the woods. I know them well. We played in them often as children. I provided Bianca with a map that will take you across the mountain to the rendezvous point where Benito and his men will pick you up. I've gone over the map in minute detail with Bianca. She's a fine soldier and will get you safely home, Lena. I promise. Do you trust me?"

She swallowed hard before nodding. "Of course. But where will Tomás be?"

"He'll be waiting for our mother and sister at another rendezvous point where he'll take them to the ship for their escape." He looked each one in the eye. "Do you have any questions?"

It seemed strange to see Pepe in a position of authority, looking so cool and competent. More and more, he was like Raoul. But it also seemed strange that Pepe rather than Tomás, the more experienced soldier, was leading this operation. Lena's queasy unease quickened.

"Good. We'll see you after then." He slapped his hand against the black Buick as Father Sierra took off with them down the road. All went well at the gate. Father Sierra was questioned, as expected, and a guard peeked inside at Lena and Bianca. They were careful to hide their boots beneath the robes. He waved them through.

Now Lena stands before Raoul's elegantly dressed mother wearing fatigues and looking back at her with the same curious, appraising look she's being given. She feels none of the warmth and concern for her son that she read in her letter. She wonders if Eva simply wanted to meet her rival. Not a rival for her son's affection, but for becoming the matriarch of the Aguilero dynasty.

"So, you are the one everyone is talking about?" Eva says with a touch of amused disdain, her gaze moving over Lena's attire. "Very soldierlike. But you are prettier than the poster. I would never have guessed you were the same woman."

"That was intentional," Lena says. She turns to Bianca, standing awestruck a few steps behind. "Please say hello to our Comrade Bianca Alamosa. She has long wanted to meet you, the mother of the Aguileros. You are much esteemed."

This is true. Though few have met her, the Aguileros regard this woman with great admiration. She's the one who raised the three brothers who are leading the revolution. She was married to their father who, along with their great-uncle, were martyrs for the cause. Bianca told Lena how honored she feels to be part of this mission to save this great woman.

"Ah, of course," Eva says, looking at Bianca for the first time. She must see the look of awe on her pale face, for she offers a regal smile and holds out her hand. "Thank you, Bianca, for your service to my sons and to this great cause."

Bianca looks almost ready to curtsy, but instead she takes the proffered hand and says with solemn dignity, "I am honored to meet you and be of service."

Eva smiles and turns to Father Sierra. "Please take our comrade here to the kitchen for refreshments while I speak with Malenque." He gives her a small bow and ushers out Bianca.

"Please, have a seat," Eva says, indicating the wing-backed chair across from her as she sits upon a red satin sofa with a carved ebony frame.

"Your home is lovely," Lena says as she surveys the room, and it is. Lovely, elegant, and cold. Was it like this, even when Raoul was a child?

"It's been in the family for generations," she tells Lena.

"Your father's home, or your husband's?" Lena asks, knowing the answer. She's not sure why she asks this. Perhaps it's to pull Eva down a peg, since she seems so smug in the power she holds over Lena, coercing her to come to her this way on what seems false pretenses, and presenting herself in this regal manner. Or perhaps it's simply because she looks at Lena the way Tomás does: with disdain.

Eva's lips, which had been parted in a smile of pride, come together. She gives Lena a long appraising look. "And what is the point of that question?"

"Only to better know you," Lena answers.

Eva looks down at her lap and moves the folds of her dress to fall more elegantly. When she looks up, she gives Lena a wry smile. "It is, as you guessed, my husband's estate. My own family home was more modest." She pauses and looks Lena in the eye. "And your family's home?"

Lena smiles. "My father, like your husband, was a modest professor. But his father was quite wealthy. We don't have an estate as you do. But the ocean view from our garden is spectacular."

Eva folds her hands in her lap. "I see why my son was drawn to you."

"And why is that?"

"For your fearlessness."

This surprises Lena and her face must show it, for Eva's smile seems quite smug.

"I'm not sure what you mean," Lena says.

Eva lifts her chin, as if feeling she's regained the upper hand in this conversation.

"All my sons are fearless. But Raoul most of all. I didn't see it when he was young. A mere bookworm, I thought. Raoul surprised me, coming back as he did after being educated in the States and seeming so . . . commanding. So much like my husband when I first met him. His strength, his intelligence, his devotion to his country, his opposition to Ortiz. I was in awe of my husband. He was the only one who could cow me, which made me admire him more, that he had that power. Raoul was the same when he returned. And I see that same quality in you."

Lena scoffs. "Surely you are not cowed by me—"

"Hardly," Eva says with a dismissive wave. "The fearlessness I see in you, which I saw in my husband and now in Raoul, is not to be intimidated by power. They were fearless in their pursuit of what they saw as the greater good. And willing to sacrifice themselves for that Cause."

She gives Lena a cunning smile, then asks, "You too are ready to die for the cause, are you not?"

Lena raises an eyebrow and decides not to answer. Instead, she asks, "And what of your other sons, do you not see qualities you admire in them too?"

"Of course. Tomás is fearless, but his devotion to the cause is more for toppling Ortiz, the man who crippled his father, more for revenge than justice or the common good."

"And Pepe?"

"Pepe could lean either way. But I see other qualities in Tomás and Pepe I value even more."

"Such as?"

"Their devotion to me."

They let that thought lie silently between them for a moment. Then Lena gives her a challenging look. "So, what is the real reason you wanted to meet me?"

Eva looks back steadily at Lena, a shrewd smile playing on her lips. Then she rises. "I think it's time to get ready for our escape, don't you?"

Lena follows her to the foyer where Eva ascends one of the curved stairways that rise on either side of the room. Her stomach squeezes with apprehension as she watches that slow, regal, rising. Was this visit merely to meet her rival, Lena wonders? Or something more sinister? She thinks of Tomás and the resentment he holds for her, which Lena saw reflected in his mother's eyes. Something isn't right.

She checks her watch. They have twenty minutes until it's time to leave. She turns toward the voices coming from the kitchen. There she finds Bianca sitting at a large country table across from the most beautiful girl Lena has ever seen. Her head is thrown back, her throat like ivory, her blue eyes dancing as she laughs in the most delightful way. Bianca is laughing too. Bianca! When has Bianca ever laughed? She's not seen it.

Bianca quickly stands when she sees Lena. "Have you met Raoul's sister, Angelica?" she asks.

The girl turns her smile toward Lena. She can't be more than fifteen. Her blue-black hair is wavy like Raoul's, but finer, shimmering like a waterfall down her back. She has her mother's fine features, but her face is softer, fuller, with a warm, rosy glow.

"You're Malenque! My new sister," Angelica cries, darting forward to embrace Lena and kiss both cheeks. "You are beautiful, just as everyone said. No wonder Raoul loves you so!" She takes Lena's hands and smiles broadly at her. "We shall be best of friends, I'm sure of it!"

Is this child-like enthusiasm the simplemindedness she's been told about, Lena wonders? If so, it's infectious. She laughs and agrees. "We shall. I feel it too!"

A short while later, Eva comes down the back stairs into the kitchen. Angelica runs up to her and grabs her arm. "Isn't Malenque wonderful, Mama? I love her already!"

Eva pats her daughter's hand affectionately. But Lena sees the ire burning beneath her smile. "We must get ready, darling. Time to put on our habits and pretend we are nuns! Won't that be fun?"

"Oh yes!" She turns to Lena. "Mother plays such wonderful games, and Father Sierra is so accommodating. But I wish we could stay longer with Malenque and Bianca," she says to her mother with a pout. "Bianca is a soldier, did you know that? She has a real gun. Or perhaps this is a game too?" She looks at Lena and seems to see the soldier garb she's wearing for the first time and frowns. "Are we playing a game?"

"Yes, we are," Lena assures her. "Your mother indeed plays such lovely games," she says, giving Eva a knowing look. "You must go with her and do as she says. We will see you again. I promise."

"And then we shall be best friends?"

"Yes, I'm sure of it."

Angelica dances up to Lena, kissing her loudly on the cheek, and does the same to Bianca. She grabs her mother's hand and leads her away. "This will be so much fun! I've never been a nun before. Do you think I will see Christ's face when I put on the habit? Oh, I do hope so!" she says as she starts up the stairs, her mother trailing behind her.

As she leaves, Eva turns to give Lena one last look—a smug, imperial smile. Then they are gone.

CHAPTER 40

At two o'clock Lena watches Eva and her daughter dressed as nuns climb into the back of Father Sierra's Buick where they'll wait for the diversion before leaving. Lena and Bianca head out the back door onto the kitchen patio where herbs in terracotta pots are growing. Bianca opens the map Pepe gave her and spreads it across a patio table, pointing across a grassy meadow behind the hacienda toward a surrounding forest.

"Where those trees part is a path over the mountain to an old dirt road. It used to be a service road, part of the San Juan National Park. But when Ortiz came into power he cut park resources, so no one goes there now."

This isn't rainforest, Lena notes. Here on the western slopes of the Sierra Madre Mountains the terrain is drier, more like the forests she's used to in California, terrain you can hike through without a machete to clear a path. But the meadow they must cross to get to the trees is wide open and unprotected. Wouldn't the Federales be watching the hacienda's back door like they do the front?

When she asks, Bianca shrugs. "Apparently there's been no sighting of Federales back here"

"But—" Lena begins before a loud explosion erupts to the south near the gate.

"The diversion!" Bianca cries. Both women start running across the meadow toward the tree line. Neither have rifles, which would have been too hard to hide in the car, but they have their pistols. They almost make it to the opening in the trees before shots ring out. Bianca pushes Lena ahead, then turns and fires back before following Lena into the forest.

"Shit!" Bianca says. "You were right. Keep going, fast, up, up, up!" she urges. She fires again, then catches up and passes Lena. "Stay close to me," she tells her.

Bianca navigates the steep hill, weaving her way through trees like a Billy goat. There's no clear, discernable path and Lena's not sure how Bianca knows which way to go, but she follows her anyway. When Bianca sees Lena falling behind, she stops to let her catch up, then takes up the rear guard.

More shots ring out. One coming so close to Lena that for a moment she thinks she must be hit. She puts her hands over her ringing ears and keeps climbing. Bianca isn't far behind. She's taken cover and is firing down the mountain at soldiers below.

"Go, go, go!" she tells Lena, who does but has no idea which way to go except straight up, grabbing tree limbs to pull herself up the slope as quickly as possible. When Bianca catches up, she takes Lena's hand and again leads the way, zigzagging as they rush through a clearing, then dive behind bushes.

"They'll have to pass through the clearing to reach us. When they do, we shoot. There are two. You take the one on the left, I'll take the right. But wait until I say go. Got it?"

They lie on their stomachs and stare down at the clearing. Lena points her pistol toward where she thinks the soldiers will appear. Her hand is shaking, and she tries to calm herself the way Raoul taught her. She remembers how his hand pressed against her diaphragm. "Here's where the shot comes from, feel it here." She feels him beside her. She takes a deep breath, and then the soldiers burst through the trees. Lena takes aim, holds her breath, and . . ..

"Now," Bianca says in her low, calm voice.

Lena pulls the trigger at the same time Bianca does. Her target jerks backward and grabs his shoulder. Bianca's target goes rigid and falls straight backward, like a felled tree. They don't wait to see what happens next but jump up and begin running again. Another shot flies by, but wide this time and they keep running. They don't hear anyone following and eventually stop and look back.

"I think they're gone," Bianca says. Then she grins. "Good shot, Malenque."

She's never seen Bianca grin so wide before, this solemn faced woman who reminds her of a younger Fiona. She's never called her Malenque before either. It's always Lena, or comrade, or nothing at all. She feels strangely gifted by this and grins back.

They head up the steep slope again, but before long Lena must pause to catch her breath. She leans against a tree.

"We can't stop," warns Bianca. "They may send dogs after us. We need to hurry to the rendezvous point."

Lena's holding her side, sweat pouring from her body so fast she feels faint. "Okay," she says, pulling away from the tree and starting up the slope again. She doesn't know where the strength to keep climbing comes from, even as every muscle in her body screams for her to stop. Eventually they reach the top of the ridge. Bianca paces along it, looking at her map.

"Here!" she says, pointing downhill where a glimpse of road can be seen. "We're almost there."

The path down is as steep as the path up—and more treacherous. Lena grabs trees and bushes to keep from falling. More than once she's on her butt, sliding until she secures a new foothold. An upslope breeze cools her face, and she feels a burst of exhilaration when she again glimpses the road and sees how close it is.

Bianca gets there first and checks her map. "This way," she says, heading south. The road isn't much more than two rut marks etched into the side of a mountain that falls away on the other side.

Bianca points to a rocky outcrop. "This is where we're supposed to wait."

Lena leans against the rock, her heart pounding furiously, her breath coming in gusts and gushes like a raging river. She tries to calm herself but can't. How can you still a body that's ready to explode?

The distant squeal of an accelerating motor and rat-a-tat-tat of gunfire break the silence. Bianca grabs Lena's hand and pulls her to the road's edge.

"Sounds like our ride has got company. We'll have to jump aboard while the jeep is still moving. Run beside it and grab hold. I'll help push you in. Can you do that?"

Lena nods. They never trained for jumping into moving vehicles. *I can do this, I must.* She looks at her hands, bleeding from the rough handholds needed to climb and wipes them on her pants. *Be calm,* she tells herself sternly. Surprisingly, that helps. She waggles her arms to ease the tension.

The Aguileros' jeep comes into sight, careening down the hill, its tires loose in soft soil.

"There!" shouts Benito. He's standing in the jeep's open door, holding out his arm. The jeep slows.

"Hurry!" Benito says, reaching toward Lena, now running beside them. She gets one foot on the running board and then is lifted inside the back seat with Benito and another soldier. Bianca, still running, grabs hold of the jeep and pulls herself in next to the driver. The roar of a vehicle comes rushing up behind them. Benito pushes Lena's head to the floor. "Stay down."

The rest is a blur. Lena hears the exchange of gunfire. Feels their jeep sway back and forth on the road, flying over bumps where her body rises for a second, then slams down again. She glances back at the pursuing vehicle and watches it fly into the air when it reaches the same steep bump they'd gone over. But their vehicle hits the ground on one wheel and starts to roll. Screams erupt as it tumbles into the steep ravine below. The Aguileros do not stop but keep going as fast as before.

Lena is elated. The men around her are raising fists and shouting in triumph. The adrenaline is pumping so fast through her body now she's shouting with glee. "We did it! Bianca, we made it!"

She turns to look at the woman in the front seat that she considers her friend now, her comrade in arms, her savior. Bianca is facing her, turned backward in her seat, her right hand with her pistol balanced on the seat's back where she'd been shooting at the vehicle behind them.

But Bianca is not shouting with glee. She's not even smiling. She's looking at Lena with shock and dismay. Her hand goes limp and her pistol falls. Her lips part, and blood spills out. She slumps in her seat.

Lena grabs at her, then catapults into the front of the jeep, her leg striking the driver as she does. The jeep lurches, then straightens.

"Watch it!" the driver shouts at her. Then he sees Bianca in her arms. "Christ," he says. Lena presses her hands over the wound, right above Bianca's heart, to staunch the bleeding.

"Stop the car, stop the car!" she screams, but no one listens.

Bianca's gaze is fading. "No, no, no!" Lena tells her. "Stay with me." She cradles Bianca's head in her arms.

"I'm sorry, I'm sorry," Lena tells her. If it hadn't been for her, Bianca wouldn't be here. Bianca's eyes focus for a moment and her mouth opens as if she wants to say something.

Lena bends her ear to her lips.

"I'm not," Bianca says. And when Lena pulls away to look at her again, to try to decipher what she means, she sees the start of another small grin on her lips before her eyes glaze over.

Lena holds her in her arms, sobbing as the jeep careens on and on.

CHAPTER 41

Sharp sheets of rain slant across the field, striking puddles in staccato bursts as they lower Bianca's wooden casket into a muddy grave, then cover it with more mud. A canopy shelters the gravesite where mourners gather. Most who came to the funeral held in the small village church do not follow the procession to the gravesite. But Lena, Pepe, Benito, and a few others, including Marta, Bianca's sister, are there.

The monsoons have come, and the fear is that this coffin and others may rise like boats from the ground and float away. Lena pictures Bianca as she had been in the church before the casket was closed, small and solemn as always, lying in her pine bed, dressed in white, hands crossed over her heart—like an angel taken too soon rather than the warrior woman she was, struck down fulfilling her pledge to the cause.

Lena imagines the casket rising from the mud after they all leave and floating away to a river and from there to the sea where it washes up on a distant shore. She sees Bianca lift the pine lid and step out—a white figure against the green jungle wall behind her—and then go about the business of living a full life, of being a whole woman. But what is not whole about the woman she was, living so purposely and so bravely till the very end?

When the graveside service is over, people begin opening umbrellas and pulling ponchos over their shoulders, stepping from the shelter into the dark downpour, their feet sinking into the mud. Lena waits behind so she can take Marta aside.

"I am so sorry for your loss," she tells her.

Marta is a softer, rounder, version of Bianca, her complexion creamier, her lips fuller. She must be sixteen now and doesn't seem to know who

Lena is. She nods solemnly. "This is the way my sister would have wanted to die, a martyr for the cause. I was told she was saving someone very dear to us when she was killed. That she had been honored to do so."

"This is true. She's a great hero and will be honored as such," Lena says, her voice thickened with grief. She wants to say more, to add that she was with her at the end, held her in her arms as she was dying, but would this have comforted the sister? Or added new anguish? So, she stays silent. Another time perhaps.

"Excuse me," the girl says as she opens her umbrella, stepping into the downpour.

Pepe dashes after her and slips his arm through hers. Lena gathers they've known each other from before. Within a few moments they're swallowed by the rain.

"Come," Benito says to Lena, "It's not safe to tarry here. You should not have come. Raoul would not have approved."

"Raoul would have come. And I have come for him, in spirit at least." *Bianca would be glad I came*, Lena thinks. She still feels her small, delicate body in her arms, the moment her breath, her spirit, seemed to depart, the moment Lena knew it was no longer Bianca in her arms, but a husk of who she'd been—this brave, solemn, and dutiful woman. Lena remembers how shy Bianca was confessing her crush on Pepe, how she laughed with his sister, Angelica, how she grinned when praising Lena for her good shot . . . and there at the end, how Bianca tried to grin again, to say she wasn't sorry to die as a martyr.

Tears rise again and Lena nods to Benito, who holds the umbrella over her head as they leave. The mud swallows her boots as the landscape before them wavers in the rain like a Monet painting. *If it weren't so heartbreaking, it would be beautiful*, she thinks as Benito holds her elbow and leads her forward.

She wants to ask him a thousand questions: Why did no one know Federales were guarding the back door to the hacienda? Why did they insist she play a part in Eva's escape? Why did Eva write a letter to ensure Lena would come? But she can ask none of this. Nor can she tell Raoul when he returns of her suspicions: that his mother and brothers concocted a plan to bring Lena there to be killed. It's too terrible to contemplate. She must rid herself of these thoughts. Even Bianca, if she were here, would not believe this and think Lena a traitor to even suggest it. The Aguilero brothers and their mother are revolutionary icons. Bianca was incredibly honored to be part of the effort to save the Aguilero mother and daughter, to get them safely out of the country. Lena will not take away Bianca's pride at being part of that.

Lena will say nothing. But she'll stay on guard when it comes to Tomás—and even Pepe. Was the sapling that could bend either way, who was as devoted to his mother as his eldest brother, bending in their direction? Or was he too duped?

Raoul returns to the safehouse two weeks later, nine days after Bianca was killed. Furious at the terrible events that transpired in his absence, he interrogates his brothers in private, then Benito and the other soldiers involved. Lena is the last one sent to face him. As she enters the barn where the interrogations were taking place, Raoul's face is as dark and thunderous as when he first arrived. But when he looks up and sees Lena—fairly trembling in her grief and guilt—he strides forward and wraps her in his arms. He tells her how sorry he is that she was made a part of this. Benito was demoted and Pepe reassigned to Camp Horchata under Bernard's command. But Tomás received the worst of his fury. If Raoul has any suspicions about the whole operation the way Lena does, he does not disclose them.

He spends the rest of the afternoon pouring over maps spread across the dining table, looking distraught and discouraged, pulling his fingers through the tangles of his hair, making it stand on end. Lena wishes she could do something to help.

"Can I get you anything to eat, to drink? You barely touched your lunch."

He looks up at her distractedly. "Pardon?"

She puts her hand on his arm. "Aren't you hungry? Can I get you something?"

He smiles, but faintly, almost painfully. "If it makes you feel better."

When she brings him a plate of rice and beans and tries to place it on the table, he motions for her to put it elsewhere. She places it on a side table and comes to stand beside him.

He stiffens. "Don't you have something else you should be doing?"

She is stunned. Never has he sent her away from him.

"If you wish," she says, unable to keep the hurt from her voice.

He touches her arm as she turns to go. "Please, don't be angry."

But when she starts to question him, he lets go and turns away.

She thinks he's angry because she agreed to take part in a plan she knew he wouldn't approve. She's angry about that too, feeling the deep guilt of putting Bianca in harm's way. Lena contributed to her death. But she will not burden Raoul with that guilt, any more than she will with unfounded suspicions.

That night when Raoul joins her in bed, his lovemaking is ferocious and tender, a strange combination, as if he wants her in every way he can take her, and at the same time, wants to memorize every part of her.

"You could have died, Malenque. It could have been you instead of Bianca. What if I had come back and you were in the ground? I would have torn up the whole Earth looking for you. I would have gone to heaven or hell to get you back."

She's stunned by his anguished fury. "Raoul don't—"

"I don't think you understand the full extent of my love for you, Malenque. I wanted to tear Tomás apart with my bare hands. He's never to come near you again."

Lena is alarmed, thinking this will make Tomás' enmity against her even worse. But she's even more distressed at how distraught Raoul appears. She's never seen this side of him. She takes his face between her hands to make him look at her. "We've spoken of this. What we're risking by being here, doing what we're doing. We agreed it's worth that risk to be with each other."

"I know there's little we can do to protect the ones we love, even in times of peace. Sometimes it's out of our hands. But when we can do something and do not . . .?" He turns away from her with a frustrated sigh and stares at the ceiling.

He glances back at her. "I have something to say to you. Something you won't like. I've been thinking much on the story of King David and Bathsheba. Surely, you've heard of it. Like all Biblical stories, it has much to teach us."

"David and Bathsheba?" she asks, confused by the change in topic.

"You remember how they met, do you not? He saw her on a rooftop, rising from her bath, and he knew he had to have her. Just as I felt when I first saw you."

"Only you were rising from your bath, not me." She smiles at him, trying to lighten his mood.

"Believe me when I tell you all your clothes magically disappeared, and all your flesh lay bare before my eyes the first time I saw you." He smiles at her. And then his face turns fierce.

"I knew at one glance you must be mine, whatever the cost. As David did. But the costs for us are as grave as they were for him. David sacrificed one of his captains, Bathsheba's husband, to have her. He sent him to where the fiercest battles were taking place, putting it into God's hands whether the man lived or died.

"But by doing so, he was sidestepping his own responsibility. Instead of doing the manly thing, the kingly thing, and sublimating his passion for Bathsheba because she belonged to another, David committed a great sin, as have I. Instead of telling you we cannot be together now, we must wait until this war is over, I put that choice in your hands, as if absolving myself of that responsibility. I knew you would choose now. I wanted you by my side, whatever the consequences. And I knew what those consequences could be."

He takes Lena's face between his hands and stares into her eyes. "What if it was you, Malenque, who had been killed? I could not bear it. And I alone would be to blame. Not Tomás, not Pepe. Not even the Federales."

She looks at the pain and guilt straining his face, the weight of it almost unbearable. "But it was my choice too. You were right to let me make it. I'm no chattel like women were in Biblical times for others to make these decisions for them. And I respect and love you for giving me that choice. You did right, Raoul. It is nothing like David's decision."

"No, it's worse. I put you, my beloved, at risk, and I can do so no longer. I must send you back to Curico. I will not risk your life here any longer."

"No!" she cries, pushing his hands away. "It's not your decision alone. It's mine too. And I choose to be with you here and now, always at your side."

"But it *is* my decision alone to make. I am your commander-in-chief, Malenque."

When she protests, he pulls her to him, tucks her under his arm. "Yes, you are my lover and my partner too. We are equals that way. This has not changed and will not. I'm not undoing your choice to be with me, Malenque. I'm no more able to sublimate my passion for you than David could for Bathsheba. But I am still the one who decides where my soldiers are stationed. How they can best serve our cause. And you are one of my soldiers. Where you can do the greatest good is in Curico.

"We're preparing a great rally. Our biggest ever on Martyrs Day, August sixth. It's not a day Ortiz's government respects, but the people love it. And this coming rally will be a cover for three major operations planned around San Balanque. We've been working on this for some time."

He looks down at her and rubs his thick thumbs over her eyebrows, as if trying to pull apart the deep crease that grows between them. "We need a good journalist like you covering this rally. That is where your talent and contribution to this great campaign lie. Will you do this for me? For the cause? It tears my heart to send you away. The danger, while less in Curico, is still there. Either way, here or there, I cannot be with you. I must lead one of the operations."

She looks back and sees a face that is tender and anxious and filled with regret. How can she say no to him, to this face, when he puts it this way?

"I will," she tells him, even as her chest tightens with foreboding.

A week later Lena arrives at her apartment in Curico.

"Lena!" Hilda cries, grabbing her into her thick arms. "I didn't know you were coming!" She pushes her away and looks into her eyes, her brows drawn into a question mark. "How were things with Raoul? I read your interview. It was brilliant! As usual."

"Everything's fine," Lena says with more certainty than she feels. "Raoul thought you could use help covering the rally."

"I'm sure we could. It's still three weeks away, but everything's looking good. The Laborer's Union and Proletariat Party are both bussing in members. We have an amazing line-up of speakers, including David Armando, a rising star with the Peace and Freedom Movement. Then there's Professor Sergio Alvarez, who's come out of retirement to speak. And Herman Estrada, publisher of *La Palabra*. But our biggest draw will be Rafael Obregon, recently back from winning that fútbol championship in France. Along with *Tres Hermanos*, who will play before the speeches start. Of course, the Federales and police will turn out in full force too. But the big stars may keep them from turning their guns on us this time." She says this last with a touch of sarcasm, even as they both know the threat is real. Still, Lena feels Hilda's excitement, and it's contagious.

Fiona comes to see her later that day. "I heard about Bianca," she says, her arms hanging strangely, lamely, at her side, as if she doesn't know what to do with them. "I am sorry."

Lena looks at Fiona and sees Bianca's face, what she might have looked like years from now, and breaks. She hasn't cried since the incident, since holding Bianca's body in her arms with her blood on her hands. Her shoulders shake, and Fiona closes in around them.

Fiona has never held her before. But the comfort Lena gets from her body wrapped around her is palpable. Even with the anguish and sorrow pouring out, she feels the wash of gratitude at being in the arms of someone who understands loss.

She tells Fiona everything she withheld from Raoul. All her suspicions about Eva and her sons. All her guilt about Bianca dying in her arms. Fiona listens quietly as Lena spills out her story. By then they've settled on the couch. Fiona finds tissues and hands them to her. Lena blows her nose and dries her tears, then looks up sheepishly at Fiona. "I'm sorry," she says.

Fiona pats her on the shoulder. The Fiona-like response, so restrained, makes Lena want to laugh. She blows her nose a second time, then eyes Fiona warily. "You think I'm crazy, don't you? About Eva and Tomás."

Fiona is silent for a moment. "No. I don't. From what you report, I would be suspicious too. Have you told Raoul?"

"I couldn't."

"Good. Say nothing until, or unless, we have proof."

"So, you think there could be something to it?"

"I've heard rumors elsewhere of Tomás' jealousy of his brother, his great antipathy for you. And Raoul's mother . . . her love for him always seemed tepid, at best. Not what you would imagine from the mother of a great leader. I've often thought it strange. But if any of this is true, I doubt Pepe knew what was going on. What lends the most credence to your suspicions is the fact they didn't position any of our soldiers at this so-called back door. We should have covered every angle."

She pats Lena's knee. "Let me see what I can discover."

Lena feels relieved, having told Fiona her suspicions and her taking them seriously. One secret was out, but another remained. Would Fiona still be supportive if she knew the identity of Lena's mother, especially after hiding it for so long? A terrible shudder passes through her. She must remain silent. A little longer, she tells herself. Just a while longer.

CHAPTER 42

"There must be five thousand people here at least, don't you think?" Lena shouts at Daniel. She's buzzing with excitement. All her trepidation since arriving back in Curico three weeks ago is being swept away in a flurry of optimism. She's never participated in a protest this huge. It's exhilarating, being caught in the swirl of pressing bodies, raised fists, and chanting voices. Signs dance above her head. "Down with Ortiz!" "Vivos Los Aguileros!" She's swept away by the passion of a people demanding regime change and is determined to help them, to capture the photographs that show the world their courage and commitment.

Somehow in the melee she and Daniel found each other—not surprisingly, both being part of the media pool. The speeches, which were held with great fanfare at the Cesar Balano Plaza, ended without incident. Now the massive crowd is heading toward President Ortiz' compound two miles north of the city, one of three located around the country. This estate also garrisons Ortiz's secret police, known as El Guardia, from which his infamous death squads are formed.

Lena is pushed into Daniel by the throng. He catches her before she falls. "Come," he says, pulling her into an alcove between buildings. They wait until most protesters pass, some with elbows locked, chanting a popular revolutionary refrain: "The people, united, will never be defeated."

"I'm glad I found you," Daniel says. "I've wanted to get a word to you. The rumors of someone high in the Aguilero movement leaking intelligence to Ortiz is growing. It's said the location of the camp that was bombed may have been leaked."

"We suspected that. Tomás thinks it was his new driver."

Daniel raises a skeptical eyebrow. "Maybe. But if that's the case, it's not from high up. Anyway, the fact that the rumors are growing gives it more credence. Something you should be aware of."

Lena wants to ask more but jumps when she hears a loud "pop-pop-pop." It's only fireworks set off by teens nearby, but her heart is in her mouth now as they rejoin the marchers.

Lena can't see a thing in the crush, so she looks for a place where she can gain height to better photograph the marching protesters. When they pass through a small plaza where a statue of a soldier on horseback rises on a high platform, she darts toward it and climbs up. Wrapping one arm around the horse's leg, she lifts her camera with the other.

Perfect, she thinks, as she begins snapping shots.

Just then three transport trucks rush up the street filled with police.

"Lena! Get down!" Daniel shouts from below.

Lena turns and shoots photos as the police jump out and pursue protesters with clubs. Many scatter, but a few fight back, using protest signs as clubs.

"Lena!" Daniel shouts again.

Two policemen run toward her. One grabs her leg, but she kicks him away. The other grabs her waist and swings her down.

"Journalist! American journalist!" she cries, trying to show them her press pass as they drag her away. But they shove her into the back of a van, along with other protesters. She scrambles for the door before they can close it. One cracks her on the skull with his club.

All goes dark.

When Lena wakes, she's lying on a cold cement floor with her head in the lap of a woman bathing her face with a wet handkerchief. The woman pours more water from a bottle onto the cloth and dabs again.

"You're awake. Good. I feared the worst." She helps Lena sit up. Her head is hurting so bad she feels dizzy. "Here, drink," the woman says, giving Lena the bottle. But after she drinks, she feels nauseous. She wipes her mouth and hands the bottle back.

"Thank you."

"You're welcome. You'll have quite an egg on your head, I'm afraid. I'm Gloria Costello, by the way. Pleased to meet you, although I wish under better circumstances." The woman looks around thirty years old, shiny black hair curls around a porcelain face. They both sit on the floor of a large holding cell filled with fifty or more people. "And you are," Gloria says, reading the press badge that hangs around Lena's neck, "Lena Landon, a journalist. From California?"

"Yes. Santa Barbara. And you . . . you were at the rally too?"

"I got separated from my husband. He's the leader of the Proletariat Party, so I should be released soon. You, too. They don't keep journalists too long, especially from the States."

"I hope you're right," Lena says. As she's speaking, a guard comes to the door and motions two people in the cell to follow him.

"They've been taking two or three at a time—to be interrogated, I assume. A few return. The others, I suppose, are released or taken elsewhere."

"Where are we?" Lena asks. The room looks too large to be part of Curico's police station.

"Debayle Prison, I'm afraid."

"What? No!" A shiver passes through her, remembering the formidable structure on her way to Casa de Amor. Where Raoul's father was tortured. "Why here?"

"Maybe they ran out of room in town. But don't worry. My husband will be here soon. He can help you too."

The guard returns. This time, instead of motioning randomly at people to come with him, he scans the room. When he sees Lena, he motions her forward. Gloria helps her rise and holds her hand as they step forward together.

"Not you," he tells Gloria, grabbing Lena's arm.

"Who shall I call to tell them you're here?" Gloria calls out as he drags Lena away. She looks back to see the kind woman's face pressed between the bars, her eyebrows a knot of concern. But she hasn't time to answer as the guard hurries her along the corridor.

Lena's head is still pounding, along with her heart, as she's shoved into a small room with cinderblock walls and a cement floor. A single light bulb hanging in the middle of the room throws an icy sheen over the pale green paint. Beneath it sits a wooden table, deeply scarred as if having lost a terrible battle, and two chairs. The guard thrusts her into one of them and orders her to wait.

Chest heaving, head throbbing, Lena tries to remember what Raoul told her to do if arrested. Hopefully, being a journalist with a press pass, they will let her go. But if not, all Aguileros are sworn to silence for seven days, even if tortured, allowing members of their cells or squads to get away. After seven days, to save their lives and end the torture, they can give up names, tell them all they know. All they know is always on a need-to-know basis, so that knowledge is limited. Their handlers or squad leaders will know what information the detainees are likely to give up and be prepared for that. This is what they tell everyone.

But Raoul was more explicit with Lena. Because she knows more than most Aguileros, he tells her which safehouses, which people, which pieces of information she may give up. "You cannot make it seem too easy, as if you already knew who to give up. Make them work for it. I am sorry. This is not easy for me to say. But I am speaking to you as a loyal soldier who understands why this is necessary and why it is important to do so.

"Let me say at the outset, if you are captured, we will kidnap a high-profile person that will guarantee your release. This I promise. We cannot do this for every Aguilero, but for you, the people's Malenque, a symbol for the cause, we must. You have to hold out for seven days to give us time to protect our people and find someone to exchange for you.

"I pray to God you will never be put into this position. But I promise you, if you are, I will get you free."

Lena startles when the door opens. Two men enter.

"I am Captain Rogelio," says one of the men, looking down at her with a polite but smug smile. He is short with thinning black hair combed straight back and thick, black-rimmed glasses. "And this is

Sergeant Batista," he says, introducing his colleague. The sergeant is burly with a bushy, reddish beard and curly brown hair. He stands with his chin down, feet apart, gazing at Lena beneath hooded eyes.

The captain takes a seat across from her and places a folder on the table between them. His hands are almost effeminate, with slim tapered fingers well-manicured. His smile widens.

"So, whom might you be?"

"I'm Lena Landon, a journalist for the *Santa Barbara Chronicle*," she answers, lifting her press badge to show him. She smiles weakly, allowing nervousness to show. "I'm afraid there's been a mistake. I wasn't one of the protesters. I was only photographing them. I can show you what's in my camera if you want. Only your men took it. Can I get it back when I leave?"

"Lena Landon," he says, drawing out the name. "Yes, we do know of you. But while you may pretend to be a journalist, we also know you are an Aguilero terrorist. An agitator recruited from the United States, an SDS member aligned with our leftist student's union, brought here to disrupt the peace in our country."

"No! I'm a journalist. No one recruited me for anything. I swear. I attended the rally to take photographs for the *Chronicle*."

Captain Rogelio opens his folder and pulls out a large poster which he unfolds, smoothing out its creases. "You were at Berkeley when Raoul Aguilero was there. That's where you met him. This is your face, is it not, Malenque?"

Lena stares at the poster, sweat breaking out on her forehead. "Of course not. That doesn't even look like me! This woman is Mayan, and I'm not. You have it all wrong. That's not—"

"No?" he asks, cutting across her. "I have it all wrong? Tell me then, which is wrong? This is not you in this poster? Or you did not meet Raoul at Berkeley?"

"No to both!" she says.

"Then where did you meet him?"

She blanches, realizing how he's trying to trick her, trap her.

"I've never met him. I don't know him at all."

He smiles. "Oh, I think you do," he says, pushing back his chair. "I think you know him quite well." He rounds the table and stands behind her, touches her shoulder. She flinches as he picks up a lock of her hair and lets it slide lightly between his fingers. She pulls away, and her hair drops. He moves to face her again.

"Yes. I'm certain Raoul Aguilero knows you quite well," he says, his gaze pooling at her breasts. "As we shall soon," the captain adds.

"Take her away," he tells Sergeant Batista. After the sergeant pulls her up and handcuffs her, the captain says, "We'll talk more when you've had time to think things through. To realize it's in your best interest to cooperate."

CHAPTER 43

B atista takes Lena to a small cell with a thick door and tiny barred window. There are no furnishings. At the back of the cell, two small, rounded bars rise from the floor with chains and shackles attached to each. Hanging from the ceiling is another iron bar about four feet wide with a leather strap dangling from each end. The whole contraption is attached to a hand-crank set into the wall.

Lena sees all this in a single glance as the door opens and she's led inside. Her feet automatically push hard against the floor to keep from entering this dark space. Batista pushes her forward. Another guard enters and cranks down the overhead bar. Lena struggles fiercely to get away. Sergeant Batista holds her while the other guard removes her handcuffs and attaches one wrist to the strap on the bar, then the other. She's kicking out with her feet.

Batista punches her in the stomach. She keels over, but the straps hold her up.

Her fear is so great, her bladder, which was full already, breaks loose. She feels hot liquid trickle down her tan slacks and feels the shame of it. Batista cranks the bar up again until her arms are high over her head. He gives it one final tug till she's standing on her toes. Then he fastens it off and looks at her.

A smile grows beneath his beard, leering at her stained slacks. "I see we've had a little accident. No worries. We can fix that."

He nods to the guard who returns a moment later with a bucket. He lowers the bar enough so the guard can lift the bucket over Lena's head. Cold, foul-smelling water rushes down her body. The last bit left in the bucket he tosses toward her crotch.

"There now. All better," Batista says as he cranks the bar up again so she's back on her toes.

The shame, the rage, the fear. They tumble and thunder through her like a furious storm.

"Don't let them make this personal," Raoul told her. "It's not you they are trying to humiliate, hurt, kill. It's our cause. What we're fighting for. Steel your heart with the love and pride that comes from that. With love comes courage, dignity, resolve. Love is what will defeat them. You are a symbol of what they hate. But what they hate, you love. And they have no weapon equal to love. Remember that."

When she's alone, she repeats these words over and over in her mind, trying to gain some measure of peace, even while her arms ache and the leather straps bite into her wrists. The only relief she gets is when she strains to push higher on her toes to take the weight off her wrists. But her legs eventually tremble with the effort, and to relieve them, her wrists and arms must bear the weight.

She's heard about this kind of suspension torture. Sometimes victims are strung so high they can't touch the floor. Sometimes they add weights to their feet to make it worse. Shoulders are dislocated. Wrists broken. She read that even fifteen minutes completely suspended like this with no toe-touching can cause nerve damage that never heals. She's lucky they've allowed her feet to touch. But for how long?

Lucky, she thinks. *Lucky*.

Hours pass or what seem like hours. She's shivering in her wet clothes and her whole body—from wrists to toes—is screaming.

"You can break my body, but you can't have *me*, you can't have *me*," she whispers as tears stream down her face. She tries to draw on the warmth of Raoul's arms wrapped around her, lifting her up. Holding her. *I belong to Raoul. He's here with me now. We can never be separated. Raoul, Raoul. He will save me.* His name rises through her like the sea's roar until she passes out.

When Lena wakes, she's shackled to the floor and propped against the back wall. The bar with its dangling straps is empty. Two buckets stand before her, one empty. A toilet? The other bucket is upside-down and holds a covered bowl. She lifts the lid and sees a soupy gruel. Its smell makes her nauseous, and she quickly covers it. There's no water, which is what she craves.

She avoids looking at her wrists. They bore the full weight of her body when she passed out and now are circled with angry red welts. Her arms are so numb she barely feels them. But the pain in her neck and back remains. She's damp and shivering despite the warmth of the room.

She must have fallen asleep again, for Lena is startled awake when someone enters the room. It's the guard who was with Sergeant Batista earlier. He looks young with gangly arms and legs. His dark head is shaved. When he was with the sergeant he leered at her. Now he avoids making eye contact.

"How long will they keep me here?" she asks, not expecting an answer.

He takes away the bowl and leaves a container of water.

"What time is it? How long have I been here?"

He ignores her and leaves. Now she wishes she had eaten the gruel, for she's terribly hungry, which makes her suspect she's been here longer than it seems.

She picks up the water he left and chugs it down, hoping it will fill her empty belly. It feels cool and refreshing on her parched throat. But when she's done, she feels queasy again. Perhaps she shouldn't have drunk it so quickly, should have saved some for later.

She notices marks carved into the walls that had been whitewashed over. Messages left by previous prisoners? Or notches to mark the length of their stay. She grows alarmed. If she can't tell how long she's been here, how can she tell when seven days have passed and it's okay to give up names? Light fills the small window, so she knows she's at least been here overnight. This is Day Two. She uses a fingernail to notch the wall.

The door opens. It's Sergeant Batista and the guard. The guard cranks down the overhead bar while Batista unshackles her. She tries to keep him from doing so. "No. Please!"

"So, you like your shackles now, do you?" Batista says with a smirk. He drags her to the lowered bar and fastens her wrists in the leather straps again. The wounds there are fresh. Panic rises through her as she stares wide-eyed in alarm at the thought of what lies before her.

She turns to Batista. "Please! Tell the captain I'll talk. I'll tell him the truth. Please tell him." She'll think of something, anything, to delay being strung up again. Not what he wants to hear, but something.

"Oh, Captain Rogelio is quite aware of that. But a little more time spent here will encourage you to tell the whole truth and nothing but the truth—as they say in your justice system. This is ours. You don't even have to swear on a Bible."

He cranks up the bar. Her arms go up, up until she's again dancing on her toes. But now he goes a notch further and her toes no longer reach. Her wrists bear the full weight of her body. Something shifts and starts to crack in her left shoulder. She screams.

He laughs as he lowers her to her toes.

"Remember. Things can get so much worse."

When she's finally brought back into the interrogation room, she doesn't know how many days have passed. She managed to scratch two more notches into the wall. But she's not sure it's correct. Time has stretched and condensed. When she's on the floor, she sobs and tries to eat what they give her, only to throw it up a short while later. When she's strung up, her entire body screams. And, from the soreness of her throat, she suspects she's been screaming aloud as well.

Her hunger has been reduced to a dull gnawing in her stomach. Her wrists are on constant fire, and her whole back and shoulders burn. Not to mention the constant hammering in her skull. The young guard from before removes the handcuffs, and Sergeant Batiste tells her to sit.

Captain Rogelio stands before her. No table now.

"All right, Ms. Landon, let's start over again. Are you ready to cooperate?"

She nods numbly.

"I didn't hear that. Try again."

She tries to speak but her throat is so parched she can't get words out. She coughs to clear her throat. How long has it been since she's had water?

She looks at the bottle he holds in his hand.

"You want water? So you can talk?" He smiles contemptuously and hands it to her.

She drinks long and hard.

"That's enough." He pulls it away. "How long have you known Raoul Aguilero?"

She draws in a ragged breath that ends in a sob. She doesn't know for sure how long she's been here, but it hasn't been seven days. Not long enough for anyone to make their escape. If she tells them she knows Raoul, they will dig deeper to get more names.

"I don't know him; I've never met him—"

His fist comes so fast she doesn't see it. All she knows is she's on the floor and her head is ringing. He's saying something, but she can't hear him. When the ringing stops, she feels her face, her mouth is bleeding.

"Get up," he tells her. She awkwardly struggles to her feet and sits in the chair again. "Now let's try again, when did you meet Raoul?"

Trembling, she rubs the blood from her mouth and looks up at him, knowing what will happen next. "I never—" she starts and is knocked from her chair again.

"I can do this all day," Rogelio tells her, rubbing his knuckles. Lena barely hears him. The ringing is louder, and she can't focus her eyes.

"Get her up here!" he yells at the sergeant, but when he goes to grab Lena by her hair, the captain reconsiders.

"Or maybe she likes it on the floor, on her back We can make her like it a little more. Perhaps the carrot instead of the stick will do the trick. Surely you can find a way to make her stay on the floor more pleasurable, can't you, Sergeant?"

"As you command," Batista says and begins undoing his trousers.

Only she's not on her back. She's on her side, curled into a ball until Batista grabs her legs and the young guard grabs her shoulders and turns her onto her back. She tries kicking at Batista and gets one leg loose, but he dodges and climbs on top of her legs. He unzips her trousers and pulls them and her panties down. She tries to buck him off, but he slides his knee between her thighs forcing them apart. He spits into his hand and lathers her with it. Then he pulls out his genitals.

She is shrieking, still trying to get away. What's about to happen is worse than being strung up by her wrists. Worse than the pain exploding in her head when he hits her. Being exposed like this, being pinned down by his weight, feeling his hand slather her with his spit, hearing him laugh at her attempt to wriggle away . . . her rage knows no end.

She tries to remember what Raoul told her to do if this happened. "It's just your body," he said. "Not your mind, not your soul. Not you. They can't violate that."

"But it's *my* body!" she wants to scream at him. "Mine!"

And maybe she has screamed this, for Batista laughs at her.

"Maybe it was. Now it's mine." He's trying to force his half-limp dick inside her and failing as she resists him.

She stares up at him with such venom. She gathers the blood that's still in her mouth and spits in his face. His fist comes down on her and as it does, she thinks, *please, God, let him knock me out, I can't endure this.*

She's not knocked out, but almost senseless. Her ears are ringing, her vision blurred. A commotion is going on that she can't make out. The room is swirling and exploding around her. She hears shouting. Feels the weight of Batista being thrown off her. The hands holding down her shoulders disappear. She scrambles back crab-like, trying to get away. She turns on her side and pulls up her pants. She rolls onto her knees and tries to stand. Someone grabs her beneath her armpits and lifts her. She tries to get away, elbows flying.

He hugs her back tightly against his chest. A voice she doesn't recognize says, "It's okay. You're safe. We're getting you out of here."

Captain Rogelio's voice is full of fury. "This is outrageous! Wait till the commander hears!"

Lena is half-carried from the room down the narrow corridor. At the end of it, a door opens, the sunlight blinding.

"Hurry! Hurry!" someone says.

She's shoved into the back of a car. Someone climbs in beside her. She doesn't know him and presses as far away as she can.

"Don't worry, we're taking you someplace safe," he says. But how can she believe him? She turns away, bringing her knees to her chest and pressing her forehead against the window as the car drives away.

It takes a moment for her to realize that the worst didn't happen. She was not raped. Then she's sobbing with relief. *I'm still a virgin,* she thinks absurdly. But that's how it feels. She's intact. Her body her own, untouched but for Raoul, the man she loves, her everything. Her first. Her only. Another sob rises in pure gratitude to whatever, whoever, saved her from the worst. They are dressed in suits, not fatigues. They aren't Aguileros. That's all she knows.

Her head is still exploding, but the detonations are duller, allowing pain from her wrists and shoulders to surface. She tries to shut it out. Concentrates on the hum of the car's engine, taking her farther and farther away from the worst that never happened.

Lena must have fallen asleep or passed out, for when she wakes, she's in bed. A seam of light shows between drapes drawn across a tall window. She's afraid to move. She lies still and listens. It's quiet. Thinking she's alone, she tries to sit up, but her body is too heavy to lift.

She's not alone. Someone presses her back in bed.

"You must rest. Sleep. It's all right, you're safe now. I'm here. I won't leave you."

The hand is smoothing back her hair the way she remembers from so long ago. A voice from her dreams. She must be dreaming.

"Hush," says the voice, the hand so soft and warm against her cheek. Lena closes her eyes and sleeps.

CHAPTER 44

Lena wakes as the room fills with light. Tall heavy drapes are drawn back by a young woman on tiptoes, dressed in a dark blue dress and white apron. Lena pulls herself up from the pillows piled around her and groans.

The woman—or, rather, girl—stops and turns. "Oh! You're awake! The mistress will be so pleased. I'm Ophelia." She makes a curtsey. She can't be more than sixteen. Her short dark curls are bundled beneath a lacy servant's cap. "She had to leave but will be back shortly. She left these clothes for you." She nods toward a chaise lounge with a dress and undergarments spread over it. A pair of ballet pumps lay beneath.

Lena struggles to rise higher in the bed and Ophelia helps her. "Would you like me to bring your breakfast now, or wait till the mistress returns?"

"Who is this mistress?" Lena asks, looking around the huge, lavishly furnished bedroom. Rich paneling rises a few feet up the wall and a soft green brocade wallpaper beyond that. Ornate molding lines the ceiling from which a crystal chandelier hangs. A dark mantled fireplace is faced by two floral upholstered armchairs. It looks like a bedroom you might find in a castle. Or one of her mother's paintings.

Ophelia's brow furrows. "Mistress Machado, of course. The vice president's wife."

Lena must be staring dumbfounded at her, for Ophelia's worried frown deepens. "Oh, dear," she says, "Perhaps I should call for the doctor."

"No," Lena says, her mind stuttering with the realization of where she is, trying to collect her thoughts. "I'm fine. I . . . I remember now. Yes, breakfast here would be nice. Just tea and toast please."

Ophelia's cheeks dimple, happy to see all is well again. "Of course, Miss Landon." She gives Lena another small curtsy and dashes off.

My mother brought me here? It must have been her bodyguards who rescued her. *But how did she know I* was *there*? Was it a rescue or is this a ploy? Did the Federales think her mother could coerce the truth from her, confess everything in gratitude for being saved?

Lena throws back the covers, anxious to escape before her mother returns. But her body resists, every muscle aching as she moves. Her wrists are bandaged, and her shoulder is wrapped in a sling. How long has she been here? She must leave before Raoul finds out where she is and who her mother is. Lena must let him know he doesn't have to kidnap anyone to save her.

But is she saved? Will her mother let her leave? Will she be followed?

She removes the sling and dresses as quickly as her aching body will allow, finding her fingers aren't working too well. She hopes her nerves weren't permanently damaged. But maybe it's the bandages on her wrists that make moving her fingers difficult. The pale blue chiffon dress, undergarments, and pumps fit perfectly. She stands in front of an oval dressing mirror. Her face is swollen, a patchwork of purple and red, parts fading to a greenish hue.

A sob escapes. They did this. Their faces rise in her mind, her breath hitches, and she pushes them away. She cannot go there.

On the nightstand are three medicine bottles. She takes two pain pills, swallowing them with the glass of water sitting beside them, then stuffs the bottles in her bra. She's learned in the field how precious medicine is, and she'll need this later when she makes her escape.

She peeks through the long drapes.

A circular driveway and lush lawn roll away to a line of poplar trees. She's on the second floor. Two men smoking cigarettes stand below her, talking softly. One crushes his cigarette before entering the house. The other strolls down the driveway, a rifle slung over his shoulder. As she starts to turn away, she sees a Rolls Royce coming up the driveway. Her mother. She's sure of it. She doesn't want to see her. Doesn't trust her. She must get away.

Lena dashes from the bedroom and finds herself on a high landing overlooking the staircase to the front door. She can't go that way. Surely there are back stairs leading to the kitchen like Eva had. She rushes down the hallway opening doors and bumps into Ophelia.

She's holding a tray with tea and toast. Stairs are behind her.

"Oh, you're up!" the girl says, dimples deepening. "Would you prefer this in the dining room?"

"Yes, please!" Lena says, turning toward the back stairs.

"Not that way, ma'am! That's only for servants. Here, I'll show you the way." She heads toward the main stairs.

By now, voices drift up from the hall below and then her mother appears at the bottom of the wide curving stairs. She and Lena stare at each other across the distance.

"Lena," her mother says, smiling radiantly. "You're up! My dear child. Come." She holds out her arms.

Dolores Machado is as beautiful as the mother Lena remembers: Dark hair falling in soft waves to her shoulders, pale skin glowing, dark eyes shining, as they always did when looking at her child. Lena's breath hitches, something raw and painful squeezes her chest. A longing and sorrow deeply buried begin to surface. Tears sting her eyes. Lena pushes away all these emotions and memories. She will not be fooled again. She must stay focused. Her mission is to leave here as soon as possible so she can tell Raoul he doesn't have to kidnap anyone to trade for her release as he promised to do.

Lena takes a deep breath and forces a small smile to her lips as she descends the stairs. What else can she do? She has a part to play. She must play it well. And then she can escape and find Raoul.

"Mother," she says as she steps into her open arms.

Lena and Dolores sit on a small sofa in the drawing room. The tea and triangles of toast have been transferred to the coffee table.

"Are you sure you don't want something more substantial?" Dolores asks. "A poached egg, perhaps?"

"No, thank you. This is perfect." Lena manages another small smile.

Her mother's brows draw together in a worried frown. "I'm so sorry about what happened to you, Malenque. I told my husband it was all a mistake. You're a journalist, that's all, just as you and your father said, although why he'd allow you to come here amid all this unrest, I can't imagine."

Lena chokes on her toast. "Daddy knows about this?"

"Only that you were arrested. He's the one who told me. Your friend Daniel Weatherly tried to get you out. When they wouldn't release you, he called your father, and your father called me, and here we are." Her worried gaze settles on her daughter. "Why would you come here and not tell me? I don't understand. Do you hate me that much?"

She must see something in Lena's face she doesn't like, for her lips purse. "Is what they say true? Is that's why you're here? You came to join that rebel group to show me how much you despise me? Is that it?"

"My coming here has nothing to do with you. I came to learn about San Balanque. To find my roots. And what I'm learning," she says, setting down her cup as her ire rises, "is that people are suffering under Ortiz!"

She presses on. "The truth is, I despise all you and Ortiz stand for, and I sympathize with the rebels. I hope they throw you all out! But I had nothing to do with them. I'm a pacifist like Daddy. I've written articles critical of Ortiz for newspapers back home. Perhaps that's why they think I'm a rebel. Don't they always imprison people who criticize them?"

Dolores studies her face, then lets out a long sigh. "I'm glad to hear you're not mixed up with them. It would be extremely dangerous, as you must know."

"Surely you know what a monster Ortiz is. Do you know what his goons did to me? They hung me by my wrists for days! They tried to rape me!" She lets out a sob of rage and anguish.

Her mother's face turns white, and she reaches across the space between them as if to comfort her.

Lena pushes her away. "Don't touch me!"

Dolores freezes, then sits back, spine rigid, hands folded in her lap. "I know what you must think. But I'm not one of them, as you put it. I don't like Ortiz and his brutality any more than you do. I never have. What they did to you . . . is unforgivable. But it was a horrible mistake. They don't treat innocent people like that. And my husband works constantly to curb Ortiz's worst excesses. Believe me, it would be much worse if my Marcos wasn't there beside Ortiz. The rebels are just as bad. They would destroy our country if they installed a Fidel-like ruler. Have you seen what's become of Cuba after he took over? No, it would be so much worse than it is now. That's why we must stop them."

Lena wants to argue, to defend the Aguileros, to tell her what they want is a social democracy not communism, but she can't if she wants to keep her cover as the innocent journalist, the devoted pacifist.

"That explains why your husband can't leave, but why do you stay? Can't you dump him like you did Daddy and me? I can't believe you chose that man over my father."

Dolores looks down at her folded hands. Lena can tell she's trying to calm herself. Finally, she looks up. "It's nothing you can understand. I hardly understood it at the time myself. I loved your father. Dearly! I still do. We keep in touch, you know. But Marcos . . . when I first met him, it was like . . . like I'd always known him. Like he was part of me already. We had to have each other. We couldn't be apart."

Lena stares in horror at her mother's revelation. It sounds too much like what happened between her and Raoul. But what they have is nothing like her mother and Marcos! It can't be.

"I don't expect you to believe me," her mother continues, "but I never thought to leave you behind. You were supposed to come with us. I always thought, eventually, you would."

"Well, you were wrong," Lena says, but with less vehemence than she wanted, her mind still reeling at her mother's revelation.

"Yes, I was wrong. And I will regret that for the rest of my life."

Dolores looks at her with such deep sadness and regret, it's hard for Lena not to want to comfort her. "I don't know if I can forgive you for leaving, but despite that, you saved my life. When I needed you most, you were there for me. And I'll be eternally grateful for that."

Her mother's eyes are moist as she squeezes Lena's hands. "I only wish we'd known sooner and had saved you from all . . . this." She touches Lena's face, the tears in her eyes threatening to spill.

"Who were the men who rescued me? I want to thank them."

Her mother dabs at her eyes with her napkin. "There's no need for that. They do what they are told, whether they want to or not."

Lena lets that sink in. "They didn't want to?"

She gives Lena a sad smile. "It's no small thing, defying a brutal dictator, as you call him. Having my bodyguards storm into an interrogation room and remove a prisoner? There will be consequences. I fear they may pay more dearly than me. But that's their job, to protect me and mine. Ortiz understands this. He says there will be no repercussions, but I don't trust him to keep his word."

"President Ortiz knows? It goes that high up?"

"He summoned me this morning. I just returned. I told him you're not a rebel, you're a journalist. You came here without telling me to shame me, as revenge for leaving you."

Lena opens her mouth to protest but stops herself. Playing the naïve, vengeful daughter is the best defense she has, so she swallows her pride.

"Ortiz understands these things," says Dolores. "He has messy relationships with his children too. His youngest son, Romero, constantly threatens to join the rebels when he's angry at his father. Can you imagine! But he's only fifteen, a child."

"So, he believes me then? That I'm not one of those rebels?"

Her mother gives her a sharp look. "He says he has intelligence that says you are. From a spy or double-agent or something like that. I told him he should be leery of such intelligence. If the rebels discovered you were my daughter, what better way to undermine the administration than to plant false intel so he would imprison and torture the vice president's daughter and drive a wedge between us? I asked him: 'Did this so-called source also tell him you are my daughter? What? No? Think on that,' I said. 'You should be thanking me for rescuing my daughter before you were made a fool.'"

Lena is taken back by that. "You said that to the president?"

Dolores smiles. "I've said worse. We've known each other a long time. He knows I speak frankly. He respects that. And it's good he does, for he says you are free to go. But you must leave San Balanque."

No! Lena thinks. She can't leave. She won't. Panic rises through her. She must find a way to convince them to let her stay. She takes a deep breath to calm herself.

"Thank you, Mother, for getting me released, but I'm not ready to go home, despite all this. I've made a life here. *This* is my home. I promise not to write about politics anymore. You can tell President Ortiz that I've learned my lesson. I'll stick to the social pages. What I really wanted to write about when I came here was art and surfing!" She lets out a self-deprecating laugh. It does seem funny now. "I wish I had stuck with that. But I still despise Ortiz and hope we can get rid of him. But not the way the rebels are doing it. Peaceful resistance, the way Martin Luther King and Gandhi did. Maybe I'll start a peace movement! Is there a Pacifist Club in San Balanque?"

Her mother laughs as she hoped she would. Lena is the naïve daughter. Harmless. Helpless. It's best she believes that.

"You can make him let me stay, can't you, Mother?" she says, taking her hands. "We've only just met again. It would be a shame to part so soon, don't you think?" Surely this will tug at her heartstrings and make her want to convince Ortiz to let her stay.

Her mother's face warms. "It would be a shame. I don't want to lose you again. I'll make him understand. I promise." She pulls Lena to her and presses her head against her shoulder, pets her hair. Lena lets her. "My little girl. Malenque Mia."

Lena stiffens and pulls back. "What did you say?" This is what Raoul calls her in their most tender moments.

Her mother looks surprised at her reaction. "It's what I called you as a child, don't you remember? Malenque Mia. My dearest one." She brings Lena's head back to her chest and continues petting her hair, and it does bring back a flood of memories, the feel of her hand on her hair, her body holding her, even the smell of her hair, the softness of her skin.

Lena lets her hold her, wishing things could be different between them. But she's an Aguilero now and she must leave quickly. She pulls back with an apologetic smile. "I'm sorry, I wish I could stay longer, but I must go."

"Go? You need to heal more. I don't want you to leave."

Lena freezes, her words triggering something dark and dangerous: Lena begging her mother not to leave. "But I must," she says firmly as she stands. "I told you, I've made a life here. And I need to make a call. I need to let . . . Daniel know I'm okay. There was a phone in the foyer, wasn't there?"

"Daniel, the journalist? Is he why you don't want to leave San Balanque?"

Lena thinks about that. Perhaps Daniel could be her excuse for staying.

Her mother sees her hesitation. "He is, isn't he?" She smiles sadly. "Love. It's a dangerous thing, isn't it?"

If you only knew, Lena thinks. "How long have I been here?"

"Three days. You slept the first two, under sedation. Doctor's orders."

"And the date?"

"It's August twelfth. What is it? What's wrong?"

So, it's been six days since the rally. She has time to stop Raoul from kidnapping someone in exchange for her and blowing her cover.

"Nothing," she assures her mother and gives her a weak smile. "It's only that Daniel will be so worried. I must let him know I'm safe." Lena heads toward the foyer, a large semi-circular room lined with her mother's paintings. These aren't the large vibrant abstracts she grew up with, but the dream-like hyper-realistic paintings for which her mother has since become known. Front and center is the painting she saw in the art journal: the girl running on the beach wearing a long dress and bonnet. The sight makes her scalp tingle.

"That's me, isn't it?" An eerie sense of déjà vu envelops Lena. Not that she's been here before, in this room, but there, on that beach.

"Yes, it is darling," her mother says, sounding radiantly alive.

Their eyes meet, and for a moment Lena feels a timeless connection between them she can't understand. And maybe doesn't want to.

She shakes off the spell and calls Daniel. "I'm out," she tells him, then adds quickly, "Please let everyone who might worry know. And quickly.

It's terribly important." She hangs up before he can say anything, ignoring the strange look her mother gives her after overhearing that cryptic message.

Wanting to forestall any questions, Lena turns toward the stairs, saying she's still tired and sore and needs to rest awhile. "In the meantime, please tell Ophelia to bring me the clothes I was wearing when I came here. I'm sure they've been laundered by now. I'll leave in the morning. And if you can get President Ortiz to return my camera, that would be lovely. It's the least he can do after torturing me, don't you think?"

CHAPTER 45

Lena sits in the back seat of her mother's Rolls Royce as her driver leaves for Curico. She looks out at her mother's estate as they pull away, nestled in the foothills near Cordoba. It's much grander than Eva's hacienda, grander than anything Lena's seen in Montecito where Hollywood's wealthiest royalty reside. *Blood money,* Lena thinks. The furnishings in one room could feed a village for years. How many hospitals and schools could the sale of her home finance?

Her mother stands on the steps outside her mansion, a small, trim figure, fragile looking against the massive structure behind her. It makes Lena's heart hurt. She can almost forgive her mother for leaving her when she was a child, now that she knows her passionate feelings for Marcos were so similar to hers for Raoul. Now she knows the grief her mother felt, leaving her daughter behind. But how can she forgive her for supporting Ortiz?

Lena's last night with her mother was awkward and sweet. They reminisced about her father and Margo. His sojourns to India and Japan seeking spiritual enlightenment. Margo's on-again, off-again relationship with Geoffrey.

"I always liked him," her mother told her, curled in the corner of the couch, her shoes off, legs tucked beneath her, a glass of red Madeira in her hand. Lena was similarly situated. The ease with which they conversed about old times surprised her.

If she weren't my mother, Lena thought, *if she didn't support Ortiz, I would like her quite a bit.* Dolores wanted to know where Lena lived so they could stay in touch and get to know each other better. She mentioned all the art galleries she would take Lena to and some "fabulous gardens."

Lena was tempted. If she was the person she was pretending to be, she would love doing those things. So Lena explained, as gently as she could, she needed more time and privacy to process everything that happened and to sort through her complicated feelings about her mother. She had been angry for so long. She needed to deal with that. But she promised she'd reach out when ready.

Her mother assured her she would clear matters up with Ortiz so Lena could remain in the country. "He will understand. And I will take personal responsibility for you while you're here. So, no fraternizing with rebels, my dear, or it may be me in prison next time." Dolores said this last part with an elfish grin, but it sent a chill down Lena's spine.

Lena tells her mother's driver where to take her, naming a busy intersection in Curico. She's wearing large sunglasses and a floppy beach hat she borrowed to hide her battered face. The drive is long and fraught with anxiety. Her stomach clenches as they pass Debayle Prison. How many people are strung up there this very minute as they drive by so blithely? She swallows the nausea rising from her gut.

She has no idea what she'll tell anyone about why they let her go. What if they already know? The Aguileros have spies everywhere, they said. The fear that Raoul might already know, might already hate Lena for not telling him about her mother, might think she's a spy . . ..

"Stop!" she cries out to the driver, and when he does, she leans her head out the door, thinking she's going to be sick. It can't be true. Raoul can't already know. If he does, if he does . . . she'll know as soon as she sees the look on his face. The hatred, the disgust. The image of his hand shooting the traitor rises. She leans over and vomits onto the street. Her body breaks out in a cold sweat. She's shivering.

She sits there, all these thoughts colliding in her head. *No, he can't know!* And if he doesn't, she can't tell him. Not yet. Not like this. She must heal first. *I'll tell him,* she promises. *I will. But what will I tell the others in the meantime?*

Nothing, she thinks. *Nothing.*

When her driver drops her off, she ducks into a store and out the back, going through the routine that comes as second nature now to elude anyone possibly following. She calls the gym from a payphone. Fiona arrives a short time later, having driven herself this time.

Lena slides into the front seat of the small sedan, waiting to see if Fiona knows about her mother, suspects she's a spy. But when Fiona looks at her, all Lena sees is concern. *She doesn't know!* Lena's relief is so immense, her eyes flood, and she removes her sunglasses so she can swipe the tears away with the backs of her bandaged wrists.

Fiona's head shoots back when she sees her face. "Jesus!" she says as she grinds down the gearshift, then jerks forward. "Those fucking bastards!" She's breathing hard. After a moment she adds, "Raoul is on his way. And Tomás."

"No! Not Tomás! Please. I was told someone high up in the Aguileros told them about me."

"And you think that's Tomás."

She nods.

"Why would they tell you that? Perhaps it's a ploy, to turn us against each other."

"No, Daniel told me at the rally before I was arrested."

Fiona's brows furrow. "So why did they let you go?"

Lena freezes and then quickly looks away. "I don't know. Maybe after all the torture they believed me, that I wasn't a rebel . . .."

"Lena . . .," Fiona says, sounding skeptical.

Lena shoots her an icy, defiant look. "I told them nothing!" she says, surprising both with her vehemence.

Fiona is silent, then says, "I believe you. What else can you tell me?"

Lena shakes her head, the tears starting up again. "Nothing."

Eventually Fiona reaches a residential area and pulls into an alley. The doors to a dilapidated garage are pushed apart by someone inside, then close quickly after they enter. Inside it's dark and quiet. Lena removes her sunglasses so she can see.

Her door opens and it's Raoul leaning over her. He halts when he sees her face. His jaw clenches and then she's pulled into his arms. They stand there in the garage, him holding her so tightly, her clinging so close.

He doesn't know! Lena sobs with relief. And gratitude.

I'm alive, she thinks. *The worst didn't happen. I'm safe. Raoul has me, and I have time to tell him about my mother myself. But not yet.*

They don't stay long. And she doesn't see Tomás. Raoul bundles her up, folding her in a blanket because she's shivering again. He carries her to the backseat of another car and holds her on his lap. They drive away, Carlos at the wheel.

Lena must have fallen asleep, for when she wakes, she's curled up on the seat, her head on Raoul's lap. He smiles down at her bruised face even while his jaw hardens, working through whatever else he's feeling. "You needed that sleep," he says.

She pushes away the blanket and sits up. They are far from town, the tangled green forest flowing by, a Gauguin painting in motion. They round a corner and the sea glimmers in the distance.

"Where are we going?" she asks.

"To Casa de Azul on Chagos Island. That retreat I told you about. Remember? Where you'll be safe. Where you can heal."

She leans against him, hanging onto his arm, thankful he's not pressing her to tell him what happened, how she got away. But he will. Her arms wrap around him more tightly. He pulls her onto his lap.

"Hush," he says as the tears start to flow again. "Go back to sleep. You're safe now. I won't let you go."

Next time she wakes, Raoul is carrying her through the surf to a small boat. Carlos reaches down to help her aboard, and Raoul climbs in after.

She's wrapped in her blanket, which she hugs around her. It's evening, the sea a slate of gray with a few white ripples where the wind passes over. There are lights in the distance. The island retreat. She fills her lungs with salty air and revels in the cool breeze on her warm face, wrapped tightly in her blanket, in Raoul's arms, as the boat skims lightly, swiftly over the small ripples toward the distant lights hovering like fireflies in the gathering dark.

The light is dazzling behind her eyelids. Lena is on a sunlit shore, laughing, running, holding her bonnet to keep it from blowing away. She's running toward a dark green jungle wall with flashes of red and yellow as macaws and toucans dart in and out of trees.

"Look, Mommy, all the pretty birds!" But as she looks, a man emerges from the jungle. He's naked and magnificent. She stops and stares.

"Come away, darling!" her mother calls. But she can't. She's hypnotized by the man whose eyes have claimed hers.

"Malenque Mia!" her mother calls again.

Only it's not her mother. It's him. Raoul.

He's brushing the hair from her face. "You were laughing," he tells her as she opens her eyes. "I love that sound. I didn't mean to wake you though."

"My mother used to call me that too, Malenque Mia."

"She did? Tell me about your mother," he says, his hand moving lightly over her broken face. She knows what she must look like, how hard it must be for him not to show it on his face. And then all the horror of what caused her to look like this comes crashing back. She turns her face away. "Don't look at me!" she says.

He moves her head back to face him. "Someone will pay for this, Malenque. But you never need to hide yourself from me. All I see is what I love. I see nothing but love when I look at you."

The night before, after he fed her scrambled eggs he made himself, he undressed her and kissed every part of her body—soft, butterfly kisses, tender murmuring kisses, sweet moist kisses that fed her soul. She felt like he was remaking her. His mouth and fingers reclaiming, remaking, every inch of her, so everywhere Raoul touched and all she was, was his, and no one else's. She felt that and believed it then.

But in the light of day, she feels . . . spoiled. Tainted. Not only by what happened to her, but by what she hasn't yet told him. What she fears to tell him. What she would hide from him forever if she could.

She covers her face. "No. I can't bear for you to look at me this way." And here come those damn tears again, sliding between her fingers. She curls up on her side away from him, bringing her knees to her chest, trying to control the sobs that want to break loose. That do break loose. She will lose Raoul. Once he knows, she will lose him. She turns toward him and clutches him in her arms. "Don't leave me!" she cries.

He holds and pets her and promises her he will never leave her.

"No matter what?" she asks, eyes wide, pleading.

His face darkens in confusion and worry. "No matter what," he tells her.

"Remember that," she says between sobs. "No matter what!"

Raoul sent for her things, and they arrive later that day: her clothes and rucksack and books. Even her surfboard. She continues taking the pain pills and anti-inflammatory medicine that she had at her mother's, although she removed the label with the doctor's name before leaving for Curico.

When Raoul asks where she got them, she tells him she doesn't know. When he tries to ask her anything, she shakes her head and turns away. Tears come. It's not a ploy. It takes all her strength to keep from crying all the time. To smile. To pretend things are all better. Why can't Raoul let her keep pretending?

Later that night Raoul tries again. They're sitting in bed, propped up on pillows, her tucked beneath his arm, him stroking her hair.

"Malenque Mia," he says softly, almost a whisper, "why did they let you go?" When she stiffens in his arms, he turns her face to look at him. "I know you don't want to talk about this, but you must tell us everything, the sooner the better. It could save lives."

Lena looks down at her hands twisting in her lap. She feels an awful chasm opening in her chest. "I told you, I told them nothing. That's all you need to know. All I can tell you."

His hand stills on her hair and moves away. His arm too. His hands are in his hair now, squeezing. "That's not enough. How did you get away? Why did they let you go?"

"I don't know!" she shouts, startling herself as much as him. "One minute he's on top of me, trying to rape me!" She glares at him now, as if she blames him. "And then he's pulled off and I'm in a car . . . and then, I don't know what happened after that. A doctor came. He must have, because when I woke up my wrists were bandaged, my shoulder in a sling."

"Okay, that's good. So, when you woke, where were you?"

"I don't know!" she shouts again and climbs out of bed and turns to face him, her face ferocious. "How many times must I tell you? I don't know! I don't remember. I don't. I can't" Tears stream down her face again.

"Let it be. Please!" she says, frantically crawling back in bed with him, like a creature scurrying for its hole, climbing under his arm, pulling it tight around her, clinging to him. "Please . . .," she says over and over until he's stroking her and then holding her fiercely in his arms.

"Hush. That's enough for now."

They spend three more days together. She sleeps through huge portions. Her wrists are healing, and they've removed her bandages. She and Raoul take walks on the beach. As her shoulder grows stronger, she begins to swim a little, and soon she can swim past the ripple of waves, turning onto her back, letting the sea's motion rock her in its arms, the sun a bright shield over her face.

They don't make love. They hold and pet and kiss each other, tenderly, even passionately, but then the sobs start up. She knows once she tells Raoul about her mother, he'll never trust her again. *This is our swan song*, she thinks, wanting to soak it all up so she'll always remember. But the thought of its ending brings tears. Because of them, she thinks, he asks no more questions.

On the fourth day, though, as they sit across from each other at the breakfast table, their plates nearly empty, Raoul puts down his fork and looks at her.

"Fiona says they told you they have an informant high up in the Aguileros. And you believe it may have been Tomás. Tell me about that."

She doesn't answer. Just stares down at her plate.

"Lena, how did you get away?"

She turns her face away. Lena, he calls her. Lena. Not Malenque. Already he's distancing himself from her. It's time. She must tell him. But she can't. She picks up a crust of bread, puts it down. She looks out the window behind him and sees the sea winking in the distance, hears the waves wash against the shore. She wants to walk out there right now and keep walking.

"Lena, where are you going?"

The sand is cool beneath her bare feet, still damp from a rain shower earlier this morning. She's wearing cut-off shorts and bikini top. Her hair flows in the breeze. Her face is a pastel watercolor now, pale pink, light greens, and yellow. It's almost pretty if you don't think of it as a face, but a canvas.

Lena will never tell him. She can't risk it. Raoul will never know. That's how it must be. She has no choice.

He comes up behind her and takes her in his arms. He pulls her back against his chest. "I know you don't want to talk about it. I wish there was another way. But we must know, Lena." And the name Lena again turns her body to stone.

He turns her in his arms so she's facing him. "If you had to tell them things you never wanted to, that's okay. It's understandable. Everyone breaks eventually."

She twists out of his arms and steps back.

"That's what you think! I gave in, told them things? I told them NOTHING!" she screams at him. "Even when they hung me by my wrists for days. Even when they starved me and beat me senseless. Even when they threw me on the floor and climbed on top . . . slathered me with spit . . . even when he . . . .. I told them nothing! How could you believe I would?"

He stares at her. "Then why not tell us what happened after that? You tell me all these horrible things, but not how you got away. Why they let you go."

"They didn't let me go!" she shouts. "I was rescued! But not by you! Not by the Aguileros. Oh, no! You didn't come for me. No one came to save me. No one but—" She bites her lip, turns, and starts trotting across the beach to the sea, then splashing loudly through the waves, diving beneath them, swimming out, hand over hand, reckless and desperate, away from Raoul, away from everything, swimming toward the horizon, as far as she can go.

He calls after her. She dives beneath the waves so she can't hear. When she surfaces and can swim no more, she turns onto her back and looks up at the sky. This is where she wants to stay forever, floating peacefully on the sea's surface, turning like a leaf in its arms, holding her up.

Raoul approaches on her surfboard, pulls her aboard, and paddles to shore. When they get close, she slides off and heads toward the house.

"Lena!" her calls after her again. *Lena*, not Malenque. She closes her eyes and starts to run, but then she hears something. An outboard engine. The speedboat they arrived on days ago reaches the island's small dock.

Someone climbs out: Tomás.

CHAPTER 46

Chagos Island is the smallest in the Santa Lucia Archipelago. It's little more than an atoll: a ring of brilliant white beaches surrounding an emerald oasis that rises six feet above sea level. That's where Casa de Azul lies, rising on stilts with a wrap-around veranda and a three-sixty-degree view of the sea, the surrounding islands, and mainland. Although called the "house of blue," its exterior walls are white, as brilliant as the sand that rings it. The blue comes from the interior, each room a different shade—sapphire, cyan, azure—while its furnishings and wall-hangings are washed with the tropical colors of fish swimming among coral in the lagoon, yellow and red birds flittering through the ferns, peach and pink stained sunrises and sunsets.

Lena stops running when she's halfway up the incline toward the Casa de Azul. She turns and watches Tomás leave the dock and head down the beach toward Raoul. She watches the two men greet each other affectionately.

Tomás turns his head toward Lena as he speaks. Even from so far away, she feels his malice.

So. It's done. He knows. And now Raoul knows.

She walks quietly the rest of the way to the Casa. She showers and dresses. She packs her bags, sits on the bed, and waits. It's over. She knows it now. Whatever lies Tomás might be telling Raoul, none could be worse than the truth, which is what she must now tell Raoul. It's her duty as an Aguilero to tell him everything she knows. All they said when she was a prisoner. All her mother told her. All Ortiz told her mother. Everything. It's done. It's over.

She looks out the window where the brothers are in a heated, animated conversation. Raoul is tearing at his hair, which Lena realizes now is what he does when he feels out of control. Now the brothers are yelling at each other.

Tomás gestures at the Casa and Raoul turns to look, sees her standing at the window.

He charges up the incline. She hears feet stomping up the veranda, the screen door banging open, footsteps storming down the hall. Their bedroom door slams against the wall as he enters.

Raoul's hair is wild, his face a fury of emotions. Anger, disbelief, betrayal. Anguish. They stare at each other across the room, then he takes her by the shoulders and shakes her.

"Tell me! Tell me everything!"

Lena feels relief, now it's out. No more worrying, wondering how to tell him, what to say, what his reaction will be. It's strange though how Raoul's wild-eyed fury has quieted her fear. There's nothing left to do but tell the truth. Yet, at the same time, something else grows in her mind: the stubborn conviction she will not go down without fighting for him, for her life. Their life together.

She lets him shake her. Then calmly, firmly, she slides his hands away. She looks him in the eye. "What did Tomás tell you?"

He looks shocked. Then angry. "No! You first! You tell me."

She sits on the edge of the bed.

"I'm waiting," she says. "I can sit here all day. Or you can hang me by my wrists. It won't be the first time. But I'm not telling you anything until I hear what Tomás told you. Because he's our traitor, I'm almost sure of it. But he's told you I am, hasn't he?"

He stares with astonishment at her. Then he sits on the bed beside her. They both stare out the window at the sea glittering in the distance.

"So, I must choose whom to believe. My brother or my lover. Is that it?"

"So it appears," Lena says, Fiona-like. *I'm turning into Fiona*, she thinks crazily. *Cool and dispassionate, as I must be.* "But," she says, gazing steadily at him, "did you promise your brother you would never leave him no matter what, like you did me?"

He looks closely at her. "Why did you make me promise that, Malenque?"

Malenque. A sweet sigh moves through her. "Because I feared when I told you about my mother you would leave me."

"So, it's true. Dolores Machado is your mother."

"Yes. It's also true she's the one who sent her bodyguards to rescue me. Not you!" she adds. "If it weren't for her, I'd still be hanging by my wrists, or dead. Or worse."

"Malenque—" he begins, but she cuts him off.

"And it's also true she didn't even know I was in the country until *Daniel,*" she pauses to let his name sink in, "told my father I'd been arrested, who then told my mother. I made my father and aunt promise not to tell her I was coming here because I hated her for leaving us and wanted nothing to do with her.

"That's why I never told you about her, because she was nothing to me. Why should I tell you something that couldn't possibly matter? I knew I'd have to tell you someday. But every time I thought about mentioning it, the more I was afraid it would put distance between us, sowing doubt or mistrust. I couldn't bear that. And the longer I waited, the worse it would have been when I did tell you. So, I . . . didn't. Because, in the grand scheme of things, it didn't matter."

Raoul sits silently watching her as she speaks. Finally, he nods. "I believe you. It's too stupid to make up. And if you were a mole, as Tomás believes, why would they torture you? Why would your mother allow you to return to us, put you in further danger? They know what we do to traitors. So do you."

He lets his body fall back on the bed and looks up at the ceiling. "Now, what am I to do?" he says. To himself, she guesses. Which sounds so strange coming from Raoul, who always knows what to do. Then he sits up again. "And so, your mother. What does she know about us now?"

"Nothing. She believes what I told them when I was arrested, that I'm just a journalist and don't know any rebels. The only reason I came to San Balanque, my mother told Ortiz, was because I wanted to shame and embarrass her for abandoning me. That's what she believes. What I let her believe."

"Wait! You spoke to Ortiz?"

"Not me. I was in bed, out on pain meds. But he summoned her to him. He was angry that her bodyguards rescued me. He told her he had intelligence that I was an Aguilero, your lover, and that was my face on that poster with you. Which matches what Daniel told me before I was arrested, about an informant high up in the movement."

Raoul rubs a hand down his face, taking it all in.

"But then," Lena continues, "my mother asked Ortiz if the informant told him I was her daughter, and he said no. So, she convinced him it was a ploy to get him to arrest and torture the vice president's stepdaughter, to drive a wedge between her husband and Ortiz. There already were serious disagreements going on between them. She thinks the rebels, as she calls us, were using disinformation to widen the rift and intensify the internal strife."

"If Ortiz believes he was set up this way," Raoul says, "then that so-called high-level informer has been compromised. Does your mother think Ortiz believes her theory?"

"Apparently—only he wanted me to leave the country. I told her I wouldn't go. That I've created a life here and wasn't going to let Ortiz or anyone else tell me what to do." She gives him a small grin. "I played up the naïve, stubborn, vengeful daughter role. Plus, she thinks I'm staying here for someone. Not you, of course. She believes it's Daniel. I called him from her house to let him know I was out. She says Ortiz will let me stay. He understands how vengeful children can be. His own son Romero threatens to join the Aguileros when he's angry at his father."

Raoul raises his eyebrows at this. "Interesting. We can use that."

"I thought so too. But what will you tell Tomás?"

He looks out the window and slowly nods his head again, like he always does when he's pondering something. "I'll tell him you came clean about your mother, but you're not the spy he thinks you are."

"Will he believe you?"

"No." He looks over at her for a long moment. "You will have to prove your innocence, Malenque, your loyalty to the Aguileros. Tomás would have told others about this. So, we must find a way for you to prove you stand with us. Are you ready to do that?"

"Of course!"

"It will not be easy. You may be asked to do something you won't like. But it will be necessary." He takes her hand and squeezes. "And no more secrets. The truth only." She nods, but then looks troubled.

His face goes dark. "What is it?"

"It's about your mother."

"My mother!"

Lena goes to her rucksack and retrieves the blue envelope with the letter inside. "I never wanted to tell you. This is how they got me to agree to help her escape. I knew you'd never approve. I wasn't trained for that kind of mission. There were others they could have recruited. So why me? When I resisted going, Pepe gave me this."

Raoul reads the letter. "You thought she was being sincere," he says with a bitter edge.

"How could I refuse to help relieve your poor mother's heart of the guilt she felt for neglecting you, right before she left the country?"

"She's clever that way, my mother."

Then Lena tells him about the conversation she and Eva had at the house. "That's when I realized the letter was a ruse. She wanted to take my measure, thinking me a rival. Not for your heart, but for the people's. By becoming your partner, the Malenque in the poster, she feared I was replacing her as the first lady of the Aguileros."

When Raoul says nothing, she continues. "When the Federales appeared at the back door, my suspicions grew. Surely your mother would know they were stationed there. So why not warn us? It seemed as if Tomás and your mother planned this together to get rid of me."

"Stop!" he says. "Enough. My mother is a cold, calculating woman, and Tomás is definitely her son, but I refuse to believe they drug you into this to . . . what? Get you killed? Remove you as a rival?"

"That's what I believe."

He shakes his head. "It's too much. Tomás would make me think you're a traitor, and now you would have me believe he is one. As well as my mother!"

She takes his hand back into her lap and strokes it. "I hope I'm wrong. I would love to be wrong. I never wanted to tell you any of this. Please don't hold it against me."

He looks at her and sighs. "No, you were right to tell me. As you know, my relationship with my brother and mother has always been complicated. When we were growing up, she was a fiery, passionate woman, totally dedicated to our father. But when he died at Ortiz's hands, she became vengeful, cold, and calculating. I didn't know this at first because she sent us away. But when I returned, it became clear.

"Tomás returned from Cuba the year before and she believed he, the eldest son, would take over where father let off and lead the rebellion against Ortiz, with her at his side. But I returned, and while she dismissed me as a mere intellectual—which she saw as our father's greatest failing—others did not. Sergio Alvarez, my father's closest friend, especially. He saw me as my father's son and the one to lead us moving forward—not Tomás, who was too much of a hothead. Under Sergio's mentorship, I become a greater force in the movement than Tomás." Raoul sits slumped on the edge of the bed, his forearms on his knees.

"My mother was not pleased. Frankly, I think Tomás was fine with it, even relieved. He wanted to fight, not lead, and I gave him what he wanted. But mother wanted more for herself. When her plans for Tomás failed, she turned her affection onto me. She wanted to become my close advisor. But I had no desire to replace Tomás in her affections and little confidence in her advice. I thought that was the end of it. After all, she had Angelica to raise. She had Tomás and Pepe. Perhaps I made a mistake in that."

"So, you believe me now, that she saw me as a rival and wanted to get rid of me?"

He takes a deep breath and blows it out. "This letter she sent is disturbing, as is your conversation with her. Also, the Federales at the back door. There was no adequate explanation of why this vital piece of information had been lacking. Still . . . what you allege goes too far."

"But you know Tomás hates me. Even Fiona found his animosity toward me strange."

"This is true. But explainable. At first, he thought you would become a distraction, interfering with our work. Then he saw how I was positioning you to be my partner, standing always at my side where he always stood. So, he does see you as a rival. And Mother also. Which explains their antipathy toward you, why she wanted to meet you, but it does not mean they were trying to get you killed. And what? Bianca too? No, it's too much."

That night, while lying in each other's arms, the lust they put on hold because of her injuries returns. They lie side by side, Raoul's mouth devouring hers while her arms pull him closer. But when he climbs on top—the weight of him pinning her down—she panics, thrown back on that hard floor with the weight of Sergeant Batista pressing down. And when Raoul's knee forces hers apart and he touches her where the sergeant had, she shoves him off.

"What's wrong? Did I hurt you?"

"Nothing's wrong. I just want you to lie there and let me look at you."

So, he does. He turns onto his back, and she runs her fingers over his finely sculpted arms and chest, luxuriating in the furry softness covering his belly. Her fingers travel down to that thicket of curly hair and the long, throbbing organ rising from it. And this erotic act of looking, feasting her eyes upon her lover's lusty body, kindles such a fire within that the memory of what happened in prison melts away. *That has nothing to do with this. With us.*

She climbs on top of him. This mountain of a man, this jaguar in disguise. She rubs herself over the length of his shaft, quivering at the delicious sensations it arouses. Then she slants it toward her entrance and impales herself, slowly, surely, rising and falling, pushing further and further with each stroke, until the whole of him is wrapped in the whole of her.

She watches him as he watches her, seeming fascinated by the sight of her taking complete control of their lovemaking. She loves how this huge, viral man, so exquisitely formed, lies so passively and pliantly beneath her. It's a powerful and delicious feeling.

She's rides him with wild abandon. His hands hold her hips as she rises and falls, his eyes full of ferocious desire. She knows how she must look with her long-tousled hair thrown around her shoulders, her breasts bouncing, her skin gleaming with the sheen of heat created between them. She leans down and passionately claims his mouth, demanding tongue and more tongue. But as the waves of delicious sensation crescendo, she throws herself back into the saddle, her movements against him frenzied and frantic. When she's about to roar her own cry of triumph, he flips her over and pins her to the bed. Her legs wrap around him as the thrusts continue, but now with him on top.

"Don't stop," she begs, and he doesn't until every rippling sensation inside her has been milked, until there's nothing more to give. He rolls them onto their sides, holding her so tightly she can't tell where he ends and she begins. He's murmuring sweet senseless sounds in her ear as he always does, and then he laughs and brushes her hair from her face, his eyes gleaming with delight.

"My exquisite warrior queen! You may ride me forever, whenever. All that strength and beauty bearing down on me. I will treasure this image of you forever."

CHAPTER 47

Lena wakes the next morning feeling light and clean. Cleansed. All her secrets out in the open, emptied of their heavy baggage. All her fears that Raoul would leave her washed away in his love for and faith in her. The anger at her mother's abandonment that festered for so long now purged in her understanding of why she left.

It's as if she had walked through fire and been purged of all that weighed her down. Even her anger toward Tomás and his mother, while not diminished, has shifted. All their conniving and manipulation failed to destroy her. The same with Ortiz and the Federales. She was stronger than ever. She survived prison. Survived torture. Survived sexual assault. The thought of the captain knocking her to the floor and the sergeant slathering her with his spit does not touch her now. She was stronger, greater, better than all of them. They could not make her give up her comrades or forsake her oath, and that fact alone makes her feel pure. Untouched. Even the memory of the pain screaming through her body when she was strung up now seems more a triumph than a defeat. Lena survived that too.

And what if they had killed her? Even then she would still have remained untouched, inviolate, pure. As Bianca was. She lived life on her own terms and died that way. Lena understands now why Bianca said she wasn't sorry when she was dying. Her life wasn't wasted. It was hers to give, and she gave it.

Both were warriors by choice. Unafraid of a warrior's death. It's clear, simple, and clean in Lena's mind now. She drinks in that cleansing feeling. She doesn't know how long this sense of clarity will last but feels it's something she can draw upon it when needed, this vibrant vision that lies at the heart of who she truly is. Of this, she's sure.

And Raoul, her warrior man, he's part of that too. Even if he had rejected her as she feared, would she have fallen apart? She no longer thinks so. She had packed her bags, ready to go.

But when Raoul entered the room, all wild-eyed, hair on fire, she knew she must fight for him, for their life together. She knew what she loved in him—that warrior spirit—was part of her too. Whether they were together or not, what he gave birth to, his vision of her as Malenque, is hers forever.

She will fight for what she knows is right, a San Balanque free of Ortiz. She will prove her loyalty and defeat Ortiz on his own ground at the same time. A plan is evolving in her mind, which excites her and makes her feel stronger than ever.

She stretches now, spreading her arms and legs over the bed, luxuriating in the silkiness of the sheets as she breathes in this new, clean, strengthened feeling. The space beside her is empty.

Raoul is gone. Off for an early morning swim, no doubt, like he often does, letting her sleep in. She puts on her bikini, thinking to join him, and slips a loose sundress over it. But when she opens the bedroom door, she hears raised voices coming from the front room. Tomás and Raoul. She steps lightly down the hall and stops to listen.

"How will this look? You were played for a fool, parading this woman about like she's our Malenque of Old, while all along she's the daughter of our enemy."

"Yes, but she's also an Aguilero. She chose to fight for the freedom of her country rather than side with her stepfather and Ortiz. This shows great passion, great courage, to stand up for what's right against your own blood. It's not like she's the only Aguilero with family who supports Ortiz. Look at Carlos, his father a captain with the Federales, and Hilda's aunt married to the minister of interior. Are they traitors, informants? Do we kick them out too?"

"But they were up front with us. They didn't hide it like she did."

He's right, Lena thinks. *If only I'd been transparent from the start.*

Raoul continues. "She made a serious mistake but that doesn't make her a traitor. Her stories about us in the *Star*, her interview of the ambassador's family, have been immensely valuable to us. . .."

Lena backs away. Let the brothers hammer this out on their own. She heads to the kitchen, pours herself a cup of coffee, and steps out onto the veranda. She loves it here. This house, this view.

Carlos is there too, leaning on the railing, smoking a cigarette, holding it daintily between thumb and forefinger, sending smoke rings into the cool morning air. He quickly straightens when the door opens behind him, then relaxes when he sees who it is. She smiles and joins him at the railing.

"I suppose Raoul told you all about what's going on, who my mother is and Tomás' accusations against me?"

He nods.

"And mine against him?"

He stiffens, and then looks at her. "But of course. I must know everything to protect Raoul."

"So, what do you think?"

"I believe what my commander believes: that you are innocent. Families are complicated and do not always align politically."

"And what about my suspicions regarding Tomás?"

He turns his gaze back to the sea. "This I do not know. Like Raoul, I tend to believe Tomás is innocent too. But," he turns to Lena again, "I was unhappy with the way he and Pepe coerced you into helping their mother escape. Had I been there instead of Benito, it would not have happened. Which makes me wonder why they plotted this while both Raoul and I were gone." He wags his head back and forth, as if weighing the pros and cons. "Perhaps it was a coincidence."

"Do you think Tomás is capable of something like that? Plotting to kill his brother's lover?"

"This I do not wish to say."

Lena leans down on the railing with him, letting that soak in. Then she turns to face him. "You know, I've never heard your story, Carlos. How you became an Aguilero."

He's quiet and then begins in a low mellifluous voice. "It was long ago. I met Raoul at the university while studying architecture. His views of the Ortiz regime and what he wanted to build in its place aligned with mine. I wanted to build something as beautiful and strong as the great cathedrals built here long ago. How could they rise so high and remain so strong? Because they were finely crafted on the principles of unity, balance, and proportion. That's why they endured centuries of hard use. That's what's needed to build strong cities and systems of government.

"Ortiz's regime has none of that. It's top-heavy with greed and corruption supported upon the backs of people caving under its weight. The only way to keep those backs from breaking is to point guns at them or starve them so they'll do anything they must to feed their families. They built an ugly bulwark of arms and exploitation to prop up a festering foundation. It cannot last. And should not."

He slowly lifts his cigarette to his mouth, blowing smoke rings into the air, as if talking to himself. "I am here so when it does fall what we build in its stead is strong and beautiful to serve the needs and aspirations of all our people."

He gives Lena a crooked grin. "So, this is my story. As you can see, I'm a dreamer as well as a soldier. And like Raoul, I see you that way too: as part of this plan to raise beauty from the ashes of war."

In all the time she's known him, Lena never heard Carlos speak so long or so eloquently. She is deeply moved and puts her hand on his arm. "Thank you for telling me."

She leaves him on the veranda, grabbing her surfboard propped against the side of the house, and heads toward the beach. She pulls off her dress, throws her board into the surf, and paddles out for the first time since she's been here.

Lena is still surfing when Tomás heads to the dock and takes the boat back to the mainland.

In a while, Raoul comes looking for her. She raises her hand over her head. He's never seen her surf, and she wants to show off. A swell rises and ripples forward, but she lets it pass. The next one feels more promising. She paddles forward as it nears, catches the crest, and rises. She darts in and out of the swell, pumping it to go further, then finally kicks away, dropping to her stomach and paddling in.

Raoul is sitting on the beach dressed in his jeans and a white tank top. He claps as she comes ashore. "You were magnificent!" he tells her. "You rode that board almost as masterly as you rode me last night."

She stands over him and wrings the saltwater from her hair onto his head.

He laughs and grabs her, brings her down on his lap. "You must teach me to ride the waves as you do."

"I will! Now, if you like. But you'll have to change. Or go commando."

"I think I'll save my men from having to endure that indignity. But before you teach me, we have matters to discuss."

"You mean your conversation with Tomás." She makes a face. "Did you convince him I'm not a spy?"

"Not yet. But he was extremely interested in what Daniel said about an informant high up in our organization. That clearly disturbed him. I asked him how he found out about your mother, and his answer was unsatisfactory. Just like when I asked why he hadn't waited for my return before sending our mother and sister to safety, or why he hadn't protected the back of the house where you were to make your escape."

Raoul gives her a hard look, as if anticipating her response. "That doesn't mean I suspect Tomás of being an informant. It means he's holding something back, and I intend to find out what. Then when I told him your suspicions about him—"

"You didn't!"

"I had to. Everything needs to be out in the open. I didn't mention you suspected our mother as well."

He shakes his head wearily. "I won't share your suspicions with others. I don't want to undermine his authority. It's bad enough his suspicions about you are moving through the ranks. But I told him, as I will tell others, if we hold your mother against you, then we will have to do so with all the Aguileros who have family members supporting Ortiz. This would reduce our ranks considerably.

"Still, it will help if we can prove your loyalty." His fingers graze her cheek as he pushes a lock of her hair behind her ear. "Tomás has an idea about how you can do that."

"What?" she says warily.

"He wants you to help us kidnap your mother to hold for ransom."

She rears back. "No! I can't. She's my mother!"

"You said you have no feelings for her, she's nothing to you . . .."

"She isn't! She wasn't! But . . .."

"But what?"

"She saved me, Raoul! Do you know what they were about to do when her men came? What I was willing to let them do to protect our people! Do you know what she risked to save me? How she stood up to Ortiz for me?"

He frowns and plucks at her hair again. "Lena, you know I could not rescue you that way. We had another plan for getting you out."

Lena, he calls her again!

She pulls away from him, eyes narrowing. "I'm not complaining about that," she says angrily.

"But you are holding it against me, I heard you—"

"I'm not holding it *against you*! I'm holding it in *defense of her*. She was the one who saved me, and I won't betray her for that! She knows nothing about me being an Aguilero! She thinks I'm a silly, vengeful daughter. She apologized for leaving us. She said she loves me, she's always loved me. Leaving me was the hardest thing she ever did, and she regrets it. She's been grieving my loss all this time . . . I couldn't . . . I would never deliberately hurt her, betray her." She scrambles to her feet, fists on hips. "I won't do it!"

"All right. We'll find another way. Come," he says, patting the ground next to him.

She sits down beside him again. He pulls her close, speaking softly, gently in her ear. "You never really hated your mother, did you? It was love, not hate, all along."

She pushes back and stares at him. Was it love all along? Her chest heaves as she realizes he's right. All that anger and hate she felt for her mother over the years, and then the feigned indifference! All because she couldn't bear to feel the love that never went away. The grief from losing her. The sting of that truth brings tears to her eyes.

"We'll find another way to prove your loyalty, Malenque—to the others. Not to me. Never to me. I know your heart."

"Yes, another way," she agrees, thinking about the plan that's been forming in her mind. But she's not ready to share it with him yet. He's not going to like it.

CHAPTER 48

The next day Raoul takes Lena ashore so she can call her father and reassure him she survived her imprisonment. She doesn't tell him about the torture or near-rape. She's sure her mother didn't either.

"Thank you for not telling her about me becoming an Aguilero."

"I hope you're rethinking your involvement with them."

"I am," she says. "At least I'm stepping back to clear my head. And to spend more time with Mom. I understand better why she left now. At any rate, I want to give her a second chance. You know, to make things right between us."

He sighs with relief. "That makes me so happy. You have uncles and cousins living there too. Have you thought about contacting them?"

"I have. But it's still extremely important you say nothing about my relations with the Aguileros. It would be quite dangerous for me. And Mom."

"I understand. I won't say anything. But please take better care of yourself and stay safe, won't you? Promise me. You know how much I love you."

"I do, Daddy. I promise."

When Lena hangs up, a heaviness fills her chest. She's never lied to her father before about things that matter so much. But she had to. For his sake as well as hers. That old line. But it's true. Deception and subterfuge are unavoidable elements of a freedom fighter's life, Lena's life with Raoul. She's resigned to it now.

She's crossed so many moral red lines since becoming an Aguilero, or at least eventually acquiesced to them. Kidnapping, hostage-taking, armed robberies, even assassinations, have been justified as necessary evils for the cause. All in the name of the greater good.

Whatever qualms she had about what was needed to survive and thrive as an Aguilero, compared with the pain of torture she had to bear to keep others safe, seem naïve now, unworthy. Her reluctance about combat training seems childish. The outrage she felt about the abduction of the ambassador's family dissipated when she saw how well they were being cared for and how it helped free imprisoned Aguileros. The image of those men hanging in trees is no more horrific now than the image of beheaded students thrown in ditches. Even the anguish she felt upon learning of Deke's assassination has shrunk to a sore spot in her mind. Bianca's death still stabs her to the core, but Lena sees it more as a triumph of her friend's warrior spirit than a tragedy.

She's crossed some kind of Rubicon. There's no going back. What they are doing is worth whatever risks must be taken, moral corners cut, or personal sacrifices made. For Bianca. For Raoul. For San Balanque. For all she believes in with her whole heart and soul: freedom, justice, democracy. We are putting our "bodies on the gears" of that odious authoritarian machine to make it stop. That horrible image from Mario Savio's speech that inspired her so long ago in the sunlight of her life is her reality now. And her future.

"I know a way to not only prove my loyalty," Lena tells Raoul that evening, "but also to find high-value targets to kidnap instead of my mother." They are sitting at the dining table, having finished their dinner and pushed aside their plates. Tall cool glasses of sweet tea leave moist imprints on the cotton tablecloth. Outside the window, a mackerel sky turns pale pink and sherbet orange. A breeze pushes sheer curtains into the room.

Raoul leans back in his chair. "All right, let's hear it."

She leans forward, her elbows and forearms folded on the table. "We need to take advantage of the situation that was handed to us when my mother convinced Ortiz of my innocence. Mother wants to see more of me and show me around, introduce me to her inner circle. I told her I was going to stick to writing for the social pages, so that could give me entrance into those circles too. And then there are my uncles and cousins.

Some may be sympathetic to our cause or have intel we could use. My eldest uncle Simon owns the Morales Mining Company and is a staunch supporter of Ortiz."

So far, she cannot read the expression on Raoul's face and rushes ahead.

"I could infiltrate those circles: spy on them, discover what they're planning, look for ways to turn it to our advantage, find high-level hostages, if that's what Tomás needs to prove my innocence. Of course, this means I'll have to return to Curico and go undercover, cutting off contact with you and everyone else for a while . . .."

She's been wanting to get it all out before Raoul objects and watching anxiously to see if he will. But she sees nothing in his face but a keen interest in what she's saying.

"You would be willing to do this? Knowing how dangerous it is? More so than anything you've done so far. You know what they will do if you are found out."

"Yes. I've thought it through and I'm not afraid. I can do this."

"And what of your mother? Will it not be a betrayal of her trust? Will you not be putting her in danger too, if you are caught and they think she helped you?"

Lena bites her lower lip. "I thought of that. But then I remembered your Gita story, what Arjuna was told when he wanted to retreat from battle because doing his duty would pit him against his own family."

She looks deeply into Raoul's eyes and reaches across the table to take his hands. "I feel I've been called, Raoul. I feel it in my bones, this is a battle I must fight and the ground I must fight it on. I couldn't stand it if Ortiz remained in power. We must do everything possible to remove him. Bianca died for the cause. And I'm ready to do so, if I must, as each of our soldiers is ready to do every day."

He nods slowly. "I've heard one of your uncle Simon's sons was part of the Student Union when he was at the University and may still be sympathetic to our cause. I'll see if I can get more Intel on him."

Lena's eyes go wide. "You mean you don't mind? Me going undercover? I was sure you'd object."

Raoul stares at her incredulously. "*Mind*? Do I mind? This is the word you choose?" He pulls his hands away from her and squeezes his eyes shut as if in pain. His head shakes wearily in disbelief. When he opens his eyes, he looks at her like she's crazy.

"Of course I mind! Do I want you to go undercover, put yourself in danger like that? Absolutely not! Do I want to object, loudly and strongly? Absolutely. Would I have asked you myself to go undercover? Never! But will I forbid it? As commander-in-chief, I cannot. As you say, this perfect set-up has fallen into our laps. We would be derelict in our duty not to take advantage of it." He takes her hands into his again. "I was not able to protect you when you were running through the forests with Bianca, so I sent you to Curico to help with a rally. But I was not able to protect you from being captured and tortured. I was not even able to come to your rescue, as you've reminded me so many times—"

"Raoul," she says softly, apologetically.

"No, hear me out. What we are doing every day as Aguileros is dangerous. I could tell you no, don't do this, and then you get blown up here on this island in a bomb raid. There is no escape from danger for any of us. We must accept our fate. It's in God's hands. That's all I can say. We can only do our duty, as you say. And each of us must make our own choice about how much risk we are willing to take on."

During the next few weeks, Lena has never been happier. The island is an exciting strategic command post by day and a romantic retreat at night, although their pillow talk now is about her going undercover, what it will involve, how it will work. Aguileros skilled in espionage were brought in to give Lena a crash course in spy craft. A few will go undercover to help her. Others will keep a watchful distance and be on hand to pass messages back and forth. As they plan and practice, she becomes increasingly confident.

She can play the ingénue to her mother, her uncles, and the social elite of Ortiz's regime. She can convince them she's innocent of whatever lingering suspicions they may have. She will win their affection and trust and become part of their inner circles, posing as a journalist covering their social events. She can use this ruse to further the cause and strike at the heart of Ortiz's regime.

She will become at last, in some significant way, the Malenque of Old they all say she is. But for real.

CHAPTER 49

Their last night together, Lena and Raoul stroll hand and hand upon a moonlit beach. It feels magical, too perfect to be real, Lena thinks: the warm balmy air on their skin, the cool soft sand beneath their bare feet, the full moon pooling on the sea's tranquil surface, the sound of surf like a soft, whispering song.

It reminds Lena of one of her favorite poems. "Do you know Wallace Stevens' poem *Idea of Order at Key West*?"

"No, why do you ask?"

"Well, it's about a woman singing as she strolls by the sea, as we are doing. And how the sea becomes her song, as if she created it, or it her. It's about what Stevens calls the 'supreme fiction': whether we create the world around us or it creates us, or if there's a kind of co-creation going on. At least that's my takeaway."

She's quiet for a moment. "When I used to go surfing, waiting for the perfect wave to carry me away, I pictured it as this strong masculine presence. Surfing in that mindset was a sensual, almost erotic experience. I always thought: That's what I want when I fall in love, someone who sweeps me off my feet." She laughs. "I was always a romantic. But that's exactly what happened when I saw you rising from the pool that day. You were who I was waiting for. Or," she adds, cocking her head coyly at him, "were you the sea I sang and singing made?"

He laughs and squeezes her hand. "I like that. You, me, and the sea, washing together."

"I wish we could stay here like this forever, that this could be our forever island," she says.

"Someday it will be."

"Let's make a promise then. To come back here and spend forever in each other's arms, shall we?"

That night making love she feels like she's back at sea, surfing. Raoul is the wave she's riding, moving beneath her, through her, surrounding and supporting her in every conceivable way. He strengthens her and makes her whole. She feels his power and her own—an irresistible force flowing through them.

The next morning as Carlos ferries her and Raoul ashore, Lena trails her fingers through the water, watching the sea separate into soft tendrils of turquoise that spread out and melt away. The breeze blowing over the bow breaks over their faces, trailing long tendrils of their hair behind them. *The patterns we make*, she muses, and lets the thought drift away into the warm air.

The murmur of a plane passes overhead. Probably a passenger jet flying to Curico like the one she arrived on, Lena thinks. How young she was. It seems like ancient history, although it's only been a year since she came here, her whole life changing forever in ways she never dreamed.

Now she's headed for a new life among people she knows capable of great cruelty. She does so with open eyes and an open heart. *Why am I not afraid?*

She looks at Raoul, touches his face with wet fingers, trails saltwater into his mouth, lifts hers to drink from his lips.

This is why, she thinks. *This is why.*

When they reach shore, Jesse puts Lena's bags into the back of his taxi. Raoul takes her face into his hands. Their kiss is long, deep and tender. Then she turns, their clasped hands trailing behind her as she walks away until they touch no more.

She doesn't look back as the taxi drives away. She doesn't have to. He's part of her now and forever will be. He's the sea she sings.

ON THE MAKING OF A NOVEL

They say it takes a village to raise a child, and the same is true for creating a novel. It certainly was for me. I want to thank everyone who helped, starting with my beta readers: Harvey Ardman, Dianne Emley, Harry Holden, Ginny Sollars, and Lena Mauveau. Then there were my incredibly talented editors: Laura Chittenden, Dana Isaacson, and Mark Paxson. Each helped hone the novel in ways that gave it clarity, momentum, and precision. A special thanks to Baris Sehri for his brilliant cover design.

Last, but never least, I want to thank my husband, Dale Brasket. His experiences fighting in the jungles of Vietnam as a Marine gave me invaluable insights into a soldier's life. I can never thank him enough for his unfailing support of all my creative endeavors.

This Sea Within was inspired by my travels in Central America when sailing around the world. I loved the lush landscapes, the warmth of the people, and the culture of the countries we visited, even while troubled by the continual conflicts and political upheavals that took place there over the centuries and continues today.

We sailed into Panama's St Andrews Bay on December 20, 1989, the same day the U.S. invaded the country. We watched from the deck of our boat while U.S. gunboats bombarded Panama City in their attempt to depose President Noriega and bring him to the United States to stand trial on drug charges. Hundreds of civilians were killed and an estimated 14,000 left homeless. When we finally were allowed to dock, the city was in shambles, all the stores empty and vandalized. The rubble and debris in the streets were piled so high that bulldozers were needed to clear them.

This wasn't the first time the U.S interfered politically in the region. Ever since the Monroe Doctrine went into effect in 1823, establishing Central and South America as under the United States' sphere of influence, it was used to justify interventions that led to much misery in the region. I wanted to throw a light on that long, sordid history of propping up corrupt dictators to benefit American corporations.

Writing a historical novel takes a lot of research, even when set in the fictional country of San Balanque. Fortunately, it's something I enjoy. My research focused on the revolution that took place in Nicaragua in the 1960s and 70s, one of the few examples where revolutionaries were able to throw out a corrupt dictator supported by the United States—in this case Anastasio Somoza.

At the same time, I was aware of how the new democracy in Nicaragua eventually devolved into another cruel dictatorship—this time, ironically and tragically, by Daniel Ortega, the leader of the revolutionaries who toppled Somoza.

Books that helped me better understand the history and politics of revolutionary warfare were:

Blood of Brothers: Life and War in Nicaragua, by journalist Stephen Kinzer. Harvard University, 1991.

The Jaguar Smile, A Nicaraguan Journey, by Salman Rushdie. Random House, 1977, 1987.

The Long Honduran Night: Resistance, Terror, and the United States in the Aftermath of the Coup, by Dana Frank, Professor of history at UC Santa Cruz. Haymarket Books, 2018.

Making History: Interviews with Four Generals of Cuba's Revolutionary Armed Forces, edited by Mary-Alice Waters. Pathfinder Press, 1999.

Books that helped me understand what it's like to be a freedom fighter, especially from a woman's point of view, or as a soldier in the field, were:

The Country Under My Skin: A Memoir of Love and War, by Gioconda Belli, a poet who became a revolutionary in Nicaragua. Anchor Books, 2003.

Remembering Che: My Life with Che Guevara, by Aleida March, his second wife. Ocean Press, 2012.

Socialism and Man in Cuba, by Che Guevara and Fidel Castro. Pathfinder Press, 1989, 2009.

Guerrilla Warfare by Ernesto Che Guevara. CreateSpace Independent Publishing Platform, 2013.

While I was writing *This Sea Within*, Russia invaded Ukraine. I followed the story closely, appalled by what was happening there, but also deeply inspired by the leadership of President Volodymyr Zelensky and the bravery of the Ukrainians who defended their democracy against against a corrupt dictator, Vladimir Putin, with a much larger force. Their struggle informed my writing and made *This Sea Within* seem even more relevant for today's readers.

Before *This Sea Within* was published, the United States under President Trump invaded Venezuela and kidnapped President Maduro, bringing him to the U.S. to stand trial on drug charges. Then President Trump made a deal with the remaining leaders of the corrupt regime to bring in American corporations to take over their oil industry.

So history repeats itself. The cyclical nature of "peace and plunder" as written about in the poem "This Sea Within All Things" continues down through the ages—even while "strong arms and stalwart hearts" rise up to resist the maelstrom, again and again.

MYTHS, POETRY, AND LYRICS

The *Legend of Malenque and Balanque* found in chapter two is my own original work, inspired by Maya mythology and the Hero Twins, Hunahpu and Xbalanque. Central components of their story involve triumphing over the lords of the underworld and a cyclical journey of death and rebirth. Highlighted in their story, as well as in *This Sea Within,* are themes of creation, sacrifice, and transformation.

The poem "This Sea Within All Things" in chapter three, as well as in the epilogue, is my own original work. I attributed it to the fictional poet Ramon Fernandez referenced in the poem "Idea of Order at Key West" by Wallace Stevens. His poem is discussed in the last chapter of *This Sea Within.*

San Balanque and its history are fictional, although inspired by the history of Central America, its landscapes and culture, and my travels to Mexico, Honduras' Bay Islands, Panama, and Costa Rica.

The titles of the three parts into which this novel is divided pay tribute to Pablo Neruda's poem "Right, Comrade, It's the Hour of the Garden," as well as the epigraph featuring those same titles.

The lyrics of "Back to the Garden" attributed to a fictional singer in chapter two is also my own original work, inspired by Joni Mitchell's "Woodstock" lyrics.

I also wrote the lyrics to "Surfer Girls" as sung by Pepe in chapter fourteen. It was inspired by the Beach Boys' song "California Girls."

I am truly grateful to poet Michael M. Burch for allowing me to quote from his poem "Floating." All other quotes found on these pages are in the public domain.

ABOUT THE AUTHOR

I spent six years sailing around the world with my husband and two children before returning to California. There I earned my master's degree at Cal Poly State University in San Luis Obispo and taught literature and composition to college students before entering the nonprofit sector.

As director of the Santa Barbara County Action Network, I was a strong advocate for social, environmental, and economic justice. During all this time, my short stories, poetry, essays, articles, op-eds, and book reviews appeared in literary and academic journals, newspapers and sailing magazines.

Now I live with my husband among the rolling hills and vineyards of Paso Robles where I write the kinds of novels I love to read. My debut novel *When Things Go Missing* was published in September 2025. Learn more at www.DeborahJBrasket.com.

What happens when the one person holding a family together mysteriously disappears?

One day Fran heads toward the grocery store and keeps going till she reaches the tip of South America, leaving an empty hole in the lives of her family: Kay, a cranky archaeology student who adores her mother but distrusts men, her father and brother in particular. Cal, a heroin addict living at home with a father he fears and no means of support. Walter, a devoted husband but distant father, who tracks his wife's journey across the continent with pushpins on a map.

Adding to the mystery of the mother's disappearance are the "gifts" she sends her family: The elated messages she leaves on Kay's phone, but never when she's there to pick up. The strange photographs she sends Cal, who studies them like hieroglyphs he must decipher to save her and himself. The credit card bills she leaves Walter, allowing him to continue caring for her, until he undertakes his own journey northward. How they fill the missing pieces in their lives to make their family whole again creates the heart of this novel.

When Things Go Missing is a masterful exploration of loss, loyalty, and knotty, dysfunctional families, told through the viewpoints of Kay, Cal, and Walter. It reveals the subtle and dramatic ways addiction affects the bonds that hold a family together. This heartfelt meditation on family is wrapped up in a propulsive page-turner that you cannot help getting swept up in.

Read more about *When Things Go Missing*, including an excerpt from the novel and reader reviews, at www.deborahjbrasket.com.

A THANK YOU AND REQUEST

Thank you so much for reading *This Sea Within*. I'd love to hear what you think and if you'd like to read more about Lena and Raoul. Writing this story was a joy, but hearing from readers is what makes it all worthwhile. You can email me at seastonepress@gmail.com.

If you enjoyed this book, please recommend it to your friends and post a review on Amazon and Goodreads, or wherever you bought the book. It does not have to be long. Just a sentence or two is fine. Reviews are critical to the growth of authors. They help others discover our books and boost its visibility on major platforms.

While I wrote *This Sea Within* to be read on its own, I envisioned it as part of a trilogy, which I'm now working on. To hear updates about my books, subscribe to my author website, where I publish a monthly newsletter and write about art and literature, nature and wildlife, and sailing around the world on *La Gitana*. You can also find me on Substack where I share similar content. Or follow me on social media.

Author Website & Blog –
www.DeborahJBrasket.com
Substack Newsletter –
www.deborahbrasket.substack.com
Facebook Page –
www.facebook.com/DeborahJBrasket/
Instagram –
https://www.instagram.com/dbrasket/
LinkedIn –
www.linkedin.com/in/deborah-brasket-39384370

www.ingramcontent.com/pod-product-compliance
Lightning Source LLC
Chambersburg PA
CBHW061415160726
47995CB00003B/622